IMPROVISING TO BEAT THE BAND

Wendolynn Jane Landers

This book touches on sensitive topics that may trigger some readers: head trauma, suicide, mental illness, anorexia, exorcisms, immigration.

Reader discretion is advised.

At the time of printing, the National Suicide Prevention Lifeline in the U.S. is 1-800-273-8255.

This book is for entertainment only. Not to be used as a substitute for medical, religious, legal, or any professional advice.

This book is fiction. Any similarities to actual people or events are coincidental.

ISBN:9781090436504

Contact information:
www.wendylanders.com
wendylanders@wendylanders.com

Please see the copyright page for disclaimer notices.

A the time of printing, the National Suicide Prevention
Lifeline in the U.S. was 1-800-273-8255.

For my mother, Patricia, and my grandmother, Ruth,
with love.

Contents

PART ONE

DIETING AFTER SHE DIED

CHAPTER ONE

After the funeral

Faustine's mental filter disintegrated. "Is it OK to go to the funeral," she hesitated, "in cases like this!" Her ruddy cheeks bled out any emotion still stored away somewhere in her soul. Sebastian's words banished any thoughts left in her mind.

"Of course it is!" Sebastian shook his head, spewing tears from his face, as though his tears were holy water that could redeem them.

Faustine jerked her head back from the splatter. Sebastian's tears on her face snapped her attention back to him. She had spaced out, talking to herself instead of to him. Sebastian grabbed her shoulder and sobbed against it. Faustine gawked at him grimly. *Is he going to use my silk print designer blouse as a handkerchief?* Sebastian sniffed, lifted his head, then stared down at Faustine, holding her tightly.

Those two never patronized this mall slightly north of the city limits. They avoided the trendy side of town with its spectacular clothing, obscure books, and other precious amenities. Yet at this seminal moment in their lives, they stood in front of a futuristic, steel-grey, open, spacy area with random stairs up against the wall in the background.

"You make no sense right now." Faustine wasn't crying.

That much was true. Sebastian's account rambled while he told Faustine that their mutual friend, Elodie, had suddenly and unexpectedly died of anorexia.

Anorexia! Elodie was thirty-eight.

———————

There were no external signs of a recent funeral, except for the lack of clutter and dust in Sebastian's car. He had carefully cleaned it for the processional, since the deceased's father had ridden with him.

"I need to tell you about an old songwriter friend of mine." Sebastian drove while Faustine stared out the window. "I never told Elodie, since I was waiting for an appropriate time. I don't think there will ever be a good time, and I need you to know."

"Can we do this over lunch? I'm starved." Faustine wiped her hands over her face. Stress blurred her vision. They cruised down a misplaced five-lane highway in the middle of their small town. The main drag had the town's main attractions attached to it, so anytime they went anywhere they had to pass the hospital, Elodie's last abode.

"Sure. Where do you want to eat?" Sebastian turned slightly to gaze at Faustine.

"Let's not go anywhere Elodie did just yet."

"OK, that knocks out anywhere we would want to go!" He sharply beat his steering wheel once. "Where do you not want to go then?" He calmly looked at her for a long moment before oncoming traffic made him put his eyes back on the road.

"I hate Mexican food. I don't think I ever went to a Mexican restaurant with her." Faustine paused before the need to explain overwhelmed her, "Too spicy." Faustine dreaded starting a war of political correctness because she didn't like spicy food.

"OK, the first Mexican place we see that isn't fast food." *What else doesn't she eat?* Sebastian absentmindedly passed Sour Cream & Burritos on the left, then catching a glimpse of it in his side mirror, whirled back right, circling an extra block before parking.

It was a small parking lot with only a couple of rows, sparsely populated with a couple of older cars: an old, beat up, canary yellow compact car, and a white sedan. In their small town, at three or four in the afternoon, restaurants weren't normally busy. As an additional dampening effect, many shops had bright, neon yellow foreclosure flyers—a few starting to fade—taped to their windows, proclaiming them to be victims of the recent Great Recession. Sebastian and Faustine needed the social protection of solitude, which in this case meant sharing space with strangers, but not a lot of them.

"It's like she died by accident or something." Faustine unbuckled her seatbelt, fumbling to get out of his car. "Like, it was all one great big fluke." Standing, she soothed her uneasiness by adjusting the strap on her sundress. Their silence let her catch her breath. The only sounds around them were the birds chirping and an occasional passing car. She frolicked for a moment in the lawn beside the sidewalk, spinning and twirling her arms like a child spinning away a nightmare, before heading towards the restaurant. She weaved around the small trees planted beside the doorway. "It's like someone made a mistake," she paused, "and now she's dead."

"Yeah, I know." Sebastian paced on the sidewalk under the neon sign. Mercifully, as soon as their feet touched the sidewalk they stopped talking about Elodie's death. Instead, they babbled about random topics while standing under the giant words Sour Cream & Burritos a little too long, almost like they were afraid to eat. This onerous meeting was the first time they had had a chance to discuss Elodie's death without immediate work to do. They could distract themselves when they organized flowers in the hallway of the funeral parlor, or replied to correspondence. Faustine acted like she understood what Sebastian was saying today, moving and nodding along with the flow of their conversation, unlike when Sebastian first told her that Elodie had died. Then, she was as cold as the futuristic steel grey walls in the mall.

"It's like the burrito is a baked potato or something," Faustine pointed at the sign. "By the way, what's his or her name?"

"The songwriter's?" Sebastian put his hands in the pockets of his tan slacks. *How did she manage to notice the discrepancy between the restaurant's cuisine and its marketing style? Marketing's not her forte.*

"Yeah."

"I know this sounds hopeless," he took his hands out of his pockets, "and corny," he put his hand on the door handle, "especially since you're not with the press," he slowly started opening the door, "but, can I use a pseudonym when I'm talking about this songwriter with you?" Sebastian held the door widely for Faustine.

Faustine waited a moment before stepping inside and pausing to be seated. "It's too late Sebastian, I already know your real name!" She smiled. "Yeah," she turned back to look at him as he entered the restaurant, "especially since I'm really going to go and sell my story to a tabloid." The dark interior was illuminated by the wall of windows in the dining area. Patrons could see cars driving by while they ate.

"I still don't feel comfortable talking about it. It's been a long time since I've talked to anyone in the band," he nodded to the waitress who motioned for them to follow her, "and I suppose it's OK now." Sebastian breathed in heavily while following her. "But you never really know when it's not OK." His eyes searched the room, especially the shaded areas away from the windows, anticipating a press attack any minute.

"Sebastian, I don't even know anyone who works for a newspaper. OK, I suppose if I were you," she paused, "I would have to suppose," she followed his eyes across the room, "that things were not OK, too." Faustine's emphatic dialect was choppier than normal.

"You sound like Elodie sometimes."

"Yeah, I would hope so. We were friends for years."

Silently they sat, then ordered, before finally chit-chatting about the dining room decor and menu options. Faustine noticed Sebastian's furrowed brow when the waitress was within earshot. After their food arrived and the waitress left, Faustine gave Sebastian a chance to eat for a minute or two before reminding him. "Now, what was your story?" Although the waitress' presence silenced him, the lettuce shreds falling out of Sebastian's mouth did not!

"Ah, her story, Manon's story, let's say..." Sebastian kicked himself for not actually having a pseudonym on ready, especially since he had just made a big deal about it, praying that pretending Manon was a fake name would be fake enough. *She's never going to meet her anyway, and it'll be one less thing to have to remember later. Maybe I can get her to take a blood oath of silence.* However, there was no way he could spontaneously come up with a name for Manon out of the blue. Mentally, he ran through a few, but rejected all of them. *Faustine's named after classic literature about a pact with the devil. I can't think of a cooler name off the cuff.*

"OK, Manon's story." Faustine smiled curtly.

"Manon was a writer for the rock band, a Slip of the Cue. It wasn't clear what she was eventually going to do with her

life, but in the meantime, she had written a few hits."
Sebastian put his burrito down and watched Faustine closely.

"Well, I can see why you're not supposed to talk about it
then." Faustine continued eating.

"Her idea, not theirs."

Maybe. This problem is where his story resides... Her stomach
and fists clenched slightly, waiting to hear the details. She
rustled her napkin.

Sebastian frowned while eating his sweet potato fries.
"This is too hot for ranch dressing."

"Why? Did she want to keep to herself?" Faustine wiped
her mouth.

"She hadn't finished school yet." Sebastian took a bite of
burrito with an absurdly innocent appearance on his face.
Faustine hadn't accused him of a crime requiring a defense.

"Well, OK," Faustine ate some lime flavored rice, "so what
happened?"

Sebastian pointed at his condiment with a sweet potato fry.
"There's something wrong with this. I'm going to ask a
waitress. For now, let's talk about the time they tried to get
Manon to start writing songs again," he placed both forearms
on the table, "after everything else had happened."

"OK, sure, whatever..." Faustine folded her napkin. *Grief
must be making him incoherent.*

The server hovered nearby and Sebastian waved. She
swooped down on their table. "There's no way this is ranch
dressing. It's way too hot."

"I'll take it back and get another," the server said.

Sebastian turned back to Faustine. "They were going to
throw her a surprise birthday party, so the band could play a
few numbers and let Manon sing along with them."

"I don't see how this can go wrong."

"I can, but then things were going wrong out of thin air for
the longest time. I was at the party. I got a couple of different

versions of the incident from the guys. The version that seems the most plausible to me was…Well, first I should say that she was told that it was going to be a small get together, since she hadn't seen them in a long time. She was in a different head space than they were. Maybe they shouldn't have switched venues on her, but they didn't have too much of a choice about it."

Faustine watched the light play off the silverware on an adjacent table while he was talking. *I don't see any potential relevance in his rambling, but at least he's talking to me. I've never known him to be a conversationalist.* Normally, she talked to Elodie while he listened. "This isn't going to turn into some weird psychopathic thriller where, at the end, you were the one who tried to kill her?" Faustine laughed.

The waitress returned with additional dressing.

"This is white, the other was tan, kind of reddish," Sebastian said.

"Yes. I'm sorry. I picked up the chipotle by mistake. My apologies," the server said.

Sebastian chuckled. The server smiled and scurried off.

By contrast, Faustine's eyes widened as she paled. Her breathing became more shallow. "Yeah, ranch, chipotle, six of one, half-dozen of the other…"

"No, no, no…" Sebastian wiped his mouth. "But, you see how this turns around in your mind quickly. It's like," he paused, "your mind is trying to force resolution on a situation that inherently does not resolve." Sebastian made circles in the air with his fork as he explained the metaphysics.

Faustine didn't see anything turning inside anyone's mind. All she envisioned was him hitting the window with his fork, sour cream, and lettuce. *A mess plastered on the window would be hard to explain to the managers…and he was vexed to explain anything.*

"OK, so long as I'm listening to a story that's not about you in the end," she said.

"It's not about me," Sebastian said.

"And, Elodie is not this Manon person." Faustine didn't even know that Elodie had been anorexic, and now Sebastian was thrashing out his alternate life in public.

"No, no, no, I'm not trying to trick you with this story, or pick on you either. I just never felt like talking about it, and had a good reason not to," Sebastian said. "I don't think that Elodie had any deep, dark secrets that she hadn't reveled to us, or at least none that I knew about."

What is the reason for this mystery? "If Elodie had any, they're in the grave with her now," Faustine took a moment and scanned the room before continuing, "and this is a good time to finally mention yours." She forced a smile.

"As long as we're not in a great mood. Before, it would have wrecked the mood of," he paused, "pretty much anything we would have been doing."

"What was one of the songs Manon wrote?"

Sebastian hesitated, remembering Manon lying face down on the tile floor unconscious, in front of the band's speakers with all the wires from the microphones entangled in her hair, wrapped around her body. Wayland had thrown his guitar across the stage mid-song when he saw her. *I can't remember if there was blood on the floor underneath the wires or not. Nobody saw what happened. Just suddenly she was there in front of the band, wrapped in wires.* Sebastian could feel his teeth beginning to hurt, and his lips beginning to crack, "Love & All Its Glory."

"Oh, that song was always a show stopper!"

"You remember it? I have the CD out in my car. It was Top 40, but not Top 10."

"Yeah I do," Faustine dabbed at her bright blue blouse, "I remember the chorus."

"At the time it was too big a deal," Sebastian put his fork

down," too problematic," he turned the paper check over to look at their bill, "to even mention."

"It wasn't hugely popular. It was kind of nice." Faustine adeptly deflected being left out of the important details of his personal life.

"Yeah, it was, especially if you were still walking around a college campus like we were back then."

"What were you scared of?" Faustine took a bite of burrito off her fork with her fingers as nonchalantly as possible.

"Losing control of the situation. You never know what's going to happen. Having a crowd to deal with once or twice is kind of nice. Having to do it every day is a chore," he said.

"That band—a Slip of the Cue—was a lightning rod," Faustine turned to look for the waitress, "but people basically supported their music." *This is like when I need to explain why I don't like Mexican food—mentioning this group could cause a riot. 'Problematic' was an understatement!*

"But once you say their name, that changes the whole conversation," he said.

"That's true, that's very true." Faustine nodded and put her fork down. "Speaking of names, I thought they were American until I heard theirs. What's the deal with his name again?"

"You're one to talk, Faustine. Made any packs with the devil lately?"

"Stop with the Faust. I'm not the lead singer for a notorious rock band."

"Ailill," Sebastian over-enunciated those two syllables, (*Ah-EEL*), "was named after a mythical king of Ireland. It had something to do with jealousy—"

"You know there's more to the Faust legend than just a pack with the devil," Faustine said.

"I only know the main gist of it."

"Well, there's a version of the story where an angel

intercedes on Faust's behalf and saves him. My name doesn't have to mean selling your soul to the Devil."

"I've never known you to be particularly ambitious, or worldly."

"The constant reminder could be part of it." Where Faustine was sitting, it was easy for her to watch the traffic outside, and as coincidence would have it, an armored truck drove past the restaurant, presumably headed towards the bank. *I don't remember the last time I saw an armored truck.*

"Did you ever hear the Johnny Cash song A Boy Named Sue?"

"I don't listen to country music." Faustine watched the street through the window. *Is a musical touring bus going to drive by now?*

"Anyway, Ailill went to high school with Wayland not far from here."

"They aren't Irish?"

"They're of Irish decent. Then they moved back. The band is Irish. I have no idea what their current U.S. or Irish citizenship status is. I think the drummer was born in Ireland. I have no idea where the bass guitarist was from originally. Meaning where he was born."

"Which one was Wayland?" Faustine nibbled the tip of a sweet potato fry to test it.

"Solo guitar." Sebastian talked between bites.

"How did you meet these guys again?"

"High school. I met Wayland in high school." Sebastian noticed the smell of roses, then tilted his head towards the freshly cut flowers that had just been displayed on the register.

"So, what happened to her? The songwriter?" Faustine asked.

"She got hit on the head." Sebastian waited a second before skipping to the result, offering no further details of Manon's exact injuries. "Everyone thought she was fine at first, but then she started having blackouts. Eventually her memory went totally blank." He stared at the wall directly above Faustine's head. "She didn't even remember her own name for a while."

"A hit can do that over time?" Faustine straightened and looked up, trying to meet his gaze, but to no avail.

"Apparently, but nobody expected it. She may have had some genetic thing wrong with her, what with writers being predisposed to having bipolar disorder, a lot of writers anyway, or post-traumatic stress. It wasn't the first time she had been attacked. All I can tell you is that it developed into a problem." Sebastian stared out the window, instead of looking intently at the perfectly white wall above Faustine's head. Faustine still had no chance of looking him in the eye.

"They caught who did it, right?" Now, even using a fork, Faustine's lettuce was in various spots between her hair, mouth, and plate. "I ask because I never saw anything in the newspaper." She twirled some lettuce shreds on her fork. "I don't think."

"No, they never caught anyone. She was hit from behind and never saw anything." Breathing deeply, Sebastian finally looked at Faustine. However, Faustine intently focused on her plate. He brushed the lettuce shreds out of her hair.

"That must make you nervous, knowing that there's somebody out there somewhere who already hurt a friend of yours."

"I should tell you about the time the band, a Slip of the Cue, tried to get her to come back to work." Sebastian munched his burrito. After a couple of bites, he said, "Now I'm humming "Love & All Its Glory" again."

"Is never gonna be for me, is never gonna be for me," Faustine mockingly sang in a high falsetto. She sportingly ducked down and grinned.

13

"Is never gonna be for me, is never gonna be for me," Sebastian's sigh puffed out his cheeks as he glanced out the window. At that point, he realized that he had gotten sour cream and lettuce stuck on the window. He tried to wipe it off. "Anyway, about the party. Maybe trying to throw a birthday party when you're an adult is a bad idea, but that's what it was. She loved singing. She had always wanted to be the lead singer, and was ticked off at Mr. Tacky Tunes for stealing her thunder."

"His name is not Mr. Tacky Tunes."

"Well they weren't the Beatles yet, you know, either."

"I guess if you're going to call her Manon then you can call him Mr. Tacky Tunes," she said.

"Helps if you don't take any of this too seriously." Sebastian's eyes pleaded for mercy.

The server danced by their table smiling broadly while singing, "Love and all its glory, is never gonna be for me, is never gonna be for me," while doing a side kick and hoisting a pitcher of water. A handful of patrons at nearby tables joined in with, "is never gonna be for me, is never gonna be for me." The patrons lifted their drinks towards the server.

"OK, keep telling me why I've never heard of this wonderful woman." She finished her burrito, but stalled for more time by pushing the stray lettuce shreds around on her plate.

"Well, she was a girl at the time. They're about a decade older than she is. That's where part of the problem came in," he said. "The other part of the problem was that she was still in school, and she wanted her own band. Other than that, what could possibly go wrong?"

"Well, they could be famous, that could go wrong," she said.

"That's not going wrong. That's going exactly according to plan," he said. "I guess you had to be there. Manon's band had gone over to her home a couple of times, which then resulted in the press trying to camp out around her house. The band couldn't risk that since they weren't around Manon enough to tell if she was getting better, or had plateaued, or had changed her mind about the whole experience, or whatever."

"They needed the chance to talk to her, in other words," she said.

"Yeah, and they didn't get it. They had to change the place where they were having the party at the last minute, the venue. Please remember that this is supposed to be a surprise party."

"You are flat out not going to finish this story, are you!" Emphatically, Faustine banged her fork down beside her plate. *He could have already finished this story, or at least outlined it by now!* Sebastian resumed attempting to hit the window with his fork without realizing it. Faustine clenched her fingertips.

"OK, there was an office building with a small amphitheater that they were able to grab at the last minute. They set up a privacy screen when they hired the catering," Sebastian said.

"You mean that Mr. Tacky Tunes didn't bake a cake for this wonderful woman? Manon? Or whoever this songwriter was?"

"Don't laugh. I can't swear that he didn't. At least, I can't swear that the lead guitarist didn't."

"The lead guitarist is part of the problem, then?"

"Well, no one ever accused him of being part of the solution." *He rarely told political jokes, much less at the band's expense. Political jokes will cost a salesman money in the music industry. However, that well worn Clintonesque allusion from their college days, or college "era" as it were, wasn't excessively political. Maybe I won't lose this sale because of it.*

"OK, they ended up doing karaoke at a small amphitheater, then what?" She leaned over to wipe the window, making sure that Sebastian had gotten all of the sour cream off of it.

"Well..." Sebastian crossed his arms. "That was the 'then what.'" He looked around the room. "That busboy can't hear us, can he?"

"How is this a state secret?" Faustine watched the local newspaper's delivery truck drive by. *He knew a famous songwriter once. Why didn't he casually allude to that person before now?*

"Well, her cover was nearly blown when she was simply expecting dinner and singing with the guys, like when they used to write songs together," he said.

"And?"

"And," Sebastian leaned over to look down the hallway that ran through the restaurant, "the closest thing to privacy they can get these days is a small concert in the park," he straightened back up, "basically." Sebastian braced his arms against the table, then wiped his mouth. *If she starts screaming, I'm running to the car.*

"They don't think they're going to be able to get close enough to her to tell how she is, in other words," Faustine half-asked, half-stated. "Not without the press knowing where she lives."

"In other words, yeah."

"OK."

Why isn't she yelling? He kept glancing around the restaurant. "I feel like I'm leaving something out."

"You probably are."

"I don't normally talk about this stuff," he said.

"No kidding. That's the point of this discussion. You probably need to. What's still bugging you about this?"

"Nobody knows if they made her worse." Sebastian's fork was on his plate, retreating from the window. "Taking someone who's been traumatized like that, and basically recreating the situation that landed Manon in the hospital to begin with, is like playing with fire."

"OK, that would be the part you're leaving out, then, the beginning." Faustine nodded. *Now, his story sounds a little more like real life.* "How is this recreating anything? She was nearly killed at a birthday party?"

"I don't want to talk about the beginning just yet. Are you done eating?" Sebastian scooted back from the table as he stood.

They didn't say anything as Sebastian paid. Then, they strolled back to his car. Sebastian's candy apple, red convertible was a perfect match for the sunny, blue sky and orange blossom scent wafting towards them on the cool breeze. The scene should have been filmed for a car commercial.

"'Tell Me About Love Sometime,' I think," Sebastian opened his car door, "was my favorite song off of that album." Faustine stepped into Sebastian's car. "A Slip of the Cue had an awful lot of songs about love on that album."

"Tell me about it." Sebastian sat down in his car. "I've got a copy of their Greatest Hits CD in the back. I always liked that album cover. Those weird colors, pink and green, swirling around." Sebastian rummaged around the backseat to retrieve a pristine, aged copy.

CD liner notes:

Love & All It's Glory
  (Is Never Gonna Be for Me)

* * *

Wendolynn Jane Landers

First verse:

I lost my taste for love
   back when people I knew
   got married before
   they should have been allowed to

It was silly to see
   them talking about forever
   when they didn't know
   what they would want next week

Chorus:

Love, in all its glory
   is never gonna be for me
   no, it's never gonna be for me
   it's never gonna be for me

Second verse:

I had wanted love to be
   like I had been told
   forever and bold

and I waited until I knew
   our love would see our lives through

Pre-Chorus:

but by then, I could see
   that love for me
   was not to be

* * *

Improvising to Beat the Band

Chorus:

Love, in all its glory
    is never gonna be for me
    no, it's never gonna be for me
    it's never gonna be for me

Bridge:

I'm still finding love
    where I didn't find you
    looking at someone
    who's a fellow creature of habit

Chorus:

Love, in all its glory
    is never gonna be for me
    no, it's never gonna be for me
    it's never gonna be for me

———————

Back at her house late that evening, Faustine stared down at the marinaded chicken breasts sizzling in her skillet. At that moment, she was acutely aware of every poster, magazine, record, CD, magazine article, and T-shirt she kept through the years having any affiliation with Manon's band, a Slip of the Cue. Suddenly, aliens had invaded her home. All of Manon's band's merchandise, which was Faustine's property this morning before she left to meet Sebastian, now belonged to Martians. A federal government investigator should be knocking on her door any minute now saying, "OK, now that you know the truth, a van is here to move their merchandise to storage to be held as evidence."

Wendolynn Jane Landers

How am I ever going to confide in Sebastian again? For him, trust is a one-way street. He kept this secret the entire time we've known each other. He heard every throwaway comment I ever made about Manon's band. I don't even remember all the derogatory comments I made about them. I bet he remembers everything. It's like finding out that Manon's band had tapped my phone to do market research or something. It's too weird to have actually occurred. Why would they have even bothered to do that?

Faustine flipped her chicken breasts. She craved a confident with superior knowledge. *Maybe my aunt?* Maybe if her aunt was too busy, one of aunt's friends would be willing to "do lunch," like the VIPs in the 1980s would say. *I'll ask her about the warning signs. I wish I could call Sebastian without appearing needy.*

A couple of days later, Faustine called Sebastian anyway, needy or not. She called on her cell phone beside her computer in her living room, right outside her kitchen door. She didn't turn on her desktop lamp with its gooseneck clip and purple shade, so the only light in the room came through the kitchen door. Even though she could have gone anywhere to talk to him, since she wasn't tethered, she sat at her desk out of habit. Her cell phone was a couple of years old, and she was still used to talking on landlines. When her cell phone was new, she had had to pay for this service minute by minute.

"I wondered if it was just me, or if you had found someone to talk to since Elodie died?"

"What do you mean?"

"I mean, I ended up calling my aunt because I think a couple of her friends also had issues with eating disorders, so she might know something about it."

Improvising to Beat the Band

"I don't know what anyone's supposed to know about any of this." He paced from his living room to his kitchen and back, holding his tan landline phone. His kitchen light was on, but he mainly paced in the darkness of his living room.

"Neither do I, but it seemed like a good time to get advice."

After the fact is a great evidence gathering time to build a retro-active *I told you so* argument.

"I spoke with her father about it when it happened," he said.

"I was wondering who sent me her obituary. I couldn't tell where it came from."

"Elodie's father sent it from her social media account, so that her friends would know what had happened. I wanted to get to you before you read it. You should find out about a friend's death in person, not online."

"Thanks," he flipped on the switch to the overhead light in his living room, "so did you talk to him?"

"Not much. He just wanted her friends to know."

"Do you think I should talk to him?"

"Nah, you didn't know him," he paused, "and becoming friends with him now would make getting over Elodie's death that much harder." He turned the light back off.

After they said good night, Faustine sautéed some veggies in a skillet, microwaved a cheese pizza, turned the pizza upside down on the vegetables in the skillet, waited for the cheese to melt into the vegetables, then flipped the whole concoction onto a plate. She took her dinner to the couch and fell asleep after eating about half of it. She had nightmares about veggie pizza.

A few days later, Faustine drove to a church that she had

attended growing up, looking for someone to talk to about anything at all. It was mid-week, late afternoon, and the church foyer was open for prayer and meditation. However instead of a prayer meeting when she got there, Faustine found herself in a line for a weight loss class which was occurring since there were no competing church functions happening at that time. She did a headcount of the line of people snaked around the room, then some rough calculations. *This should take about half-an-hour.* She asked the woman in front of her, slump shouldered and carrying a bag full of paperwork, about how long the wait should be.

"Is this your first meeting?"

"Yes," Faustine said.

"Then go up to the side desk. They'll get you signed in," the woman said.

"Thank you." Faustine worked her way up beside the main desk. There were four women altogether at the two front desks, two to each desk, generals overseeing the troops. *Is this like an alcoholic's meeting? What's said in the weight loss meeting stays in the weight loss meeting?* Looking around, no one immediately stood out. She ended up staring at her ankle for a few minutes, since she didn't know what else to do before the meeting started, without making extended eye contact with people she didn't know. Women predominated, with an occasional guy visible. Glancing at what other women were wearing, Faustine finally saw a teenage girl by herself in the corner with the extra folding chairs, pushed as far away from everyone else as possible. She was thin. She was really, very thin. *Sebastian needs to see this girl.*

Roughly a week-and-a-half later, at home, Faustine was brushing her teeth, eyeing herself in her mirror. The day of reckoning had brought impending doom. She hadn't weighed since the funeral, out of respect for the dead. She didn't have to weight-in at the first weight loss meeting, just sit and listen. When she stepped on her scales, she hadn't lost any weight, in fact, she had gained 10 pounds. "How, in the name of anything, am I supposed to lose weight!" After looking around the bathroom, she walked around her house, gathering data, searching for a way to lose weight. In college, she had taken a psychology class, so she tried to analyze her problem in psychological terms. She only had so many options: stimulus response, personality, and environment. She really didn't remember anything else without looking it up. *I must need a structural change in my environment, since I'm sure there isn't a fat personality trait.* The environmental effects were close to the stimulus response part. "Well, if I'm going to lose weight, I'm going to have to rearrange the living room." She analyzed the amount of room she had to exercise. *My house is cramped. There's no extra space to stretch.* She needed a comfy place inside her house to workout on the days the weather was too bad go outside. She went for a walk outside every day, but needed another indoor routine instead of additional sit-ups. *I don't trust my back on the floor.*

In the meantime, Sebastian isolated himself. *Telling Faustine was a mistake.* Sebastian strained to expunge their conversation from his head. He imagined this coming back to haunt him from different directions. *How many newspaper articles had innocently appeared out of nowhere in the past? I've got to be careful who I confide in.* Occasionally, having a reporter around could be worse than having bad press itself. There were a lot of things he could do to get it off his mind: he could go running; he could cook an elaborate dinner; there was a popular book he still hadn't read. There was a recent blockbuster he avoided watching, since he had personal issues with the actors involved, but prominent people in the music business had already reviewed it. He needed to watch it to get up to speed if he wanted to talk to decision makers later.

Why didn't a connection opened up between us? Maybe some kind of understanding? I thought that one of the reasons we had never been close was because I had too many secrets. He couldn't reveal to Faustine and Elodie the events that had haunted him. Naively, he had let Faustine in on his "state secret." *My own family doesn't even know as much as I confided in Faustine, and we still can't discuss any problems, mainly because she just doesn't care.* But right now, he had to keep moving. Sebastian's plethora of memories raced inside his head. By way of contrast, Faustine had merely sat, staring blankly at him during lunch. *Maybe I left something out? It hasn't been so many years that nobody cares anymore. Manon's songs still play on the radio. I know that if another woman Faustine's age had told her Manon's story, she would have been shrieking, yelling, and cussing "Mr. Tacky Tunes," swearing to never listen to the band's songs again. Does it not sound real coming from me?*

The scenario in Sebastian's head explained why Manon had never revealed herself. She would have been fighting an army of girls like Sebastian imagined, now women, so obviously, it was reasonable to conclude that she should keep quiet. *I wonder if she's still in love with Wayland?* Sebastian and Wayland had been fairly close, but not close enough for Sebastian to have definitive, specific knowledge of Wayland's relationship with Manon. *She might not really believe it's over with him.* Forever is longer for a lyricist than it is for most people, even longer than it is for lead guitarists.

Sebastian searched several old music books, from the couple of years he had majored in music during college, and found a reference to an Aeolian harp. An Aeolian Harp is a wind harp. Today, they're typically park sculptures, but during the romantic era (turn of the 18th century Europe), households had their own. The frame is set up so that the wind will blow across the strings. They're in a minor key, so they sound cool and creepy. *I should make one for old time's sake.* The most famous part of Love & All Its Glory was the sampled wind harp introduction. *It'll memorialize Elodie and maybe even let me contact its namesake, the ancient Greek god of the wind.* He thumbed through the book. *At least it'll guarantee a periodic moment of silence for Elodie.* He started looking up how to make a wind harp online. *This is complicated. I'm going to have to make a temporary one first for practice. Craftsmanship is a complicated endeavor.*

Fear and heat are two things that don't combine well, so Sebastian waited until the summer sun set before taking his new wind harp outside. He wandered around, trying to figure out where to hang it. At first, he hung it from a tree, but then the wind blew it around too much to play. *I need to find something to lodge it on.* He tried the door, then the porch. Manon's amnesia inspired his obsession about forgetting Elodie. He temporarily positioned the wind harp on top of a storage unit, where he couldn't see it, but it lay flat, so he could hear it. *It'll be easy to take inside when it rains. I may move it again later.* He put his hands on his hips and looked around his yard.

He needed sounds that he couldn't control to listen to, making the wind he normally couldn't hear a little louder. The smell of cut grass with the twinkling stars lightened the night. Nothing heavy weighing anything down. The jasmine from his neighbor's yard wasn't overbearing, unlike most nights, and the creosote scent blowing in from the desert meant that it had rained in the last hour. *Why didn't I notice the rain? It's normally such a big deal, people can't ignore it.* So he lingered, waiting for an answer from the night about how much of life he had missed.

———————————

Faustine drove over to Sebastian's house after the weight loss meeting with a thick pile of pamphlets. *I need to do this before I lose my nerve.* She rang his doorbell. Nobody answered. She heard him in his backyard, then crept towards the noise, since her arrival was unexpected.

As she rounded the corner of his house, he jumped. "I thought I heard somebody pull up." Sebastian started putting up his garden hose, and turned on his porch light.

"Let's do something to remember Elodie by." Faustine's speech was even more abrupt than normal.

"We had the funeral. That's supposed to be where you do that sort of stuff." Sebastian tensed.

"Yeah, but it hadn't really sunk in yet that she had died," Faustine said. "I mean, I can't even realize that this has even happened. Part of me still has no idea. I keep expecting her to come back."

"I understand, so what's your idea?" Sebastian started putting up his garden hose.

"I went to a weight loss meeting at the church I used to go to. It was the first weight loss meeting I had ever gone to, so I had no idea how it would work out, and that's where I got this idea. I don't think any memorial could be more perfect," Faustine said.

"Well, I made an Aeolian harp in her honor. I have it playing out here. Do you want to hear it?" He walked over to the pale wooden structure. *Did she see me working on it when she walked up?*

"Sure," Faustine said. "How do you say it again?"

"Ee-oh-lee-ann."

She followed him through his yard. He had moved the wind harp all over his yard, testing it in every spot. He had finally stuck it near a window where he could see it, as well as hear it play in the breeze. The wind harp whispered. They had to stand beside it before they could hear anything.

"It's like a lot of notes all at once," Faustine said.

"Yeah." Sebastian listened, gazing off at the night sky.

Faustine looked up as well. *It's strange to turn away from an object you're listening to.* The wind harp had a soothing sound, in its own way. If it had been any louder, it would have been annoying. As it was, the cacophony of notes wasn't any louder than the breeze.

Faustine abruptly blurted out her idea. "We should go to the weight loss meeting together."

That broke Sebastian's trance.

"In honor of Elodie," she said.

"That's your memorial idea?"

Faustine exhaled. "Yes." She smiled. She looked right into his eyes. She stood close. If there were any proximity effect in sales, she should have the wind at her back at that moment, while it was blowing through the wind harp, remembering Elodie, no less.

"What do you do at a weight loss meeting? Since we should do something that will help us stick together through this," he said.

"Learn to eat right."

———

Sebastian stood in front of Faustine in line at the following weight loss meeting. *Why is she standing behind me? This was, after all, her idea. She should be leading the way.* "Don't we need to go to more than one meeting? I mean," he glanced back at her, "isn't this a thing that we're supposed to do together? To remember Elodie?" He repeatedly looked over his shoulder at Faustine.

"Yeah, but I don't think you need to lose any weight. You look pretty fit to me." *He didn't notice my compliment.* She could smell his cologne once he turned around, like a nice breeze.

"We'll see when we get up there." Sebastian was curt, formal, like at Elodie's funeral.

I'm surprised he isn't wearing black, to go with his attitude. At which point, Faustine realized that she had on black shorts. *Why am I wearing this?* It was a hot day, without wearing black, which made it hotter, even if they were only shorts. *Do I own so much black that I can pick anything up, and it would happen to be black?* "You don't have to do this forever." Faustine strained to smile. "Is there any place in particular you'd like to sit?"

"No." Sebastian searched the auditorium with its array of folding chairs.

Faustine found the overly thin teen again, off in a corner of the room. "How about over there?" She pointed in the general vicinity of the teenage girl.

Sebastian saw the girl and stared a hole into Faustine's eyes. "Anywhere over there would be fine," he said.

———————————

After the meeting, Faustine, Sebastian, and a few other potential dieters had to stay behind for an orientation session. Faustine wouldn't leave without him. That meant that when they were finally walking out to the car, there wasn't anyone else around. Faustine's bravado kicked in. Visually, wearing black in a church parking lot should have made her more cautious. However, talking to Sebastian without Elodie's around was still a new thing for Faustine.

"What happened to you and Manon?" Faustine stood beside his car. Their eyes didn't meet when she asked him. She timed it that way.

"What...?" Sebastian looked over at her, having a hard time catching his breath.

"What happened between you and Manon? Did you ever date her?" Faustine opened the door and reached around behind the car seat, trying to find the CD, while attempting not to look at him for a minute. "Are you," she found the CD, "were you," she turned the CD over in her hand, "still," she put the CD back down, "friends...?"

Sebastian looked over her shoulder at the CD. *I knew this was going to be weird. It's too private, like a date. It's like a pre-date date. A get-to-know-you meeting, except that we already know each other. Asking me if I've ever dated Manon is supposed to get at what? The reason I haven't asked her out yet?* After a pause, he finally answered, "I don't know."

"Let's not mince words then, and get straight to the point." Faustine stood up, crossed her arms, and backed away from him a bit. "You don't want to talk about it." She pointedly smiled at him for emphasis. "Did you want to go eat, workout with me, or go home?"

Sebastian laughed. Inwardly, he doubted that she was going to give him an eternity to make up his mind about Manon. "I'm having a hard time staying on diet right now, so I was thinking that I probably wouldn't go out to eat right after my first weight loss meeting."

"You're having a hard time staying on diet right now? Did they even let you join? All they did was give you pamphlets. What did you tell them your target weight was?"

"You're surprised they let me join? What about that girl?"

Sebastian paced towards the brick columns.

"I know. I don't know what the deal is with her. I've seen people bring doctor's notes, but they were all quite heavy. Maybe they made an exception for her?"

"Maybe she's still within their target weight range. She could have a larger frame than she told them," he said.

"Maybe, but someone's making a tough call with her right now," she said.

"Do you think she's on maintenance?"

"That could be. You start paying again if you gain your weight back, but I don't know if they make you pay if you lose too much."

"I guess they don't have that happen too often," he said.

"It hurts to look at her," she said.

"I know. Maybe we're too sensitive to this since Elodie died? Maybe she looks thin to us."

"Let's hope so. Are we going to the store then, on the way to dropping me off? Looks like you're going to have to buy fat-free everything now."

"Fat-free. The supermarket's on the corner, near you?"

"Yeah."

The following meeting, the weight loss class co-ordinator lectured about how motivation effects dieting. She was prompted by a group of women in the back, near the door, getting out their cigarettes and lighters. One of them lit up, so the class co-ordinator told them to go outside to smoke. They protested on their way out. Once they left, the class co-coordinator reminded everyone how difficult it could be to become motivated to change a bad habit like smoking. She started relating quitting smoking to losing weight.

Faustine wasn't following what the class co-ordinator said.

Improvising to Beat the Band

It sounded like a lecture on creative visualization. However, Faustine knew she didn't hear part of it correctly. *Did she just say that if a person visualizes themselves being thin, then they will never lose any weight? She seems like an otherwise responsible person. Maybe I misheard.*

While the class co-ordinator counseled the remaining dieters, making sure the smokers stayed outside, Sebastian quizzed Faustine. "Didn't we skip going out to eat after my first weight loss meeting so that you wouldn't be tempted to break diet?" He listened to her answer more closely than the class co-ordinator did when she weighed at the beginning of the meeting. "Are you off diet?"

"Sort of, it's been over a week now. I keep thinking that I'm going to go back on the diet, but I never do."

"Anything I can do?"

"This would be it, apparently." Faustine furrowed her eyebrows.

While the weight loss class was breaking up, Faustine chanced asking the class co-ordinator one last silly question. "When you were talking about those women who were smoking near the door, did you say something about not picturing yourself thin? I thought we were all supposed to put pictures on our refrigerators of a supermodel's body with our own head attached to it." Faustine smiled while laughing nervously, watching for Sebastian's reaction. *For all I know, he's friends with a supermodel too, just hanging out with me to pass the time.*

"That's right. It's part of the motivation problem. You simply visualize yourself doing the very next thing required, nothing past that," the class co-ordinator said.

"Don't worry about next week, just worry about today." Sebastian echoed the weight loss meeting co-ordinator while nodding at Faustine. He seemed to understand what the class co-ordinator meant. Faustine had no clue.

The weight loss meeting co-ordinator turned to counsel a dieter individually, while most of the dieters were getting up to leave, folding their brown, metal chairs together, then placing them by the wall. Faustine decided to stand and gather her pamphlets. Sebastian stretched his legs. They lingered long enough for most of the dieters to leave. They finally drifted outside.

"I'm only going to come to these meetings if you actually want to lose weight," Sebastian said. "How much are you trying to lose? Twenty pounds?"

Faustine leaned back on her feet and put her hands on her head.

Sebastian elaborated on what the weight loss meeting co-ordinator meant when he said that dieters shouldn't picture themselves thin, using a plethora of examples from when he played sports. "Don't worry about winning or losing, just play the game. Do your best at every point along the way."

Faustine stepped back a bit more, then covered her mouth to keep from saying anything.

"I don't think you're even trying to lose weight," Sebastian said. "You're on a pseudo-diet out of habit, because Elodie was always on a diet. I don't know why you wouldn't want to lose some weight."

Faustine's hand flew up above her head. "This is not a P.E. class. I want to lose weight, I just don't care how fast I do it!"

"That's not being on a diet. You're used to being Elodie's diet buddy. Elodie put up with anything since she was anorexic." Sebastian paced between their cars.

Tears started streaming down Faustine's face.

"Unlike Elodie, I'm eventually going to have to stop coming to these meetings," Sebastian said, "and you're going to have to have lost some weight by then."

The weight loss class co-ordinator casually strolled past them as they were arguing a few steps outside the door.

Improvising to Beat the Band

Faustine reached out her hand to stop the instructor, since she wanted a second opinion. Sebastian pulled Faustine back because he didn't want the class co-ordinator to see her crying. Now Faustine was too bleary-eyed to have a conversation. She heard the grey gravel crunch under his feet as he walked to his car.

Faustine waited until Sebastian drove off, as though he might stay all night in the parking lot if she didn't watch him. "I'm sorry I ever asked any questions about Manon!" She screamed obscenities, paced and shook with rage, waving her arms in the early evening air. Getting into her car, she looked into the rearview mirror. *Why am I doing this? Why am I acting like any of this even matters?* She wiped the makeup circling her eyes with a tissue.

Faustine's distraction barricaded her memory. She previously planned to inform Sebastian of her discovery. She had been measuring rice in the half-cup measuring cup instead of the quarter cup measuring cup, which explained why she wasn't hungry since she had been eating twice as much as she thought she had. She finished wiping her eyes and tried to figure out what to do with the tissue. *Guys should not be allowed to go on diets. It's way too complicated for them to deal with.* She had never gotten into a fight with Elodie because she hadn't lost weight on time, as it were.

Faustine had to wait until the weekend to have enough time to make the trip across town to find the last remaining tub of fat-free ricotta cheese in the state. *I'm scared I might have to make my own.* Driving like a speed demon was not Faustine. She would have never gotten a food DUI even if there had been such a thing, so this errand blew her weekend. She strained to concoct an excuse to go cruising for fat-free cheese. *Why should I drive 50 miles for an item that costs less than five dollars?* Her mind was blank while she tried to think of reasons. *I could go to the movies and buy some fat-free ricotta afterwards.* There was an art house that had a specialty shop next door. Although it was hard to say when she was going to use her cover story. It was unlikely anyone was going to walk up to her and ask.

Faustine spent the next day eating foods that weren't on the official diet list, but weren't particularly fattening either. Commonplace food items she had in the house before she decided to start the diet. The day after that, she ate even more of the non-recommended food she usually ate. By then it was safe to say that she was off diet. Not badly off, just not on diet.

I can't believe how easy it was to stay on diet the first week. Maybe it was the novelty of a new adventure? The magazine and pamphlets made it seem special. Faustine remembered the colorful diet magazine with its exotic recipes in it. *Their editors aren't a bunch of shills who don't care if their readers gain weight.* She had spent an entire day eating off of one recipe since it made enough for two people. That meant eating the same meal twice, freezing it, or letting it go to waste. Faustine knew what her options were: *eat it now!* She used half-a-carton of egg substitute.

In spite of her trip, she still hadn't found any fat-free ricotta cheese. She had found other low-fat cheeses and substituted them instead. *That'll have to do.* She couldn't find the fat-free ricotta at the store, although she remembered seeing them in grocery stores years ago.

Faustine's lunches with her aunt were turning into a ritual cleansing, like a baptism or burning sage.

"Guys should not be allowed to go on diets. It's way too complicated for them to deal with." Faustine explained life to her aunt.

Their food arrived, but its aroma had yet to stop their flow of conversation. Faustine's aunt reached for an undisclosed, mysterious object inside her purse several times, but so far had not resorted to hiding in the bathroom to keep from listening to her niece.

"How can it be too complicated?" Faustine's aunt put her purse down.

"When I saw Sebastian, he was trying to explain to me why you shouldn't visualize yourself thin while you're on a diet. I've been told my entire life that that's one way to motivate yourself, but the weight loss meeting co-ordinator insisted it was bunk! Sebastian agreed. I was trying to explain why that was wrong, but he wouldn't listen. So, I started crying in the car." Faustine reached for a napkin to wipe her face. "That's when I realized that I might not be able to talk to him again..."

"I'm not following how having a disagreement about motivation is going to keep you two from speaking." Faustine's aunt picked up her fork. *I doubt anything could keep her from babbling on and on.*

"Motivation," Faustine stirred her diet soda, "no longer has any meaning. It's a cliche." Faustine dug deep inside herself to mine her last ore of motivation in order to sip her soda, instead of stirring her drink to watch the bubbles rise. She intensely scrutinized them, in case they were little crystal balls with pictures of what she should do next inside.

"Your disagreement about motivation made you cry?" *How close to the psychotic edge is she?* She eyeballed the bathroom door, in case Faustine started sobbing. *There's no reasoning with Faustine, but there's no telling what's wrong with her, either.* "How about your salmon? Is it good?" Faustine's aunt's fork directed her attention to her plate.

That reminded Faustine of the last time she ate salmon, back when she started to go off her diet. *Why is there a problem with me and salmon? I'm not even having rice with it, only veggies.* "The last time I ate salmon, I went off my diet. It started my fight with Sebastian."

"Why would salmon throw you off your diet?"

"I went out to celebrate after work, but I had already eaten before dinner," Faustine said.

"So, you're using food as motivation at work?" Faustine's aunt face brightened while the tension left her shoulders for a moment. "That could lead to problems," she finished a bite of broccoli, "if you aren't careful."

"No, not motivation, it's celebration!" Faustine smiled. "Motivation is a cliche without any meaning."

"OK, well, you're going to have to find another way of celebrating your days at work, as well as celebrating being on a diet," Faustine's aunt said, "before celebrating becomes a cliche, too!"

"It may be, now that you mention it," Faustine said.

"Then live the cliche!" Her aunt smiled and raised her glass.

CHAPTER TWO

Starting a Bucket List

While parked on the silent sidewalk in front of Manon's house, Sebastian visually inspected her neighborhood before taking a deep breath, decamping, and carefully scrutinizing her yard as he crept towards her door. He cautiously knocked on her front door instead of her garage door side-entrance like he used to do. Their current relationship was unknown, therefore more formal. He didn't discover anything unusual or worrisome in the yard: green grass, nothing overgrown, nothing obviously missing, a tabby cat. The healthy cat strode towards him.

"Talk about a surprise! Come on in." Manon greeted him at the door.

"Sure, cool, uh," Sebastian petted her cat, "we can talk out here if you need to." Sebastian offered neutral ground for his own protection.

"No, no, quite alright now," Manon said. "You know, Wayland came by the other day. I was wondering what had happened to you."

"Did he say anything was wrong with me?"

"No, it's just that you weren't with him. He came by himself," Manon said. "That made me think you could be

37

sick. No one would tell me if you were, so I didn't bother to ask."

"So, you know he's doing fine then?" Sebastian glanced over her head and scanned the darkened room behind her. He was looking for clues when he really didn't know what he wanted to find.

"Yeah, yeah, he said they were all doing fine. Everything's alright."

"Not losing money on the tour then?" Sebastian chuckled.

"Not that I know of. I think they're fine. If they're not, he didn't mention it. The press gave them good reviews," Manon said.

"Good. Good news then," Sebastian said.

After Sebastian came in, they settled around Manon's kitchen table. Manon reflexively furnished Sebastian a diet soda, for which he had equally reflexively thanked her. Sebastian did a double-take when he noticed fast-food sandwiches in her refrigerator, after its door opened for a split second. *How often does she go outside?* For a year or two after the incident, she didn't go anywhere. Sebastian kept scanning her kitchen and fidgeting. *Maybe Wayland brought the sandwiches over?*

"What's wrong with me? Of course you think that we wouldn't come by unless there was a problem." Sebastian smiled at her broadly, abruptly forcing himself to sit still.

"Well, that is the first thing I think of, truthfully," Manon said.

Sebastian calmly pondered her situation. "Do you have a car?"

"Yes." She shrugged her shoulders.

He mentally calculated how far she might drive it. "You're not going to believe this."

"Not in any way. What is it?" Manon twisted a lock of her hair. Out of habit, she took a sip of her diet soda, using the food-as-distraction gambit when she didn't want to talk.

"I want you to go to my weight loss class with me."

"You," she paused to sip her diet soda, "want me to go to a weight loss meeting with you!"

"Just to look around. I want to introduce you to a friend of mine," Sebastian said.

Faustine had been home from work maybe half-an-hour when she was ambushed by Sebastian pulling into her driveway. She saw his car, choked, then went out on her front porch to meet him. *Please don't walk up to the door!*

"Why are you here?" She watched the sunset instead of turning towards him. This wasn't subtle. She had to lean way over to one side in order to look around him.

Sebastian focused on her. *I'm not looking at the sunset, no matter how often she glances over at it behind me.* He put his hands into the pockets of his tweed sports coat. "I came to find out what happened to you. You went missing. Where have you been?"

"I keep losing track of time. I've been running errands before the weight loss meeting, then enjoying the sunset once I realize I've missed the meeting. I drove over to the bridge one evening, parked on this side of the river, and watched the birds flying over the river for a few hours." She avoided eye-contact with him.

"Do you want to talk out here?" Sebastian's voice implied she should invite him inside her house. He glanced at the door. Faustine pushed back against his manipulations harder than Mannon did. Manon had more leverage over him that Faustine did.

"Sure." *I don't want to talk to him at all, much less invite him in.* Faustine glanced past him, then started striding towards his car. "You know," she rested her knuckles on his car hood before turning her gaze back to his eyes, "I realized that I was using a half-a-cup of dry rice when the standard serving size is a quarter-cup." Then, she pushed her fist hard enough into the hood to turn her knuckles white.

"You think you're good with half as much rice now?" He followed her.

"Since I'm rarely hungry, I'd say so." Her t-shirt and shorts combo was decorated with friendly, glitter-outlined pastel flowers, which was too frivolous for her to pull off being haughty.

There was a natural lull in their argument. Since they had been fighting, the conversational space was yet another problem they had to fix later.

"I need you to come to the next meeting, anyway," Sebastian said.

"I didn't say I wasn't coming to the meetings anymore."

"Anyway, be sure not to miss the next one." He sounded pointlessly urgent. Out of nowhere, the niceties of life had new meaning to him. Avoiding the rest of this fight had value.

"Why? What's going to happen at the meeting?"

"I'm bringing a friend that I want you to meet."

Faustine paused. "Who?"

"Someone I don't want you to know, but I'm doing something stupid and introducing you anyway." Sebastian started to get back into his car.

"Who?" Faustine lifted her knuckles from his hood.

Sebastian hesitated a moment before closing the car door behind him. "Show up and see."

———————

Sebastian picked Manon up and drove her to the next weight

loss meeting. *I don't know if Faustine plans on coming back. I hope she'll be a little late, since I need to acclimate Manon to the building. I'm not sure how Manon will cope with being in a novel location. I don't know how much she goes outside anymore.* They arrived early, before the diet co-ordinator did, so they could watch the dieters walk from their cars into the red brick building. *It should help Manon's feelings to know who she's sharing the building with, but I also want to know who might show up uninvited just because she's here. One of these days, I'm going to catch that guy red handed.* Never mind that it would be almost impossible for a hacker to get this kind of detailed information about their lives.

Nevertheless, Manon's heart raced as Sebastian pulled up to the vacant building and empty parking lot. *I hope he doesn't turn to me and say something trite about having never suspected him, before attacking me with a blunt object.* Manon had trouble falling asleep the previous night, visualizing being thrown up against a wall. *I don't know if I can trust Sebastian, or what he wants. He's part of the band, and therefore, part of the problem. Logically, not all of them could be out to get me. If he'd wanted to kill me, he would've already taken advantage of the opportunity.* Sebastian lived the perfect distance away from her if he wanted to kill her: on the other side of a moderately sized town. He could always drive by, and he could always have an alibi. The things that crossed Manon's mind were nerve-wracking, and they never went away, not even after all these years.

"You're beautiful," Sebastian said.

Manon took a deep breath. "Thanks."

I don't know if she's having issues with how she looks or not, so it's better to play it safe. After all, she could probably take being invited to a weight loss meeting the wrong way. They sat in the car while Sebastian talked about them being early enough to watch everyone enter the building, so that way they would know who the other dieters were. He even made a joke about being able to tell if the other dieters were "packing heat" or not. Apparently, he didn't notice how she worriedly searched his back seat after he parked the car. If he had, he might of pulled the CD of "Love & All Its Glory" out of his glove compartment.

"We have to go get in line, now that everybody's here," Sebastian said. The class would be starting in about five minutes. He still hadn't seen Faustine. *Did I will her away?*

"The woman I want you to meet," he opened his car door, "I had a fight with her," he got out of his car and stood beside it a moment, scanning the parking lot before walking towards the building, "I thought she'd be at this meeting though," Sebastian said.

Interestingly enough, Manon didn't seem to care. She beamed and strode beside Sebastian into the building, like she knew what to expect. A bit of confidence born from childhood acting experience in local stage productions and commercials. This time it was Sebastian's turn to explain about the multiple lines.

"OK, you go over there to weigh. That's where I'll be. I'll go sit down after I get weighed," Sebastian explained. "You need to talk to the people at the side booth about your medical history and why you want to lose weight, that sort of thing."

"I don't want to lose weight. I'm here with you," Manon said.

"Well, tell them you want to be healthy then, or make something up. You can just sit in on the first day, before they start getting bossy," Sebastian said.

———————

After the meeting, Sebastian kept pacing and saying that the woman he wanted to introduce her to wasn't there that afternoon. He didn't know why. Sebastian dropped Manon off at her house, and then went to find Faustine.

At home, Manon played piano trying to make sense out of what had happened between her and Sebastian, letting her thoughts race smoothly through her mind, and out her fingers to exorcise the negativity. An improvised motif to take her mind off the past. Improvising was what she was good at. Anytime she wanted to write a song, she just started playing something on her piano to see what was already there, sitting out in the cosmos waiting for her. Once she had a melody flowing, she would check to see if it would fit with what she was looking for. Kind of like trying on clothes at a store. Who knows how long it would take her to find what she was looking for as she tried out various melodies, discarded a few, put a few to the side to check later to see if she changed her mind and liked them after all. A few she would choose to keep. Then she would try it all again the next day to see if the melodies still fit.

Manon arrived at the next weight loss meeting five minutes before it was supposed to start. *That should be reasonable, but I don't know how these meetings typically run.* She searched the parking lot for Sebastian's flaming red sport's car before deciding to enter the classroom without him. If he were late, she could catch him afterwards.

Mannon didn't know what Sebastian's friend looked like, so she wouldn't be able to introduce herself. *I wonder if she'll be here this time. Sebastian left me in line at the last meeting wondering why I was there. This time, I'm wondering why I'm here in the parking lot. If I start wondering why I'm going before I leave the house, I won't come.* She sat down and waited in the back of the room near the door, so she could see Sebastian when he entered. Sitting there in her blue jeans and tennis shoes, she crossed her arms while resting her foot on the lowest rung of the folding chair in front of her. She tapped her foot constantly, staring at the door.

The meeting barely adjourned when the door slung open and Sebastian marched in wearing blue jeans, complete with a large belt buckle of the university's emblem, and boots.

He must have changed clothes after work. Manon waved him over.

He hovered near her.

"The class just ended," Manon said.

"I know, I'm late, sorry," Sebastian said.

"It's OK, how are you doing?"

The dieters sorted through their pamphlets and weight charts. Scanning the room, Sebastian didn't find Faustine. *I wonder why?* He absentmindedly meandered towards the front of the room. *I need a minute to talk to the instructor alone.*

"What was her name?" Manon called after him. *I'm still wondering why I'm here.* This was her second chance to meet someone who, apparently, didn't go to the meetings.

Sebastian hesitated for a minute. *It's OK to tell Manon Faustine's name, even if it isn't OK to tell Faustine Manon's name.* He said, "Faustine."

"Well, if anyone says her name, I'll let you know." Manon stood by the side of the open doorway.

"You don't have to wait," Sebastian said.

"I might as well. I came to see you." Manon smiled and shrugged her arms broadly.

"You're not on a diet?"

"No," Manon pointed at the registration desk, "and I

weighed, too."

He looked at her blankly.

Manon cocked her head. *What's he expecting me to say?* "I don't think I could deal with it, emotionally, right now, anyway."

He shrugged.

That's my built-in, all-purpose excuse that he's expecting to hear. But why would someone who isn't overweight need to be on a diet? Manon paced.

Sebastian crossed the large meeting room to catch the weight loss meeting co-ordinator. "Why did my blood pressure go up once I lost 15 pounds?"

The instructor looked at him, blinked, and said, "Have you been watching your salt intake?"

"Not yet. I have no idea where to start."

A blond woman in her late thirties made an entrance by blocking the doorway while scanning the room. She wore a loud, print dress with high heels that clacked on the tile. Manon noticed her canary yellow pumps first, since she had been looking down, then smelled her designer perfume. The woman saw Sebastian and stopped. Sebastian nodded towards Manon.

Is this the right person? Manon looked at Faustine and smiled warmly.

Faustine turned around and stared at Manon. *She's the only one here who's already thin.* "Are you," Faustine shifted her weight in her pumps, "with him?" The woman pointed towards the front. "Sebastian?"

"Yes, I'm here with Sebastian," Manon said.

Faustine's mouth hung open a bit.

Manon yelled across the room, waving and pointing at Faustine. Sebastian looked over, and nodded again at Manon.

Faustine looked over at Sebastian, then back at Manon. "You're the songwriter, then?"

"Yes, Sebastian," Manon waved her arm in a large circular motion, "mentioned me?" *I thought he wouldn't mentioned me at all before I met his friend. Hadn't he signed a confidentially agreement?*

"No, he didn't say anything. What he said was confusing. I don't even remember what he said your name was. I think he just called you the songwriter," Faustine said.

Manon smiled, and held out her hand to shake. "I'm Manon."

Faustine's mouth flew completely open and she started shaking in a large forward and back motion. *I can't even trust him when he's making something up!*

Manon felt the shockwaves Faustine sent off and started rocking back and forth too, holding her crossed arms. Sebastian hurried back across the room as he heard Faustine screaming unintelligible phrases. Manon fled the room.

Sebastian stopped and looked at the weight loss meeting co-ordinator to keep himself from cussing in public. *I can't believe she scared Manon off!* Every cuss word he knew ran through his head.

Talking to Faustine didn't calm her down either.

"Why are you yelling?" he asked.

"To get your attention. You just ignored us," Faustine said.

The weight loss class co-ordinator told them to go outside, made a comment to Sebastian about his blood-pressure, and left. Apparently, no one wanted to be the person to call the cops on them. Filling out a police report gets you more involved in a scene than you really want to be. But now, since they had been officially warned, if they stayed, they would be trespassing. That's not as complicated a complaint to make.

Sebastian opened the door for Faustine, to get her to follow him. "Let's go outside. Maybe we can talk about it out there." It was late enough in the day to be chilly. The colder wind calmed them down a bit.

Improvising to Beat the Band

"No, it doesn't go on like this," Sebastian said.

"What?" Faustine asked. "What doesn't go on like this?"

"You having a fit every time we talk," Sebastian said.

"I am not talking to you anymore. You have been horrible to me ever since we started trying to do this. I don't think we can be friends without Elodie. I think we should just let it go," Faustine said.

"I don't think we should, but I don't know how to get around this either," Sebastian said.

The wind blew Faustine's hair backwards into her face. *I'm through trying to be on a diet. Sebastian's already lost more weight than I ever will. Once he stops going to the meetings, I will too.* Faustine rocked her feet back and forth for a minute.

"I hate the idea of never seeing you again. That's like losing two friends at once," she said. "There's a lot of things I still planned for us to do together."

"Like what?"

"We've never eaten at Foothills Foodie. We never went to the Halloween Haunted House downtown."

"Friendships don't have bucket lists," he said.

"There's not anything else you want to do together?"

"Sure. We can try one more time," he said.

"But it should be sometime next month. I honestly think you heard me the first time I tried to get your attention, and are passing it off like you didn't," Faustine said.

"Second week, next month?"

"See you then," Faustine said.

They stomped off to their respective cars.

Manon had the good sense to leave the premises once she ran from the room. One thing that years of working with the band had taught her was what a fight looked like. This was not going to be a constructive dialogue that just happened to be at 95 decibels. *I don't know the woman, and I don't know the man all that well anymore, someone else can the cops on them.*

Manon didn't know how it started, but they were suddenly at each other's throats. Best she could tell, Faustine had said, "I measured how far I've been walking. It was four-tenths of a mile when I thought it was one-half." Then Sebastian nodded distractedly. After that, Manon couldn't quite make out what Faustine had screeched.

Manon had smiled at Sebastian, waved, and said good-bye all at once. *I don't think he saw me leave. Good.* She heard the first part of their argument as she left. *They don't make any sense to me, and I don't want to know. The one thing about keeping to yourself, you miss a lot of fights, plus, you get to choose your battles. I'm lucky to have my own car to escape in, and even luckier to be driving it, myself, alone. Sebastian was right about that, although it was rude of him to quiz me for details.* She breathed deeply, shut her eyes, and took a minute before she put her seat-belt on. It took at least 15 seconds for her to shut out their argument in her mind. Then she backed out and pulled away. Mercifully enough, she could watch the sunset as she drove home. Manon didn't enjoy being used as a ploy to help Sebastian break up with a girl. *But that's what men do, don't they?*

Sebastian went grocery shopping after the weight loss meeting, while he was still inspired to eat correctly. He wandered up and down the aisles aimlessly. Violin and flute versions of various popular songs played in the background on the store's overhead speakers. *I'm supposed to get as much fat-free stuff as possible, especially the cheese.* But the store management had started rearranging the items so that the vegetarian food was all in one place, with a lot of the diet food in that general area as well. He wasn't vegetarian and had trouble isolating the diet food. He cruised past the magazine rack, grabbing one of the diet magazines. He flipped through it when he noticed an article called "Is Your Diet Making You Crabby?" He decided to buy the magazine. *Faustine said something about having gotten a subscription. Anyway, it will give me something to talk about with her at the next meeting. Maybe the magazine will expose fat-free cheese as a mood altering drug. I've been getting angry really easily lately, and the fat-free cheese must have something to do with it. I should cut Faustine a little slack. She's typically unreasonable, but maybe she's eating too much fat-free cheese.*

Sebastian stopped to weigh, as long as he was in the store. *Never hurts to get a second opinion.* He weighed a little higher on the store's scales than he did on his scales at home, but then he also weighed heavier at the diet meetings. No real change. *Nothing to it.* He managed to lose 15 pounds in the first month without trying. All he did was stop eating out, and start running again. The machine automatically took his blood pressure when he weighed. *Maybe I should've waited a little longer after my fight with Faustine to find out what my blood pressure was. I didn't realize it could shoot that high that quickly, especially since I've lost the extra weight. Maybe the extra weight was holding my blood pressure in? In any event, I should cool down before driving the rest of the way home. No sense hitting a stop sign.*

Getting a cart, he started towards the cafe area to sit for a minute and read the magazine. On the way, he crashed into the soda display at the end of the aisle. He sat and looked at the display for a minute before putting the boxes back together. There was too much racing in his mind all at once. Then he saw an older man he knew in line at the cafe for coffee. It was his father. If the point was to calm down before going home, Sebastian needed to avoid him.

Sebastian sat in the cafe area of the supermarket, looking at his diet soda and magazine. His cart, which had recently been drinking its own diet soda after the run-in with the isle display, was sitting there beside him, like a faithful horse in the Old West. *I don't know how long to wait before checking my blood-pressure a second time.* He flipped through his magazine. The article about diet induced crabbiness discussed diet induced fatigue. *Apparently, skipping meals is not the way to go. Unfortunately, fat-free cheese is not being covered at any length.* Suddenly, a man stood over him. Sebastian looked up to see his father.

"Mind if I sit down?"

"No." Startled, Sebastian pushed his cart away from the table, "Go ahead." Sebastian tried to hide the diet magazine in his cart since he didn't want his father to see it. However, his father carried coffee, so he steadied himself against the cart to sit down. Then, he saw it.

"You're reading women's magazines?" His father sat down with his coffee across from Sebastian.

"Love & All Its Glory" started playing on the store's overhead speaker system. Sebastian started to shiver. "Yeah," Sebastian took a second to decide how much to tell him. "Faustine is on a diet, and I've been going to the weight loss meetings with her."

"Have you been on a diet long? It's only been a month or so since I've seen you." His father squinted, and leaned forward to look more closely at him. "You look thinner in the face."

Sebastian sat there for a minute, not knowing what to say. "Do you think fat-free cheese makes people angry?"

At first, his father was going to decline to comment, but he saw a look in his son's eye that he didn't like. "I don't see how it could. Everybody sells it. It's bought all the time. Everyone eats it, at least sometimes," his father said.

"Yeah, but it could be like smoking and cancer, where they let it go on for years," Sebastian said.

Improvising to Beat the Band

"Cancer takes decades to develop. Getting angry only takes a minute. Besides, people are more suspicious of diet food since saccharin was associated with cancer." *There's no convincing him.* "Why are you worried about fat-free cheese anyway?" He placed his coffee on the table. *I'm glad I got groceries! I would've never known.* Then, Sebastian's father started slowly turning the cup clockwise. "I haven't heard of any research, or anyone complaining about fat-free cheese."

"I always end up angry after I eat it," Sebastian said.

"How long have you been eating it, a couple of weeks? You would have to stay angry all the time then, if something you ate caused it," his father said.

"OK, even before I started the diet with Faustine, I picked up some fat-free cheese by accident. Then I started reading this band's website, which aggravated the life out of me. It was a bunch of stuff that had to do with Manon." Sebastian tried to explain. "Manon used to write for that band," Sebastian leaned forward and drank his diet soda. He forced himself to keep from automatically mimicking his father by not turning his plastic cup! He realized his father was not going to comprehend the full import of his anger about Manon. This was a little bit like talking to Faustine. *Why suddenly no one cares is beyond me.* Sebastian continued, "Then after I started the diet, I went to this political rally, and they had fat-free cheese there, and I ended up ticked off for the rest of the evening. Then, when I ended up buying a bunch of it for the diet, I was raving mad about Manon, the band, and Elodie. I was scared I was going to break something, the way I was banging into stuff at the house." Sebastian concentrated on his father. "That's when I realized it was probably the fat-free cheese that was making me upset." *I feel better.* Sebastian opened the magazine, turned to the article, and pushed it in front of his father. "So, this article is supposed to be about how your diet might make you, quote, crabby, but all it ended up being about was how you shouldn't skip meals."

Sebastian's father started flipping through the magazine. He was figuring out how to take it away from Sebastian, since he stopped listening after he couldn't make sense out of what Sebastian was saying. The best he could tell, Sebastian was doing a lot of stuff that would make anybody angry. *How am I going to get through to him? He's already scapegoated the fat-free cheese.*

"Honestly, I don't see how Elodie died of anorexia," Sebastian said. "Every time I turn around, there's someone telling me that I don't have to skip meals to be on a diet. How can you ignore all that?" Little did they know that in a decade or so fasting would be faddish.

Sebastian's father read the cover, then picked a random place to start flipping through the magazine. *Surely he knows that people believe whatever they want to believe.* "Who did you say used to write for this band?"

"Manon," Sebastian said. *This is the first time I've told my father her name.* The words felt weird. He rarely said her name out loud.

"And neither of them are on diets?" Sebastian's father attempted to untangle this web a strand at a time. He had no idea what band Sebastian was referring to. Talking about Manon to Faustine had tricked Sebastian's mind into thinking that he had been talking about Manon more than he had.

Sebastian sat up a little straighter. "Well, I've started getting Manon to come to our weight loss meetings with us," Sebastian said.

"You and Faustine?"

"Yeah. So me, Faustine, and Manon are all on a diet together."

"You all need to lose weight?" Sebastian's father shook his head. He flipped through the magazine faster, then he started backtracking through the parts he had already flipped through once already.

"Well, I'm at the weight I'm supposed to be at. Faustine hasn't started losing any weight yet, and I asked Manon to tag along so she could meet Faustine. I don't know if she'll lose any weight."

"You all go to this weight loss meeting, but none of you cares if you lose any weight?" Sebastian's father stared at him for a minute.

"Yeah, that's basically the size of it." Sebastian sat and looked at his dad. *It sounds a little cold coming from him.*

"Why did you start going to the weight loss classes then?" Sebastian's father put the magazine down. *He's going to find a reason to get up and leave. I'm asking direct questions of someone used to keeping secrets.*

"Oh, it was Faustine's idea to remember Elodie by," Sebastian said.

"You remember an anorexic by going on a diet?" *There's a little bit of a disconnect going on for him, as well as his friends.* He shoved the magazine towards Sebastian.

Sebastian explained while fanning himself with the magazine. "It didn't sound so weird when Faustine asked me. I put a wind harp, like this band had in their song, up in my backyard to remember Elodie. Faustine came over and asked me to go to the weight loss meeting. Then, she saw the wind harp."

"No chance of her being anorexic too?"

"Not that I can see. She doesn't ever lose any weight. She only talks about being on a diet."

"I'm taking the diet magazine to your mother." *I should ask him more about this band. He seems ready to fill in the details.* Suddenly, he lost his nerve and avoided asking anything. Finding out what happened to his son would have to wait.

Sebastian shuffled his feet and scowled when he lost his new magazine, but didn't argue. In theory, Sebastian could talk to Faustine about this article in the diet magazine without having it open in front of him and reading from the magazine directly. *She won't know which article I mean if I can't point to it.* He could see her looking at him vacantly and smiling already.

His father relaxed his grip on his coffee once he got the magazine away from Sebastian. It sounded like his son's friends were trying to start their own cult.

Sebastian's father whiled away the next hour with him, going up and down the aisles, talking about what Sebastian could and couldn't eat.

"This should be similar to the diet they put diabetics on," Sebastian's father said.

"I don't think it's exactly the same," Sebastian said.

"I thought they had more fat-free stuff than this." His father picked up a brick of reduced-fat mozzarella, then scoured the cheeses for fat-free ricotta. He found reduced fat, but not fat-free.

"I think there used to be, back when being fat-free was new, but I can't tell," Sebastian said. "I wasn't paying that much attention. After 9/11 I was focused on the Iraq war. Besides, I don't think they do national surveys of how many Americans diet during the year, not just in January."

"There's gotta be a survey out there somewhere about it. But I don't think there are as many people on diets as there used to be." Sebastian's father helped him put the diet soda in his cart. "People used to talk about being on a diet all the time. Kind of like talking about the weather. Now, no one mentions it, even if they're on one."

"Well, when everybody wore leg warmers, they were supposed to be taking dance classes," Sebastian said.

"The last two dance studios that opened up went out of business after a couple of years," Sebastian's father said.

"I don't remember the last time I saw someone wearing leg

warmers. By the way, I ran into the display earlier."

"You ran the cart into the display?"

"You can see where I hit it." Sebastian pointed to a crumpled edge on the display. "It was right after I took my blood-pressure."

"You should take it again tomorrow. I don't think it's accurate now," Sebastian's father said.

"I'm not taking it again tomorrow."

After picking up a few more items, Sebastian waited in a check out line. "I'll wait 'till another time. It'll be fine." Sebastian looked over at his father who had gotten into another line with a hand basket full of steak and peppers.

"I hope so," his father said. "You know I didn't get high blood pressure until I was about 10 years older than you." He eyed Sebastian suspiciously from across the aisle.

"Ten years from now I'll be fine, don't worry," Sebastian said.

His father didn't argue out loud. *There's no way.* "Maybe you should go home and take it easy," his father said. "You should go home and read or watch TV, maybe work in the backyard. I'm going to go grill."

Sebastian finally made it home after the weight loss meeting and ensuing grocery shopping expedition. Taking your groceries in from the car by yourself gives you too much time to think: like why Corporate America stopped making so much fat-free food. Before people complained about Big Tech, they complained about Corporate America. The first time Sebastian saw fat-free cheese he was in high school. By the time he was in college, it was on every label. But tonight, he couldn't even find fat-free ricotta.

As he was opening the fridge to put the eggs up, from his memory he heard Elodie's voice, "I ate an entire dozen eggs in junior high. I found out that it took more calories to digest the eggs than they actually had, so if you ate them, you had to lose weight. My mom found out what I did and nearly killed me. Nearly everybody in her family had died of a heart attack. Doctors had only recently found out that eggs had enough cholesterol to kill you." *I want to talk to Elodie, not listen to her ghost ringing in my ears. Talking to Elodie is never going to happen again. That's the awful reality of time passing.*

———————————

Sebastian sat on the edge of the examination table. No music was playing. He was surrounded by white walls. The doctor confirmed that his blood pressure was high: 142/92. "So, you took your blood pressure at the supermarket and it was... "

Sebastian breathed in sharply. "145/93."

"Have you had any chest pains, gas, sharp pains in your arms?"

"No, no sharp pains. None in my chest or arms. I haven't been having gas either." Sebastian looked away from the doctor to the white wall. *Which is weird, since I've been eating four times as much vegetables as I used to.*

"Any feelings of heaviness in the chest, or shortness of breath?"

"No, and I run every morning," Sebastian said. *Is he going to go on all day?*

"OK, we need to have you wait a week, and then come back in," the doctor said. "It may be high today, or you may be experiencing more stress than normal."

"Come back in next week to check it again?"

"Yes, and in the meantime, you're going to want to get one of those home blood pressure machines. They sell them at the large supermarkets, or you can order one online."

"You want me to take it at home? How will I know the machine's accurate?" Sebastian looked back to the doctor. *Maybe it's a clerical error.*

"Bring it in next week and we can check it against ours here. You are also going to want to get an accurate scale. You know how much you weighed today, so you can use that as a guide."

"I've been on a diet. I think the scales I've been using at home are pretty accurate," Sebastian said.

"So you've been losing weight?"

"Yeah." Defensively, Sebastian tried to hide whatever inadvertent clues he might be giving off by sitting straighter.

"Did you have high blood pressure before you started losing weight?"

"No, no abnormally high cholesterol readings either. I wasn't expecting this. I thought, if anything, it'd be lower." Sebastian ground his teeth and crossed his arms.

"Well, watch what you're eating this week for extra cholesterol and salt. Salt can sometimes increase blood pressure. Something in your diet may have changed when you lost weight," the doctor said. "Keep track of the amount of sodium you eat, and try to keep it below 1500 mg."

Sebastian sighed. *One more thing to keep track of.*

"And if it's still high next week, we'll do an EKG then. In the meantime, if you experience any of these symptoms," the doctor handed Sebastian a yellow sheet of paper, "go to the emergency room immediately."

Sebastian looked down at the list of dire warnings. The yellow sheet of paper reminded him of the yellow foreclosure notices put on building after building during the Great Recession. *I hope I'm not going to be foreclosed on.* "How can losing weight cause a heart attack?" He remembered the small bits he'd been told about Elodie's death.

"Lots of ways: salt, cholesterol, lack of potassium...those are the common ones," the doctor said.

"I guess you have to be about careful losing weight." Sebastian thought he was telling a joke, and chuckled.

"Yes, you do." The straight-faced doctor emanated motionless seriousness. "Be careful on the way home, too." He left Sebastian with the nurse.

Faustine scooted into the booth at the restaurant across the table from her aunt. She psyched herself up to describe what occurred with Sebastian. *Just tell her how he started yelling.* There was a very real chance that she might not be able to spit it out, since she really didn't know what had happened, even though she was there. "Why does he think he gets to act like an abusive…?" She waved her hand in circles in the air. Maybe she should have let her aunt order her drink first.

"Well, at least now we know why you didn't know anything about him. He never talked to you because he didn't respect you. That's why he never told you anything about himself," Faustine's aunt said.

"So, he's belligerent because he doesn't value me," Faustine said.

"Would seem that way to me." Faustine's aunt put down her purse, and fished around for a napkin.

"Man, that's harsh." Faustine gave the waitress her order. "Maybe he's just suppressing grief or something."

"I didn't know why you were making such a fuss about him to begin with. You were oblivious to these big gaping holes in his story. I wasn't worried about him so much as I was worried that you didn't know enough to call him on it. I'm getting the shrimp entree with soup, salad, and fruit."

I can't make up my mind. "I'll have the same thing." Faustine closed her menu. "Why would he try to be friends with me all these years if he didn't appreciate me? What's the point?"

"It's childish behavior, trying to be friends with everyone all the time. He didn't feel like cutting you lose, and you weren't putting any demands on him," Faustine's aunt said.

"Being nice to people is childish?" Faustine cocked her head to the side, tossing her hair back.

"No, trying to keep them around you in case you might need them one day is childish," Faustine's aunt put her menu down, "especially if you can't stand the person."

The waitress strode quickly past as she put down their drinks. She continued moving beside the rest of the tables, but she kept glancing over her shoulder, like she wanted to double-back to their table. Once she got to the corner of the room behind the cash register, she hovered, taking a long look back at them. They had gotten a little louder, and more threatening than they had realized.

"I don't see how we could have been friends all of those years if he didn't appreciate me." Faustine pointlessly stirred her diet soda with her straw. She gazed at the bubbles like they were a hundred mysterious tiny crystal balls. "I think you're being presumptuous."

"I don't think you were friends. He only told you what he wanted you to know. And, I'm only going by what you told me, is he, or is he not, being abusive?"

———————

Since lunch with her niece was a bit of a debacle, Faustine's aunt called her later that afternoon when she got home, which was an irregular move on her aunt's part. Faustine didn't expect to see her aunt again until Christmas.

Faustine decided to rely on her aunt, so she stopped searching for another source of information. There was no way she knew what to do next, plus her very evasive aunt must already understand her situation. Her aunt avoided all the right questions. She changed the topic at all the right times. She knew what food to order. She knew when to look away. Next time, Faustine was going to completely level with her, then question her for all she was worth.

———————————

"I don't get why you say you're friends with this man." Faustine's aunt had taken on a harsh tone mid-way through lunch. Although this was an attempt to re-do the previous lunch, it was turning into a rerun of the same show, including eating the same food.

"We've been friends for years." Faustine did not see this hardball coming when it hit her from right field. She had been trying to get her aunt to tell her if she had ever had any friends who were anorexic. In order to do so, she had started talking generally about her aunt's friends. Now she was stuck justifying her own friend's lives to a distant relative. Probably not the best situation to be in, especially since it can't be done.

"You don't know anything about him," her aunt said.

"Yes I do. I know everything about him. I know all about his past. I remember how hard it was for him to get a job right out of college—"

"You don't know half of what he does! You haven't told me anything at all about this person, except that you think you know everything about him," her aunt said.

"What could I possibly not know about him?"

"You know why you're friends with him, I get that. You know he's busy. He probably is. He tells you enough about what's he's doing to keep you from wondering about him. Whatever it is is probably none of your business anyway, so there's no point in asking..."

"What on earth do you think I'm supposed to be asking him about?"

"Who his other friends are."

"I honestly don't think he has friends that I don't know

about. I wasn't always friends with all of his friends, but that doesn't mean that there's a bunch of people running around that I don't know about."

"I don't see why it wouldn't," Faustine's aunt said.

The waitress returned and wrote down their order on her notepad. A Slip of the Cue started playing in the background, but instead of "Love & All Its Glory," they heard "Just Let Time Pass."

"I'll buy that there could be a couple of acquaintances that I haven't met, but I know everyone important to him, and I'm sure I've met all of them at some point."

"There are 24 hours in a day, which is a lot of time in a busy person's life. I know people I would consider to be lazy who have thousands of friends. There's no way I could possibly know everyone that my friends know." Social media was not a big part of her aunt's life, nor did she expect it to be.

"It could be that we don't get out much," Faustine said.

"I doubt it. It's most likely that you don't talk too much. And honestly, why should you?" Faustine's aunt ate a bite of shrimp, then dabbed at her blouse with a napkin. Even if she had accidentally gotten something on her clothes, it wasn't noticeable against the maroon paisley fabric. She nervously tugged at the tie her blouse had near her throat.

"Well, I think I'm friends with this person. If it turns out that I'm not, like you're saying, I think I should want to know about it."

"I'm not saying that you're not friends, I'm saying that you're not getting the whole picture of who he is. And the fact that you can't pick up on that is bothering me."

"I've never felt like he was hiding anything."

"I don't think he wants you to wonder about what he could be hiding from you. If you're close to him, you should be able to talk to him about Elodie's death. As it is, it doesn't seem like you are comfortable talking to him at all."

"What do you think I should ask him?"

"Honestly, I don't think you should ask him anything. Don't make suppositions about him for awhile and see what happens."

"Sure. Not a problem." Faustine had stopped wondering why she didn't see her aunt more often.

Faustine stared at her desktop computer screen. What she read guided her mind back in time:

Anyone want film festival tickets for tonight? Got sick at the last minute & can't go! :(

Faustine moved her mouse around on the computer screen. *I know those aren't Elodie's last words. Her last words were something unknown uttered to a doctor or nurse before she lost consciousness.* Faustine's hand hovered over her mouse for a minute. *It doesn't sound like she was planning on dying. It sounds like she was having a good time. A film festival is a enjoyable event. I wish I could've gone with her.* Faustine clicked on the next post. *Elodie always seemed happiest when we were all watching movies together. Maybe she was less self-conscious in the dark? Maybe the movie took her mind off things? It's not a bad habit to have if you need to forget. Drinking is worse, but drinking has calories.*

She carefully, slowly, clicked on the screen. *It'll be easier to see who Elodie's been following first, then I won't be blindsided by the posts themselves.* She put her hand on the screen to keep from reading more than one post at a time. Elodie had been following quite a few people, one of which was the movie theater, another was the hospital. *It's strange that she's following the hospital where she died.* Faustine clicked a few more times. *I didn't realize that the hospital made announcements on social media. That explains why Elodie never mentioned her social media account to me. It was how she kept up with the hospital's programs.*

The answers to Faustine's questions about Elodie's death had been hidden by Elodie herself, specifically concealed from Faustine. "Managing to focus in on all the details at once." This post had no further explanation.

That's a weird post coming from a dying woman. In retrospect, it seems odd that someone that detail oriented, and that driven, should wind up dead.

"There is no way that breakdancing ever makes it onto this list!" Sebastian pointed at Faustine from several car lengths away in the church parking lot.

Sebastian and Faustine had agreed to meet after a month's cooling down time. They decided to stop eating fat-free ricotta, and to stop going to weight loss meetings. Since they doubted they would be on speaking terms much longer regardless, they started working through the part of Faustine's bucket list that dealt with Sebastian. So far, they had had a mock engagement party at Foothills Foodie, in spite of Faustine's reluctance to mention that engagement parties were typically thrown there. (Sebastian started asking questions once he noticed that they were surrounded by frosted champagne flutes on the restaurant's balcony.) They had gone ice skating with a married couple who were friends with Sebastian, without him bothering to mention the additional couple he invited beforehand. After going ice skating with Sebastian's married friends, Faustine stopped doubting her aunt's suspicions.

Manon was their referee. She wrote down everything that they both agreed to, keeping the official list herself. If there were any disagreements about what they had agreed to, or what the terms were, Manon made the final call. They alternated picking their adventures. All the reasons they were still clinging to each other, afraid to let go, were made concrete operational by this list of outings they still wanted. But at this moment, the only thing that was definitely on the list was the making of the list, and they couldn't accomplish that alone. Mercifully, Manon was there to help them. Plus, there was no way to hear an old a Slip of the Cue song in an empty parking lot.

"I have put several reasonable requests onto the list, like you asked me to. I'm only doing this so that I won't have any regrets once it's over. People used to breakdance when we were kids. It could be our one exotic thing to do together before we never see each other again," Faustine said.

"I honestly think this is how people stay friends when they're kids. They absolutely know it isn't going to last."

"That may be the truth, but I'm not backing down from break dancing. You asked what things I would always see ourselves doing together, and that was one of them," Faustine said.

"So that's supposed to be our extravagant dancing with celebrities moment? Breakdancing?!" Sebastian could argue this one point the remainder of their meeting. Never mind the fact that if he continued arguing, he wouldn't have to finish the list.

"You would never want to do anything romantic. I still want to go dancing. Breakdancing is a happy medium. It's fun. It's dancing. It's not romantic!" Faustine stomped up and down in front of her car.

"We could go ice skating. When you ice skate to music it's like dancing." Sebastian put his hands on his hips.

"As if!" Faustine pantomimed ice skating, then disco dancing, then back to ice skating.

Improvising to Beat the Band

"It's going to get tabled. You guys aren't going to be able to get through this all in one day." Manon read her notes. "You've got stuff to do that you've agreed on. Meet again next month to hammer out the rest of it." As referee, Manon could call time on any public meeting.

"What!" Sebastian stood there with his mouth hanging open. *You're supposed to be on my side.*

"You heard me. I'm the ref. What I say goes," Manon said. "We meet again next month and try and finish the list."

Sebastian wasn't used to her drawing a hard line. "Sure, why not? What are we doing next?"

"We can either go to a local concert, or we can go skydiving, your choice," Faustine said.

"How about we go running, so I can show you how I lost the weight?" Sebastian jogged in place.

"Let's try to make this as enjoyable as possible, or else it'll be one more thing that we regret," Faustine said.

"I'm unnerved by both the skydiving and the concert. Why was 'local' specified anyway?"

"Because I always saw us making a road trip together," Faustine said. "There's no way we could be cooped up together in a car all day now."

"We both have to agree to this, right?"

"Yes, pick it apart, and there'll be nothing left," Faustine said.

"I can see you both going to a day spa without getting hurt," Manon said.

"Not on either of our lists, Manon." Sebastian glared at her.

"Yeah, but I can see it." Manon countered.

"Not seeing it." Sebastian shook his head at Manon.

Manon watched them with awe. She memorized the details of their fight, especially since neither knew where their relationship was headed. If they got it to work, meaning if they made it half-way through their list, she would ask

Wayland to try it. "Taking time off my fight with the band to watch you two rip each other apart is primo. I need the change of pace. I spend too much time worrying about my own problems."

"Happy to oblige," Sebastian said. "Have you been fighting with the band, or with Wayland?"

Manon cocked an eyebrow. "I'm simply trying to remind you that this," she gestured to the empty parking lot while swooping down into a bow, then continuing in a conspiratorial stage whisper, "is none of my business."

In the interest of time, Faustine opened her tote bag and handed Manon a piece of paper with the rest of her bucket list on it. Manon took the list, and let Sebastian read it over her shoulder. Manon attached it to the clipboard she brought with her. She had thought about asking Sebastian if he had a video recorder that she could use to tape the entire ordeal, since she didn't own a cell phone. She changed her mind, since she felt too awkward asking him for a favor.

"How did you get through an engagement party?" Manon didn't see how Sebastian could have ignored a tiered cake.

"Later, Manon," Sebastian said.

"Not hard," Faustine mouthed at her.

"I'm not doing that, that, or that." Sebastian pointed at various things on the list. Manon crossed them off.

"OK, I'm done then. Should I leave and let him write down whatever he wants on the list?"

"No, you have to stay and agree to it." Manon eyed Faustine warily.

"Water skiing, hiking, and there was something else, give me a minute to think of it," Sebastian said.

The entire meeting took less than 15 minutes. Sebastian took photos of the finalized list and emailed them to all three of them. Things go much faster when you have no expectations.

CHAPTER THREE

Jar glasses & yoga class

"Hi, I'm Wayland. I'm calling to tell Sebastian how he can reach me." Sebastian's father returned from errands after lunch to hear this unknown, urgent, commanding voice on his answering machine. As he paced over the tan carpeting, he weighed the pros and cons of writing the contact information down and informing his son. *The voice sounds tense, first name only, no mention of calling back, no best time to call. Sebastian needs to hear the man's voice in order to recognize the caller, much less know whether or not to return the call. I don't want my wife to touch the phone before Sebastian does.* He wrote a note saying, "Don't erase this," and put it on top of the answering machine. *Just to be sure. The voice sounds familiar, but I can't place it.* Then he called Sebastian, and left a message to return the call.

————————————

It took a day or so to get Sebastian on the landline phone. "Hey, what's up?"

"We got a message for you. There's contact information, but I can't tell who it is. I think you need to listen to it before I erase it," Sebastian's father said.

"What did it sound like?"

"It didn't sound like a sales call. It didn't sound like work, or anyone I knew. A man sounded like he knew you, and he sounded urgent. Maybe an old friend from school?"

Sebastian trekked across town after work. *What's so important that he couldn't tell me over the phone? It can't be a ghost, so rule out Elodie's last words coming back to haunt me. Maybe somebody died. It always runs in threes.* Worrying made him hungry. In an unusual move, he stopped and bought fried chicken for supper for him and his parents, in case the news was too bad to cook anything. *I've gotten no news from anyone for years. What makes me think that hearing someone's died is going to keep me from eating now?* Sebastian pulled into the drive, alongside his father waiting by the garage door. "Well, let's go hear it," Sebastian said while he was getting out of his car. Sebastian's red convertible sat in contrast to his family's austere, tan sedan.

"Glad you made it. I was worried your mother might erase your message if we waited too long."

"I brought fried chicken."

"Great."

Sebastian left the chicken on the table, then wandered through their house to their old answering machine. Light steamed in through their bedroom window. Their neatly made bed showcased a embroidered, pastel bedspread. Their open curtains had the same pattern. In contrast, the spooky voice waiting for him was obviously a flash from the past. The red light blinked omnisciently. In that moment between knowing and not knowing, Sebastian braced against the existential threat. *What am I going to hear?*

"Hi. I'm Wayland. I'm calling to tell Sebastian how he can reach me." Wayland's voice emanated from the answering machine.

Improvising to Beat the Band

Sebastian exhaled. It was a Slip of the Cue calling. Once that sunk in though, he started hyperventilating. He broke his pencil lead writing too hard while he copied the message onto a notepad on the dark wood bedside table that held his parent's landline phone.

The voice continued. "I hope he's doing OK. It's been a long time since I've seen him. I'd like to get together sometime to catch up." The voice paused. "I'd like to find out more about how Manon is doing, too, if he knows. Tell him he can call me at," and then the voice trailed off with the magic numbers no one ever knew, the constantly changing private phone numbers, the ambiguous mail drops.

"Yeah, Dad, thanks for saving this for me. Where's another pencil?"

"There's one by the phone with some paper. Are you going to need to keep the recording? We hardly use this phone anymore."

"I don't think so. Let me get a hold of him, then I'll tell you when it is safe to erase it," Sebastian said.

"Your mother doesn't know," his father said.

"OK, good. We can keep this between you and me?"

"Is this anything I should know about?" His father sighed and crossed his arms.

"I can tell you after I've talked to him," Sebastian said. "Right now, let's eat. This can wait until tomorrow."

"OK." His father trudged back to the kitchen.

"I have to double-check when I should call them. I think I have to wait until three in the morning here," Sebastian said.

Sebastian took a couple of days to collect his thoughts. *What can I tell dad about Wayland? Not that he's the lead guitarist for a Slip of the Cue. I can only say the bare minimum since I haven't gotten Wayland on the phone yet. There wasn't anything definitive about privacy on the message on the machine, so I can tell dad what he needs to know, good faith being what it is and all. Dad needs to know who was on the phone, and why that voice called. Taking the fifth isn't an option. Some things you don't say on the phone.*

Pulling in the drive, Sebastian's father was watering the purple bushes in the yard.

Sebastian got out of his car slowly. *This is not a time for sudden moves.*

"Hey, how's it going with—" Sebastian's father didn't finish his sentence, waving around and pointing instead.

The irrigation system must be broken. Sebastian stepped over some purple shrubs in order to stand beside him. "I know I was vague about who was on the phone the other day."

"You weren't vague, you simply didn't tell me," his father said. "Who was it?"

"Believe it or not, he was a guitarist in a band," Sebastian said.

"Why wouldn't I believe it? What's unbelievable about being a guitarist?"

He stopped watering to look at his son. All the color had drained from Sebastian's face. He was standing there, looking at his father, motionless. "What's the name of the band?"

"The I-can't-tell-you-their-name-because-you-haven't-signed-a-confidentiality-agreement band. I always call them 'the band' although I shouldn't, since there's a group by that name," Sebastian said.

"I'm supposed to be concerned about this? You're acting like you're trying to tell me you have cancer," Sebastian's father said.

"Cancer? I wouldn't worry about telling you that!"

"Why is this worse than cancer?"

"Because," Sebastian said, "you hated rock music."

"Not so much that you couldn't tell me if one of your

friends was in a band."

"Well, yeah," Sebastian searched the clear blue sky. "You hated it that much!"

He stopped watering and looked directly at his son.

"You're still calm, so it must not have sunk in yet," Sebastian said.

"Yeah, but if one of your friends were in a big band, you would mention it eventually." His father turned off the spigot.

"No, the bigger the band, the less likely anyone is to mention it."

His father nodded. "So, how big is the band?"

"Big enough for me never to bring it up," Sebastian said.

His father stared at him. "I take it I don't like the group then?" His father smiled at his own attempt at a joke.

"I have no reason to think you're going to be civil once you know their name." Sebastian frowned.

"And this confidentially agreement is what's keeping you from telling me their name?"

"No," Sebastian said, "it's the only legal excuse I have to keep from having to tell you their name!"

"Well, I wish you had told me this before." Sebastian's father waited for his son to reveal more information, then concluded that Sebastian wasn't legally required to say any more.

Sebastian stood and silently stared at his father. *Why hasn't he ordered me off his property yet?*

Sebastian's dad studied him, trying to read his son's face. *I should water him too, since he's told me as much as the plants have. Obviously, he feels like he's imparted important information. I have no idea what it is yet.*

"OK, so I don't like the band." Sebastian's father flung water randomly around his yard. "Although, honestly, I think you should let me know who the group is before deciding that I don't like them—"

"Uh-huh, that's what they all say when they can't remember the songs anymore. Honestly, Dad, you know who the group is. You don't like them. Remember, I know who they are, you don't." The only point Sebastian clarified was the fact that he hadn't told his father anything. He stepped around the water as it pooled beside the plants.

"Your friend being in this band hasn't seemed to effect our lives very much. Especially since I don't know who this friend is, much less who the band is." Sebastian's father. "So, why the theatrics?"

Sebastian leaned over to smell a rose. *Being an adult is coming into play. Not wanting your kid to listen to a band is apparently very different than not wanting your kid to work for that band. Maybe through my years in marketing, dad's already come to grips with the fact that my life's work isn't going to be very holy.*

The next day, Sebastian continued attempting to return Wayland's call. *I wish I'd simply picked up the phone and heard Wayland's voice when he called the first time.* Now Sebastian had to steel himself repeatedly to dial the numbers. He had pencil and blank paper to write down anything Wayland might want to say: a crisp, freshly sharpened pencil, no less. *What on earth could he possibly want to say?* Sebastian wore jeans and a thin, black sweater as he quickly paced and banged his hand against the wall. *I'm just going to get his voice mail again. There's no way I can time a call.* Breathing deeply, he dialed the number.

"Hey, Sebastian, you called me back." Wayland picked up on the second ring.

"Hi, Wayland. Of course I called you back. I've always

called you back. What was I going to do? Sit around and wonder why you wanted to talk to me?" Sebastian laughed. "What's going on? Is everything OK?"

"OK, everything is fine." Wayland echoed Sebastian's nervous laughter. "Couldn't be better. I wanted to touch base with you guys and see how you're doing. You're calling from your parent's house? How are they?"

Has he programmed his phone with a special ringtone for U.S. phone numbers? Sebastian stiffened and rocked back and forth on his feet. "My parents? No, I'm calling from my cell phone." *I don't know what I can tell him.* "They're fine. They're both still living, thank God. I don't live with them anymore. I've been living across town for a few years now." Sebastian started pacing the full length of his darkened living room. He had the room memorized, so it didn't matter that he kept his curtains closed. There was enough light spilling in through the kitchen door to keep from tripping over his heavy, sangria furniture set.

"So is there a better number for me to call?"

"I mean, you can still get a hold of me here, but I'll give you my newer number, so you can call it."

"You're working across town?"

"Yeah. The commute is too far from here, so I moved closer to work. It's in marketing. I'll tell you more about it when I see you. Are you guys going to be around here soon? Is that why you're calling?"

"The tour is not coming by your area, I am. I need to try to...catch up...with you guys if I can," Wayland said.

"I haven't talked to Manon in a while. I had a friend die, and it's been taking up most of my time right now, with the funeral, and processing it." Sebastian picked up the pencil beside the phone, but then had second thoughts about keeping anything traceable. "You know I told my father you called. He wondered who was on the answering machine. He was worried."

"Tell him not to worry. We're not mobsters. At least he knows you're not on drugs by now," Wayland said.

"Yeah, that was always a concern with weird random phone calls before." *I was terrified.* He could felt the panic rise in his throat. *Certain people still make me panic, even after a decade.* The left side of his head started to ache. "So, when are you going to be in town?"

Which is how Sebastian ended up at the motel in the early afternoon, sandwiches in hand. He had ordered from the same fast-food chain that he had seen in Manon's refrigerator. *Maybe I can find out if Wayland brought them to her?*

Wayland drove up in a nondescript car, alone.

Sebastian pulled back the orange, flowery curtain. *It must be a rental.*

"Hey, looks like I found it." Wayland slammed the car door.

"Been a long while," Sebastian said, as they embraced for a long moment. "Let's go inside. I don't trust being out here, too exposed."

"Oh, you didn't have to. I've eaten," Wayland said when he saw the sandwiches on the dresser.

"It's supper. Don't worry, it's good cold. We can eat it later," Sebastian paused, "if we want."

"How've things have been going?" Wayland sat on the edge of the bed.

"Well, I'm working in marketing. Which is ironic, considering what happened," Sebastian said.

"I don't think it's ironic, You look OK. You look like you've been keeping in shape."

"Yeah, health-wise, I have no complaints."

To Sebastian, Wayland was a ghost sitting on the edge of the bed. "I never thought I'd see you again."

"Why not?" Wayland shook his head.

"Well, last time you tried to visit Manon, things did not go as planned. So why would you try it again?"

"Either she has gotten better, and can remember more things, or her memory has gotten worse and she will still have no idea who I am. If she doesn't have any idea what happened, I'm home free, I'll just introduce myself," Wayland said.

"A rock star happens to drop by." Sebastian pulled out the desk chair and sat down.

"Sure, why not?"

"OK, but I don't have any idea where Manon's memory is right now," Sebastian said.

"I've dropped by. It freaks Manon out when I call. She doesn't know who's on the phone," Wayland said.

"Always presuming the worst," Sebastian said.

"Well, the worst did happen once, so it could happen again you know," Wayland said.

"You know as well as I do that you don't have any idea who attacked her or why, so don't go presuming that you know—"

Wayland's laughter cut him off. "And no one's ever going to find out either. Which is the weird part."

They both stopped to eat a bite of sandwich, using the dark brown dresser as a table. Mainly because they needed to keep from talking.

"Have you changed your mind about what you think happened? Anything new turn up that I should know about?"

Wayland shook his head to keep from talking with his mouth full.

Sebastian continued, "Do you think she was getting sick anyway, and made it all up? She was in her early twenties, and I read this book about how highly correlated writers are with being bipolar. She had quite the imagination."

"Please don't start with the bipolar issue. I'm a writer too, remember? I don't want people saying that I made Manon up," Wayland said.

"I would never do that." Sebastian fleered: a smirk.

"Only because you've met her. If I started talking about co-writers who have no memory of me," Wayland put the leftover sandwiches in the small refrigerator, "I would be in as much trouble as she is."

"Still no idea then?"

"I'm sure a person did it. It simply wasn't my former wife," Wayland said.

"But how would Manon know that?" Sebastian picked bits of jalapeño pepper out of his sandwich.

"She wouldn't. How would anybody know that? She's never met my ex-wife. Our fans have never met my ex-wife! The world," Wayland waved an arm around the hotel room, still holding the sandwich with the other, "has never met—"

"Wife finds out. Goes on a rampage." Sebastian eyed the floor, waiting for Wayland's sandwich to fall.

"Yeah," Wayland said.

"It does seem plausible," Sebastian said.

"Especially since there was probably a deranged lunatic following Manon around," Wayland said.

"See, that's harder to prove because you have to speculate the existence of a person that no one has heard of before or since." Sebastian grimaced. "Anyway, Manon wouldn't want you calling anybody names. Neither would Jane."

Wayland nodded and ate. Sebastian had started his own personal backlash, so Wayland wasn't sure where Sebastian stood anymore on several issues. Philosophically, Wayland was having a difficult time learning how to love where he was in life right now.

"When I see Manon, do you want me to tell her how you're doing?" Sebastian wiped his hands.

"Nah, tell her 'hi' and that I'll be by to see her soon." Wayland ate slower and slower.

"It's good that you're trying to stick by her. What are you going to tell her if she does know what's going on?"

"Anything she lets me tell her. Probably talk about her, and her plants and whatnot," Wayland said.

"You don't talk about your family then?"

"Never. She does know things about them."

"That they exist, to be sure. Not even I know much more about them than that, and I watch the news," Sebastian said.

"Life's a lot easier when you know what you can and can't let in. The reality is that she understands that she doesn't have to know anything about them."

"If she starts working with you guys again, you'll have to tell her what's happened over the years. I can't imagine that she'll be too thrilled to know you've remarried."

"That's one of those things I let her bring up, and then I only answer direct questions. Then I change the subject as soon as possible," Wayland said.

"I don't know if I would talk to you if it were me."

"We still owe her money, remember?"

"That's interesting. Does she know that?"

Wayland mulled over their possible discourse as he drove to Manon's house. Many times when he visited her, he passed himself off as a Christian fundamentalist, passing out pamphlets. Manon tended to try to convert him when she was in a good mood. There was one thing that Sebastian had been wrong about concerning Wayland's arrival. The car was not a rental. The car was his. Wayland never got over either Manon, or what had happened to her. He went on with his life, but he kept a house near hers. On occasion, he would drive by. The house was officially in the name of a property management company. He even rented it out to people he knew from time to time. Plus, it was cheaper than a hotel. Part of him had always tried to stay in touch with her, with whatever means he had available.

So, he knew that Manon still walked, and that it would be easier to catch her in the evening. *What am I going to say?* There had been so many times when she flat-out did not recognize him. Usually he could remind her of things he knew about her, or something they had done together, and it would spark her memory. Those times the wheels in her mind would catch, and they could talk. Other times they wouldn't. When that happened, he would only end up upsetting her. Some days he felt like taking the chance; some days he didn't. Either way, he didn't try it too often, for her sake.

He glimpsed Manon walking back up her drive. The bright, sunny day matched his good luck. Her front yard flower garden danced in the breeze. He parked and ran to catch up with her before she went inside. "Do you know how I'm blessed today?"

Manon turned and looked at him. "Hi Wayland. How have you been blessed today?" She smiled directly at him, broadly.

Wayland took a minute to look at her before he answered. "Because you knew my name today." He smiled and kissed her cheek.

"Believe it or not, I've been watching the videos." She didn't immediately embrace him. *I can remember knowing him, and I can remember not knowing who he was.* "I can recognize you now." She gave him a quick, short hug.

"So, let's see, it's been twenty years, and you finally broke down and watched a video of us." Wayland's mind spun a web of nervous incredulity, expecting a flukey one-time deal. *Did someone mention the band to her recently?*

"I told you I never watch anything until it's a classic. It's been twenty years now, so I can watch your show."

"A couple of years past twenty. More like thirty. Are you feeling better?"

"Yes," she said, "are you?"

"Yeah, I'm fine." Wayland laughed.

"Come on in. I will prove to you that I have watched your show."

"You have the videos to prove it."

"Not only do I have the videos, I am willing to put one of them in the DVD player right in front of you." She opened the door wide.

He went in to see what he looked like, decades ago.

Manon threw herself down on the couch. Wayland settled in a chair. After watching a couple of concert movies, Wayland went to her piano. Wayland was working on a new song idea with Ailill, the band's lead singer, and wanted to know what Manon thought of it.

"It's called 'Take Me Home.' What do you think?

"'Take Me Home?' How does it go?"

Wayland started humming a motif, with oohs and aahs thrown in for good measure. Manon saw him turn on his cell phone, and thought he was just recording an idea. Actually, he was on speakerphone with Ailill, while Ailill softly strummed his guitar overseas.

"Sure. Why not?" Manon paused. "It's supposed to be about the past?"

"Yeah. Trying to come to grips with the past," Wayland said. He started writing on Manon's musical notation stationary, flipping papers back and forth. To Ailill on the phone, it sounded like Wayland was trying to take out the trash.

"Hey, hon, did you ever think about getting a new computerized phone? They have video calling now. That way you could practice with us," Wayland said.

Manon paused for more than 10 seconds.

"Wayland, I'm broke. Not so bad that I'm sitting on the curb, but not enough to have the latest, greatest gadgets. Mail doesn't work anymore? I thought it was under a buck."

"It is," Wayland said, "but this is as good a reason as any to send you money. Where do you want it sent?"

Manon couldn't believe he was talking specifics. "Send a paper check to my address. It'll go towards past royalties."

"'Past royalties?' Do you want that written on the check!"

"Yeah. At some point we should figure out how much the total is, until then, just write me a check," Manon said.

"You're sure you don't want it to go through your lawyer?"

Manon sighed. "Write the first one, and I'll start looking for a lawyer." Manon had no legal representation. For others, she was adamant, for herself, not so good.

"Maybe we should do the binding arbitration thing? If you die your family could still sue us for back royalties."

"Maybe. I wouldn't want to stand in front of a jury trying to explain this. But maybe an expert could figure out how much you guys are supposed to pay me. Who would be an expert on royalties anyway?"

"Someone in show business with no axe to grind."

Manon veered off the topic of money. "Speaking of things we ought to do together, Sebastian and his girlfriend Faustine are breaking up, and they're working through a bucket list together."

"Bucket list? Because their relationship is dying?"

"Yeah, why not? I was thinking if they got theirs to work out, maybe we could try it," Manon said.

Wayland stopped playing. He didn't even have a bucket list for himself. Ailill's guitar chords continued to drift faintly into the room.

"I still can't believe you finally got that Aeolian harp part to work." Manon reminisced about life before digital recorders. "You guys had to cut and splice it." Hearing the faint guitar, she walked over to Wayland's cell phone. "Is this a four-track recorder?"

Wayland didn't want her talking to Ailill yet. If he pushed her memory too hard, it might stop working. "There's an app that works like a four-track recorder on it, but right now I've got Ailill's guitar part playing." Ailill heard them talking about him and stopped. Wayland hovered over his cell phone, looking like he was punching buttons on it. Manon retreated to her couch to keep the guys from finding out that she didn't know what an "app" was, then started watching another video of the band. Wayland said something inaudible to Ailill, who started playing again.

"We had the synthesizer playing over it. It masked where the tape was cut." Wayland didn't want to tell her that the synths were her idea because she didn't like the transition from wind harp to guitar, but he wasn't knocking it. At least she knew who he was today. "The Aeolian harp part was creepy for a rock song. You remember we recorded the wind harp at that monument? We were on vacation."

The band used the recorded wind harp sample for the vinyl album as well as their live performances. They made a few backup copies, but they had to be careful with it, since there was no way of replicating that exact sound. They tried though. Wayland used a half-a-dozen linked guitar pedals to replicate most of the tone with his electric guitar, but for unknown reasons, it never sounded quite the same. Wayland and Manon took the chords in the wind harp sample and elaborated them into a simple melody.

Manon stopped the video and went into the kitchen.

After several minutes, she said, "Come here."

Wayland took Ailill off of speaker phone, then walked into the dimly lit kitchen to view a set of bottles that had been cut into glasses. Magic suffused the room as light shimmered across the glass. Wayland tossed his cell phone in a chair with Ailill still listening.

"It was jarring my memory, no pun intended," Manon said. "We had started talking about playing a song by blowing across bottle tops. We were going to have a harmonica go with it because I saw a commercial for cutting your own drinking glasses from glass soda bottles. That commercial stuck in my mind until I had to do something with it. It reminded me of something that happened seven or so years before we wrote the song. Which doesn't sound very long at all anymore, but was forever back then."

"Even I thought that seven years was a long time back then." Wayland watched the light streaming through Manon's kitchen window. It highlighted the herbs and flowers growing in her windowsill flower box. The spring flowers matched the ones growing in her yard.

"The song did the weird, creepy, haunting thing all right. I still can't believe that any song that started out with corny commercials could end up with that hauntingly beautiful melody. At the time it felt like I was trying to tap into pre-conscious space," Manon said.

"Well, it turns out that we did a pretty good job of tapping into that space, and turning out something that a lot of other people have used for years to tap into that same space." Unfortunately, Wayland sounded like a magazine interview from time to time.

"Weird," Manon said.

"You wanna play the glasses," he pointed at the table full of them, "as long as you have them out." He picked up a glass beside him.

"Sure. How much water do you put in each?"

"Don't know. Pour and see how it sounds."

———————————

In a few minutes, or maybe it was an hour, they had put together the intro to the song using water glasses instead of the Aeolian harp. It still had a weird, eerie, uncontrollable sound. They sat for a minute, looking at each other, wondering. They had never tried to recreate the wind harp with anything besides a guitar before, since that's what Wayland used on tour. Wayland, Manon, Ailill eavesdropping from the chair, and a bunch of half-filled bottles sat stupefied around Manon's kitchen table.

Ailill held his breath for a moment. *All those years of trying, and all we needed were some water glasses. I wish Wayland was recording the sound to use later.*

"You were able to watch the video," Wayland shifted in his chair, "of the song we wrote," he thought twice before asking, watching Manon's reaction, "about your suicide attempt?"

"Yes, and it did not make me feel suicidal!" Manon pumped her fist to reassure him, even though he couldn't see her over the phone.

"It's a little scary, doing something like that..." Wayland said.

Ironically, scarier than attempting suicide. Manon juxtaposed an interview being given over a grave in her mind, with a TV camera propped on the tombstone.

They both paused, looked at each other, then at the glasses, then back at each other. The room dimmed with the setting sun, but they didn't turn a light on

"I wonder if they would sound the same with candles in them," Manon said.

"You mean those floating candles?"

"Yeah, they shouldn't sound too different, but they might." Manon interrupted her own train of thought. "You know, the fundamentalist Christians know where I live."

"How do they know where you're at? Did you tell them?" Wayland didn't want to know where this was headed.

"No, but Someone did," Manon's eyes indicated the heavens. "When they've been in the neighborhood recently, I've been walking out the door, so they catch me. They don't want knock on the door because of the sign."

"I'm surprised that you have one of those signs up. Didn't you hate them when you were growing up?"

"Paintballs on the house, and vandals in the car drove me to it. I explained that to the fundamentalist Christians as well, so that they wouldn't feel too badly."

"But everyone else can drive by 'No Trespassing' in block red letters, even though they had nothing to do with the paintball vandals."

"It's the problem with broadcasting a message. It goes out to everybody," Manon said.

"You ready for your suicide attempt to be broadcast, or is there still a 'No Trespassing' sign over it." Wayland smelled the flowers in the window box by the sink.

"I don't want it broadcast, however, I'm not doing my level best to try to avoid it either." She straightened to level with him.

"That's not an answer." Wayland picked a sprig of parsley. "It might not be mentioned anytime soon, but one day it will be. What do you do once it's out there?"

"Dealing with it once it happens is not the answer that

you're looking for, I take it." Mannon got up and started taking dishes out of her dishwasher.

"That's right. I want to know how you think you're going to react once other people eventually know."

"It was so long ago, I can't see people as caring anymore. And I'm much older now. I think I'd be viewed more like a depression survivor or something."

"I can't swear that there would have been a big crowd in an uproar about it back then." Wayland munched the parsley. "I'm sure I would have been overwhelmed, but then, I get upset about things..." He smiled.

"You guys would have made sure there would have been a protest. You would have had signs up at my funeral saying I shouldn't have done it."

They laughed.

"That might have been good for the video of the song, but..." Wayland tilted his head towards her. "You're willing to go outside and tell everybody that this part of your life is over? You think that you're well enough to do that?" He leaned further towards her.

"Yeah."

"What about relapses? What are the chances of it happening again?" Wayland reached towards the glasses. *Are you going to be overwhelmed by what the public might think?* Wayland turned a water glass on Manon's cedar table slightly. "That's an obvious question a reporter might ask." Wayland turned the water glass back the other way. *She knows no one's going to ask.*

"That's an easier question than what I might do about public opinion, when no one in the public even knows me." Manon stood stoically in the middle of her beige, ceramic tile floor for her brief oration. "I finally found a treatment that works for me. No more hit and miss, then pray that something finally works. I'm sleeping fine, no problems."

"You always complained about not sleeping before."

"Sleeping's the first thing that goes. Once it's gone, you're over," Manon said.

"You sound like you're confident it's over," Wayland said.

"I know it's over now," Manon said.

Manon followed Wayland to his car as he was leaving. She folded her arms against the cold night breeze since she was wearing shorts and a loosely draped designer print top. Wayland was warmer in his standard blue jeans and long sleeve white button down shirt. No kiss goodbye tonight.

"I don't know what gods I'm crossing by trying to see you again." Wayland shook his head, looking outwards into the night while sliding into his car seat.

"Yeah, I know. I haven't even asked about it yet, you know." Manon picked a flower, even though it was dark.

Wayland looked at her as directly as possible. She looked down, kicking gravel around on her long, winding, dirt driveway. The shrubs and trees on her property cast dark silhouettes against the night sky.

"Manon, I don't have any idea what happened. If I had any clue, I would tell you. Or I would tell the police. Anybody..." His eyes were pleading while he was gripping the steering wheel. He twisted his hand around it like a motorcycle.

"I'm surprised you haven't given up and let it go," Manon said.

"And run into whatever it is in the spirit world that is messing up your life on my own? No way. No thanks." Wayland glanced at the nearly full moon and shuddered.

---

* * *

Improvising to Beat the Band

After Wayland left Manon's house, leaving her the extra veggie sandwiches that Sebastian had brought him, since that was her favorite, he drove to his house nearby to spend the night. He didn't have anything personal there but toiletries and a change of clothes. He had vintage clothes that, to date, had never appeared in a photograph. He even wrote songs there, while he was bored and waiting for his ride.

The next day, Wayland tried to sleep on his return flight. Normally, Wayland had no trouble with airline seats since he was a little short for a guy, only slightly taller than Manon, but today he couldn't get situated in his seat that was abruptly tiny. He adjusted every knob he could, but nothing was right. He had the morning after blues, never mind the time. In the darkness of sleep, he could process seeing Manon before he had to go back to pretending nothing happened. *Why are fundamentalist Christians visiting Manon! That's my schtick. I hope they don't blow my cover. And of course, there's some mysterious spiritual force hanging out by her house, still waiting to direct traffic her way. Even if the spirits don't seem nefarious yet, they will be soon.* He tossed and turned in his seat. *She must've been attacked by a demonic spirit, bitter and murderous. I can't believe Sebastian thinks it might have been Jane. Whatever it is, I hope it doesn't keep me from seeing her. She's feeling better. She's got a lot going for her this time. She has concert films. As long as she doesn't throw them out, I can always play one of them and show her the band playing on the video. Maybe next time I'll be a fundamentalist Christian who happened to carry old rock videos with him.* He adjusted his seat. *This can't last, but next time I'll take a guitar to her house. Who knows, maybe she'll do some songwriting.*

Wayland never knew what to do about the perpetual unfinished business with Sebastian. Wayland tried to prise Sebastian open like a storage chest that had rusted shut. *Sebastian could help me with Manon, but by the same token he could turn around and tell Manon anything. There would always be a chance that she would believe whatever he said, good or bad. Why shouldn't he know? He was there, right?* It was absurd to think that he might not want to see Manon; they had been friends for years. *Plus, like I told him, the band still owes her money. When she's well enough, I'm going to write her a check for my part of it, at least.*

Wayland finally stopped fidgeting in his airline seat with the snapshot memory of a previous time in his mind. He had been playing guitar with Ailill and Manon. His memory turned into a dream as he fell asleep.

Ailill had turned to Manon and said something like, "What's his problem?" They had had a fight he had long since forgotten.

Manon turned to Ailill and said, "I didn't know what his problem was back when I *was* his problem."

Not once did Manon realize that she had never stopped being his problem.

Manon phoned Wayland a few days later. "Did you take my digital recorder?" She turned the long length of white, coiled cable in her hand.

"No, you never found it?" Wayland had no cord attached to his phone. It was a black brick. *Why didn't she ask me while I was there?*

"Why in the name of anything did I mention my mother's necklace on the recording!"

"Since I don't have the recording, I wouldn't know," Wayland said.

"I was hoping it was you. I'm not mad at whoever it was. I think I may even understand why they did it. But it's been ages. You would think they would bring the necklace back eventually. It only had sentimental value to my mother," Manon said.

"Thanks for accusing me of stealing a necklace for no other reason than it had sentimental value to your mother," Wayland said.

"What should I do? I've asked everyone. No one knows anything. But I swear I did have that recorder."

"Can I presume that you had finished material on this recorder?"

"Of course, why else would I have a fit?"

"I wasn't there for the original fit, you know. You weren't speaking to me at the time," Wayland said.

"What did I do? What did I do," Manon started hyperventilating, "that was so wrong? Why did I ever start writing?" She wiped the tears from her eyes.

"Don't start with the 'writing caused all my problems' thing again." Wayland's studio wasn't large enough to pace around in, since it was specifically designed for acoustics, so he stepped out into the hallway, a corridor specifically designed for walking. Wayland shook his head while he paced through the long, grey empty hallway that seemed to go on for a least a quarter mile. No family photos along the walls since this house was for work only: writing and recording music. There were publicity stills of the band in the living room, along with the gold records in cases, where band members would give magazine interviews.

"Why not!"

"Because you had a motherlode of problems before you ever started writing." Wayland leaned his hand against the wall at the end of the corridor before turning around. "Writing let you ask more people for help," he kicked the wall, "than you could have otherwise." He continued pacing the hall. *I'm certainly not a contributor to your lifelong misery. Besides, that weird, evil spirit keeps stalking her. That thing would have attacked her regardless of the line of work she went into.* "Why bring it up now?"

"I finally told my mother why her necklace went missing," Manon said.

"You slipped that into a casual conversation!"

"Oddly enough, it was easier to say than I thought it would be," Manon said. "Especially since I pointed out that I thought that whoever it was would have returned the necklace by now."

"Maybe you should have left well enough alone?"

"Maybe it's been so long, no one will care anymore," Manon said.

"Except your mother. She wants her keepsake back." Wayland paced to muffle his irritation on the phone.

"Yeah. You'd think someone would leave it on the door or something," Manon said.

Wayland paused a long moment before he finished his thought. "Manon, have you ever thought a demon might have carried it away?" He walked back into his studio. This recording room was sparsely furnished, but comfortable. The furniture set didn't match. The walls and ceiling were decorated with fabric acoustic panels, also non-matching, but an attempt was made at shabby chic so that the room would look put together. Cables ran through the hallway from this room into the room beside it down the hall. Both rooms would have been bedrooms in a normal house.

"A demon?" Manon's crisp voice was followed by a heartbeat of silence.

"Yes," he said.

"You guys never did figure out who knocked me down, did you? Not even amongst yourselves?"

"No." He heard Manon slam something down.

"I had hoped you guys had figured it out, and didn't tell me because you thought I'd overreact," Manon said.

"Manon, I've said it every time we've talked about this. If I knew anything, I would tell you."

"So, you're down to a demon stealing my stuff."

"Yeah."

"You don't know what's going on?"

"No. I don't know any more than you do," Wayland said.

"Then I guess I shouldn't wait around for a demon to bring back by mother's necklace?"

"You should probably think about it like a stolen car. It's probably in the same category by now," Wayland said.

"Gone but not forgotten," Manon said.

"Basically," Wayland said.

———————

Manon heard someone banging on her front door. She didn't move. *It might be a fundamentalist Christian proselytizing in the area. There are so many devout Christians in the area who remind me of Wayland. I must not have gotten over him.* Reflexively, she took the song she had partially written off the piano to hide it. If she had had a record coming out with an artist under contract, she would be required to guarantee that no one else had seen the song already. The fact that it didn't matter anymore would not sink into her head. Her life wasn't any different after all these years, so why would anyone else's life have changed that much? Sometimes "going on with your life" is just pointlessly rearranging other people's lives.

Manon opened the door to see a delivery truck. There was a delivery man, dressed in brown work clothes, holding a rather large bouquet of long-stem red roses. He was holding out an electronic signature pad for her to sign. She waited until he had left to try to figure out who sent them. She looked at life through fun house mirrors. *I had hoped that the weird part of my life was over and done with.* She looked at the roses and knew she was going to find out for sure, one way or the other. She eventually figured out that the signature read "Ailill," the lead singer for a Slip of the Cue.

"Thought you might like these. Still sorry about that time Wayland sent you roses and you didn't know who they were from. Let me know when it's safe to get together."

When would it be safe to get together? Mercifully enough, Ailill's handwritten note had a return address and phone number, unlike the time Wayland sent her roses with no note. She didn't know who had sent them for five years. For five long, scary years she hid from a non-existent, rabid admirer. The police didn't start dealing with stalkers until after she had graduated from college. She found out Wayland had sent them when she started complaining about it one Valentine's Day, and he finally mentioned them. He was a guitarist. Talking to people was not in his contract, so to speak.

Manon could remember the incident Ailill had referenced. *It must be safe for us to talk since he won't be talking about stuff I can't remember. I don't care if I get his wife on the phone, whoever she is.* She looked down at the signature and thought for a minute. *It's been over twenty years. The band doesn't hang out anymore. They just work together. Plus, they're old enough for early retirement. I'm not going to get anyone but Ailill on the phone. It's his private line. Best to decide what to say before I call.* She looked around the room for a minute, then put his note on her refrigerator. *What am I going to say?*

Manon had her living room windows open, along with her kitchen windows. There was enough natural daylight in the middle of the day to not need to turn on any additional lights. The weird dark maroon print of her couch really didn't go with her lighter colored kitchen furniture. Standing in the kitchen, you could see at least part of the furniture from both rooms with the door open. Her house had been decorated one room at a time, not as a coherent whole.

Improvising to Beat the Band

Manon dialed Ailill's number. His greeting sounded upbeat. "Are you having a good day today?"

"Yeah, why?" *How did we manage to skip saying hello.* Manon clutched the phone with both hands.

"I wanted to know if it was safe to talk to you?"

"I'm calling, so it must be." She started pacing. *That's not obvious?*

"Didn't know if we were putting pressure on you is all." *I hope she doesn't relapse.* Ailill was on speaker phone since he despised having to hold something while he was talking. Since he was on speaker phone, he had to be alone to talk to Manon. So he was at the office in his house, as opposed to going over to the recording studio. He wouldn't have to explain making a short phone call to anyone. His office was oddly business looking, trimmed in black with a medium colored wood paneling. It didn't seem to match his personality. Ailill decorated it to impress businessmen he needed to ask to sponsor their tours.

"Ah," Manon pulled her hair away from her face. She habitually looked down toward her feet when she heard his voice. She didn't realize that she did that until she had to pull her hair out of her eyes in order to talk on the phone. *How long have I been doing that?*

"Yeah, there's pressure. But there's going to have to be, isn't there?"

"I don't want you doing this if you're going to be feeling too much pressure," Ailill said. "You need to be concerned about your health first."

"Well, I go outside and everything these days." Manon paced to the living room window and pulled back the curtain further to peer outside more. *I don't know how much I need to be worried about my health anymore.* She let go of the curtain and moved back to the kitchen. "So it seems like going on should be in order."

There was a long awkward silence. The kind of silence that inspired people to write letters instead of talking on the phone.

"Ailill, I don't have anything to say. I'm presuming that you want to write me a check for my part of whatever's left." She picked up a pencil from a jar on her kitchen table that held loose coins and rubber bands. *I wish I had planned out the conversation after all.*

"Well I do," his voice slowed, "but that's not it," he paused, "I'm worried about your frame of mind."

Manon sighed. *There's money left over. I never thought there would be.*

"Oh, good. There was something left after the last tour."

"I've bad news. We did have corporate sponsorship on the last tour. So I doubt you'd consider us to be truly independent anymore. But, we are still in business, if that's what you mean."

"Yes, that's exactly what I mean."

"Because I hate it when you mean the other thing as well."

"You mean the 'drinking it all up' thing."

"Yeah, that thing." Ailill had the sheer white curtains to his business office open. They showed off his glass block windows. Normally, this type of window would be relegated to the bathroom, but regular glass is too easy to take a picture through. Shadowy photos don't sell for as much to tabloids.

"Do I want to know how close you came?"

"Not that close, truthfully. I know I give the impression I've got one foot in the grave, and the other in rehab, but, everything's fine." He waited a moment before clarifying. "Personally, everything's fine for me."

Aside from being wrong about the band going deaf, she was also wrong about how long each of them would stay married. So, the way things ended up was not the way she had expected.

"You're still married then?" Manon specified his clarification.

"Yes, I'm currently married," he said, "and have been for a long time now."

"Anyone I know, or knew?"

"No. Can I talk about it in person? This is hard to do on the phone," he said.

"OK, so what do we do now?" She twirled the long telephone cord like there was a kid skipping rope in her kitchen. *He better know.*

"You don't know?" *Doesn't she plan everything she's going to say in advance?*

"No, I don't know what comes next anymore." She could not have been more truthful.

"Do you want to try to write together? I don't know how to say this without sounding like I'm coming on to you, but I really miss writing songs with you. How much time do you have right now?"

CHAPTER FOUR

The Hospital

A nightlight shone through the western styled swinging doors that led to Faustine's kitchen. She slumped over her computer wearing her faded bluejeans. That evening, the reading light in her living room came from the desktop lamp beside her computer. She rapidly tapped her foot while retrieving a copy of Elodie's archived social media posts. Faustine inhaled sharply and clicked on Elodie's saved favorites. The first archived web page was a photo of the chapel at the hospital. The next was a post from the hospital reminding the world at large that eating disorders have the highest mortality rate of any mental illness. *Anorexia isn't a mental illness. That makes it sound like people aren't supposed to talk about it. Anyway, the chapel's stained glass window is beautiful.* Next on Elodie's favorites list was a yoga class. There were several people in the photo, none of whom Faustine knew. *Another group of friends of friends I missed. My aunt will chide me over lunch. I didn't even know she was in a yoga class.* Faustine's cat tried to jump in her lap, even though her knee was still bouncing from her nervous toe tapping. She picked her cat up to carry her outside. *Why didn't Elodie ever ask me to go to yoga with her? The chapel is pretty. Maybe I'll go there and meditate.*

Faustine entered the hospital, making note of the chapel inside on the left. The stained-glass dove soared above her in its pastoral sky. Faustine unceremoniously entered the open chapel doors, which emanated a welcoming organ playing gospel music. A dry erase board by the doorway on an easel had the announcements. *Maybe the pastor knew Elodie? Should I leave a note on the dry erase board?* There was a service at three that afternoon, and a later one at six. *I'll meander around the hospital a bit, then check back before the service starts.*

She went back through the door she came in. She turned right, since she had gone left to begin with, only to discover that she was in the hospital's gift shop. She tried walking through it, but ended up going through a door that led to a parking lot instead. *Where did the hospital go? No one misplaces a hospital, it has to be back in there somewhere.* Faustine turned around and headed back. This time she lingered in the gift shop, pretending to browse. A couple came in through a door she hadn't noticed, discussing a baby shower.

"We should get them blue diapers," the man said, "the ones with the indicator strip."

"You don't give diapers as a present," the woman said. "Take some time and figure out how you want the baby to remember you. Maybe a small cartoon hairbrush that he can still use when he gets a little older."

Faustine couldn't focus well enough to read the back of the box she was holding, so she put it back on the shelf. It didn't even register with her what was in the box. *People actually wonder how other people are going to remember them?* Faustine decided to leave the way the couple came in, which put her in a long, grey, empty hallway. It seemed to go on for a least a quarter mile. *This would be a great way to meditate, if I didn't have so much to think about.* She stopped for a minute and stared at the gray walls. *I wonder if this is where Elodie came to die?* Faustine had no way of knowing if Elodie had ever walked down this particular hallway. The air conditioner echoed from somewhere far away. It was as though she were the first person to ever walk down this space-capsule corridor. It showed few traces of prior human existence.

Faustine finally came to double-doors. When she went through, she walked into a hallway that was half-glass. There was a regular wall on her left, and a wall of glass on her right. The hallway window peered out over yet another previously unknown parking lot with a few scattered, small, palm trees. As she walked along, running her left hand against the dark tan wall, looking through the glass into the sunlight, she heard a recording from behind a half-opened door. She stopped for a moment to identify the tune. She heard feet shuffling across the floor to the beat. She leaned her head inside the doorway a bit. The room was full of mirrors. The floor was polished wood. The dancers stretched on mats. All the mats made a jigsaw of faded primary colors on the floor. *This room looks familiar for some odd reason.* She stayed a moment too long, and someone from inside the room asked her a question. "No, I don't know where I'm going." She forced an introductory smile on her face.

The yoga instructor had a policy of first class free, so potential enrollees could check the place out before having to commit. It reminded Faustine of the weight loss meeting. But she wasn't trying to make a new relationship work with someone else after an old relationship had gone bust. *Wait, I don't have to do this, I'm here because of a post. It's amazing what you can convince yourself you have to do.* She watched the dancers stretch beside a ballet balance bar. They didn't look at themselves in the portable mirrors.

Improvising to Beat the Band

"Can I watch from the sidelines?" An angry tremor pulsed through Faustine. Her foot started tapping without her realizing it. *I should join yoga class...but that's crazy, way too much!* She shook her head, winning her internal argument.

The yoga instructor looked askance. "You'll get more out of the class if you participate."

Faustine stopped and smiled. "I can't work out right now. I'm passing though. I didn't even know this was here." She pointed across the room, generally towards the wooden double doors. "Maybe I'll leave and come back another time." She was on the verge of tears, but her anger had subsided, and her foot remained still. "Do you have a brochure with the times listed?"

"Stay and sit for a while." The yoga instructor beamed. Her crying concerned him, but he hid behind his smile. Smiling could be its own form of yoga meditation: an intentional pose. "You can meditate to the music while the rest of us stretch out a bit." He sat down on the floor before realizing that he had forgotten to put the music back on, and got back up. "You'll want to check out our instruction times online. I don't have any brochures." He sat down on the floor again. The music filled the empty space. "I don't think anybody has brochures anymore. Everything is online these days." He closed his eyes and sat with his back very straight, before he thought to say, "You don't look like you're old enough to know what a brochure is, anyway." He opened his eyes for a moment to smile and emphatically nod like the conscientious instructor he was.

Faustine breathed a sigh of relief. She went over and sat in a folding chair, near a wall without a mirror. She shut her eyes, took a deep breath, and tried to listen to the music. She couldn't quite hear it. The room was dimly lit and cool. It felt very relaxing. *That's the first time anyone's ever commentated on my age. I don't know what to make of it. He's probably trying to get people to join the class. Why doesn't he know that comments like that aren't going to do it?* Faustine's breathing eventually calmed down enough, with her eyes shut, to hear the music. She let her breath rise and fall with its sound, slowing to the beat of the music. She opened her eyes slightly to see the shadows of the dancers going through their yoga moves. It was all very soothing, and very distracting.

"There's a service at the chapel in an hour or so, depending on how long I've been in here. I was planning on going there next." Faustine explained her schedule to the yoga instructor after class since he was trying to sign a form for her, but she didn't have any paperwork for him to fill out. It was turning into a comedy of errors with him asking for paperwork that she didn't possess.

"Most of my clients are here to fill a prescription," the yoga instructor said.

"You can get a prescription for a yoga class?"

"I don't think I can tell you any more than that without breaking client confidentiality, since you were here and have seen everyone. I do have nonprescription students as well, but most of them are at another site. The ones that are here are usually with the patients, though," he said.

"Well, I guess my patient died then," Faustine said. "I had a friend, who has since passed, who posted about coming here, and I was following her old posts, looking around, trying to figure out what happened. She never told us anything was wrong."

"You need grief counseling," he said.

Faustine recoiled slightly and grimaced.

The yoga instructor took no notice of her reaction. "They have an introductory seminar in the cafeteria. I don't know what their entire schedule is, but I think their initial meetings are on Tuesday nights. They should have more information about it at the front desk. You passed it when you came in."

Improvising to Beat the Band

"I didn't pass anything on the way in. I got totally lost. I passed the parking lot twice while going the same direction, which logically should be impossible, but that's how it happened. I'm not entirely sure I'll be able to find the chapel again. I need to know where the exit is," Faustine said.

"I'll walk you there. I'll try to tell you a little more about the class in the hall, where we can speak more privately," he said.

The yoga instructor bantered about several upcoming hospital activities while he took Faustine around many circuitous corridors. Eventually, they walked past the chapel, and out an exit.

"I figured this was the way you came in, since you had mentioned wanting to go to the chapel." He smiled warmly while he walked away, letting the door shut behind him.

Faustine scanned the parking lot. There was a giant glare in her eyes that she covered with her hand. *Is the sun shining brighter now than it did when I arrived?* She went back to her car, dropped off her things, then slowly returned to the hospital. She managed to circumnavigate her way to the chapel. It was about half-an-hour until service. *That's not too long to wait.* The sun's beam lightened Faustine's face as she stared up at the sky blue stained glass, praying. Eventually, the service started.

Faustine and her aunt decided to meet at the Foothills Foodie Cafe. It was the same restaurant Faustine took Sebastian to for their bucket list, a mock engagement party. At that time, Sebastian had only been told that they were going out to eat. Somewhere between the steam dancing off the sizzling fajitas in the night air and the champagne toast on the balcony, another couple's engagement party toasted the happy couple, since Sebastian and Faustine had toasted them when the rest of the room did, and the jig was up.

Faustine analyzed her situation. *A normal engagement party would have had lots of people. Even if Sebastian and I got married, we wouldn't have any friends to invite.*

Today, the cafe was in a small, side room, which was partitioned from the rest of the restaurant during the day, and catered to shoppers. In the midst of the subdued ambience, an earth tone, beaded curtain with petite, mirror-like wind chimes jangled. Faustine had been reduced to eating lunch with her aunt again. For the third time, they had the shrimp entree with soup, salad, and fruit.

"So, did you bring a print out of her social media posts?" Faustine's aunt asked.

"I didn't bring them." Pale, Faustine shook slightly. *Why did I ever start doing this?*

"If you need me to help you read them, I'm here." Her aunt nodded along with her singsong voice.

"I'm OK, I just need to know what some of them mean." She pulled her purse across her lap, and put it down on the bench. Her brow furrowed.

"You have to read all of them to know what they mean, Faustine." Her aunt's voice became monotone and hypnotic.

"We talk," Faustine paused, "you and I do," she looked directly at her aunt, "when we're eating." She took a breath. "Did I even talk with Elodie? And when we talk, do people even know I'm there? I don't remember people saying my name much." Her mind raced. *Are all of my relationships fake?*

Faustine's aunt looked away from her niece's imploring eyes. "OK, just because I knew there was something more going on with Sebastian doesn't mean that I can play ESP with all your friends." (ESP stands for Extra Sensory Perception. It means a person can read minds, tell the future, and bend spoons with their thoughts. It was a popular concept in the 1970s.)

"But that's why I thought I could talk to you about it. You knew more about what was going on with Sebastian in ten minutes than I had in ten years." Faustine started rustling her silverware.

"That, I think, is more you than me," her aunt said.

Faustine dropped her silverware on her plate, then took a moment to drink her diet soda. "So, why wouldn't I presume that there was something missing? I mean, I still don't know why she died. Or even how…" Faustine rustled her menu.

"The part that's missing is reading the posts that are left," her aunt said. "Did her father ask you anything before he gave them to you?"

"No, he didn't say anything. Sebastian thought I might like to have them," Faustine said.

"So, that's it?"

"Yeah, why?"

"His daughter dies, and he doesn't want to find out what her friends might know about it?"

"Guess not." Faustine shrugged for emphasis.

Her aunt studied her niece. "There's more to it than that. Why don't you ask him what he wants to know from you?"

"I didn't want to say anything to him because I didn't know him and I thought it would be rude," Faustine said. "Sebastian said it would make getting over Elodie's death harder."

"It's been long enough. It's no longer rude," her aunt said.

The waitress approached them. "Are you guys ready to order?"

Wayland and Ailill's conversation required a dedicated afternoon. First, Ailill had to find Wayland's "new" house.

Wayland had lived there for three years, but since they had always met in the studio, Ailill had never been inside his house. Ailill could not find anything "new" before noon: he was directions-phobic.

Wayland had the windows open and the lights on in the middle of the afternoon as they sat around his kitchen table, which was covered in fast food, sandwiches piled high. Wayland was vegan and brought his own food everywhere since very few people followed the same dietary guidelines. He always had leftovers to offer to others to take home.

Ailill focused on Wayland, transfixed. Ailill drank some beer to stall for time, with his foot propped up in the seat of the straight back chair beside him, then he put his foot on the floor and leaned forward to make his pitch. "I want you to write a song about Manon." Ailill concentrated on Wayland while he waited for his reply. *C'mon, if it's about Manon, it should be OK.*

"You're killing me." Wayland did not break into a smile at his own joke. "'Take Me Home' sound like a good title to you?" Wayland gently kicked Ailill's foot.

Ailill caught Wayland's sarcasm. Wayland took a counter swig of beer, trying to smile. "Take me home," was the last thing the band members heard Manon say during the last "accident." That phrase wasn't what they expected her last words to them to be. Quite frankly, they felt cheated; she had been a good writer.

"Sure." Ailill wasn't joking.

"Amen to that, then." Wayland said, and took another drink, mock-toasting Ailill. *As long as we cut it close to the bone...* He swiveled in his chair. His kitchen set had mismatched pieces. Some chairs were straight backed while others swiveled. They were all roughly the same shade of yellow wood.

"We can sing it to her, and see if she likes it." Ailill

frowned, thinking out loud. "And if she likes it, she might sing it."

"Instead of making her write it," Wayland said, turning to look straight at Ailill.

"Yeah, I don't think she's in a writing mindset." Ailill took another drink while avoiding the sandwiches. Ailill tried to avoid the obvious. *She feels used. If we write our own music, and let her sing it, she might feel more like talking to us. Turnabout's fair play...*

"She hasn't written in years—"

"She hasn't written anything in years that you know about," Ailill countered, pointing at Wayland, pointing at him while holding his beer.

"She said she hadn't. I was over there. You heard her," Wayland said.

Ailill's short-term memory was, unfortunately, amazingly bad. "I was playing guitar. I didn't hear her say anything. Getting her to sing is the only plan I can think of," Ailill said.

Wayland nodded his head, knowingly.

"It's all that we have as far as options," Ailill said.

"Yeah," Wayland agreed. "It seems like there should be a good idea out there, somewhere..."

Ailill nodded. "But I guess not."

Wayland got up to look outside the window at the trees surrounding his house for a minute or two before coming back to the table.

"I still can't believe what happened to CD sales after she stopped writing," Wayland said.

"I can see our record sales slumping, but how did this effect genres we weren't even dabbling in?"

"An economist at the university explained it to me once. It just seemed so weird, because I think of competition as driving out business, but apparently you have to have a certain amount of competition to keep an economic sector going," Wayland said. "Everyone playing similar songs all the time, after a while nobody cares. Her songs were really unique."

"Economic stuff like, the more players, the more advertising, which makes sense to me, but we didn't cut down on our advertising," Ailill said. "I don't get his point about competition."

"That was as close to an answer as I got out of him." Wayland nodded. "It made sense when he said it."

Wayland decided that as long as Manon was excited about bucket lists, he should do a wellness check on her. She swore she wasn't suicidal, but bucket lists were currently popular, so the only people not making them were potential suicide victims. *I hope she doesn't start a trend.* Wayland pulled up beside her house and parked his car. It was odd for him to be walking up to her door without a calculated script. He had already called her the day before, then again an hour before he was supposed to arrive. *Nothing sudden. Nothing unexpected. This is so unusual, I'm about to freak out.*

Manon cracked her bright white front door and peered around it at him while he strode up the wooden steps to her door. She had been watching for him.

Wayland didn't know what he was going to say. *That's a pleasant variation. It beats seeing her there, not saying anything, making sure she's not getting worse, and leaving.* He hadn't brought his guitar. *Manon needs to have a spare guitar. For emergency jam sessions, clearly.*

The lack of a guitar was what she noticed first. "Where's your guitar?" Manon finished opening the door for him.

"It wasn't on my bucket list," Wayland said.

"Yeah it is, we're supposed to be writing together again."

Manon grabbed his jacket to hang it up, and pulled back the heavy drapes.

"But we've written together before, so it doesn't count as a bucket list item," he said.

"Bucket lists are things you want to do before you die. You could want to do the same thing over again. It could count," she said.

The temperature of the house was a little cool, which reminded him of the morgue. *Cold doesn't correlate with suicide.*

"You're hand delivering the check instead of mailing it?"

"I'm making sure you get a lawyer. And we're ordering new computer equipment together online." *I hope we don't get into a fight about me being so bossy. We used to make joint decisions.* He shivered.

There was no fight today. *Are we risking a catastrophe through inaction?* She looked him in the eye, which was always hard for her, then said, "Let's go in my car."

All Wayland could do today was be extremely pro-active in making sure Manon got a lawyer, mainly because too many people knew that this issue had never been resolved between them. Otherwise, Wayland would take his cues from Manon. Hand her the check, and let her get her own lawyer, or even let her keep the check in her bedroom drawer. They cruised the small town for lawyers, although any lawyer would do. There was an absurdly large number of lanes given the town's size. Most of the lanes remained empty. They stopped at a random lawyer's office. Coincidentally, it turned out to share the same parking lot with the church where they had the weight loss meetings. From the looks of the facade, this lawyer was best suited for making wills. Afterwards, they dropped a small, relatively speaking, check off at Manon's bank.

———————————

Cruising back through the town, Wayland and Manon stopped at the church's parking lot for a minute, then got out to walk around, stretch their legs, and watch the sunset for a minute.

"Sebastian always wondered why you made references about me when you knew I wasn't watching your show," Manon said.

"We were always worried about what had happened to you. We wanted you to know we were thinking of you, if you happened to be watching anyway." Wayland paced, kicked a few rocks, then studied the traffic driving by. He was a little warm in the sun, since he wore blue jeans and a long-sleeved black shirt.

"I never knew what to say to him. The situation always made him mad." Manon gazed at Wayland studying the cars.

"What's to say?"

"He acted like he thought you guys were gloating, even though that was never the word he used for it," Manon said.

Wayland turned for a moment to look back at Manon.

"I guess I was too worried about someone showing up to kill me to be worried about you stealing money from me," Manon said.

"Someone's gotta be worried about the practical things. It might as well be him." Wayland sighed.

"I guess he figured you guys would never keep tabs on me." There was a pause while Manon waited. "There'd be no point in mentioning anything if you wanted people to forget."

"I'll grant you that much." Wayland opened the car door.

"If we weren't planning on seeing you again, we wouldn't have mentioned anything."

This conversation should have happened several years earlier. Any emotion either would have felt at this long awaited moment of truth had long since drained away.

"I don't think Sebastian believed that anyone tried to kill me." Manon stood as still as an empty lane of traffic. "My life wasn't worth a check. Until I knew who it was, I didn't want any of your money."

"I know." Wayland reflexively ran his hand through his hair, which messed up his hair since he had a ponytail. He sat down looked at himself in the rearview mirror while he tried to straighten his hair back out. "That's why we didn't start wiring money into your account, and be done with it."

"Why would anyone think that holding the money for me all those years would be a problem?" Manon waited a minute, then shook her head. "I guess I can't make it sound like he did, all nervous and tense." The parking lot reminded her of refereeing during Sebastian and Faustine's fights.

Wayland took a breath, then gazed into her eyes long enough to know that what he was about to say was going to register with her. "You're the one with the check."

Manon thought a moment. "I'm also the one who didn't try to get in contact with you. Did he? Was he mad you guys wouldn't call him back?" Manon stepped into the car and slammed the door.

Wayland took a moment to gaze at the steering wheel before starting the engine. *I appreciate why our arguments kept repeating, but how many times will we have this same fight before I feel real to her again?* He finally pulled out of the parking lot.

"Have you ever noticed the resemblance between a haiku and the 12-bar blues structure? Not to change the subject, or anything." Manon's angelic eyes sparkled with the light from the setting sun.

Wendolynn Jane Landers

* * *

Faustine turned on the T.V. to watch the news while eating her pizza on the couch. There was a hullabaloo about fracking (gushing water through subterranean rocks to force out natural gas) happening on the east coast. Completely out of place, "Love & All Its Glory" started playing. It was being used in a car commercial. A brown, oversized family vehicle sped through the wooded backroad while the audience's omniscient view from the sky pulled away.

"That has got to be the weirdest song ever used in a car commercial." The air around Faustine felt heavy and chilly. She couldn't tell where the extra pressure was coming from. She wiped her mouth with a paper napkin between bites, and dropped part of her pizza on the carpet. "Do they mean that the car is never going to be for," she picked the pizza up off the floor, "anyone watching the commercial? No one's ever going to be able to afford the car? No matter what you do, they won't sell it to you?" The sermon Faustine had heard bugged her, but she couldn't quite put her finger on it. *I need to talk to my aunt again, but I don't need her version of "I told you so," to go along with trying to explain Elodie taking yoga classes at the hospital.* Having memory problems made her think of Manon. Faustine decided to call her. She shivered. *Yes, it's crazy, but so is Manon. It's not like she's going to notice that this is weird. She hasn't spoken to anyone in years. She won't notice that I'm stepping over the line of decorum. Besides, Sebastian has introduced us.* The air in the room waxed dense, while the temperature continued to plummet. Although her cell phone beside her computer was closer, Faustine went to the landline to call, since that's where she kept Sebastian's number. She had put Manon's number in the phone book beside it. *A flash from the past songwriter needed a phone from the past to compliment her age.* She figured she would leave a message. *Don't get up Manon, wherever you are.* While she dialed, the kitchen lights flickered slightly. *I need to check the thermostat when I get off the phone.*

On the third ring, Manon picked up, "Hello?"

"Hey, Manon, this is Faustine, I heard your song on a car commercial. Way to go!"

"My song was on a car commercial? What car commercial!"

"It was 'Love & All Its Glory.' I forgot which car. The commercial came on during a segment about fracking, and I thought of you, so I called," Faustine said. *This is the weirdest reason to call somebody, ever.* The air lightened while the florescent lights steadied.

Manon hesitated, lowering her voice, embarrassed. "I had no idea they were making a commercial. I'll ask the guys about it, thanks."

"I'm sorry to bother you like this. I know we're not friends. But it's like," Faustine cocked her head to one side," I felt this pressure, or something," then she looked around the room. "I was thinking about calling my aunt, but called you instead. Do you believe in ghosts?"

"Wayland, this is Manon," she said.

"It's good to hear from you. I can't believe you called me." He paced through the long, grey hallway of the recording studio. He was already at work for an early meeting, dressed in his typical business attire of long sleeved black t-shirt, printed with long ago concert dates, and black jeans.

"Yeah, I guess I had to."

"Why?"

"I found out I wrote a car commercial." Manon hunched

over her kitchen table, trying to keep from falling asleep while talking to him. She was used to going to bed early and this was way past her bedtime. She was still dressed in a loose fitting dark blue blouse and tan shorts,

"You have a lawyer and a bank account. Now you have a new car, unless you want Ailill to drive it," he said.

"I haven't ever had a new car before, Wayland," she said. "Not one that was my own."

"Not many people do, from what I hear." Wayland got all the way to the end of his hallway, then turned around as though he were talking on a landline whose cord only went so far.

"Why a car commercial? Seriously. You guys hate car commercials. What about the fracking protests? You haven't changed that much over the years. No one could," she said.

Wayland stopped to kick the white wall trim that housed the cables running through the house. The hall was grey because of a lack of lighting, not because of the paint color. *She has faith in a continuous universe for other people.* He leaned back against the wall. "All of us have made money from the album over the years. We could either try to figure out how much we owe you from past receipts, or we could generate new income and hand it over to you."

Faustine lay flat across the kitchen table, barely propping her phone up enough to talk into it. *He has a way with math. He sounds sincere. He also sounds like he has no idea how much he owes me.* She closed her eyes. "Does it turn out the same?"

"I sure hope so. It's how we're planning on making payments on your part of the royalties," he said.

Mannon paused. *It sounds legit. If I ask any more questions he'll tell me to ask my lawyer. My lawyer. Not his lawyer. Not their lawyer. Not the band's lawyer. **My** lawyer. Sounds like a divorce, but we're really getting back together. Sort of. As long as that strange breeze that ruffles my life doesn't blow too hard.* The silence while she was thinking had gone on too long. "I should tell you, Wayland...," Manon said.

"Yes," he said.

"The woman who called me to tell me about the car commercial said that she thought a ghost had put her up to it," Manon said.

"You didn't see the commercial yourself? Who told you about it?" Wayland's eyes popped open and he started walking down his hallway again. *She shouldn't find out what's going on from someone else. That's too much like it had been before.*

"Ghost, Wayland. Focus," she said.

"I am focusing. I'm focusing on you losing the car because someone said the word 'ghost.'"

Manon sat at her digital piano in the middle of her new home recording studio waiting for Wayland to come back from her kitchen. In was a home recording studio in as much as it was inside her house. Most novice recording engineers do not have a 24-track console with overhead boom microphones. Manon had no idea how to turn any of the new equipment on or off, much less how to do anything else with it. She sat at her piano pecking at the keys. *Why don't they sound?* She looked at the sign printed on a white sheet of paper taped directly above the middle of the keyboard. When she sat down at her keyboard, she couldn't miss it. She also couldn't see anything else when she looked up. *They're going to have to take that down soon.* The sign said what order the equipment had to be turned on in. It also said what order the equipment had to be turned off in. *Why don't you turn it off and on the same way?* Plus, there was a lot of equipment in the room that was not readily identifiable from the list of turning things on and off. Manon looked around at all of the stuff she didn't recognize. *I'm glad I still have my baby grand in the living room.*

Wayland walked down her hallway into her new recording studio, sipping the diet soda he brought with him. He had just put the sandwiches that he always brought into her refrigerator, since she wasn't hungry. The hallway light shone on pictures of her family and friends that lined her hallway. He stopped to look at a couple of new ones that he hadn't seen before.

"They brought the mics in and set them up before they left. It took two guys all weekend. There's a seminar I'm supposed to go to in a couple of weeks about how to use them. Until then, they posted those instructions." Manon waved her hand at the wall above her computer.

"Wow, you've got it already set up." Wayland put his diet soda into a drink holder attached to a microphone stand, then roamed around her studio picking at her state-of-the-art equipment. "You know you can feed a digital piano into electric guitar pedals."

Manon found a piece of loose paper and put it under his diet soda to use as a coaster. *It must have taken him some time to unpack his box of recording supplies. He doesn't know what he's saying.* She watched him turn a knob on a flat black box. "Look, they assembled it. You're still going to have to show me how to use it."

"Sure." He walked back and finished his diet soda. "But you're going to have to tell me who your friend is who told you about the commercial, and why she said a ghost told her to call you." Wayland started taking his cup back down the hall to her garbage can in her kitchen.

After Wayland left, Manon sat alone in the room, staring at three different microphones. She was supposed to decide which mic she liked best. There were several different colored strips going across her computer, one for each mic, like a Mobius strip (a curved object with only one side created by taking a strip of paper, twisting it once, and then taping the ends together), as though the room itself were a continuous play tape. Her eyes glazed as she stared at this great big electrical surface turned back around on itself.

"She's Sebastian's friend. He either unloaded her on me, or me on her before disappearing," Manon said.

Wayland could still hear her talking down the hall. "Ghost, Manon. Focus." Her recording equipment comforted Wayland, just like at his home, enveloping them like an electronic blanket.

"She had been to a hospital, trying to figure out how her friend had died. Apparently, it was quite sudden. She was making dinner after she got home when she heard the commercial. She thought of me and called," Manon said.

Wayland returned. "You make it all sound so normal." Wayland's voice waved up and down, mocking her.

"I'm going to have to deal with rock stars again," Manon said.

"Yes, you're going to have to deal with rock stars again, Manon. Now let's play."

"We should write a song about the ghost, since you're all worried about him," Manon said. "Do you want to turn everything on? I don't know how."

Wayland eyed her with curiosity. "You don't know how to turn any of it on?"

"They came in, plugged everything in, and taped that there," Manon pointed to the sign over the computer. "I said you would be here and could show me how to do the rest."

"Take it down and pass it around," Wayland said.

"Not even funny." Manon handed him the sheet of paper.

He scanned it. "Where did you put all your other stuff that had been in here?" He still had a visual image of her bedroom set.

"You're not being here with me now, Wayland. Mentally

you're outside putting up scaffolding to paint the house and fix the roof," Manon said. "I doubled up the furniture in another bedroom."

"Don't worry, I'm here, inside with you. You know we're going to have to board up that window." Wayland pointed at the open window with sheer white curtains across from her piano. Then he dramatically peered over the paper at her. "I've done this many, many times. I had wondered what directions they'd left you."

"I told them you'd be here, so they didn't leave many instructions. According to them, they didn't leave many. Personally, I still can't make heads or tails of everything on that list. Plus all of the manuals are online, so I can't start flipping though them," Manon said.

"Why not?" Wayland put the sheet of paper on her desk, leaned over, and turned her computer on.

"Is the computer supposed to be turned on first?" Manon tried looking over his shoulder to read the paper.

"Yes. It's the closest to the wall plug-in. It follows the flow of electrons around the room." Wayland sounded like he was quoting a textbook. "You don't have to worry about the computer. It's the peripherals that you don't want to blow out." Wayland pointed to the steel filing cabinet that housed who-knows-what in it. Wayland took a minute, and walked around the room. He pulled one microphone out the cabinet, attached a cord to it, clicked a button on the computer, and said, "We're all set now."

"There are more directions here than that, Wayland!" Manon waved the sheet of paper at him.

"This is all we need to start with," Wayland said.

"Who gets to talk into the mic, me or you?"

"We can put it on the stand. Neither one of us has to hold it," Wayland said.

"You know what I mean. Who sings lead and who sings

back-up?"

"It doesn't have to be like before, love," Wayland said.

"Well, to start in with, maybe it should be," Manon said.

"It's not that I won't eventually show you how to use all of this," Wayland was looking at a couple of items pointedly, "but I think I should go to the hospital first."

"Why, may I be so bold as to ask, should you do that? We haven't broken anything yet. No one's been electrocuted," Manon said.

"No one's going to be electrocuted. We aren't soldering anything," Wayland said.

Manon sighed. *I'm joking! There's so much stuff lying around.* She shrugged her shoulders.

"Look, your friend who told you about the commercial said she had been to the hospital?"

"Yes," Manon said.

"And she was talking about a ghost?"

"Yes," Manon said.

"She hadn't been talking about ghosts before she went to the hospital, right? The most likely place to find a ghost at a hospital is the morgue."

"I was joking about writing a song about the ghost, Wayland, joking."

"It can be difficult to learn how to love where you are in life right now. Sometimes we need fans, and sometimes we need friends..." The preacher dramatically waved his arm across the room, indicating the entire congregation.

Wayland and Manon were sitting in a pew nodding. Manon figured that Wayland was nodding because he had a lot of fans to deal with. Not something he normally got a lot of sympathy for. Manon, however, was nodding along with the bobbing foot of the pianist in the front row.

I can't believe we're in church together. Manon was mentally rationalizing what they were doing. *As long as neither one of us wants to go to church, here we are.*

When they walked into the hospital, the chapel was the first thing they saw. Manon agreed to step inside, since the service was about to begin. That also kept Wayland from heading straight to the morgue, which was his first impulse. After the homily, Wayland stayed to talk with the preacher. Manon tried chatting with the pianist. Neither got anywhere, and they ended up back out in the hallway with nothing to show for their work.

"Wayland, I'm not going to the morgue. You think a ghost is trying to kill me. I'm not going to make it easy for him," Manon said.

"There's nothing going on," Wayland said. "We always have problems with crowds. This should be OK."

"This is a hospital. There are a lot of people here. They're all hiding behind closed doors, working," Manon said. "Wandering around looking for a ghost in the morgue is not OK. We've been here. Now we're leaving." Manon started trying to find the exit.

Wayland followed her. They went through double-doors that led into a hallway.

"Does this hall look like it should be in a spaceship to you, Wayland?"

"It does look like we're trying to enter the international space station," Wayland said.

Manon and Wayland glanced at each other and kept walking. Manon wondered why art wasn't exhibited along the empty walls, while Wayland compared the sunlight streaming through the wall of windowpanes to the shadowy corridor at his recording studio.

"I bet the morgue is this way," Wayland said, staring at

Manon out of the corner of his eye. "They are—"

"It better not be!" Manon said. "This is probably a service entrance. Once we get to the end of the hall, there should be a door to the outside." As they got to the end of the hall, the walkway turned left, then started rising. They ended up on the next floor up, without trying. No exit in sight. They could hear music in the distance. Wayland started humming along to it.

"I know what that is," Wayland said. It took Manon a second, but she recognized the twenty-year-old tune, too.

"Well, at least it's not one of ours," Manon said.

"Speak for yourself," Wayland said. "You didn't have to negotiate the car commercial contract."

They were walking towards the upbeat tempo when they ran into a hall lined with windows on one side. For some reason, the windows overlooked a parking lot.

"That's a lot of work for very limited viewing. I wonder why they don't plant trees, or make a little park out there," Wayland said as they walked past. The view was on the right, and there were no doors on the left until they got to the end of the hall.

The rock anthem blasted from the door at the end of the hall. Since neither Wayland nor Manon liked the song very much, they were not inclined to see what was going on in the room. However, they didn't know where else to look.

"This better not be the morgue," Manon tensed up as they got close to the door. "I'm going to stop and ask for directions. Maybe they have a map."

"OK, sure," was all Wayland said as he sighed. *I'm going to have to come back alone to look for the morgue. This is probably too traumatic for her to deal with.* He knew better than to say what he was thinking.

The door was slightly ajar. She opened it and stuck her head in. There was a yoga class stretching. One of the students complained about how bright her neon pink leotard was.

"Bright is beautiful," the yoga instructor said, smiling broadly.

Manon pulled her head out of the doorway, and glanced back at Wayland. "They're doing yoga," she stage whispered.

"You make it all sound so normal," Wayland said.

Wayland took Manon home after she refused to enter the morgue. As they walked down her hall towards her studio he detailed his itinerary. "I'll drop back by on my way to the airport," Wayland said.

"I don't think you should go back to the morgue," Manon said, "Flat-out. We were there. Nothing happened."

"Why not, Manon? I can get to know the doctors around town, in case we ever need them."

Wayland strode down the space station-like corridor near the service entrance of the hospital, again. The yoga instructor had given him directions to the morgue from the yoga studio, so he was headed back to the studio, as a starting place, for following the directions.

Once he got to the yoga studio, he looked inside for a minute. No one was there. Lights on. No music. No people. He took a minute to walk around inside. *Look at all the reflections in the mirrors. I should take off my shoes and go sliding across the room.* The polished wood reminded him of Manon's tabletop where she put the glasses filled with water. The mirrors made the room look twice as large as it was. Since the mirrors were on the hallway wall, it gave the room the optical illusion of sticking back into the hall, somehow or another, when he walked into the room. As Wayland looked around, he saw many lists taped up on the studio walls. He read several. *This yoga studio is for women who are anorexic.* There were all kinds of tip sheets on how to exercise safely. There were even places in the room where there were partitions, in case a patient could not exercise in front of a mirror.

"You don't know what you look like, you only think you do." *That's the best tip of all of them. That's pretty good advice.* He put his hands on his hips and looked around the room. *I wonder if it came from a book, or if it's the yoga instructor's personal take on the situation. Weird that they have a guy teaching this class.* He shook his head to himself as he was walking towards the door.

Wayland stumbled out of the room, and back into the hall. *I don't know how I tripped. It must have been because of the mirrors.* He turned left, and headed further down the hall, towards an exit and left turn that didn't look like it went anywhere. *I should make a tip sheet for Manon on how to safely write songs again.* He got to the door of the morgue, and checked to see if it was locked. *She needs her own sort of partition before she has to work in front of mirrors again.* He pushed open the door.

Wayland was in the morgue by himself. He couldn't say what had drawn him back to the place, only a hunch. Maybe it was more wishful thinking than a hunch. *I need an incantation to drive this all away.* The morgue was white and stainless steel. Empty as a vacuum. He started walking across the room. The door on the other side was open. That door seemed to lead into a hall. Wayland could see the stainless steel gurneys from where he was standing. *I don't have to go any further.* "Is anyone here?" *I'll say I'm lost if a nurse appears.* He did notice a security camera pointed away from him, presumably towards a rear entrance. His experience with security cameras was that no one ever looked at the video unless they were obligated to do so. He heard no reply. "Any ghosts around here I should know about?" All he heard was his own voice echoing slightly in the hall, followed by the hum of florescent overhead lights. He had spent decades listening to different styles of reverb. Long halls, small rooms, high ceilings all echo differently. Otherwise he would not have noticed how his voice sounded in the room. Very light. A short hall. "You don't have to worry about Manon performing, if that's what concerns you." Wayland was addressing white walls and stainless steel cabinets. He hadn't seen or felt anything funny. But on the off chance that the ghost was there, he was going to explain his side. "You didn't think I'd tell her about the car commercial? I didn't get to surprise her with the good news. I had planned on flowers and balloons, at least, probably a cake and dinner, too. Now I'm dealing with an upset woman inside a room full of electronics. Hearing the news from someone else makes me look cheap, if not downright dishonest. You don't want her trusting me again?" His face flushed red, so he started to leave. "Getting her friend to tell her instead of letting me do it." Wayland's voice was a stage hiss. "I don't know what to expect out of you next." Wayland scanned the area before walking out the door. *A ghost should be more mature. After all, a ghost has had the experience of dying, which should make anybody grow up.* He went back the way he had come in, down the hall, turned right and walked a few steps before tripping, again, in front of the yoga studio door.

The first time Wayland tripped in front of the yoga studio, he thought it was because of the mirrors. He walked around the studio entrance, scrutinizing the doorway. The entrance door's adjacent wall was covered in reflective glass on the inside of the room. Not only did it make the room look twice as large as it actually was, it gave a person the optical illusion of the room sticking back into the hall when a person entered.

Improvising to Beat the Band

This time, there was nothing physically amiss. *This time I can't blame it on the mirrors.*

———————————

"So did the ghost tell you anything?" Manon pecked at her keyboard, frowning. Her headphones that let her hear her digital piano were around her neck. The light was still coming through her once bedroom window, although a large piece of plywood sat beside it, waiting to be nailed up. The room that used to be colorful was now shades of black and grey studio equipment, with an occasional metal box that was manufactured in a primary color.

"No, but I gave him a piece of my mind." Wayland rummaged around her microphone cabinet, turning on a light inside it.

"Well, he was here while you were gone," she put one earphone at her ear, "I think," Manon said.

Wayland quickly turned two shades lighter, closing the cabinet door. "What did he do? Did he say anything?"

"The streaming service I have on my cell phone kept going back to the same song for no reason. Really obvious mid-song switches. I thought maybe I had the automatic shuffle on, but no." Manon stepped around the recording equipment to hand him her cell phone. He started flipping through it. "I was scared to start playing along with it."

"Well, OK, I guess we see what happens next." Wayland stared at her phone lying on top of her piano, about to fall off since the digital piano sloped. "If he's here, he's here."

"This is probably not the greatest time to bring this up, but I had an idea about how we could get back in the writing groove together."

"This is a good time. I mean, that's what we are here for."

"When Sebastian and Faustine were breaking up, they made a bucket list for their relationship. They did all kinds of crazy things that they'd never do, like break dancing and throwing an engagement party. They went to carnivals and Halloween attractions that they always wished they had gone to. We could put together a list of things we've never done before, and go through them." Manon grabbed a piece of paper from the pack of blank sheet music that she was using to write down lyric ideas, tore it in half, and handed the paper to Wayland, then waited for him to start writing down his half of their bucket list.

"They threw an engagement party and then broke up? How would that even work? People would bring presents. You're supposed to give the presents back if the deal falls through." Wayland looked around for something to write on. He grabbed a stool to sit on, then looked sideways at Manon before scooting it a couple of feet away. *I shouldn't sit too close.* The white of the paper stood out against the darker background of her studio. He could barely see the electric guitar he had left in the corner even with the window curtain open. "You're going to have to get some more light in here, hon."

"I don't think people brought presents. It was just them. They had dinner reservations at a restaurant noted for its extravagant engagement parties. The weird thing was I don't think Sebastian knew about it until they got there. Faustine just presumed he had a clue."

"They got to do the toast and everything then. Did she pick out a dress to wear?"

"I don't know if she went that far, although now that you mention it, I don't know why she wouldn't. I was just refereeing them setting the date and location. I didn't get a lot of feedback about how it turned out. I actually found out more about what happened from Faustine than Sebastian, which was weird. I thought their trip to the Halloween carnival Twice as Fun sounded like it might have actually been fun. I'm surprised that their relationship didn't revive after everything they were doing together."

"I can't believe they named a carnival Twice as Fun as Doin' Nothin' at All."

"You've got no room to talk. 'Love & All Its Glory?' Maybe love could be for you, maybe not?"

"You agreed to the title, longwinded though it may be. Songs can be ambiguous, or sarcastic. An actual business name is supposed to be clear and straightforward."

"Maybe you were a bad influence. It opened after the song was released. Anyway, we're going to have to start writing something."

Wayland found a clipboard left in the microphone cabinet. Manon used the notebook that she had been writing lyrics on for her list.

"One question before we start, is this something I can take my wife and family to?" Wayland adjusted his stool.

Manon sighed and looked up at him. "I don't know, we haven't made the list yet."

But instead of her half of their bucket list, Manon doodled. Then, she started a grocery list. Wayland wrote directions for Manon about changing guitar strings. After half-an-hour, they checked with each other and realized that neither one of them had any meaningful items.

"We should wait until we've both had a chance the think about it before we totally hash out the bucket list," Manon said.

"Yeah, 'cause nothin' is coming to mind. But I'm sure it's because I haven't thought about it," Wayland said. "I mean I've thought about things I've wished we've done, but never in the context of a list before. I'll put the directions I wrote for changing guitar strings up over there." Wayland got up and started rummaging around in the microphone closet for tape.

"Until then," Manon drew a flower, "what was the song you were working on?"

"What was which song?" Wayland taped the guitar directions to the wall beside the other equipment directions. "You can change my guitar strings," he pointed to his guitar in the corner, "every six months or so, depending on how much you practice."

"The song you were working on when you came by and we put the water glasses together. We were trying to recreate the Aeolian harp part of 'Love & All Its Glory.'"

"'Take Me Home,'" Wayland said. "But don't feel obligated to work on it. The other guys were none too into it."

"What made you pick that title?"

"It was the last thing you said to us."

"At the party? I asked someone to take me home?"

"Yup." Wayland still avoided talking about it with anyone.

"Maybe not a good song," Manon said.

"It was all I was into," Wayland paused, "It was what I felt deeply about."

"Maybe helping me move my furniture around is something you can feel deeply about?" Manon pointed around her studio. "Because I don't want to talk about it either."

"Your furniture?"

"Yes, these." Manon pointed at her microphones.

Wayland jumped backwards. "That's not furniture. That's a mic!"

"Well it's about to be a clothes rack unless it gets moved."

"You're supposed to go to a seminar in a couple of weeks, right?" Wayland jerked the stand away from her. *She's making plans without me knowing about it beforehand.*

"Yeah, it's out in Indiana. Weird place for rock-n-roll."

Manon rocked back and forth on her half-sized piano bench. *I'd've never thought to go to Indiana for a concert, much less a professional music seminar.*

"Hon, they've got a ton of stuff out there." Wayland situated the microphone stand ever so slightly away from the mic closet door. "What I'm hoping is that you'll find people that you wouldn't mind working with on one of our albums." Manon had always been exceptionally picky about who produced their albums.

"A meet-and-greet?" Manon glanced over at his guitar. *This time I can control the compressor knobs myself.*

"Yeah. There are real quality people working there, and they do this all the time. It's not a one shot thing." Wayland verbally laced together a pitch he hadn't completely finished weaving in his mind.

Manon's stomach started to cramp. *Will my house be OK if I leave it for a week?*

"How 'bout we get something to eat?"

"Sure. I didn't stop anywhere coming back from the hospital."

"I have frozen pasta, pizza, or vegetables," Manon said.

"Or we can order pizza," Wayland hesitated, shifted back and forth on his feet, and watched her, "already warm," he put his hands in his pockets, "and I can pay for it."

"You don't trust my taste in frozen food?"

"You weren't planning on company."

"Can we agree on toppings?"

"Mushrooms and whatever you want."

"Mushrooms and black olives it is then. I'll call." Manon walked to the phone.

No, she doesn't carry a phone on her. We have to change rooms. Wayland sauntered down the hall, flopping on the living room couch. *She's trying to change the subject. She thinks she's being subtle, but this move towers above us like a city skyline.*

Wendolynn Jane Landers

Anyone else would have stayed in the same room to make a call. She's inadvertently living in the past. I hope she catches on fast when she's at the recording seminar. Wayland sat and meditated for a minute. *Maybe she doesn't trust my taste in recording seminars?* He sat and stared at the abstract painting on the wall. Her curtains were open, plus there was an accent light situated above each print. There were three different abstract art prints on her bright white walls. There was no attempt to match them to the furniture and curtain set, which was a heavy dark color that Wayland couldn't quite figure out. *Is this maroon? It's too grey. It's too quite. Should I turn on the television?* He glanced around for a remote control. "Hon, you're not worried about going to Indiana, are you?"

"Why should I worry about going to Indiana?"

Wayland gawked at her holding a landline phone. *I can't remember the last time I picked one of those up. It's not like the last time you use a landline phone is a momentous occasion. There's no ceremony for it. Nobody's written a song about it. Nobody plans to either.*

"If I don't like it I can leave," she said.

"No pressure," he said.

"No." She addressed the phone: "Large, mushrooms, and black olives."

I should should tell her that they have an app for that, but maybe she should find out from somebody else. Maybe somebody in Indiana. I don't want to tell her my ideas for her future just yet. I want her to find out on her own. If she does stuff that would've made me jealous before, she should probably be OK now. Wayland started looking around for more paper and pencil. He opened the coffee table drawer.

Manon joined him in the living room. "What are you looking for?"

He looked up at her, dubiously. "Paper and pencil."

"It's on the kitchen table." She went to get it. "Did you

finally think of something for the bucket list?"

Wayland strained to hear her. "Are you going to sit down?"

"I guess so." Coming back, Manon was about to make the most important decision she had made in a very long time. *I have to decide if I'm going to sit beside him on the the the couch, or sit in a separate chair? Why be presumptuous? Or ambiguous? Go for the chair.* It took her a full minute to make up her mind as she walked slower and slower.

Unfortunately, Wayland noticed that she was having a hard time deciding where to sit. *That decision can't be blamed on ordering pizza.*

Manon leaned over the coffee table, handing Wayland the pen and paper, then she sat in the chair, well out of arm's reach.

She needs a minute to work it out. Old habits die hard.

"So, what did you want to write down?" She crossed her arms.

"Thank you," he scribbled on the pen and paper.

"You need to put a seance on it." Manon laughed, running her fingers through her hair. Wayland wrote more.

"Oh, you don't have to put that on—"

"You said the only ground rules were that it'd have to be stuff we would actually do," he said.

"You would have a seance?"

"Yeah. And write another song together." Wayland doubted the writing part.

"I don't know if that has to be on the list since that's what we're going to do anyway."

"I'm writing it down. We can edit it later." Wayland started writing. *I don't like the fact that songwriting suddenly sounds optional to her.* He paused. "We should write a throwaway song together. We've never done that before." Wayland laughed.

"I thought everything we did had to be deathly important."

"Nah, something stupid."

After a pregnant silence, Manon looked him in the eye before continuing. "That should be OK since I'm not trying to impress you anymore."

"Ouch. Maybe not a good idea." Wayland smiled. *She's willing to discount our relationship out loud. What does that mean?*

"Why? Why not? We can write one," she said.

Wayland's pout wavered.

"One," she said, "to see how it goes."

"A seance and a stupid song, plus our regular work," he said.

The pizza arrived. Wayland was good for his word and paid.

Manon had headed towards her pocketbook in the back room anyway. "We should put food on the list. Sebastian and what's-her-name—Faustine, um—they made going out different places to eat a lot of what they did." Manon coughed while swallowing her pizza.

"It'd have to be an ensemble production number." Wayland picked up a slice. "It'd have to be with family."

"Maybe towards the end of the list?" She wiped her mouth and sat in her own chair, instead of with him on the couch. *This is complicated enough for one day. There's a gravedigger pulling me towards an open pit.* She reached for another slice of pizza. "What did you want to do?"

"You mean beside the seance?" Wayland laughed and relaxed for a moment. "I always wanted to go on a Ferris Wheel with you." He closed his eyes, remembering. The vacation where they found the wind harp was etched in his mind.

"It'd have to be at a theme park. I won't go on a Ferris Wheel at a state fair," she said.

He opened his eyes. "Excellent." He paused and scanned the room. "You need a chandelier or candelabra for your piano. It looks naked beside the abstract art."

"We've got a lot of stuff that's going to fall into the production number category with family." Manon got up and walked over to look at one of her prints. "Maybe we should start small."

"We've got the stupid song." He looked at the now filled notebook paper. *This was quite the blank sheet to have to stare down.* "Dancing lessons," he said after a long pause. He smiled, writing. In the past, he had gotten into stomping mad arguments with Manon about whether or not they should hire a choreographer.

"You never taught me how to play poker," she said.

"That's because we could never agree on what to play for." He sighed. *Well, she can remember some things.*

"If we have an issue with the bucket list, you can teach me to play, and then we'll play poker instead of flipping a coin," she said.

"I don't think we're going to have an issue."

"I don't know if we're even going to think of anything to write," she said.

"We always think of something. Eventually. Writing a song eventually comes to you," he said.

"I'll tell you what I'm thinking," she said.

"What?" he said.

"I'm thinking we should re-write 'Love & All Its Glory.' I never did like the first verse, to be honest," she said.

"You don't remember that? We never finished it. We just played the demo with the dummy lyrics still in it anyway. People loved it, so we stopped messing with it," Wayland said.

"Well, maybe we should finish it then," Manon said.

Wayland flew back home, pretending to read a rock magazine while dozing. *I always have too much time to think every time I want to be distracted the most. I can't believe I still have a headache. Am I about to have a stroke?* Wayland's head had hurt off and on while he was visiting Manon. *At least now we have a game plan with Manon.* He had known the guys at the recording studio in Indiana since they produced his solo guitar album. Wayland flipped through the pages, looking at the photos without reading the text. *There are a lot of different possibilities for her career right now.* The magazine distracted him from his headache a bit. *What am I going to tell my family once I land?* It was a mental block he could not get around. *I should try to paint an abstract of what I'm feeling now and put it on Manon's wall.*

Every time he came close to falling asleep, he would remember something about Manon that would scare him and wake him up. Like her wanting to re-write one of the verses to "Love & All Its Glory" after all these years. *Which verse did she want to redo anyway? I can't remember.* Taking a prescription sleep aid was not an option since they only made him groggy. He would have to out wait his nerves. *I don't have to worry about checking up on her until after the recording seminar in Indiana. That won't be for another month.* He had gotten accustomed to going that long without hearing from her.

I wonder if the song that Manon's streaming service kept bumping back to was symbolic? The streaming service only did that while he was gone. *If a ghost wanted to kill her, and there was obviously a ghost there messing with her cell phone, why didn't the ghost try to kill her while he was at the morgue?* That hadn't occurred to him while he worried over Manon's bucket list.

Bucket lists are strange things. I don't think I'll have any problems selling my family on it. He had spent so much time worrying about Manon anyway, they might as well have her around.

He wasn't going to test how Manon's nerves were going to take being around his kids until after the recording seminar was a success. Any bugs in the system could get worked out on those guys. Wayland closed his eyes. Finally a good idea came to him. He made a note of it in the margin of the rock magazine. *I wonder if I can put that in a song later?*

PART TWO

LOVE & ALL ITS GLORY (IS NEVER GONNA BE FOR ME)

CHAPTER FIVE

Prologue

A chapbook is a poet's notebook. Manon's chapbook has completed songs, half-done lyrics, and initial musings in it. It's more official than her doodle notebook. It has the bits she thinks she's going to keep.

It's interesting to watch Manon's chapbook grow over time. Unlike Sebastian's pristine copy of the band's CD liner notes, which look dead by never changing, Manon's chapbook keeps getting crossed out and scrawled over, like a plant sprouting and growing on its own. Wayland, of course, refuses to entertain the notion of rewriting anything decades later, regardless of whether or not a particular song was ever finished.

Manon still hasn't finished "Tell Me about Love Sometime." It needs a second verse, which is the hardest part of a song to write since it has to fit in with everything else in the song, as well as stand on its own. The second verse usually has bits and pieces that mismatch and don't overlap nicely. Technically, Ailill could start singing this verse as an intro or ending to another song during a concert. If the song fragment caught on, Manon wouldn't be able to stop him. Wayland could finish the second verse without telling her. It's possible that the next time she heard her verse, it would be on a streaming service. They might not even tell her before finishing the song. Why make her worry it in case it isn't a big hit?

Tell Me about Love Sometime

Tell me the joy of
　　Holding someone's hand
　　Faraway feelings
　　While gazing in their eyes

Tell me something
　　I'm going to understand
　　Tell me about love sometime

"Just Let Time Pass" was included on A Slip of the Cue's Greatest Hits CD.

Just Let Time Pass (The Hammock Song)

First Verse

Drove home last night
　　Saw the rainbow's end
　　Close enough to look for gold
　　Changed my mind again

Chorus

You won't mind
　　Me sitting here passing the time

Improvising to Beat the Band

* * *

My hammock sways
   As I turn the page
   Or reach for my drink on the grass
   Just lettin' the time pass
   Just lettin' the time pass

Just let time pass
   Just let time pass

Second Verse

My hammock is my headspace
   Swaying me into a trance
   The mist from the lawn
   Fanned out in the sun
   A rainbow there
   Starts to dance

Chorus

You won't mind
   Me sitting here passing the time

My hammock sways
   As I turn the page
   Or reach for my drink on the grass
   Just lettin' the time pass
   Just lettin' the time pass

Just let time pass
   Just let time pass

Wendolynn Jane Landers

At Ailill's prodding, Manon started writing a song commemorating her cell phone, which kept disappearing. She never knew when she'd see it for the last time. This song fragment hasn't been performed by a Slip of the Cue yet. Manon's not sure of its title. She's toying with "You're Not A Cheap Cell Phone," or possibly "I'm A Cheap Cell Phone," along with the song's current title. The first verse and chorus interchange in her mind. She has doodles over the words, extending into the margin of the paper.

You're A Cheap Cell Phone (unpublished)

There's nothing left to do
　　But give up on you

Take a minute
　　Take a breath
　　Before you say "Goodbye"

I never know
　　Where you are
　　Or where you're going to be

Take a minute
　　Take a breath
　　Before you say "Goodbye"

There's nothing left to do
　　But give up on you

Take a minute
　　Take a breath
　　Before you say "Goodbye"

Improvising to Beat the Band

Once Wayland and Manon unofficially dissolved their romantic union, such as it was, they decided to commemorate someone else's relationship in song. Manon's direct experience of watching Sebastian and Faustine's comradeship unravel prodded her creativity.

Manon kept her notes from her suicide attempt in a separate chapbook. She told Wayland the No Trespassing sign over the incident had been removed, but she kept her original notes out of sight anyway. She never talked to Wayland about it, but oddly enough, mentioned it to Ailill instead. Ailill had threatened to have a protest march for her in lieu of a funeral. He showed her a black and white "End Suicide Now!" placard he had printed, just in case. She's contemplating writing another song about it, from the perspective of the incident being several decades in the past. The contrast of the two signs intrigues her. She doubts she'll tell Wayland she's working on it.

No Trespassing

First Verse

The sign on the lawn
    People step around
    No Trespassing
    Not meant for a funeral

His placard read,
    "End suicide now!"
    An odd protest
    After the fact

* * *

Second Verse

The line of mourners
  With their protest signs
  "She shouldn't have!"
  "We were there for you!"

Manon is taking her time rewriting that one since she has no plans for its use.

CHAPTER SIX

Indiana

It had been nearly a decade since Manon left her house for more than 24 hours. Her mother and sisters always came to visit her! They ate at nearby restaurants to make sure she definitely left home occasionally. She didn't shop more than once a month, maximum. Manon had received partial payment for a few songs before her accident, but not the full amount owed her, and certainly no royalties incurred after "the accident." Manon budgeted tightly, since she had no current income, therefore never bought anything she didn't need. She owned every shoestring budget book available. So this trip was miraculously impracticable for her.

Wayland wasn't going to be there. There was an upcoming tour that needed planning. *She doesn't need me since she's gotten used to me not being around over the years. I'll drop by before the tour starts.*

However, Manon wasn't actually making the trip without Wayland. Since she ignored cell phones and other contemporary items, she got Wayland to make a list of things she might need for her recording master class. Toothpaste and pajamas she could remember. But taking her computer was not something that would have occurred to her. In one respect, though, she was going without Wayland. It wouldn't matter what he thought about anything that happened there. He was no longer in the review process of her life.

"My laptop's expensive. Are you sure other people will be bringing theirs? I don't want to be the only one." She complained to Wayland via mail, which usually has a week's lag between being sent and delivery. Manon had a salient memory of having money. She didn't realize it was so long ago, the stuff that would have been putting on airs back then was commonplace now. *I'm going to bring too much equipment and be a laughing-stock.* However, she knew it had been a long time since she had been in college, which was her last similar experience, so she went online to see what people currently told kids to bring. Plus, she ruffled through a couple of summer camp lists, including a summer music festival list. *I'm going to need a similar list.* Manon mentally checked off items as she read a college dorm room supply list. *I have no idea what a flash drive is.*

When Wayland dropped by before she left, she pointed in the direction of her laptop computer. "Which one is the flash drive?"

"It looks like a small stick of gum. People put it in the side of their computers, where you plug in the mouse and keyboard. I don't know that the guys who assembled your studio would have brought one. Usually people have their own," Wayland said.

"Do I have one? Do I care if I have one?" Manon paused. "Where do you plug in the mouse and keyboard then?"

Manon flipped through a few pages in her notebook she labeled "Critical Notes." *I'm only going to get out of this professional seminar what I put into it.* She started writing things down about her equipment that she didn't understand. Thus, she would have a clearer picture about what was going on in her spare bedroom when she returned. *I intend to start working again.* Hunkering down over her notepad, she had to study enough to go it alone.

Before leaving, she had to remember to lock everything, unplug everything, and turn everything off. Unfortunately, she spent a solid hour the first day of the trip completely convinced that she left the stove on, when she knew full well she microwaved an egg and cheese muffin before she left. She kept having coughing fits. *It's weird to know I'm this anxious. My sister will be by to check on the house.* She breathed deeply. Once she talked to her sister on her cell phone, the idea that she wasn't abandoning anything started to sink in. This was her first experience using a cell phone regularly. In college, she talked to her family once a week for an hour. Two or three times a year she would mail a set of twenty to thirty pictures she had gotten developed. This was not the same. *I could call every day if I wanted to.*

Unfortunately, Manon had stopped talking to her family altogether after the accident, or whatever it was, occurred. Figuring the fewer details they knew, the safer they would be, she didn't tell them anything. Maybe whatever it was that was after her would leave them alone since they weren't involved, whatever it was.

Manon hadn't flown since before the last war started, and she wasn't about to start now. She drove across the heartland! She stopped the car every 50 miles to get out and stretch, anticipating the possibility of having flashbacks while driving. By the time she kept that routine up for a day, Manon could eat supper her first night on the road since her nausea had begun to abate. Her coughing fits had slowed down. She had a hard time sleeping, since she recounted everything she brought instead of counting sheep, trying to figure out if she'd forgotten anything. *I can always go back home if I've forgotten an important item.*

When she arrived at the conference, her hotel was

surprisingly close to where the recording conference was being held. She drove around the area before classes started. Once she was there, she really didn't need a car. She gawked at the newness and brightness of the hotel and conference area. One of her favorite surrealist paintings hung in the hotel lobby. She smiled.

In the conference room where the masterclass on audio recording was being held, Manon sat towards the front, near the teacher.

"Can you snap to the grid?" The demand came from the teacher at the front of the class. He appeared younger than Manon by a decade.

Manon deployed her strategy for coping with this class. She took copious notes, which she sifted through to find an answer. To the teacher, it looked like she was stalling for time as she leafed around in her notebook. He walked over to see what she was doing.

"What are you looking for?"

"My notes on how to make the grid snap." Manon turned the pages in her notebook faster. *Why would I want it to? The other option of having the spliced digital recording slide around in the computer program like a skater on ice sounds better anyway.*

"You don't need notes. It's right there." He hovered beside her, then moved her cursor to a small square on a very busy computer toolbar.

Manon looked up from her notes to follow the cursor on the screen. *There's no way I could've found that.* She thumbed through her marked up copy of the text. Hers was the only copy of the textbook in the room, yet the other students could "snap to the grid," but not her. She clutched the mouse and started moving the cursor around like she thought the teacher

Improvising to Beat the Band

did, then she started coughing and couldn't stop, so she went outside to catch her breath.

Manon paced in the hall while she focused on the window at the end of the hallway with its evergreen fake plastic plant. *I want to talk to someone about when I used to write music. Then maybe talk about the new stuff they're doing now.* That's how they used to get older people to do new things. Nobody ever liked the new stuff back when it was new. It didn't matter what it was. Manon felt it in her bones now, although she didn't get it when she was younger. It wasn't that she was afraid of the new technology, she simply didn't care. She had done the same thing too many times without the cool new gadgets. *But how am I going to keep from making a fool of myself in this class? I can't remember anything!* Manon opened the door to go back inside the conference room.

A few hours later, Manon relaxed when it turned out that she definitely needed her laptop and credit card after all. There were some additional computer programs she needed to buy called "sample libraries." They were what made the computer sound like a realistic instrument. She bought "sample libraries" while in class and had the teacher help her download them. The people giving the seminar weren't the ones selling the sample libraries. *At least I don't have to worry about getting ripped off. It's odd that people didn't worry about being ripped off like they used to.* Time was, anytime anyone suggested that you buy anything in a class, a chorus of "rip-off" would ensue. *This must be the part that Wayland is paying for.*

The instructor had to explain how to load the audio samples into her computer. She had not gotten the hang of calling a computer program a "DAW" and didn't remember where anything belonged. (DAW stands for Digital Audio Workstation.) Manon got the part about "midi" being the same thing as a perforated paper roll inserted into a player piano. (Midi means Musical Instrument Digital Interface.) However, she did not get the thing called the "midi editor." Presumably, it edited the player piano inside the computer. She put her hands over her ears to escape the jargon.

Manon opened the computer program, looked at it, edited one or two notes, then something went wrong for no apparent reason. She edited a note on one verse, and it changed the same note in two different places as well, which would have been great if she had wanted it to do that, but she didn't. *Did the ghost follow me here?* Manon actually couldn't tell when the "select" button was depressed. She would have had more luck taping and re-punching a player piano paper roll. It would have been faster.

"I know you've only been working on this for a week, but I'm certain you all have music you can share with the class." The teacher wanted a presentation out of everyone.

Manon figured she would go last. Unfortunately, at the end of the week, the seminar instructor called on her to go first. Manon sang in recitals long enough to understand what that meant: novices go first. Getting up in front of the class scared her. It was a still, closed room. A cute guy wearing a faded polo shirt sitting near the back wall caught her eye for a moment too long. The man sitting beside him punched him and laughed. She thought she heard the man say, "Jacob." For someone who was expecting metal door keys, and instead received something like a credit card when she checked in at the hotel lobby, she did a good job of finessing her presentation. Manon sang over the audio samples for her final recording project. Manon stood in front of the class. The room lights were dimmed, and the lights directed at the front of the classroom shone directly in her face. Once the instructor hit the play button on her assignment, all eyes stared at her. All of her mental processing stopped. She blanked out. It was a good thing she didn't have to speak.

After her recording finished playing, the instructor asked if she had anything to add.

"No." Manon looked around at the students in the classroom. *What question could I possibly have about my own work?*

The instructor then opened the discussion up to the class. "What changes would you make to this, or is it OK as it is?" The instructor scanned the class to cue the students.

Manon braced for this, since she had been warned what was coming. Several people had been talking about it out in the hall. The point was to have something to add to the discussion.

"I would put more reverb on it?" The question came from the man sitting beside Jacob. Manon did not fully realize as of yet that this was a standard statement, or in the case of this student, a standard question. There are few sounds on earth that a sound technician couldn't add more reverb to. Many current music producers would add synthetic reverb to french horns recorded at Carnegie Hall, which has been celebrated for its superior acoustics for over a hundred years.

"The guitar sounded a little dry to me." Another student concurred: safety in numbers.

Manon had no idea what they meant. *I love the guitar sound.* She absolutely adored the idea of fussing around with the notes without having to ask Wayland to play the same lick over and over. *Nothing sounds better.* She had no idea why they called the guitar "dry." *If that's 'dry,' what's 'wet' mean? Or 'sweet?' Is this a martini reference?*

"OK, that's something we could change. Is there anything we can point out that she did right?" This gruesome question displayed the instructor's pedological enthusiasm.

Manon gasped, then she couldn't breathe at all. She waited to see if she was going to start coughing. She never had stage fright this bad before, not even the first time she sang in front of a crowd. *Where is this stage fright coming from?*

"I like the xylophone." A disembodied voice added from the other half of the room. Otherwise, Manon couldn't tell the difference in the speakers, as though they had the same voice.

"It could use more reverb, too," the second guy said.

"OK, presume we could add more reverb to all the tracks." The instructor looked stern. "What else about the xylophone makes it matter?"

"The listener can notice it over everything," Jacob said.

A xylophone can always be heard over everything. Manon didn't dare say that thought out loud. She was the worst student in the class.

"That's right," the instructor said. "She panned the xylophones left to keep them distinct from the guitar on her right."

OK, panning I've got. Although Manon decided that panning should be called something else as well. *But what's wrong with my reverb?*

"I'm not getting this reverb thing. To me, the guitar sounds fine," Manon said.

At that point, the instructor said, "Listen!" Deathly silence swept the sound from the room. Then he clapped his hands once loudly. "Can you hear the sound after the clap?"

Even listening with all her might, Manon only heard the sound of his hands clapping once. She didn't hear any echo in the room. All she could do was shake her head and frown.

"Well, that's something to work on, ear training," the instructor said. "We can all always work on our ear training." He searched the room for confused faces. "What else about the xylophone?"

"Ear candy," another disembodied voice came from behind Manon.

Everyone grunted affirmations.

"Absolutely. Great ear candy, Manon," the instructor said.

Improvising to Beat the Band

Manon had always taken her work extremely seriously. *I don't like being called any sort of candy.*

If he could have said anything to make Manon feel worse, she had no idea what it could have been.

A few months later, Manon settled into her engineer's chair in front of a 48-track mixing board in a darkened auditorium. A crowd of people hopped and clapped to the beat flowing from the stage. Chairs kept bumping as the audience got up and down. The ambient lighting made it difficult for Manon to mix in the darkness since she wasn't completely comfortable with the mixing board yet. Unlike in rehearsal, when the concert spotlights shown down on them, the drums overpowered the two guitarists plus a singer. It was Manon's job to try to even out the sound by sliding 24 levers around, each connected to a separate microphone, from the opposite side of the auditorium.

The fact that the mixing board looked really cool and spooky with its blue and white penlights drew hangers-on behind her to watch. The partially lit mixing board, her, and the fans standing behind her resembled a seance, but instead of channeling a ghost, Manon was trying to channel the song that the group was performing. Moving the faders, which were in long, thin rows, up and down, she dare not blink her eyes. *I should have brought night vision goggles.* This was her third live show to mix for the local rock band, DD&PF.

Ideally, Manon would be touring as a road technician with a Slip of the Cue in order to monitor crowd response to various songs performed. But she still couldn't fly, so she needed to watch groups performing locally. After asking around, meaning she made Sebastian ask around, she found a job running the sound board for a low-key rock band, DD&PF. This job was supposed to be a half-way house for her between being a stay-at-home songwriter and an actual performer. Unfortunately, she tended to be mesmerized by the light show while the band played. Since she had to reset the sound levels for each song, she strained to keep from wandering too far away mentally, but the blue flowers made of light beams ran idyllically across the wall. *Like they're running through a field.* Manon's thoughts danced along with the flowers. Everything had gone alright in practice, so as long as everyone did the same thing that night, nothing could go wrong.

The idea of Manon being in charge of anyone's mixing board for any reason was more than a little odd. Whoever is in charge of the mixing board is the de facto conductor for the concert. Manon being at the mixing board made her the Music Goddess. The band had to trust whoever was at the mixing board; they had no choice. Manon could control every little sound that anyone in the band made. She controlled the power going to the microphones. She controlled how easy it was for the microphones to pick up sound, as well as how loud each person was. She could control how close the singer sounded to the audience. If she wanted to, she could make the lead singer sound like he was near the rafters when he was actually glad-handling fans in the front row.

Manon's fingers touched the mixing board like she was playing piano. She pulled down the volume of the singer's microphone to keep him from being heard over the band. Personally, she was not comfortable with that arrangement, having spent too many days in her life being very picky about Ailill's word choice. *I can't believe they don't want the words heard over the lead guitar.* Her skin started to itch as she slid the mixer fader knob up for the guitar. But that was

Improvising to Beat the Band

Dissent Dissonance and Phosphorescent Freckles', DD&PF's, musical style, so she wasn't messing with it. *It's their concert.*

Manon watched the doors as best she could from where she sat. The band's security stood by the main entrance, so she wasn't the only pair of eyes searching the room. The lit doors beamed on the audience while they came and went between songs. The strangers standing behind her remained silent. The board had an uncanny presence. People with limited interest in music tended to peer over the edge of it. It had a surreal look in the dark with the pen lights focused on it. There were blue and red colored lights flashing periodically, mainly when the inevitable unexpected mishap would occur. If the drummer getting nervous and playing too loud counts as unexpected.

Manon took a deep breath and raised the level of the lead singer a smidgen. One great thing about this band was that the lead singer's girlfriend didn't care if her beaux could be heard above the rest of the band. However, the lead guitarist's current girlfriend had wanted her boyfriend's part louder than the lead singer's, which made no sense. The lead guitarist's girlfriend had, mercifully enough, been shouted down in practice by the bass guitarist's father! It gave Manon a new perspective.

Manon mixed all night, but had no idea what the highlight of the band's performance was. She wasn't connected to their songs, only to whether or not she was going to get yelled at afterwards. *They aren't yelling at each other.* She was giving the band exactly what they had asked for. *No one's waving at me.* That was no guarantee though. Several of the major yellers had already been smiling and talking to the regular fans. Regular fans, as opposed to the few uninitiated who thought DD&PF stood for the initials of two performers, and were surprised to hear a rock band perform instead of a couple of singer-songwriters.

Wendolynn Jane Landers

Mannon planned to record her own material after tonight's concert. She rearranged the equipment in the concert hall quickly after DD&PF finished their last set. Keeping the drums unchanged, she unplugged the bass guitar to use its amplifier on her acoustic guitar's microphone. She had an hour to start recording the songs she had drafted. This was a decent hall, no one was in a hurry, and the equipment was already set up. She would bang out a few takes before tearing the set down and going home. That way, she could record the song with its reverb still attached to it, instead of splitting the song from its echo.

Since DD&PF for wasn't completely set up to record live, Manon brought her computer to plug into their mixing board. She still didn't have the microphone placement around her drum kit at home correct, so borrowing their setup made her life a lot easier. She emailed a few experts from the recoding seminar in Indiana, and got a reply from Jacob. According to them, her drums sounded "boxy." To Manon, DD&PF's drums sounded too loud, which was probably the opposite of "boxy." She had no idea what they meant by "boxy." All the songs she liked sounded "boxy" to them. She put that in the same category of not knowing what they meant by "reverb" either. She checked her microphone placement, which was by the book, literally, following the pictures she had taken in class. To her, it was strange to stick that little microphone that looked like a mat into the kick drum itself. *Because the mic wasn't going to be loud enough sitting immediately outside the drum? How?!* She concluded it must be her room's "reverb," since her ignorance continued as to what that actually meant.

DD&PF drifted off to their dressing rooms. A handful of fans milled a few feet from their gear. Manon wasn't worried about getting a completely clean take, just enough to show Wayland. She hunkered down behind the drums to beat out a groove. *I hope I can get this software to work.* She couldn't quite get the demo of the software to take off like she wanted, so she started banging on the drums, on stage with the stage lights in her eyes. Fans stood around taking pictures of her on their cell phones and posting them online. The fans had no idea what she was doing. She hadn't played drums before. She tried a tat, tat, tat in the middle of the snare. Manon didn't realize there were metal beads underneath the snare. She thought the snares rattled because of how tight their drum heads were.

Once she finished the drum riff, she took out her acoustic guitar. She didn't think she was going to get the level right since she was in front of the microphone instead of behind the board. And of course it was deathly important to get the level right. She had experienced that during her singing days. Whoever ran the show had to sing a bit first to make sure the microphones were set up right. The loudest part of the song had to register as the loudest sound the microphone would pick up. Louder than that, and the microphone would start to veer dangerously off into its own world of screeching limbo.

Inspired by fans taking pictures of her, when Manon got back home she tried to finish writing some songs. It's hard to rest against a piano and think, so Manon sat at her kitchen table, hunched over a notepad. *I need to write something popular. Love songs are perennially fascinating. I've composed several love songs over the years. This should be a comfortable topic for me.*

Then the part where you stare at a sheet of paper and no ideas come into your mind arrived.

Unfortunately, she spent two days staring at the same notepad. Clearly, she was going to have to start writing anything, anything at all. She hadn't even doodled on the page. It was still completely white. *But I don't want to talk to anyone.* Part of writing a song is having something to say, even random words will do. *I wouldn't dare write a love song about Wayland. That would be screamingly bad.* So, given that she couldn't write a love song about the love she knew, she was going to have to make something up altogether.

She was streaming a new release. The song felt quite old. It had an emotion from another decade. The words were in dialogue form, so Manon could erase one singer's dialogue, and replace it with another actor. *That would at least be half a song to start with.* As she heard the new release, she became psyched. *I can nail the other half of the song in minutes.*

After 10, or was it 15, minutes she had no luck. She decided to get a diet soda from the refrigerator. Manon started thinking about the car commercial. *I wonder what it would have been like if we had tried to write a love song that could be used as a car commercial?* She opened the door. *It would have been a better fit, that's for sure.* Manon stood there with the refrigerator door open for a minute. It was not a good time for an epiphany. It was a careless afternoon. The sun was shining brightly through the kitchen window. *The only thing I care about right now is the refrigerator.* She stared at the refrigerator. It had been a touchstone in her life for years.

It was quite the moment of reckoning for her. She froze at the thought of never feeling anything for anyone again. *No one exists in a vacuum. I should expand on what emotions I have left.* If all she loved was the refrigerator, then she would write a love song for the refrigerator. People would never know. She got her soda, and went back to her blank paper.

On it she wrote:

Let me find something sweet inside you today
    Talking to you was all the feeling I had left in me
    When I didn't know what to do you came through
    I didn't know what to say and I would pray
                    * * *

Improvising to Beat the Band

I never heard a single reply from you
    Yet you stood there and saw me through
    You didn't have to say anything
    You knew how to keep things cool
    You were stable when I wasn't able

I'm glad I found a heart within me
    To pour out to you
    I thought there was nothing left inside
    I put myself in your shoes
    To know what you had seen
    The serendipity within your coolness

You help me connect my past to other people's pasts
    You were easy to open and hard to close
    I would stand there for hours just looking at you
    There was always an excuse to go back to see you

I would lean on you and think in the night
    You would shine a light inside you
    You kept the sweetness of my life inside you
    The sweetest things of my life inside you
    Let me find something sweet inside you today

I go looking for the same things every time
    How do I know I'll never find anything new in there?
    Do I need the light or the coolness?
    It's probably the sweetness and the familiar
    That I need to find

Manon didn't know what to do with the lyrics that came to her. *The first part's OK, but I don't know about the rest.*

* * *

———————

The songwriters were video conferencing their call on three cell phones even though Ailill and Wayland were sitting in the same room overseas. A person who kept up with the times might not have found that situation to be unusual, but Manon thought it was extremely extravagant. Manon watched two different views of the same room behind each of her co-writers. At this point, Manon was using a cheap phone she had picked up at the grocery store. She marveled that the video conferencing worked as well as it did. To her, that was still an enigma. Manon wasn't clear on how Ailill had found out about the source of her inspiration. *Wayland must have told him, but maybe Ailill's clairvoyant. Sometimes musicians are like that.*

"Yeah, that's a great song Manon," Wayland said, "but it sounds like it was written in the seventies."

"I was trying to sound serious with it."

"Try to sound like yourself," he said.

"I do sound like myself."

"Try to sound like yourself right now. Not yourself thirty years ago, or however long it's been."

"It's not been thirty years, Wayland. I don't sound like regular people now. I've been by myself too long." Manon's time for having friends had run out years ago. A natural part of aging, friends move, start families, then die. The spare time for friendship occurs when you're young.

"That's what you're going to have to work with, so run with it. It's pointless to try to write something that you're not feeling. Write the stuff that's inside you now. Save the song you're trying to write for another day." It was good advice, but Manon was in no mood to take it.

Wayland said, "Can we incorporate the lyric 'Take Me Home,' into this? We've been working on it for a while now.

"Sure, 'Let me find something sweet inside you today,' doesn't necessarily conflict with 'Take Me Home,'" she said. "Of course, they have nothing to do with each other."

"If this song is about the refrigerator, am I a magnet on it?" Ailill had invited himself to this songwriting session. "I'm stuck on you, and I feel like people come along and pick me up and move me around however they want me to be on the face of things." Ailill's face brightened while he started tossing his arms around. "You know, thinking of the refrigerator as a person's face."

Thank God he's just using it as a metaphor! Manon tried to hide how callous she had become through careful word choice and prolonged silences.

Ailill nodded knowingly at Wayland when he had heard that Manon had written a song about her refrigerator. *She doesn't want to say that it's about Wayland since that would be awkward.*

"You need to start writing a song about the ghost at the morgue," Manon said.

"I don't need to write a song about a ghost," Wayland said.

"Yeah, you do. You keep trying to talk to him. Write a song for him. See what happens," Manon said.

"When you write a song for someone, you at least entertain the idea that they might listen to it." Wayland crisply pronounced every word.

"The ghost will eavesdrop. He messes with stuff, so he must be nearby," Manon said. "What did you say to him when you went over to talk to him? Did you pick a fight with him?" Manon never found out exactly what happened at the morgue. She had expected Wayland to be verbally cited by the hospital security, or possibly arrested, for trespassing since he had wandered into an unauthorized area. She also couldn't fathom how to ask him once it was over. They had merely started talking about bucket lists instead. She started to take notes on her cell phone. *Don't expect Wayland to take notes for you.*

"The ghost started it," Wayland said. "I had plans on how I wanted to tell you about the car commercial, but out of the blue your new friend calls with the news. I blame it on supernatural interference in the lives of mortals."

"Faustine happened to see it." Manon bristled and ducked her chin close to her collarbone when Wayland referred to Faustine as her "new friend."

"Uh-huh, and happened to call you immediately," Wayland said.

"Faustine did say she thought she was spiritually influenced, I remember," Manon said.

"You don't need me yelling at you, and your new friend, Faustine, doesn't need me yelling at her either," Wayland's voice rose, remembering, "but I definitely needed to yell at someone after that happened."

"What did you yell?"

"I don't remember. How I wanted to tell you. How stupid I felt about the way you found out." Wayland avoided narrating the bit about telling the ghost that the spirit world need not worry about Manon ever performing again.

"Love songs are about being stupid. We can work that in," she said.

"I am not writing a love song about this idiot. For whatever reason, he's got it in for you. We never wrote a song that would wreck anybody's life."

"Maybe he heard the song after his girlfriend or wife left him?"

"The song! We did write more than one you know," he said.

"You get the idea. Our most recognizable song," she said.

"I think he's a suicide victim who hasn't moved on," Wayland said.

Improvising to Beat the Band

Suicide wasn't a topic he typically broached with Manon. She suddenly dropped the idea of drafting this song.

After they hung up, Ailill and Wayland drank and mulled their conversation with Manon around for the rest of the afternoon.

"I cannot call you what I'm thinking right now!" Ailill banged his hand on the table.

They had been friends long enough that they were no longer allowed to call each other names. Not ever.

"Why is that?" Wayland took a swig. There was a footlong sandwich on the table that neither one of them touched. The sandwich reminded Wayland of Sebastian, and the footlong sandwiches he took to Manon's house. He glanced around the room to avoid looking at it, just like if Sebastian had been there, he would have avoided eye contact with him.

"We do not see eye-to-eye in this matter." Ailill spoke crisply between swallows. The more he drank, the more sense he made, unfortunately. He needed to be a little loose to tell off Wayland. "I think we need to at least be respectful of the trust factor at this point."

"After what she's been through," Wayland continued for him, nodding his head.

"Yes, after everything she's been through." Ailill nodded his head along with Wayland, waiting for Wayland to change the subject on him any second. He might not have the guts to start down this road again. "And when she finds out that not only your son was at this recording master class," Ailill glared at Wayland, "but one of the instructors produced your solo guitar album..." Ailill pointed his beer at Wayland. *I don't know what she's going to do. Bad enough that Wayland remarried, but he also recorded an entire album without any lyrics. Clearly, he's thrown her away. Maybe she'll take it better because she's a girl?*

"What's she gonna do?" Wayland had already lain awake at night asking the ceiling what it thought Manon would do. So far, the ceiling had made no reply. *Ailill's guess isn't going to be any better than the ceiling's.*

"It's gonna look like everyone was put up to this." Ailill spat his words out while banging his beer down.

"I told them she would be there," Wayland's whine rose, "they came out and put her equipment together."

"You let your son put her studio together!" Ailill pointed his beer directly at Wayland.

"No, no not him, two of the other guys at Jacob's studio," Wayland said.

"She gonna find out," Ailill's voice boomed, "and then you're going to be in trouble!" His beer dropped to the table with a thud.

"Yes. She's going to find out. Either she meets my son before she finds out who he is, or afterwards," Wayland said.

Ailill nodded, then drank. He finally reached for a sandwich. He noticed that Wayland wasn't eating.

"She has no chance of liking him once she finds out he's my kid," Wayland said.

Ailill started eating in earnest, once he realized that Wayland wasn't going to bother. Wayland sat there, drank, and watched Ailill eat.

Wayland reasoned that Manon presumed his son, Tadgh (pronounced like "tiger" without the "er"), worked as a sound technician. *Has she noticed that we look alike?* Tadgh, named after several medieval Irish kings, lived a couple of hours away, so inviting him over was not completely casual.

When Wayland tried to think of activities he could do with his son, the only thing that came to mind was coloring books. There were several yellowed half-scribbled books kept in a closet full of storage boxes. He made up an excuse about finding a new tree to plant in his front yard, since he saw an ad for landscaping in one of the rock magazines he was reading.

When Tadgh arrived, they went outside to figure out where to plant it. No way they could be overheard. Never mind the fact that their family actively discouraged Wayland from wandering around the yard, given his penchant for absentminded mishaps, or even wanted new plants by their driveway for that matter.

Wayland asked Tadgh several open-ended questions to which his son gave curt replies. *Why doesn't he just blurt out what happened during recording class? How long are we going to play twenty questions before he tells me what I need to know?*

"Did she seem to get how it's done?" Wayland calculated how much of the equipment Manon should be able to use by now, then concluded what tasks he could assign her. *A current project should take her mind off of how much of life she's missed.*

"She was in the class," Tadgh said. "It's not like I was grading her or anything."

"I don't know what she's going to know," Wayland said.

"I'm sure she can figure it out. There are videos online," his son said.

"She's not used to watching videos online," Wayland said. "Plus she thinks half the world is out to get her."

"She's sure that the half the world that's out to get her knows how to use the internet?"

"I don't think they would need to use the internet, personally." Wayland had not told his son everything that had happened to Manon.

Wayland's son was treating Manon like the step-mother he

never had. He knew the drill. Don't expect his dad to be completely rational when dealing with this woman. As long as he wasn't forced to take sides in their fights, he could still help out occasionally. A bullet dodged.

"She wasn't noticeably impaired." His son thought to offer this information, since his dad didn't seem to be asking the questions that were on his mind.

"I didn't think she would be," Wayland said.

"She seemed to be making friends," was the only other thing that Wayland's son could offer. He was guessing what his father wanted to know.

"She's going to be stressed when she tries to use all of that equipment on her own," Wayland said. "We shouldn't have gotten her so much."

"I don't think you got her that much dad." Tadgh put his hands on his hips. *Where is this going? I don't know what he wants.* "She needs to be able to work on her own. She can't do that if she has to borrow a mic all the time. Who would she borrow a mic from anyway? Is there anybody out there with her? Someone who lives nearby?"

"You know, a couple of people figured your mom did it." Wayland shoved a boulder for no apparent reason.

"They thought mom had done what?" Wayland's son pulled a few strands of grass growing underneath the rock.

"Tried to kill Manon," Wayland said.

His son looked sharply at him.

Wayland stood up to look for another rock to move.

"What are you talking about? No one's said anything to me about anything like that." Tadhg stared at his father who had just put three boulders together to form a triangle. *Is he going to put all the rocks into one great big pile?*

"Can't image that they would," Wayland stepped on top of the pile of rocks, put his hands on his hips, then looked down at Tadgh. Wayland rarely played sports or went camping with his son, so he was making up this outdoor activity as he went. He waited for his son to start making a similar pile of rocks.

"How did Manon seem to you?"

"She never got stressed," his son said. "She didn't miss any class either. She seemed to socialize with everybody." Tadgh wasn't catching on to what all his father was expecting him to include in this check-up. He took a pass on mentioning that Manon spent a lot of time talking to Jacob, who was an audio producer. *This is too weird.*

"I've promised to take our family to an amusement park with her." Wayland stretched out his arms towards a couple of puffy clouds in the distance, as though he were welcoming the upcoming rain.

"An amusement park?" His son was too old for this, nor did he have kids of his own yet. It didn't occur to him to make his own pile of rocks either.

"Yeah, I need to go on a Ferris Wheel with her. I'd prefer it if the rest of you were around." Wayland stepped off the rocks.

"I don't see why anyone would think that mom had tried to hurt her." Tadgh switched the topic back to search for the missing pieces in Wayland's story. He eyed his father, who was shoving another small boulder around for no reason, with suspicion.

"We may also end up playing poker with her, so you should probably learn how," Wayland said.

"Why are we doing this?"

"Bucket list," Wayland said.

"Maybe Jacob can go with us to the amusement park?"

"Jacob? Why Jacob?"

"He seemed to get along with her OK at the recording seminar," Tadgh said.

"Are you supposed to be telling this? What happened?"

"I'm thinking that if mom's going to be there, and you were in a relationship with Manon, maybe another person should be there to break the ice," Tadgh said.

"Maybe Ailill? She already knows Ailill," Wayland said.

"Ailill's taken," Tadgh said. "It won't be the same."

"I need this to be a good experience for her. If we start setting her up before she's ready the whole thing could blow up," Wayland said.

Tadgh put his hand on his hip and stared at his father. He wasn't worried about how Manon was going to take it. Tadgh's mental picture was of his mother pacing around the house, not eating for days. She had always made off-handed remarks about how secure her marriage to Wayland really was.

Sebastian paused for a moment on his porch to look up at the stars. He heard the Aeolian harp whistling as though it were far, far away, although it played few feet from him. In his mind, he filled in the rest of Manon's song. It felt more like having her there than listening to the recording. He closed his eyes to hang on to every note. There was a variation in the whistling on the wind that wasn't on the MP3. When he opened his eyes, he noticed that the stars were blinking on and off. They weren't in time with the music at all. Their rhythm being off satisfied him.

For Sebastian, too many years of running from one event to another had taken its toll. Now he naively envisioned himself solitary for decades without feeling alone. Too much had happened. It was like the Aeolian harp: once he heard the beginning, he could fill in the rest of the tune himself.

Sebastian took an awfully deep breath. *I'm glad I don't have anyone to meet with tonight. I don't want to go back to my living room though.* Not having a chore waiting inside didn't help matters. *Maybe I could stay out here all night? I could put a mic on the wind harp, and either record it or send the signal via cable to an amp in the living room.* There was something in the night—the darkness and aloneness—that soothed the burning in his soul.

As long as Manon's back in touch with a Slip of the Cue again, I should start working on my own career. A band that Sebastian previously performed public relations work for, Phosphorescent Freckles, was back in town. *Their name is longer now, DD&PF. Wonder why? Probably got some new band members.* He could peruse their merchandising table to see what kind of posters they were selling.

He pulled into the stadium parking lot. *Are they going to deny me entrance?* But truthfully, they wouldn't even know he was there. *There's a marketing meeting I really should be going to instead.* He needed to learn how to use one of the products that consumers found difficult to use, but all the experts were completely sold on. Sebastian strained to maintain a professional level in more than one field, even if they were somewhat related. He had the same 24 hours in a day everyone else did. He needed to figure out which was more important to him and only focus on that. *I dread making that kind of a commitment in my professional life. A client wakes up on the wrong side of bed one day, and there goes your career.*

Sebastian's main diversion was ice skating. He usually took acquaintances from his office. It was a novelty, so people didn't mind being asked. It forged bonds. Sebastian didn't have to interact personally with anyone, yet they would be spending the day together. He went ice skating with potential clients, trying to network. He went ice skating with former clients, trying to keep in touch. Of course, he went ice skating by himself. On the rink, he knew he would never think about that adorable rock band, a Slip of the Cue. Faustine never realized that putting ice skating on the bucket list was Sebastian's most vulnerable moment. Instead, she thought he was blowing her off.

———————————

"Hey, Faustine, this is Manon." Manon was using her nifty new cellphone! She had researched her options and bought a new model with her commercial money. It was candy apple red, just like Sebastian's sports car. *I shouldn't splurge on myself. Who knows when I'll need the money?* "We're having the seance next Saturday. Can you make it? We still need a referee to run interference between me and Wayland."

"This Saturday?" Faustine wrote it down. "I don't think I heard you correctly. I don't remember anything about a seance."

"Next Saturday, next Saturday," Manon excitedly corrected her. "It'll be around midnight. We're having it at the Fleer Casino and Resort. You'll want to park around back, near the band's equipment trailer."

"Why are you having your seance at a casino!" Faustine said.

"We decided to use a mixing board instead of a Ouija board. The band I've been working for has a pretty big mixer. We can use it after their show. We can slide the levels up and down to get messages from the other side, as it were."

"Pret-ty cool," Faustine's accent time traveled back to the 1980s. *I have no idea if that could work. What about Sebastian? Where did this extra band that Manon was talking about come from anyway?* "Is anyone else going to be there?" It was the most diplomatic way Faustine had of asking where Sebastian had gone.

Improvising to Beat the Band

"Well, there's the band I'm working for. It's their mixer. I presume they're going to want to know what people are doing with it."

"A Slip of the Cue, I mean," Faustine said.

"So far, Wayland, Ailill, and Wayland's son. I supposed they all could show up though," Manon said.

"No Sebastian?" Faustine asked.

"No, Sebastian won't be there. You're safe," Manon said.

"I bet it's been a while since you've seen Wayland's family. The kids are probably a lot bigger by now." Faustine took a deep breath, waiting for a good moment to change the subject.

"I've actually never met his family. This'll be the first time I've met his son," Manon said.

"That's a lot to look forward to!" Faustine was smiling as hard as humanly possible as she said it. *I hope Manon catches my drift.* Working as a receptionist in her youth, her supervisor had warned her that listeners could hear her facial expressions change the tone of her voice through the receiver.

"Yeah, it's going to be quite a night," Manon said.

Faustine parked behind the casino, as per Manon's instructions. The gig had ended over an hour ago. The two back doors were wide open. She watched people traipsing in and out, lugging stage equipment. *I shouldn't simply walk in. There has to be proper protocol.* It was a cool evening with a slight breeze and jasmine in the air. *Perfect.* The stage was poorly-lit. People were still deciding whether or not they wanted to stay for the seance. DD&PF were talking themselves into leaving early. Many fans weren't sure if they were supposed to leave yet or if DD&PF was going to continue singing. Random people milled around the stage

169

area. Faustine walked over to stand around with the fans.

Wayland's son, Tadgh, flew in with a Slip of the Cue, although he had not said hello to Manon yet. Manon still didn't realize she met him at the recording seminar she attended in Indiana.

Manon and Wayland rolled the mixing board out onto the stage. They put different colored electrical tape along the side of the mixing board. That way, each level could slide to any letter of their color-coded alphabet.

"I like this better, the mixing board not being ours," Wayland said, "that way we'll know it wasn't rigged."

"I guess people could still say I tampered with it," Manon said.

"Yes, but I will know that no one from outside, as it were, could have arranged it to say anything in particular," Wayland said.

"I don't think that anybody but Ailill would even try that," Manon said.

"If this says anything important to us, I don't want to wonder about it later, whether what it said was true or not," Wayland said.

Ailill wandered over to where Manon and Wayland were having their tête-à-tête. "What should we play?" Ailill had a long, thin scarf that he was waving in the slight breeze. "In order to entice the spirit world into our presence this evening?" His flair for the dramatic was coming out. Probably because there were fans within earshot. He was making large swooping motions towards the make-shift audience who could not make up their minds whether or not to stay. The scarf billowed in the breeze. Ailill could smell the jasmine.

Faustine walked up behind him in the semi-darkness, noticing how expensive the silk scarf was with its designer print. She hadn't met him yet, and thought that answering his question first might be a little much. Once she realized that she was going to have to walk past the famous rock star, with his wall of fans, to get to Manon, she went ahead and said, "Something that goes with jasmine. There's a lot of it in the air tonight." Ailill turned backwards to look at her. He hadn't realized anyone was standing behind him.

"Yeah, I believe she's right," Wayland said. "I think I saw a bush near the entrance on the back wall as we came in."

"Yeah, it's there," Manon agreed. "I'm still allergic to the stuff." She smiled knowingly at Wayland, who returned the look in her eyes. They held each other's gaze for a beat.

"I think that's all we have to do, Ailill." Wayland made a point of slowly over-pronouncing his name, (aye-yill), to make sure Faustine knew who he was.

"No candles?" Ailill asked.

"We're using the lights from the mixer. They're low," Manon said.

"Oh, come on now. You can't have a high-tech seance! It simply isn't done," Ailill said. "I'm going to go get some candles. I'm certain there's some in a drawer or suitcase somewhere." Ailill took off to the equipment trailer past the stage doors. Everyone else stood around waiting to start.

"How do you say his name again?" Faustine asked. "Is it Aye-yill or Ahh-yill?"

"Aye-yill," Manon said.

"It can be pronounced 'Ahh-yill,'" Wayland said. "I've heard it pronounced both ways."

"He wouldn't have let me say it wrong for years," Manon said.

"It's not worth fighting about. Say it as best you can." Wayland cut them short since he thought he heard Ailill coming back.

Ailill situated the candles on either side of the mixing board. Wayland's eyes met Manon's as they both touched the fader. As soon as they moved the fader, they closed their eyes. Ailill played a medieval chant on his cell phone. *Wayland and Manon are going to bicker about how far the spirit's told them to move the fader any minute!* Ailill's sense of intrigue piqued when they started picking out letters. They got an *n*, then an *o*. The first thing Ailill thought of was, *no way.* They kept going and spelled out "notseb" instead.

Wayland's son, Tadgh, positioned himself between Ailill and his father, gazing intently at the board. Several other family members of a Slip of the Cue scrutinized the mixing board. Half of DD&PF stayed after watching Ailill's scarf show. Part of the observers were family while part of them were uninitiated in this conflict.

Wayland gradually opened his eyes to move his hand to the next fader. Since Wayland was next to Manon's face, he looked at her closed eyelids for a moment while he waited for them to open. Without warning, Manon's shoulder abruptly had two more eyes staring over it. Wayland blurted out a shout. A grizzled man with a scruffy week-old beard was smiling sickeningly at Wayland.

Manon flinched. "What is it?" She was unaware of the person looking over her shoulder at Wayland.

Wayland reached out to push him away from Manon as he vanished. Wayland pushed Manon aside a step when he darted into the night chasing this banshee, yelling. The mixing board was on rollers, so it swayed away as Wayland ran. The candles overturned. Tadhg ran around the swerving board to grab the candles.

Ailill looked Manon in the eye. "What happened?" Instead of chasing Wayland, Ailill focused on remaining calm. He expected chaos this evening. Manon was still upright. That fact alone made tonight different. The fact that the place could catch fire eluded him.

"He yelled and ran," Manon said. "I don't know why." She

turned around and wobbled towards where Wayland disappeared into the dark.

Ailill then lurched the same direction. "Wayland! Wayland!"

"Who was that?" Wayland returned from the darkness. He grabbed a candle and threw it at the shadow behind him like he was trying to throw a boomerang through hell.

"We didn't see anyone, Wayland." Ailill tried to get beside Wayland so he could grab him. Tadgh chased the rolling candles through the darkness.

"You didn't see him?" Wayland asked.

The bystanders closest to the mixing board only saw Wayland's reaction in the semi-darkness. They saw Tadgh run after him. They jumped slightly when the men started running across the stage, then huddled closer together, backing slowly away. Ailill declared the seance to be over and set up the table for the appetizers.

"We need to figure out how to put this evil genie back in his bottle." Ailill took an emphatic swig of beer.

Everyone sitting around the table gawked at him. Chasing this "evil genie" was not the first thought that crossed their minds, never seeing the ghost again was. Having a seance was their outer limit, and they had already done that. They knew Ailill meant literally grabbing the thing, whatever it was, and physically and shoving him into a small, round, opaque glass object with a cork. The fact that it couldn't be done didn't impress Ailill. Even calm, cool, collected Wayland tried, physically, to run after it.

"Ailill," Faustine hesitated before pushing herself into the conversation. *But I just witnessed the thing!* "The only being I've ever heard of successfully grabbing one of those things was an archangel. I think most exorcists only shoo them away."

The entire party's jaws were open like they were about to sing, only there was silence, since their faces were frozen, while turning a shade lighter.

"What's the 'notSeb' mean? It wasn't Sebastian who hit me? Why would the ghost who scared Wayland want to write that?" Manon understood that the ghost had scared Wayland. However, no one had told her that the ghost stared over her shoulder at him.

"Maybe he didn't know we could see him?" Ailill scrutinized her face. *How does she deal with this thing all the time and not notice?*

"Maybe it wasn't him. Possibly, there's another one." The cool breeze bothered her legs, since she was wearing a dress, so she crossed them. The smell of jasmine made her nauseous.

Manon fumbled for her cell phone. *I need to write 'notseb' in my own notes. I shouldn't presume Wayland will keep track of it for me.* Her cell phone wasn't in her pocket. She started having an asthma attack as she bent over to reach around the corner of the table leg for her purse. It hadn't been that long since the seance, and they hadn't gone anywhere. She hadn't left the room, only walked from the mixing board to the table where they put the food. She felt in her small purse, and didn't find her phone.

Manon had finally bought an expensive cell phone. Her sporty, candy apple red cell phone the guys had gotten her with her commercial money.

"Hey, has anybody seen my cell phone?" Manon said.

All their eyes focused on her.

CHAPTER SEVEN

Vacation

Immediately following the seance, Faustine searched the stage with Manon for her missing cell phone, then attempted to make a graceful exit. Somehow or another, Faustine kept getting turned around. *Why is it so hard for me to find the door?* Faustine wove through the band, family, and friends milling around with their mouths open like a choir that's about to start singing, but one that was wandering around the stage like a pop-up concert, waiting for an unknown event to happen that would explain everything.

Ailill definitively decided that it was time to go. "Leave now! Or else no one ever will." He motioned them away with his arm.

Wayland stood slightly behind Ailill and nodded.

Faustine straightened her thin pastel, lace dress, fortified with a substantial lace petticoat. It was long sleeved, but the hem hit above her knees. She remembered the chill that she had felt on her legs around the time that Manon realized that she had lost her cell phone. *I shouldn't still be cold.* She reached down to rub her calves and ankles while looking around the room to see where the draft was coming from. *The room should be warm, especially filled with so many people.* She didn't see anyone shivering or complaining about the cold. There was a breeze from the open stage doors, but she was completely across the stage from the doors when she felt it. "Ah—huh?" There was suddenly a shortness of air in Faustine's lungs. She was able to catch her breath, but it threw her off guard. *What's going on?*

Meanwhile, DD&PF finished loading their equipment into a trailer attached to the drummer's truck. They had waited to load their equipment because they thought someone might still need their stage lights. The drummer and lead singer found themselves alone for a moment.

"Nobody but Wayland saw anything," the drummer for DD&PF said to his band's lead singer. The drummer zipped one of his toms into its carrying case, and shoved it tightly into an upper shelf in the trailer.

"I don't know, Ailill might have seen something." The lead singer swung a light stand around, folding it into its compact traveling case.

"It's bright red. There's no way they could miss it. Manon must have lost her purse," the drummer said.

"She might've left her cell phone at home. She'll probably find it later," the lead singer said.

"I'm not going to worry about it," the drummer said.

"Neither am I," the lead singer said.

"Now if the lights start falling on us during a performance, then, well…" the drummer said.

"Yeah, then we'll have to do something about it." The lead singer gave him a curt nod. They closed the back of the trailer, locked it for the night, then headed back to the stage to say goodbye to the rest of both bands before leaving.

Dissent Dissonance & Phosphorescent Freckles obtained their

name the hard way. Dissent Dissonance had been touring locally when their drummer dropped out. Phosphorescent Freckles had been touring in a neighboring state when they lost their bass guitarist, who never really recovered from a vague illness merely described as "the flu." The band remnants met at a state fair. What was left of both bands had already spent too much money on equipment to stop touring. They decided to combine forces. Both bands still needed to keep their fan base, minimal as it was, so they kept both band names. They started opening with first one band and then the other. Dissent Dissonance would use Phosphorescent Freckle's drummer. Phosphorescent Freckles would use Dissent Dissonance's bass guitarist. Eventually they started playing musical combinations together towards the end of their concerts. That's why they were willing to pick up Manon as a mixer. They knew the problem; they had been there. Although she belonged to another group, the arrangement was familiar. In fact, they never knew when they were going to break up, either. Plus, they might get an extra writer out of the deal. Who could tell?

DD&PF nearly got into a car wreck with their equipment trailer the day after the seance. The drummer, Chad, drove his truck pulling their equipment trailer, while his lead singer, Scott, rode shotgun. They noticed a tall, thin, elderly man on the right shoulder of the state highway about a quarter mile ahead of them, near a traffic light. As they approached, the grizzled man with a scruffy week-old beard smiled sickeningly at the drummer through the windshield, meeting his eyes. For no apparent reason, the man strode into the crosswalk. The drummer didn't have time to stop. He veered and swerved to keep from hitting him. The elderly man stared them down the whole time he crossed in front of them. He hopped up on the opposite curb, then skidded out of sight.

"What was that about!" Scott said.

"Whoever it was almost got hit," Chad said.

Scott said nothing more, giving silent thanks that they didn't collide with him. The man acted like he wanted to be run over.

Later that evening, they switched drivers after they had gotten fast-food. It was twilight. As they were getting closer to home, Scott swerved suddenly.

"Hey!" Chad spilt coffee on himself.

"It looked like a head!" Scott turned in his seat, straining to see what happened. "It looked like that guy we almost hit before. I wonder if somebody finally hit him, although I don't know how he could have gotten in front of us. I'm going back to figure out what it was." He made a u-turn through the grass dividing the highway. He crept along, carefully watching the median. "We haven't gone far, so the head should still be there."

"Maybe it was a rock we saw instead," Chad said, "the shadows are getting long right now."

About a mile later, they were still driving. They still hadn't seen whatever it was.

"I don't know what else it could have been. I saw his face," Chad said.

"I'm going to turn around. We missed it," Scott said.

They exited and went over an overpass, then around to the other side of the state highway, backtracking. They stared at the median expecting to see what caused the image.

"Must have been a shadow," Scott said.

Then suddenly they both saw the object again on their left. The head had a slack, open-faced mouth, as though it were saying "ah." They turned to each other, each knowing that the other had to have seen it.

"We turn around again." Scott made the same u-turn for the second time.

They studied the median carefully.

"This is about where it should be," Scott continued, "I can tell from the shrubs."

"I don't see anything," Chad said.

"It was here," Scott said, "I saw it twice. Now it's gone."

"Are we hallucinating?"

"No. I'm driving. If I were hallucinating I would have hit something already." They turned again at the overpass. This time they pulled into a fast-food restaurant.

"I'm calling my wife," Scott said, "to be on the safe side. I don't want this to be a sign that something bad's happened."

Chad nodded. "I'm walking around."

Scott went inside to use the pay phone. He didn't remember that he had a cell phone on him until he wandered around the restaurant long enough to realize that they didn't have pay phones anymore. Chad couldn't stop pacing rapidly beside their van. He kept shoving his hands in his pockets and immediately jerking them out again.

The day after the seance, Faustine spent her day off nervously pacing. *If I only knew what was going to happen next...* Her stomach tightened into a knot. A dry hacking coughed started, then she began having dry-heaves. She picked up the phone four or five times before she finally completed the call and invited her aunt her to lunch. *She always seems to have a sixth sense. Maybe I can borrow some precognition for an afternoon?*

In contrast to her niece's expectations, her aunt's standard claim was that Faustine never paid enough attention, therefore Faustine believed whatever she wanted to believe.

When Faustine entered the restaurant, she mentally noted the intricate, eggshell, linen, lace tablecloths. The draped segment of the tablecloth that swayed beneath the edge resembled a doily which appeared hand-crocheted. The loops resembled figure-eights. *Why haven't I noticed the tablecloths before?* Faustine looked around at the empty tables. She saw her aunt seated near a window and waved. Faustine's aunt waved back and smiled as Faustine walked over to her table.

"The waitresses haven't sat us at the same table twice. Isn't that strange? Do you think they did it on purpose?" Faustine asked.

"No, they fill the tables depending on which waitress is working. We've never arrived at the same time twice." Her aunt smiled knowingly as she remembered.

"I never realized before how excellent these tablecloths are." Faustine pointed to the side of the table. *The coils of the doily look like figure-eight infinity signs.*

"Well, they've been here the whole time, Faustine," her aunt said, "Why are you focusing on the tables this minute! Read the menu. The soup of the day is new."

While standing beside the booth, Faustine clutched the tablecloth tightly, pulling the infinity signs closer to her eyes.

Is she going to let go of it? Faustine's aunt reached out to take the tablecloth from her.

Suddenly, as Faustine threw down the tablecloth, her arms flew up over her head, and she slid into the booth. Then, she picked up a menu like nothing odd had happened.

"Have you had watercress soup?" Faustine's aunt asked.

"Watercress?" Faustine shook her head, reading the menu. "Sebastian's band had a seance the other night." As creases returned to her eyebrows, she put down the menu, gasped and clutched the edge of the tablecloth again, pulling it around the table. *The doily circles look like eyes staring at me.* She pulled it closer to her face to double-check. "Wayland said he saw eyes staring at him over Manon's shoulder."

"A seance?" Unfortunately, Faustine's aunt couldn't focus on the seance with her niece trying to tear apart a tablecloth in public. "You should let go of the tablecloth. You'll stretch it." Faustine's aunt reached over to grab Faustine's hand.

"Yeah, the band was trying to unearth who bludgeoned Manon when this ghost appeared and terrorized Wayland." Faustine tried to straighten and smooth out, the tablecloth.

"You met Sebastian's friends? The ones in the band?" She leaned towards Faustine. *I had given up on her ever figuring anything out about them.*

"A ghost is involved," Faustine said. *Maybe she didn't hear the part about the seance?* "This tablecloth reminds me of him." She lifted the tablecloth towards her aunt, turning over her spoon. "The circles look like infinity symbols, which remind me of his eyes."

"Had you met the lead singer before the seance?"

The lead singer was more important to her aunt than the seance.

"I introduced myself at the seance." Faustine put the tablecloth back down. "Everyone ran when the ghost appeared. I told Ailill that he couldn't put a ghost in a bottle. It wasn't a genie."

"Maybe the stress of meeting these past friends of Sebastian affected you?" Faustine's aunt asked. *Something certainly has!*

"The ghost took Manon's cell phone," Faustine said, "She arrived with the cell phone, and it was gone as soon as the ghost left. We think he took it."

Faustine's aunt patted her niece's hand. *Who does she mean* by 'we?' "Well, now we know why Sebastian never told you about his friends."

The waitress appeared.

"We'll both have the watercress soup and tea to start," Faustine's aunt said.

Faustine's aunt decided that their lunch was over when her niece tried to poke a hole in the tablecloth's lace with her fork. She followed Faustine home, expecting her niece to start making u-turn after u-turn the entire trip, trying to make her own infinity symbol. When they got to Faustine's house, her aunt made her lie down on her couch. It was the first time she had ever been in Faustine's house.

"The letters at the séance spelled out 'notseb' meaning 'not Sebastian,'" Faustine said.

Her aunt dropped a pillow over Faustine's eyes, then pulled a blanket over her. While her niece rested, Faustine's aunt searched her house. Her aunt slipped quietly up the carpeted stairs to find Faustine's computer. She looked up Elodie's old social media posts. Though she had no idea what they said, she was betting on her niece never looking at them again. After she found the link to Elodie's father's social media account, she emailed him. In her note, she put a link to her own social media account. *Hopefully, Elodie's father will get back in touch with me.* Then she sneaked back downstairs to the kitchen to get a drink. She looked for hard liquor in the cupboard, then for wine. She settled for the diet soda she found in the refrigerator. While she was looking around, she saw the remains of a cold veggie pizza, turned upside down in a skillet, still on the range. *I'll have to talk to her about that later.*

"It means the ghost was trying to tell us that it wasn't Sebastian who tried to kill Manon." Faustine still had the pillow over her eyes.

She doesn't know I've left. Faustine's aunt sat down in a chair near her niece.

"I think the ghost was trying to tell us that because I had asked Sebastian if he was the one who tried to kill Manon. I didn't know why he hadn't mentioned it before. If he had done anything wrong, that might've been why he never said anything about it," Faustine said.

"Okay Faustine, lie there for a little while longer. I'll get you something to drink," Faustine's aunt said.

Manon was on speakerphone with Wayland and Ailill. A Slip of the Cue was working on a throwaway song for Wayland and Manon's joint bucket list. Not that the song would literally be thrown away, but it would never be released to the public. Since it was on the bucket list, Manon had invited Faustine over to referee.

"You're calling this 'trip-hop' but it sounds like punk," Manon said.

"You can play punk rock, we'll play trip-hop, Manon." Ailill videoconferenced from overseas.

Since Faustine had already met Ailill in person, she was prattling one dumb joke after another. Once Ailill started to laugh a bit, the volume of her jokes slowed down. They were attempting to record in Manon's spare room, transformed into a lost artist's colony, as though all of Salt Spring Island in Canada with its artists, musicians, and writers, could be shoved into one room. Faustine didn't know what to do, so Manon let her sing "oohs" and "aahs" into a microphone.

Manon was still learning how to turn the knobs displayed on the computer screen so that she could hear Faustine's voice, but not her breaths. *This is the weirdest thing to practice, ever.* Manon wasn't sure what she was supposed to be listening for, but she slowly raised the lever on the screen anyway. So far, moving the lever didn't make anything sound any different to her.

Wayland and Ailill were shouting encouragements over the video phone.

"I never thought I'd be a backup singer for a Slip of the Cue!" Faustine's joke fell flat.

"Technically speaking," Wayland said, "this is our throwaway song. If we pay you, it's got to be on an hourly basis."

Manon mouthed to Faustine, "if you get paid!" Faustine started nodding and Manon also nodded in agreement.

"I meant it as a joke guys. I'm here as a friend of Manon." Faustine cautiously hedged her bets. *These guys don't like to talk about money.*

"She's right though," Ailill said, "we have to get a signed agreement from her on pay and confidentiality."

"Guys, there is no way this song ever gets released. A Slip of the Cue does not perform trip-hop." For a moment, Wayland had a vision of a 1950s rock-n-roll audience breakdancing to 1980s muzak and chuckled.

"You know," Faustine decided to take advantage of the fact that they were not in the same room, "Ailill's scarf show at the seance would have looked good in a trip-hop video. Maybe it's something you should consider?"

"I'm emailing Faustine a non-disclosure agreement, along with a work-for-hire form. You should get it in a couple of minutes, Manon," Wayland said.

"I'm wondering if she'll accept a trip to a theme park as payment?" Manon strained to obtain the details on their upcoming vacation. She envisioned waking up suddenly one morning in her pajamas, opening the front door for a courier holding airline tickets with a departure time within an hour, and not being able to get anyone on the phone to ask questions.

"That's right, we have to put that together," Wayland said.

Improvising to Beat the Band

"This'll work out then. We'll pay her what the trip will cost. That way she can make her own arrangements if she'd like," Ailill said.

"Yeah, that sounds good, I'm following," Faustine said.

Manon finally slid the lever so high that she couldn't hear Faustine's voice at all. *They want to use the money as a paper trail, in case things go wrong.*

Tonight, the group, DD&PF, was playing a gig out of state. With only a week's notice, Manon couldn't mix for them, since she would've had to have driven to the gig location. Any time Manon thought about flying, she envisioned the Lockerbie bombing. Never mind how many decades ago the bombing was, in Manon's head, the plane was still in the air, intact, right on the verge of being ripped apart.

The lead singer, Scott, unloaded the mixing board—the same one they used for the seance—since he needed to mix that night's performance, impromptu, while he sang. He wasn't going to try to find a temporary person to mix for him on the spur of the moment. This mixing board was an entire panel of the levers similar to the ones that Manon was having a hard time getting adjusted to. Manon couldn't hear anything yet, and she was a noted songwriter. If the lead singer handed this mixing job over to someone who had never actually performed themselves, the overall sound would be too loud, plus the singer would be heard over the lead guitar.

"I wish Manon would learn to fly." Scott lifted the mixing board to situate it. *But by then she'll be back with a Slip of the Cue. You can't win, even when you're helping someone out.*

The last thing the lead singer for Dissent Dissonance & Phosphorescent Freckles expected was to unearth was

Manon's cell phone, especially since he hadn't found her cell phone on the night of its disappearance. Tonight, as Scott was unloading the mixing board, he found Manon's cell phone shoved underneath it, mashed as though it had been run over by a bulldozer. Turning the candy apple red pieces over in his hands, Scott couldn't understand how it ended up under the mixer. Their drummer, Chad, wasn't into that style of humor, and neither was anyone else in the band.

"Any idea how her phone got there?" Scott asked.

"Are you kidding me? No way," Chad said.

"Do we start wondering when the lights are going to fall on us?" Scott asked.

"Give the phone back to Manon and see what happens," Chad said.

"Now that we've touched it, does the bad luck rub off on us?" Scott asked.

"I don't think so, but don't mess with it too much. Put it in a plastic baggie," Chad said.

"How does a plastic baggie keep voodoo away?" Scott asked.

———————————

Once DD&PF got back from their gig, Scott waited until the next rehearsal to give Manon her smashed cell phone. *It would be bad luck to overreact.* He carefully calculated his steps across the long hall their band rented for practice space to make sure they weren't too fast, and that his stride wasn't too wide. He made sure not to swing his arms too often.

"Where did you find it?" Manon took the baggie from the lead singer.

"Underneath the mixing board in the trailer," Scott said.

"It can't have gotten there by accident." Manon held the baggie up to look at the cell phone through the clear plastic without touching it. It was smashed, but all the pieces were there.

"If you want to take it to the police, you can," Scott said, "it's got my fingerprints on it, but I've got witnesses as to when and where I found it."

"Who was there?" Manon's faint voice sounded like she was whispering at someone's deathbed.

"Our drummer," Scott said, "he had loaded the mixer. I unloaded it."

As Manon inspected the bag, she felt the lead singer's cold, clammy hand touch her shoulder to comfort her while she watched his arm tremble.

Those eyes pierced Wayland in the darkness. Those eyes. They smiled so sickeningly. Wayland's whole arm grabbed for them, almost hooking the eyes with his left hand. It was like when he reached over Manon's shoulder during the seance. He couldn't quite grab what was underneath those eyes. He yelled. Then he realized he was sitting up in bed, looking at his bookcase. His arm dangled above his head. No one was in the room with him. The stillness crept back into his mind. Wayland only had dreams about Manon when he was alone. He started breathing again. Wayland pushed himself up against one of the pillows in order to steady himself. Then he got out of bed and stumbled to the bathroom. He stared at his own eyes in the mirror. They seemed smaller than the ones staring at him in the night, more human. The eyes he saw in his nightmare reminded him of car headlights.

It was like a car was coming straight for Manon. In Wayland's dream, he was trying to push the car out of the way so it wouldn't hurt her. But now that he was awake, he needed to push Manon out of the way instead. *How am I going to get her out of the way when she can't see the car?* Wayland opened his medicine cabinet to hide its mirror against the wall. *Manon couldn't see that fiend behind her no matter how close he was.* "Dear God, save us from people who hate love songs." Wayland addressed his bathroom ceiling. His stomach felt like he might throw up, so he lingered. He didn't have a headache before going to bed, which made it weird to wake up with one. His migraine throbbed in a rhythm that was faster than his heartbeat. *Maybe I should take aspirin? Would I even keep it down? Does aspirin work when the banshees have come for you?* The only thing that would've made Wayland's nightmare any more Kafkaesque—being caught by an unseen tyrant—would have been if the ghost had left Manon's cell phone beside his bed! Wayland didn't know that her smashed cell phone had already been found.

The next day, he called Manon, just to make sure she'd pick up her phone. She answered on the third ring.

"I've been having nightmares, so I wanted to know how you were doing," Wayland said.

"Nightmares about what?" she asked.

"Car wrecks and Ferris Wheels," he said, "I hope the Ferris Wheel isn't a reference to Fortune's Wheel. I don't feel like leaving my life to chance right now."

———————————

Faustine went to sleep that Saturday night planning on getting up bright and early Sunday morning and heading out to the hospital's chapel. About three in the morning she woke up screaming. She dreamed of headlights with their center blacked out. The headlights were menacing, shadowy eyes wearing old-fashioned, cat eye style glasses made from the car headlights. She opened her eyes and knew what it meant.

Improvising to Beat the Band

I'm next on the ghost's hit list. Her head was splitting. She took migraine pills, determined to sleep. *One way or another, I'm going to make it through this.*

Faustine stared transfixed at the now familiar, ivory, stained-glass dove the chapel had flying on its blue-sky, stained glass background. She shifted her weight from one foot to the other, marking time until the service's end, waiting to demand a personal briefing from the minister. The pianist still bobbed her foot to the arrhythmic sermon. The hospital's parson droned about the upcoming holiday. A few solitary people scattered themselves strategically around the room, listening. Everyone positioned themselves to stay out of everyone else's way. No one knew each other. They were like autumn leaves, fallen and dried underneath an oak.

After the sacrament, Faustine stood in line to shake the minister's hand. *I wonder if there's a special way I'm supposed to broach this topic?*

The minister beamed at Faustine, shaking her hand. "How are you this holiday?" It slipped the parson's mind that she had met Faustine earlier in the year.

"Not so good. I wanted information about exorcisms. I hope it's OK to talk about this today, but there is this thing—"

"Exorcisms!" The minister was expecting to greet the bereaved during this minor holiday. She hadn't prepped for this. "I'm not an expert on exorcisms."

"If you can find anyone who might have experience with this, I have an acquaintance who keeps getting death threats from this," Faustine paused to look around, "thing. Whatever you want to call it, it's not living. I thought an exorcism might be the most direct—"

"Exorcisms are not done very often." The minister

immediately grabbed a hymn book and held it between them. "I only have historical information about them." The phrase "death threats" did not mentally register with the preacher.

"Actually, anything would be great. Could I meet with you sometime?" Faustine mirrored the preacher by picking up a hymnal and thumbing through it. That gave Faustine something to do while she waited for the preacher to finish greeting the rest of the congregation, after which she followed the preacher back to her office.

Apparently, the various clergy who occupied that pulpit used the same room to prep. The office smelled of musty books, but Faustine didn't see any. There were no bookshelves. There were a couple of different styles of competing religious symbols to mark the territory. There was a patchwork memorial quilt on the wall. Faustine sat on the love seat. The space was cramped with a small coffee table shoved into Faustine's knees.

"I'm not an expert on this," the pastor paused for emphasis, "but I can give you the name of a historian on the subject. He may be able to talk to you."

Faustine got the message that it was not hospital policy to perform an exorcism! "Anyone who knows anything would be great."

"I'm also giving you the name of a doctor you can see about your nightmares." The cleric handed Faustine a sheet of paper with both the name of the historian and the doctor on it. Faustine could not take one without the other.

The historian's office was at a university extension site. Faustine was early for her appointment, so she stood outside his office reading the various signs posted on the bulletin board in the hall. Apparently, a band from the university was having a concert in a couple of weeks. The professor walked up beside her and unlocked his door.

The physical key caught Faustine's eye. *With all the crazy nouveau electronics on campus, he has an actual key!*

"Hello? Did you have an appointment to see me?" He carried several old books under his arm.

Faustine nodded.

They went inside, and he put the books down on his desk. Faustine sat down on the other side. A small sky light illuminated his desk. There was a wall of book in various shades of tan and brown. Unlike the hospital cleric's office, she could see the books, yet nothing smelt musty.

"What do you want to learn about exorcisms?" He suppressed a chuckle.

"Is it still possible to have one? Or is it all ancient history?" Faustine asked.

"You would have to ask a priest who still does them to find out for certain. There are reports of different protestant organizations having them. I can show you two or three current books on the subject." He took one book out of the pile and pushed it across his desk towards Faustine. "If you want to know, you would have to email him." The professor pointed to the author's name on the book cover.

"I'm not asking you to make an exorcist recommendation, I just need a place to get started." Faustine opened the book. *He must be worried about his liability.*

"Don't worry, I'm not giving you one. If you're wanting historical information, that would be one of the books to read to get started." His carefree smile glowed.

Faustine turned a page in the book. She took out her cell phone to make notes. Her cell phone reminded her of Manon. She sighed.

Wendolynn Jane Landers

* * *

When Faustine got home with the books, she absentmindedly got blank paper and a pencil out to make notes instead of using her cell phone. She had the email address of one of the authors. *I'm going to finish reading the book before I start asking questions.*

She tossed the name of the doctor that the cleric gave her into a drawer. *If the exorcism doesn't stop this metaphysical game, I'll try the doctor. How would anyone even know if they'd successfully gotten rid of the thing anyway?* Now the couch where she had previously had nightmares involving veggie pizza was repurposed. It cradled her quest to understand Manon while she read the books on exorcisms. *I wonder why Manon hasn't tried an exorcism herself? It'd apparently occurred to Ailill.* After Faustine finished the first book, one of the newer ones, Faustine turned on the bronze desk lamp with the green shade beside her computer and started to write an email to the author. Then she deleted it, and started all over again a few times. After that, she started writing it out by hand in a notebook before copying it over to her computer. *He made several references to current exorcisms, so he should know someone I could contact who had performed one recently. I wish I had more than one real, current reference. I hope it pans out. But what should I ask him?*

After having addressed him with a degree of formality in the email, she said, "Would you be willing to perform an exorcism for us?" *That's too easy to say 'no' to.* She erased it. *I need to be very specific, or else he'll change an important detail on me after we've gotten started. I need a contact person as soon as possible.* She continued writing. "A friend of mine has experienced unexplained occurrences, and we're wondering what the criterion is to determine demonic influence. Could I talk to a priest personally?" *That way he'll know that I need help without having to commit to anything.* He was a stranger, so she was forced to keep an appropriate social distance. *This is a little like trying to talk to a rock star. I should ask Ailill about this. He seemed sympathetic to the idea at the last seance. I'll call Manon.*

Faustine called the same number she used when she heard a Slip of the Cue's car commercial. The phone rang four times and the answering machine picked up before Manon got to her landline phone, not her second expensive new cell phone that the car commercial had paid for! The second one was sapphire with rhinestone hearts.

"Hey, Manon, I was working on the exorcism and thought it would be a good idea to talk to Ailill about the logistics. Is there a number I can call to talk to him?"

"I'll let Wayland know that Ailill should call you," Manon said. *I doubt Ailill knows his own number.*

Technically speaking, she was supposed to go through Sebastian, but currently, no one was speaking to him. Sebastian's public relations duties included hoarding their contact information so they never had to give out their phone number to anyone. Manon wasn't sure what the distinction between being a PR specialist and a personal assistant was. Wayland hadn't said anything about getting a new public relations person for her to contact.

Until they hire someone else, deal with the questions yourself. Manon would call Wayland since they were still working together. *What a mess!* "What makes you think he'd be interested in an exorcism?" There was a slightly bitter taste in Manon's mouth.

"He said he wanted to 'put the genie back in the bottle' at the last seance. That would be what an exorcism is for," Faustine said.

---

* * *

The priest who authored the exorcism textbook emailed Faustine the next day. "What made you decide you needed an exorcism?"

Faustine replied, "We saw an apparition at a seance. The band thinks it's the same ghost that hurt Manon several years ago. We want to know how to get rid of him." *What kind of detail is he looking for?*

He got back to her the next day. He was a once-a-day email type, not at all like Ailill. "Why were you having a seance? What were you trying to ask him? How did the band know it was a ghost that hurt your friend originally?"

She emailed, "I don't know. Two of my friends were working on a joint bucket list, and a seance happened to be on it. I don't know who's idea the seance was specifically, or what they wanted to know. I think it was something they hadn't done before and they were curious. I think they were still trying to figure out if a ghost hit her or if somebody else did."

She didn't say what the hit involved. For all the priest knew, she was talking about a car.

He emailed, "Well, don't have a seance to get rid of a ghost!"

Apparently he thought his joke was funny.

"Well, how do you get rid of them then?" she emailed.

"Do you know anyone locally?" the priest emailed.

At this point, it had been about a week since the priest first made contact.

"No, I'm emailing you! I got some books at the local college. No one said anything about knowing anyone personally," Faustine emailed.

"The real key is getting the poltergeist to tell you how to get rid of it," the priest emailed.

"They tell you how to get rid of themselves? Why would they want you to know that?" Faustine emailed.

Improvising to Beat the Band

"They don't want you to know. You have to ask them," the priest emailed.

"You ask them?" Faustine felt a trick coming on.

"For an exorcism, you ask them their name, how many of them there are, when and how they entered the person, and when they are leaving," the priest emailed.

By now, they had been emailing for almost two weeks.

"Manon's not possessed. Is that still going to work?" Faustine emailed.

"If you happen to run into the poltergeist again, it's something you could try. I wouldn't go looking for trouble though," the priest emailed, "you never know when you're suddenly going to be in over your head."

"You can't order the thing into a bottle, but you can ask it when it's going to leave?" Faustine emailed. *I hope I've gotten the directions right.*

Faustine texted Ailill. *I need to let somebody else know about this.*

"Ask it when it's going to leave?" Ailill texted.

"That will make it tell you how to get rid of it," Faustine texted.

They had a disposable email account set up for Faustine to contact Ailill. It was cumbersome for Faustine to be held at a distance, especially since it was in a completely traceable fashion. Ironically, she had already been invited to go on vacation with him and his family, yet he wasn't sure if he could trust her with his private email address.

Once burned, twice shy is one thing, but they presume everything is going to end up in court. Faustine sat at her desk beside her kitchen door with her computer off, texting. She looked around her living room. *Why do I have so many computers?*

"So when we see the thing, we ask it when it's going to leave?" Ailill texted.

Faustine noticed that Ailill tended to get business issues over with all at once. Dragging a conversation on for days via email was not his style. *He could just pick up the phone instead of texting. After all, you have to use a phone to text anyway. Does he text from his computer?* Faustine glanced at her blank desktop monitor. There was dust across the top of it.

"Yeah, that's basically it," she texted.

"We only had a minute at most when he appeared last time," Ailill texted, "when someone's possessed, the demon's with them all the time. So you have longer to ask them questions. Or a priest would. We've got a ghost who's a hit-and-run driver."

Ailill hadn't gotten the story straight from DD&PF about nearly hitting the old, grizzled man and then not being sure if there was a head or not in the median further down the road. He recollected that there was a car involved and a person died.

"The priest suggested holy water, crosses, and other holy objects," Faustine texted, "the idea being to cover an entire area in holy, religious symbolism."

"Did he say anything about singing? As long as you mentioned covering, we can cover a few religious tunes and play them on the speakers," Ailill texted.

Faustine was not familiar with musical jargon, so she didn't know that when a band records a song that another artist has previously released, it's called a cover song.

"He didn't specifically say to do that, but it couldn't hurt," Faustine texted.

"Wayland may not be able to ask him anything. He jumped on the ghost last time. I wasn't expecting him to lash out like that." Ailill texted the little surprised looking emoji.

* * *

Improvising to Beat the Band

———————————

Remember when Faustine's aunt followed her home after lunch the day that Faustine attacked the tablecloth? She spied on Faustine's computer while Faustine was resting on the couch. Which is how Faustine's aunt ended up reading Elodie's old posts, instead of Faustine. She wasn't so close to Elodie that she couldn't take the bad news. She had no preconceived notions about what they should say. There were the posts about the hospital. Elodie had been involved in several hospital programs, the dance program being the most prominent one. There was an innocuous nutrition program. It didn't shout that Elodie was anorexic.

Well, Elodie's father finally returned Faustine's aunt's message.

Faustine's aunt tapped her pencil while she thought about how to reply to Elodie's father.

The kids are too young to know that nothing ever works out. Faustine's aunt pressed a button on her cell phone.

Elodie had been openly involved in several hospital programs. There was certainly enough going on that Faustine's aunt couldn't fault Elodie's father with her death.

Maybe she had gotten a bad case of the flu after having gone to the hospital so much? Faustine's aunt put her cell phone on her kitchen table while she kept tapping her pencil.

There weren't any posts about guys.

That's unusual since she was single. Were they hidden behind the other posts? Faustine's aunt stopped tapping her pencil, and pushed a few more buttons on her phone.

The chapel at the hospital had its own social media account, and would post devotional readings. Elodie had a couple of other motivational social media accounts that she had been following. Faustine's aunt deduced that Faustine wasn't following any of the same accounts that Elodie was, since that way she would have found out about Elodie's social media account. Oddly enough, Elodie followed Sour Cream & Burritos, apparently to get its coupons. It wasn't the sort of thing you would expect a person who was watching her weight to do.

Did she do it to give away the coupons? Faustine's aunt decided to use one of the coupons.

Elodie had additionally been a candy striper at the hospital, volunteering occasionally on the weekends. She practically lived at the hospital, while covering up her anorexia.

There was no good reason for Faustine's aunt and Elodie's father to meet at Sour Cream & Burritos. The coupon wasn't that much of a deal, financially. Maybe they picked the place because it was near the hospital? Subliminal mental processing working? There was an orange and red banner hanging underneath the bold, neon sign that read "Sour Cream & Chicken coming soon!"

Faustine's aunt turned to Elodie's father, "Why didn't you stay in touch with the kids after the funeral?"

Elodie's father glanced at her, startled. "The doctors never wanted me involved in her therapy. I presumed it was best to stay out of her friends' lives too."

Faustine's aunt didn't know what he meant by that, but figured he had decided to let the doctors do what they needed to do. "I don't think her doctors would have approved of the way I got in touch with you."

Since the restaurant was crowded, they sat on the patio. Elodie's father graciously opened the patio door for Faustine's aunt.

"Did you mean that Faustine and that other kid didn't

want you involved in your daughter's therapy?" *I can't see her as having figured that much out. Maybe I missed a detail somewhere?*

"The doctors don't want you involved in the therapy," Elodie's father said, "they don't know if you're part of the problem."

"So you weren't acquainted with my niece then," Faustine's aunt said.

They sat down with the sun shining directly onto their table. Squinting made it harder for them to chitchat.

"I wasn't close to any of them after Elodie got sick," he said, "I believe Elodie had a virus. She was over 100 pounds when she died."

He doesn't have anyone to talk to about his daughter's death. It's best not to argue. Faustine's aunt unwrapped her burrito. "Well, the kids have started having seances to try to get in contact with your daughter. Your daughter's spirit, I mean."

Elodie's father tried to eat a bite of taco, but choked for a minute, looking at her.

———————

Faustine's aunt handed Faustine a coupon for Sour Cream & Burritos. *I'm not going to tell Faustine that I've gotten in touch with Elodie's father, but I want to know what her reaction to the coupon's going to be.*

"You want to eat at Sour Cream & Burritos? We never eat at Sour Cream and Burritos. It's like fast-food, you know. Plus, you have a coupon. Wow." Faustine's delivery of her soliloquy was remarkable dry.

"Yeah, I found their social media account, and they post coupons regularly," Faustine's aunt said.

"You know, it's a pity that Sour Cream & Burritos doesn't have a flower garden near their restaurant." Faustine stared at the coupon. *Why did I say that? It's been a while since I've thought about the type of flower garden they used to have.*

Faustine used to pick flowers with Elodie after they ate out.

A flower garden reference was not what Faustine's aunt expected. "Maybe you should post that idea on Sour Cream & Burritos' social media account."

"I don't know if they take suggestions," Faustine said, "places like that have social media accounts to put out information, not take information in."

"It wouldn't hurt. Restaurants used to have suggestion boxes. I haven't seen any around lately. I guess they went away with the advent of social media," Faustine's aunt said.

It was time for a Slip of the Cue to attempt to go on vacation. The group agreed to fly to the influential megalopolis near the sea on their own. Manon, Faustine, Jacob and Tadgh were at one hotel. The rest of the entourage of a Slip of the Cue stayed at another. Manon shared a room with Faustine. They were too old for this summer camp arrangement, but it was only for a couple of days.

Manon realized they had separate lodgings when they checked in. *Why is this on Wayland's bucket list if we aren't literally going to the amusement park together?* Manon walked around their room, pulling the curtains back, trying to see what their view was like. "I need to get a ruling from you about this trip. Once we get Wayland by himself, I will get your opinion." Manon was crisply matter-of-fact.

"You've finally found a flaw in Wayland's bucket list? Way to go!" Faustine beamed.

"I don't have any idea why we're here." Manon unzipped her suitcase at the foot of the bed. She took out her rhinestone studded flip-flops and changed shoes.

"Sebastian quizzed me about going to Foothills Foodie once we ordered. I never knew why he waited 'til then to ask," Faustine said.

"I think we're supposed to go on a Ferris Wheel together? He had a nightmare about it. Theoretically, this is the easiest way to do that. He said he had to take his family, and I refused to go to a state fair," Manon said.

"Just from that, it sounds like you're right on target." Faustine hung her coat in the closet closest to her bed.

"I need to check with him though, that this is what we're supposed to be doing," Manon said.

"You can wait until we leave," Faustine said, "I was totally weirded out by Sebastian asking me what my real reason was for going was. He asked between the balcony and the fajitas."

"But you guys needed a referee to get through your bucket list. Wayland and I were able to start ours without anyone wondering if they should call the cops," Manon said.

"We always had to meet at the designated location. We couldn't ride together. Sebastian thought we would get into a fight and not finish the list," Faustine said.

"I have to say," Manon got her shampoo out of her bag, "there were a couple of times I wondered if I was going to have to call the cops, and we were meeting outside." Manon zipped her bag. "I'll call Wayland in the morning to coordinate."

Manon wasn't completely reconciled to an extended weekend at an amusement park that was not at all amusing.

"You do know Jacob though, right? Jacob said you two had met," Faustine said.

"Yeah, I met him at the recording seminar I went to in Indiana," Manon said, "Wayland knows him too."

"So it's only Tadgh you don't know." Faustine said it like a concluding argument in court.

* * *

It was the same dream. This time, the head-lights were red. Wayland woke up reaching for the nightstand. He found his cell phone and called Manon.

"Are you alright?" Wayland asked.

"Yeah, I'm fine. What's wrong?" Manon asked.

Wayland hesitated a moment. *I shouldn't've called her in the middle of the night.* He checked the time in the dark. "I had that nightmare again. Only this time the headlights that turn into eyes were red." Wayland's shallow breathing started to even out.

"My cell phone is fine right now, but I'll keep an eye out for him, so to speak," Manon said.

"Not funny," Wayland said, "I'm worried about tomorrow."

"We have general plans, and Faustine is here with me now," Manon said.

"Let's go on the Ferris Wheel first thing and get it over with," Wayland's voice was strained, "that way if one of us needs to leave later on, we can."

"OK, Ferris Wheel first thing in the morning," Manon said, "are you going to be able to go back to sleep?"

"I don't know. I usually end up with a migraine after one of these things," Wayland said.

"I don't have migraine pills. Take aspirin," Manon said, "it could be the stress of the trip. Once we hit the Ferris Wheel, you should be able to relax."

"OK, I'll go downstairs and get aspirin," Wayland said.

After they hung up, Manon stared at the ceiling. *Does Wayland feel as weird as I do talking with his wife within earshot?* Then she remembered that Jane wasn't in his hotel room. She didn't know the name of the woman he had remarried. *This is*

Improvising to Beat the Band

like waking up in bed with a stranger.

———————————

Manon, Faustine, Tadgh, and Jacob arrived together in the hotel van. They slowed down to stop a good quarter mile from the entrance. Manon wasn't sure where they were supposed to go next.

"Tadgh, did you guys do this before?" Manon craned around to study him. *Is this a repeat of a previous family vacation?*

"Oh yeah, we all came here in the spring when I was 15," Tadgh said.

"Is this on the list of contraband information you can't tell me?" Manon tended to think of the trivia she wasn't supposed be cognizant of as ammunition.

"I don't think so. I think I can tell you about me! It's not like you don't need the info. I wouldn't have guessed how to get in here if I hadn't done it before," Tadgh said.

"Aren't we going in the main entrance?" Faustine smiled forcibly.

Jacob glanced at her from the corner of his eye. *She is extremely expert at smiling.* "Was Wayland divorced by then?"

Since it was a very obnoxious question, Tadgh gave him a reproachful look and stalled by taking a deep breath. "I'm not sure," Tadgh turned away and started looking at the amusement park as they approached it, "that I know the answer to that question at this time." Tadgh looked knowingly at Jacob. "They let me do this because they trust me." He lifted a corner of his mouth.

"I'm not your lawyer, and I'm not a journalist." Jacob returned his hypocritical smile.

Everyone was smiling too much. The driver of the van started to scrutinize them in the rearview mirror.

"Why do they need to trust you?" Faustine asked.

"Manon's on a need-to-know basis," Jacob said.

"Sebastian didn't keep her on a need-to-know basis," Faustine said.

"Oh yes he did." Jacob laughed.

"They didn't come over that much after a while," Manon demurred defensively, then shot a glance out the van's window.

For it to have been on Wayland's bucket list, he was surprisingly quiet as the Ferris Wheel lifted Manon and himself heavenward. Several of the band's kids had gotten on the ride at the same time, along with Faustine and Jacob. Tadgh shared a seat with his older half-sister. No one but Wayland understood why they were there. After Faustine told Manon how awkward it was for Faustine once Sebastian had asked Faustine why they had gone to Foothills Foodie, Manon didn't want to risk it! The whole vacation was uncomfortable enough, Manon didn't want to make it more perplexing.

Manon held back her questions. *But when else am I going to ask him?* Manon turned towards Wayland in the ride's seat. She had a panoramic view of the city behind him. He stared at her because of the seriousness of her voice. "Wayland, why are we here?" Her voice was a solemn monotone.

"Meaning, why is this on the bucket list?"

"Yes, it can't be because you simply wanted to go on a Ferris Wheel. It certainly can't be that you were in a romantic mood," she gestured towards Tadgh and his half-sister, "I don't know why we're here. What was your nightmare about?" She emphasized her blank look towards him by leaning forward and staring. *Maybe I can communicate through telepathic glaring.*

"I thought it would be cool to write a song from the top of a Ferris Wheel," Wayland said, "maybe bring back memories of recording the wind harp sample for Love & All Its Glory."

"We aren't going to be at the top of the ride long enough to write a song." Manon's voice rose into a whine.

They had not brought a recorder. She didn't have paper. It didn't occur to her to use her cell phone, or even check to see if she had it.

"I don't think we're going to be able to pull it off," he leaned towards her conspiratorially, "but it was a cool idea, and I'm glad I'm here with you." Wayland smiled and kissed her cheek. "I had a dream about writing a song with you at the top of a Ferris Wheel. I thought if I could get you up here, I could remember how it went." He hummed softly to himself.

Manon's gripped the metal frame enclosing them tighter. *Maybe he thinks I won't remember any of this later?* From the corner of her eye, she could see Tadgh and his half-sister swinging in their seat to and fro. To Manon, they looked uncomfortable and distracted.

Wayland took out his cell phone to take a picture from the top.

In contrast to Wayland's carefree waving and laughing at his kids, Manon's knuckles turned white clutching the bar which held them in. Manon watched Wayland fumble with his phone, then started to take hers out too—the sapphire and rhinestone one—to take a picture as well. Manon squirmed around in her seat trying to take her cell phone out of her back pocket. *Are we actually allowed to have cell phones out during the ride? What if one of them dropped? Could the radio waves jam the computer running the ride?* She put hers back up.

When the ride stopped, Wayland got off the Ferris Wheel and held the door open for Manon.

Manon felt nauseated as she grimaced and glared at him as she ducked her head while sliding out of the car. Manon scooted in two parts, so she did not look gracious as Wayland held the door open for her. *Why is he letting his family see him do this?* Manon tried to smile when she looked Wayland in the eyes as she slid past him. The fact that this wasn't his previous family, except for Tadgh's older half-sister, eluded her again.

"Thanks." Manon thought she should say more, but couldn't think of anything.

"Did you like the ride?" Faustine stood behind Wayland slightly to one side.

"The view was great." Manon had no enthusiasm. She staggered towards Faustine.

Wayland watched the women begin to walk towards the next ride, the bumper cars. At that point, he let them get ahead of him. Then, he turned to Tadgh.

"It was a great view from the top." Wayland beamed.

"It's awesome," Tadgh's brow furrowed, "where are we going?"

"Let's go over to the water park with the kids," Wayland said.

They stopped following Manon and Faustine and started veering away. Jacob got off the Ferris Wheel after everyone else had. He was following the group when he saw Manon and Faustine wander to his right, while Wayland and Tadgh suddenly made a sharp left. Jacob figured they had decided not to follow the women. *I don't know who to catch up with.* Jacob kicked around the idea of chasing Manon, but then second guessed himself. He started running after Wayland. Jacob was out of breath when he ran up beside them. Maybe he jogged a little fast for a casual day at a theme park.

"Hey, where are we going?" he asked.

I need to be alone right now. Wayland was paler now than

when he got on the Ferris Wheel, and not at all steady on his feet. "I'm following the kids." *I hope they find another ride together.*

"Was there anything you wanted to do, Jacob?" Tadgh asked.

"No, I thought we were all going to stay together today." Jacob glanced back towards where the women went. *Why are we off schedule already? What have I signed up for?*

"You can catch up with Manon, if that's what you want to do." Tadgh made a point of matching his uneven stride. *I doubt dad will ever be that direct. Jacob's clearly trying to get along in spite of his own agenda.*

"Yeah, I don't think we'll be staying together all day. Go talk to Manon. Or Faustine." Wayland motioned in the direction of the women. He held his stomach.

Jacob looked back over his shoulder at Wayland as he headed towards the women. "Tadgh, do you want to come with me?" Jacob sounded like he needed a favor.

"Sure," Tadgh's voice echoed the resigned determination in his stride. He marched with Jacob towards their uncertain fate.

Talking to a girl who hadn't realized that her boyfriend had broken up with her wasn't easy.

Manon and Faustine casually chit-chatted while they strolled from the Ferris Wheel to the bumper cars.

"Why don't we go on a roller coaster?" Faustine asked.

"Because I can't stand heights," Manon said.

"You seemed fine on the Ferris Wheel," Faustine said.

"It was a special occasion," Manon said, "besides, I was hoping my fear of heights had cleared up. You have to try it out periodically to double-check how it's going."

"Why did he want to go on the Ferris Wheel?" Faustine asked.

"He wanted to write a song," Manon said.

"How did you do on the ride?" Faustine asked.

"When he asked me a question, I would open my eyes," Manon said, "I still feel pretty shaky." After a few steps, she continued, "I didn't worry about it. I figured if I started screaming uncontrollably, Wayland could explain it to people."

"I went up in a hot air ballon once. That was the last time I was that high up," Faustine said.

By then, they had talked their way over to the bumper cars. A trio of cats sat on top of decorative boulders, staring at them.

"Hey, do you think Wayland's part wizard or something?" Faustine pointed at the cats.

"Not anything you don't already know about, I don't think," Manon said, "the cats chase mice here."

The cats crouched, visually tracking the women, but were too far away to pounce on them.

"I don't know why they're all sitting there together," Faustine said.

As the women got closer to the ride, one of the cats jumped to an adjacent boulder, which kept the women in the cat's line of site, but did not jump down to approach the women.

"We can get the park staff to chase them off after the ride. I'm sure we'll run into them. They've been staying pretty close," Faustine said.

"It's empty." Manon pointed at the vacant attendant stand. The chain that would indicate the ride was closed was clipped to the side so patrons could go through. "We can sit down and wait 'till they get here. They can't be gone more than a minute."

Manon got into the bumper car first and started to slide

over. Faustine hopped in right after her, but Manon shrieked suddenly, then stopped. A sharp pain ripped into Manon's leg. Faustine backed up, and a grayish-green object slid beside her. She tripped backwards stepping out of the car and fell on her side.

While Jacob and Tadgh were walking towards the women, they had a heart-to-heart talk. The women, as well as Wayland, were far enough away that they wouldn't be overheard.

"So now we're through with the reason we came here," Tadgh said.

"How do you know?" Jacob asked.

"I overheard Manon talking about it. Apparently, my dad wanted to go on a Ferris Wheel with her," Tadgh said.

"So is she free for the rest of the trip?" Jacob asked.

"Define free," Tadgh said, "she's not with Wayland now, but she's not talking to anyone else either."

At the same time, Faustine tumbled back out of the bumper car, screaming. The men broke off their conversation and started running towards her.

"Are you OK?" Tadgh ran at full speed. He looked for the ride attendant but didn't see anyone.

"Faustine?" Jacob hurtled past Tadgh. He caught up with Faustine first and grabbed her arm.

"Did you see it?" Faustine pointed. "Get Manon!"

"I don't see anything. Are you OK?" Jacob asked.

Three voices screamed. Tadgh grabbed Manon and started pulling her from the bumper car.

"Help. Help me." Overwhelmed, Manon neither moved nor yelled.

"What happened?" Tadgh yelling in Manon's ear was not making her move any faster.

"Something bit me," Manon said, "it bit my thigh."

"That thing—it went that way." Faustine caught her breath and resumed yelling. "Snake!—it slid over me." Faustine kept pointing towards the corner of the room that housed the bumper cars.

"Are you hurt Manon?" Jacob asked.

"Yes. It bit me. Whatever it was." Manon was the only one talking in a conversational tone.

"Let me see it." Tadgh started twisting her in the seat to get a better look at her thigh. "Jacob, call somebody."

Faustine lay on the ground where she fell. She rolled gently from side-to-side to see if she could move before starting to get up. *Falling backwards is a strange sensation!* She managed to grab her head to cushion the blow before hitting the concrete. Jacob hovered over her. Ignoring the corner where Faustine pointed, Jacob texted the theme park administration via the VIP app that there was a snake bite on the bumper car ride. A minute later, the ride attendant showed up.

"Where's the snake bite person?" The ride attendant sprinted towards them.

"Here," Jacob waved.

"Don't do anything. Our emergency staff will be here in a minute," the ride attendant said.

I should call 911 anyway. Tadgh started to take out his phone.

Manon struggled to slide out of the bumper car. Jacob pulled Faustine up. Manon leaned on Tadgh. Faustine was not at all certain she hadn't been hurt as well.

The ride attendant addressed Manon. "Sit back down in the car until the staff medic arrives. That way she can look at the snake bite better." The ride attendant pointed at Faustine.

"Does your staff know what to do about snake bites?" Jacob asked, "I can call 911 myself."

"They texted me an emergency pamphlet. It says to loosen clothing and brace the bitten area, but not to do anything else," the ride attendant said, "don't put ice on it."

The guys exchanged curious looks. Tadgh arched an eyebrow and Jacob nodded.

Jacob looked over at the open gate. *Maybe he had already seen the snake and was looking for someone to catch it?*

Jacob and Tadgh thought it was eerie for the attendant to have gotten texted an emergency pamphlet so quickly. There wasn't a sign saying the ride was closed. Of course, no other customers were there when the women walked up either. At that point about five minutes had elapsed, and a golf cart drove up with a big red cross on it. Two guys with an emergency medical bag got out.

"I'm not going to lie to you, I don't do snake bites that often," the first medic said, "we're taking them to the helicopter." The ride attendant looked relieved.

"I'm not sure an air-vac is necessary." Manon's fear of heights had already kicked-in on the Ferris Wheel. An uncontrollable scream was rising in her throat.

"There's no way we can get an ambulance into the park quickly once it's opened. It's too crowded," the first medic said, "since we need you out in a hurry, the air-vac is actually the easiest way."

"The park has its own helicopter on standby. I'm going to put the girls into the cart with us and take off. They can phone you guys from the hospital. We're taking them downtown. It's the closest hospital," the second emergency medic said.

"We came in the courtesy shuttle," Tadgh said, "how do we get to the hospital?"

"Take the shuttle. I'm texting them."

After they left, Tadgh and Jacob stood there looking at each other for a minute.

"How do we go after them? They're going too fast." Tadgh watched them as they disappeared. *I can't run as fast as an electric cart.*

"Meet them at the hospital, I guess," Jacob said.

They both started running towards the VIP side entrance.

"I guess we try to take the van to the hospital," Tadgh said.

"How did Wayland miss seeing this happen?" Jacob asked.

"He doesn't have his eyes glued on Manon." Tadgh laughed morbidly.

Jacob scowled. "He was right behind her on the Ferris Wheel."

"He took off with one of the kids the other way towards a different ride. He doesn't know what Faustine screaming sounds like, and apparently Manon doesn't scream," Tadgh said.

Manon lay on a stretcher in the helicopter while flying over the city. Faustine enjoyed the scenic view as best she could. Manon clenched eyes and teeth shut, praying it would be over soon. The pain in her thigh had started to subside.

One emergency medic tried to talk her through her repeated anxiety attacks. "Once you're at the hospital they'll give you an anti-venom shot. We've called them. They should have one on ready once we get there. This should all be over soon."

The other medic who picked them up at the bumper cars flew the helicopter.

"I can't believe the view from up here." Faustine prattled on distractedly to pass the time.

Improvising to Beat the Band

It was the close social proximity with compete strangers that made Faustine nervous instead of heights.

Manon clutched a pillow tightly. She hadn't opened her eyes since they put her on the helicopter. Manon felt the helicopter going up and down. She imagined an elevator cable breaking, and the elevator crashing to the bottom of the shaft. She didn't dare say a word.

"How did you get on the Ferris Wheel with Wayland?" Faustine looked at Manon lying there, nearly catatonic with fear.

Manon didn't reply.

You must have been in love with him. Faustine watched the city bustle from her mobile skyscraper.

CHAPTER EIGHT

Seance

In the hospital hallway, Wayland strode towards his son and Jacob while the color drained from his face. "I talked to Faustine in the cafeteria. She was getting a soda. She'll be back here in a minute."

"They immobilized Manon's leg," Tadgh said, "she's sedated. She might have gone into shock when it happened. They're more worried about that than the bite. Faustine told the nurse that Manon had some mental issues—"

"What mental issues did Faustine tell them about! Manon doesn't have anything they should try to treat her for." Wayland stamped his foot, lightly. His foot had a slight, short echo against the white cinderblock walls.

"They're not treating her for anything," Tadgh said, although the nurse hadn't told him anything definite. "They wanted to know what medication she had been taking, also whether or not she was allergic to horses. Apparently, the antidote serum is derived from horses."

There was enough light from the humming florescent beams overhead for Wayland to pull out his cell phone. He attempted to call his current wife, but suddenly held a sapphire and rhinestone studded case instead. "This isn't my phone!" Wayland started pushing buttons on it.

"Where's your phone?" Jacob asked.

Wayland glowered at him. "I don't know. I thought this one was mine. This phone's a different one." He continued pushing buttons on it, then smiled. "There's not much on it." He started trying to look for his number.

"If there's nothing on the phone, it's probably Manon's," Jacob said.

"The phone's not locked," Wayland said.

Tadgh and Jacob started scrolling through the apps on their phones.

"I spoke with Faustine, but I didn't notice anything wrong. I don't remember her taking her phone out while I was talking to her. Me and Jacob used our phones to call for help," Tadgh said, "I didn't see either Manon or Faustine with theirs."

"Did they download the amusement park's VIP app?" Wayland asked, "they would've been looking at the map on it. The VIP app also had the tickets and itinerary."

"Did you two break up?" Jacob stood in front of Wayland with his hands on his hips.

"Yes, and I've remarried since then." Wayland stared Jacob in the eye, then emphatically beamed.

Jacob returned a frown.

"Speaking of which, I need to call my wife and tell her where I'm at." Wayland turned away.

"OK, well both Manon and Faustine are upset about being in a hotel away from everyone else. Plus, Manon's been asking for you the whole time, even though everyone else is here," Jacob said.

"Well, we are on the trip together!" Wayland's smooth voice sounded like he was giving a magazine interview. He flipped a switch in his head and went into "everything's fine" mode.

* * *

Faustine chauffeured Manon back to the hotel from the hospital in Manon's white compact car. Manon didn't know how she would react to the new medication and didn't want to find out the hard way on the open road. The weather was excellent, and Manon enjoyed sight-seeing.

"I need to stop and get toothpaste. I bought a trial size and just ran out." Faustine turned into a superstore parking lot. "We can get something to drink, too."

"There are dishes I wanted to look at as long as we're here." Manon shook her head and frowned, remembering the doctor at the hospital who attempted to have her admitted to the psychiatric wing. *I shouldn't've told him about throwing the dishes out when I hadn't gotten around to washing them after a couple of weeks.*

"Dishes?"

"Yeah, I broke several dinner plates and never got them replaced." Manon got out of the car and looked at the summer sky. *I don't want the same thing to happen in a follow-up visit.*

Once they were in housewares, Manon continued her confessional. She admitted to Faustine that she was down to disposable plates and glasses since she had dropped several drinking glasses on the floor, plus some silverware down the garbage disposal. Additionally, several dishes had to be thrown out since she hadn't washed them before they were covered over in a malignant green and white film. Manon downplayed the hospital psychiatrist's interest in this story. "As long as I was talking to the psychiatrist, I thought of the kitchenware that I've lost or broken or damaged. That was the only crazy thing I've done that I think someone would actually worry about. Most people would've done their dishes before having to throw them out, I think."

"We can get you a new kitchen set and have it shipped back to your house." Faustine picked up a box full of plates from the shelf. *A road trip in a small packed car isn't OK.*

"I think it's strange that the first time I go on vacation in years, someone decides I'm in need of psychiatric help—for not getting out enough." Manon picked up a package of utensils and looked around the isle for a stocker to ask a question about shipping.

"As long as we're in a shopping mood," Faustine pointed towards the towels, "what is the status of your laundry? Do you need new sheets and towels?"

"I could use some more socks," Manon said, "all mine have holes in them."

"Stuff like that can be a sign of depression," Faustine said.

"Or of being lazy. I don't want to be put on medication because I haven't kept up with things."

"Better get with the program then."

Manon nodded.

The next day at the hotel, Manon took her suitcase and boxes of housewares down to her car, packing to leave. Jacob watched her carrying her luggage back and forth.

"Do you need any help with the bags?" Jacob asked.

Manon slammed the trunk. "Uh, no, not really. We're having the housewares I bought yesterday shipped. We're stopping at the post office on the way out." Manon started walking back to the hotel room.

"You don't have to ship them. There's room in my SUV. Do you need any help driving back?"

Manon stopped and turned to look at Jacob for a moment.

"You shouldn't be putting any pressure on your leg," Jacob

said, "besides, you could have a reaction to the antidote."

The doctors presumed she would be flying home, then catching a cab. Her driving cross-country didn't occur to them.

Manon shifted her weight from one foot to the other, while raising her hand to block out the sun, although its rays were nowhere near her eyes. *He's right.* "I'm going home with Faustine," Manon stuttered, "we live near each other."

Manon went back upstairs to the hotel room. She wanted to get Faustine alone to ask, since she didn't want Jacob putting any more pressure on the situation. Back in their room, Faustine was pushing too many belongings into her overnight bag. The room was almost empty, but her bag was already completely full.

"I'm going to have to ship part of this." Faustine grimaced while shoving the top of her suitcase down and zipping it half-way with her other hand.

"Jacob can take part of it if you don't have a box to ship it in," Manon said.

"It's not necessary." Faustine heaved and flipped her suitcase over on the bed to finish zipping it closed from the other side. *I'm not going to track down my stuff at Manon's house.*

Faustine planned on a veggie pizza and sleeping on the couch with a magazine or book. It wasn't a good sign that she couldn't make up her mind what to read when she got home, and they hadn't left yet. Her indecision set in many, many hours too soon.

"Jacob wants to drive me home. He says we can put my boxes in his SUV." Manon's face was deathly pale.

"Now that you mention it, that's not a bad idea," Faustine said, "I don't know what I was thinking. You can't drive home on that leg, and your car is too small to hold the housework we bought. If he drives you home, we don't have to do any shipping."

"I've been walking on it just fine," Manon said, "I don't see how driving's going to put that much more stress on it."

"It'll distract you while you're driving. What if it started to itch or something?" Faustine stopped packing for a moment. "It's not a bad idea."

Manon caught her meaning, which was that Jacob wasn't a bad idea.

"Did you want to fly home instead?" Manon said it with as much seriousness in her voice as she could muster.

"No, we've got two cars to take back, and the point is you're not supposed to drive, although I've never been big on car rides. They're boring after a couple of hours. It's aggravating being stuck inside for that long, especially in a small car like yours," Faustine said, "I don't want to interfere if Jacob's asked you. I can drive your car back, and you can ride with him."

"OK, I wanted to make sure." Manon reluctantly searched the room for any items she might have left, shrugged, hugged Faustine, and walked towards the door.

"OK, bye then. See you when we get home."

"It's no problem. Actually, it's a lot easier than if you drove me to the airport." Faustine gave Manon a short hug. "Bye. You can call me when you get in, if it'll help."

"I will." Manon turned back before leaving. "You never got Sebastian to do an overnight trip with you on your bucket list."

Faustine stopped for a moment, finished zipping the suitcase, and said, "Yeah."

Manon opened the passenger's side door, and stepped up to get in. *I hope this isn't awful.*

"We didn't get to spend any time together this week."

Jacob climbed into the driver's seat of his big SUV.

"Do you know where I live?" Manon asked.

"It's where Wayland lived," Jacob paused, "and Sebastian."

"Wayland doesn't live there," Manon said, "I didn't realize he bought a house near me."

As Manon buckled her seat belt, she realized that part of her brain was confusing the two men. However, she couldn't run around with a day planner open with notes about them on hand to refer to. *Pay no attention to the memories you've been having.* She planned to spend the trip with Wayland and rarely spoke to him. Now, she would be alone with Jacob for most of two days. She hadn't talked to him alone since the recording seminar in Indiana. *I hope I don't start thinking that Jacob's married to Wayland's first wife, Jane.* "I didn't expect to see you again after that seminar. How did you meet Wayland?"

"I recorded Wayland's solo guitar album for him."

"He recorded a solo album? He didn't tell me." Manon felt a punch in her stomach. *Why is he still trying to write with me if he has a solo career!* "How did it do?"

"Well reviewed. Obviously not a best seller like the band's albums. But decent. I don't think he'll record another." Jacob shook his head, looked sideways, then turned his SUV into the street. "Mainly to have gotten the guitar pieces he had written for bridges into one coherent form. Where were you wanting to eat lunch?"

"Pizza is fine. Any pizza shop." Manon bobbed her head and searched the road through the windows.

"I mean, what town? How far are we going today?"

"Two-hundred miles from here is the state line. That's a good place to stop."

"Do you mind if we do a little sight-seeing on the way? There's a scenic trail I've always wanted to hike but never had the time," Jacob said.

Improvising to Beat the Band

"Don't you want to go ahead and get home soon?"

"No, not particularly," Jacob said, "I'm still on vacation. Want to listen to Wayland's guitar album?"

He turned on his cell phone which was plugged into his SUV's audio speakers.

"Sure." Manon clenched her folded arms. *This is not a good time to daydream about Wayland.*

"You'll like it." He smiled at her, then looked around as he merged into the interstate traffic.

I'll bet. Manon closed her eyes and imagined Wayland on stage playing. Manon fell asleep remembering Wayland playing guitar in her house. She had only watched him playing in front of an audience once or twice.

"Soothing, huh?" Jacob glanced over at her sleeping.

Jacob propped his feet up on Manon's foot rest to show off the orange sunset he had the nail technician paint on them. Manon had never been in a salon with the opposite sex before. She had always been around women gossiping, especially when she went with her sisters.

"Wayland spends money because he has all those wives and kids and people like me around to bug him into spending it all the time." Jacob waved a toe in Manon's direction. "If we left him alone, he'd probably stay cooped up in the house all day like you."

"I like this song," Manon said, "do you know who it is?"

The nail salon had adult contemporary playing.

"Nah, I'm not an A&R guy. I never listen to anything," Jacob said.

Manon looked at her toes while her nails dried. *I don't believe that. Managing artists and their repertoire sounds like it would be right up your ally. Especially since you have no problems overseeing me.*

They were back in the car, heading towards the state line. Manon was sitting up straighter, looking around, and talking more after her pedicure. She left her paper flip-flops on while Jacob continued driving. *I wonder if I should look at the snake bite?* The bite was under her shorts, since the snake had bitten her upper thigh. *I don't want to scoot around too much in front of Jacob.*

"What was the name of the movie you wanted to see?" Manon asked.

"You sure? I figured I pushed my luck with the mandatory pedicure," Jacob said.

"There must be a reason you brought it up," Manon said.

"It could be showing at an art house. You'll need to search for it while I'm driving," Jacob said.

"I don't have a cell phone," Manon said, "not a real one anyway. I got another one of those cheap ones at the super center when Faustine and I picked up some kitchen supplies. I don't know what happened to my blue one. I put those stick-on rhinestones on its case. I think this is my fourth one, now. I'm not even sure. I don't know how to use it yet. I hadn't even found everything on the cell phone I got with the car commercial money before it went missing."

"I thought Wayland had yours at the hospital," Jacob said.

"I don't know what happened," Manon said.

"Use mine then." Jacob banged his hand against the dash board. "I've got a theater app downloaded on it. You can kind of see how they're supposed to go."

Manon reached around to the back seat and started digging through his overnight bag. *This is not OK. I don't want to see his stuff.* She dug through his bag while he drove. She pulled out his cell phone and started looking at his apps. She recognized the name of a theater chain and clicked it.

"Wayland's phone is officially missing then?" He looked over at Manon who nodded while looking intently at his cell phone.

"Which movie?" she asked.

"It's a concert film of one of your competitors. Hope you won't mind," he said.

"Anyone I've met?" Manon asked.

"Manon, I'm not going to pretend that you've listened to anyone since you asked me who was playing in the pedicure salon," he said.

"Was I supposed to have heard them? Are they famous?"

"I couldn't answer the question in front of everybody without people noticing, becoming distracted, then coming over to see what was wrong." He frowned his disapproval at her.

"A critical blind spot of mine. I'll take note of it," she said.

"Look up the theater chain first," Jacob said.

Once Manon was home, Wayland and Manon started working on their bucket list again. The next item was dancing lessons, which was great, except that the only place they knew that had dancing lessons was the hospital where Elodie died. The hospital web page said that general ballet lessons were available to anyone. They would be held on Tuesday nights at 6 pm.

Manon called for more details, and was told that participants paid for each session as they went, in cash at the hospital's front desk immediately before class. *That's a weird setup, but I could never follow insurance regulations.*

Manon attended her first class alone. Wayland wasn't

going to be able to attend every week, even with having a house near hers. A 12-hour plane trip for an hour of dance was a little much even for a Slip of the Cue's guitarist. However, he did think to get Manon to ask the dance instructor if it would be OK to video conference the lessons. He was willing to pay, if bribes worked. So Manon arrived early the first night to get her registration in order, and ask the dance instructor for a special favor. Manon appeared at the door, watching the other women milling around in matching leotards. Faint classical musical played in the background. Dancers warmed up with stretches.

Manon looked at two or three groups of women talking quietly. *Who should I ask?*

It turned out there was no time to talk to the instructor alone before class, and the instructor asked her to stay afterwards to fill out forms. After class, Manon broached the subject. "Would it be alright to have my cell phone going during class? I have a friend that wants to take the class too, but he couldn't be here tonight."

"I'm sorry, but for confidentially concerns, I can't have any use of cell phones during class." The instructor wasn't entirely certain he remembered seeing Manon, and thought it best not to say anything more.

A few women waited around after class to introduce themselves. Manon suggested that they all go over to Sour Cream and Burritos, since it was nearby. The irony of going to a fast-food restaurant with a bunch of closet anorexics didn't occur to Manon. She was hungry after dancing.

———————

"When you said you wanted to put dancing lessons on the bucket list, you did not imply they would be ballet!" Manon stretched out in her living room.

Improvising to Beat the Band

Wayland used a kitchen chair for his balance beam. They had a half-a-dozen changing mirrors propped up on barstools between them. Wayland thought about the dance room at the hospital in which Elodie had recuperated. He already taped one of the motivational messages of the set he wanted leave on her mirrors. The sheer curtains were pulled closed, leaving the room in diffused light.

"I did want to take dancing lessons, and I wanted you to start taking dancing lessons too," Wayland said, "but I play guitar and you're a lyricist. We need elementary moves before trying to do anything more than," he hesitated, "stretching."

"Your wife didn't suggest this?"

"I totally said that everything on the bucket list had to be family friendly," Wayland said.

"Which dance class would we've taken before the theme park trip?" Manon's hand rested on her chair as she went into a plie.

"Country Western line dancing." Wayland wasn't completely certain, but figured it was one of the options. A quick answer worked best.

"How is Country Western line dancing too risqué?"

"We aren't ever going to perform a line dance at a concert," Wayland said, "ballet is basic for any choreographed movement we may want to put onstage."

"Does. Not. Sound. Fun. In other words." Manon's arm curved around her head.

"She's had ballet. She knows the moves. I can tell her what happened in class." Wayland smiled to himself. He pulled his left leg around himself in a semi-circle, letting go of his chair for a second.

"You can tell her what happened in a line dance class, too." Manon paused. "You can tell her it's easier to get rid of me in a line dance class."

"I don't want to get rid of you," Wayland said.

"What's the deal with Jacob at the hotel then?" Manon stretched her arm over her head.

"I don't want to get rid of you, but I don't want you sitting home alone either," Wayland said.

"This is an appropriate conversation for former lovers?" Manon's look was stern.

"I've proved you don't have anything to be jealous of," Wayland said.

"Au contraire," Manon said, "you've proven that I have everything to be jealous of."

Wayland paused to face her.

"I'm not supposed to notice that you've set me up with someone at the hotel? I met him at the recording seminar in Indiana, and he happened to go on vacation with you guys!" Manon swooped into a demi-plie.

"Do you like him?" This reminded Wayland of Jacob asking him if his relationship with Manon was over. He crossed his arms.

"I don't know. I don't know if it's possible to like someone with that kind of set up," Manon said.

"Manon, was there anything else I could have done?" Wayland uncrossed his arms and stood beside her.

"I don't know. But I honestly don't think you're worried about it," Manon said.

Wayland's leotard was uniformly black. In contrast, Manon's leotard left big blue dots all over her. She swirled a maroon scarf as she went through the positions. *That outfit doesn't go with that mood.*

"Isn't line dancing too square for you? Shouldn't you be twerking?" The hip shaking twerking moves were gaining popularity, even among exercise enthusiasts. Side-stepping line dancing had ebbed around two decades previously.

"You're right. We need twerking lessons for the show," Wayland said.

"Is someone else controlling your bucket list? It doesn't count if it's not your bucket list! It's actually really stupid if it's not your idea," Manon said, "didn't you want to do ballroom dancing at some point?"

There's something inherently disconcerting about trying to go through another person't bucket list, even if you're close to the person. Manon hit her limit.

"I don't think we should do this any more." Manon had her hands on her hips.

Manon's hands happen to fit over two light pastel, blue, giant dots, which looked comical. Wayland stifled a chuckle looking at her.

"What's wrong with dancing lessons? You like the teacher." Wayland started plies again. *She's getting along with the other women in the class. The plies are toning her stomach, too.*

Somewhere in the back of Wayland's head was the idea that Manon had a hard time getting along with other women. He completely misread her latent resentment towards his spouses.

"We aren't going through your bucket list? I don't know what we're doing." Manon started snapping her maroon scarf at him.

Wayland grabbed the end of her scarf and held it. *This might not be a good time to put the rest of the motivational signs up.* "We should keep up the dancing lessons." *I don't care if they're on our bucket list or not.* He let go of her scarf.

"No. We should stop trying to go through a bucket list." Manon draped her maroon scarf over the back of the chair.

———————————

A few weeks later, after Wayland defended his argument with bouquets of daffodils, anemones, and cherry blossom branches (all of which carried notes with his signature and rationales), he and Manon were at back ballet lessons together. They weren't at the hospital, but the lessons were from the same instructor, although across town. Manon's argument had not won the day, since they still had a music business to maintain, which necessitated forming a new working relationship. Manon did not bring her sassy maroon scarf to class. When the class was over, and Wayland was walking out the door, he tripped, catching himself as he hit the floor.

He remembered tripping outside the dance studio near the hospital's morgue. He looked down and saw a printed piece of paper. He picked it up. It was a coupon for Sour Cream & Burritos.

Manon choked when she saw the coupon. "It's where Sebastian told Faustine about me. I hope he's alright."

Wayland held the coupon and stared at it for a while. "It looks normal."

Is he having doubts? Should I call Faustine? Manon took out her cell phone. "I'm stepping outside to call Faustine. I want her to call Sebastian and see how he's doing."

Wayland nodded as she walked outside the hallway door. *Where did she get another cell phone? I still have her old one.*

"Faustine, guess what happened?" Manon asked.

"Your cell phone materialized in the dishwasher for no apparent reason?"

"Even better, the ghost gave Wayland a coupon for Sour Cream & Burritos," Manon said.

"How?"

"We were leaving dance class, and something tripped Wayland. Then he looked down and saw the coupon under his feet. I was right behind him. There were no other coupons for Sour Cream & Burritos around. Nothing it could have fallen off of. No tables or chairs around or anything," she said.

Improvising to Beat the Band

"I have no idea what that means," Faustine said, "especially since you still have your cell phone—"

"It's just a cheap one," Manon paused to look around, "well, I took Wayland to the hospital chapel we had gone to a couple of times. Once he went by himself to yell at the ghost in the morgue, and tripped outside the dance studio. Also, Sebastian told you about me at Sour Cream & Burritos. Since you're alright, I think you should call Sebastian and see if he's OK."

"A coupon materializing is weird enough to call him," Faustine said. *This is like when my aunt gave me a coupon.*

Ailill picked up his phone to call Manon. *What is going on between Jacob and Manon? We better end up touring together. Manon's writing a throwaway song with Wayland, supposedly trip-hop. If they get the demo together in time I'm going to play it at the poker-seance. A good enough reason to call. Besides, she didn't seem to be suffering a relapse. This shouldn't set her off. Manon not having any setbacks blows my mind.*

Manon answered her phone to hear Ailill's voice. "Taking any more classes with Jacob?"

"You're blunt." Manon stopped to remember and added, "As a matter of fact, we did finish the recording class together."

"What else are you doing?"

"Dancing lessons with Wayland, but you know about those, right?"

"Are you taking dancing lessons with Jacob as well?"

"No, the dancing lessons are on our bucket list! Jacob doesn't have to go through my bucket list with Wayland," Manon said.

"Why don't you invite Jacob to the dancing lessons, or take

another recording class, or something else that Jacob might be able to show up to?" *I hope I'm not being too subtle.* "You guys seemed to be getting along at the amusement park."

"I was in the hospital! I don't see how I would have had much of a choice about getting along with anybody," Manon said.

"How did the hospital think you were doing anyway?"

"It was a problem because I was from out of state," Manon said, "they released me to receive follow-up care at home, but I hadn't been seeing anyone for trauma."

"Who are you seeing?"

"Let me get his card." Manon went looking for her paperwork. "I've seen him once already." She shuffled some papers around.

"You've seen him already? How'd it go?"

"It was OK. I had to explain that I didn't go to the doctor before because no one knew what had happened. I didn't know what to tell a doctor."

"You should send me his card so I can put him on our insurance plan." Ailill picked insurance carriers and negotiated policies for the band and its employees.

"You want me to mail you the information? I need to keep the card. I'm still seeing him." Manon hadn't written Ailill in years.

"No, keep the card. Email me a photo of it," Ailill said.

Manon looked up from her phone. *I didn't realize a person could do that. Jacob gave me a song-and-dance in Indiana about how he had left his business cards in his condo. He could've simply emailed me a copy.* Manon struggled to breathe.

Ailill continued, "Do you have a cell phone right now? Wayland ended up with yours at the hospital. No one knows what happened to his. I don't know if you kept the cell phone after that."

"I bought another one. I didn't want to say anything

because I got one of the cheaper ones. So far it's working OK," Manon said.

"I meant that literally," Ailill stammered, "I didn't know if the phone you're using had disappeared on you again." *She might not want to keep a cell phone at all after enduring the witchcraft surrounding it. She might prefer to do without.*

"If anything happens to this one, I won't feel badly about losing it. I was upset about losing the first one," Manon said, "it felt special."

"I can imagine. Losing your first one of anything new has got to be bad." Ailill stopped himself since he could've been talking about Wayland as well. "Especially since you and I can both remember when a computer took up an entire room."

"Yeah," Manon said.

"Maybe you should think about writing a song for your cell phone," Ailill said, "since the refrigerator song went so well."

A Slip of the Cue was having a rehearsal. This rare and momentous event was when they wrote music. They had built what was in essence a large garage on the property with the recording studio. It was a large hall that would hold all their on-stage equipment at the same time. When they were recoding, only one instrument had to play at a time, so they didn't need as much room. The drummer arrived first since he had the most equipment to set up.

Wayland was next, so the drummer took advantage of the relative solitude to ask, "Did Manon try to kill herself?"

"She never told me if she did," Wayland said.

"I've wondered about that for a while. Maybe she tried to kill herself and that caused the ghost to start following her around." Even though they were the only ones in the room, the drummer whispered.

The bass guitarist arrived.

The drummer cleared his throat. "I was asking Wayland if he knew," he paused to consider his words, "if Manon had ever tried to kill herself."

"I don't think she did," the bass guitarist said, "I think somebody tried to kill her! Pretending it's a ghost is just letting somebody out there get away with it."

"I was wondering if a suicide attempt could cause a possession-type situation." The drummer turned a knob, trying to tune the drums. *I feel like I'm being interviewed for a tabloid.*

Wayland said, "If she had tried to kill herself, I think she would have eventually succeeded."

Ailill walked in, which stopped their conversation.

Since everyone was there, Wayland called Manon on video phone. To keep Ailill from asking more questions about her cell phone, Manon went ahead and bought another brand new one that had everything on it. At the moment, her new, expensive, emerald green cell phone was still intact.

Ailill was humming and bobbing up and down to find a groove. Wayland tried to play something on his guitar along with him, just anything. Neither the bass guitarist nor the drummer had been given lead sheets, notes, or any kind of sheet music. They didn't know where to start, so they were waiting until they heard a good place to come in. That was a holdover habit from when copies were expensive and you had to run to a speciality shop to have them made. And you might not want a speciality shop to have an unfinished copy of your lyrics that the clerk might try to dance to behind the counter.

Manon frowned. "Wayland, I'm texting everybody a copy of the lyrics I have. I've been singing it in F, then modulating to B-flat."

"Get her up to speed and she becomes a petty tyrant." Ailill mumbled to Wayland under his breath while he bobbed and hummed.

"Is this a secure line?" Wayland asked.

"No," the drummer shook his head.

"Which is fine as long as there's nobody out to get us." The bass guitarist smiled sarcastically at the drummer.

"Are we smashing these lyrics together?" Wayland said, "I don't see how it flows."

"It flows because she's talking and we don't want her to stop," Ailill muttered to Wayland again under his breath.

The bass guitarist looked at the drummer who was apparently thinking the same thing. "Ah, guys," the bass guitarist started delicately, "we can hear you over here."

"Yeah, no private conversations," the drummer said mocking them, "if you can't say it in front of the class don't say it at all."

"Am I missing something?" Manon asked.

The drummer started cussing.

"Where did you want to switch chords, Manon?" the bass guitarist asked, "wait, never mind. I own a cell phone too." He smiled and dialed Manon's number. *There's something to be said for a change in power.* The bass guitarist didn't have to go through Wayland to find out what the chord sequence would be.

The drummer laughed at him. "What was the name of the song we're working on? As long as we're going to be transparent today?" He was banging his sticks together hard enough to break them.

"'God Save Us from People Who Hate Love Songs,'" Wayland said, "either that or we're going to call it 'Take Me Home.' Nobody's decided which one yet."

"I like singing this song for the ghost," Ailill said, "it's a perfect exorcism song."

"I don't see how you get an exorcism out of it." The drummer was still banging his sticks. His patience had run out, and they weren't five minutes into rehearsal.

"We want Someone," Ailill looked heavenward, "to take the ghost Home to a place where there is light inside him."

"And sweetness," the bass guitarist said, "since Heaven is normally a place associated with refrigerated sweets." He laughed at the drummer.

"OK, it's an exorcism song because that's what we want it to be," Wayland said, "it's how we mean the song. That's what counts."

Manon remained silent on the phone. Wayland had Manon's previous cell phone—the sapphire and rhinestone one—propped up on a music stand on a riser. She had a fairly good view of the room. She was too small and far away to be seen by anyone in the group while they played.

Manon's chapbook entry was scribbled over and scratched out. There are doodles of album cover ideas. This is how it currently read:

God Save Us from People Who Hate Love Songs

First verse

God save us from people who hate love songs
    Who don't know when the party's over
    And they're supposed to leave

God save us from people who hate lovers
    When they go into fits of jealousy

Improvising to Beat the Band

* * *

Let me find
   Something sweet inside you today
   Throw away the bitter
   That makes my thoughts splay

Second verse

Let me find
   Something sweet inside you
   Someone in passing
   Won't take it away
   Something for me
   I don't have to share
   Something sweet
   Where your soul is laid bare

Chorus

Let me find
   Something sweet inside you
   Take me home
   Where there's light inside you

Take me home
   Take me home

Ailill texted Faustine. They were finalizing their plans for the exorcism since they were the only two who had actually done any research on the topic.

Faustine was still trying to get back in touch with the priest to get him to come to the seance, but he stopped returning her calls. She had never gotten the brush off from a member of the clergy before. *That's harsh considering how desperate we are.*

"What all do I need to bring?" Ailill asked.

"Anything you can get your hands on," Faustine said, "I have holy water, but I don't think we can have too much of that."

"I'm bringing the candelabra," Ailill said. "Can you believe they tried to have a seance with electric lights from the mixer!"

"It worked. They are awfully spooky looking." Faustine paused a moment to visualize their upcoming seance. "Bring scarves. Your scarf display helped set the mood last time."

Ailill called the lead singer for DD&PF. *Everyone's plans for the exorcism should be consistent.*

The lead singer for DD&PF, Scott, had one major question for Ailill. "What are you going to do with Manon's cell phone during the seance?" He still had a visual image of the pieces of her candy apple red cell phone looking like it had been run over by banshees. *Her cell phone looked like blood on my hands.*

"I suppose she'll have hers with her," Ailill said, "I hadn't thought about having her leave her cell phone at home. I don't know why the ghost is obsessed with her cell phone anyway."

"I want to know where Manon's cell phone is at all times," the lead singer said, "did they tell you we found her cell phone smashed in our equipment trailer a couple of weeks after the last seance?"

"I don't remember who told me, probably Wayland." *Sometimes I wonder if our problems aren't simply a lack of communication. For that, a crushed cell phone would be an apt metaphor.* Ailill could never say for certain what had happened when things went wrong. There was always a predicament that no one bothered to tell him about that everyone else already understood. *You can't hang up on someone who's not telling you what's going on.*

"We also saw a head in the median of the highway the day after the seance," the lead singer said.

"Did you give her back her cell phone or throw it away?"

"We put it in a baggie and gave it back to her. What she did with it after that, I don't know," the lead singer said.

"Jacob told me that Wayland's cell phone went missing at the hospital. Wayland started using Manon's at that point, since it materialized in the place of his cell phone. I think. Either that, or he's kept it and is using his wife's or something. Maybe he got another one, but if he did, no one's given me the new number. No one knows what any of this means, and I can't get Wayland to talk to me about it," Ailill said.

On poker-seance night at Fleer Casino and Resort, both bands were at hand. Only close friends and relatives were invited. Wayland's second wife decided not to come. Her absence was a mystery. She didn't say why, and Tadgh didn't understand it either. The owners of the resort watched. Once they realized that they might have an actual poltergeist on their premises, they wanted to see first-hand for themselves. The owners turned on the auditorium lights, which showcased the crushed, red velvet curtains and matching wallpaper. The owners left the grand piano on the stage in case anyone needed one. Manon took the opportunity to play a little in front of strangers. She got used to mixing in public, but had started to give up on playing in front of a crowd, however small. Everyone asked Manon where her cell phone was constantly.

Playing poker should lend consistency to the event, making it sound less eccentric. Ailill carried scarves, looking for Faustine. *I might be able to get Manon to dance with the scarves later.*

DD&PF went ahead and brought their mixing board in case they needed a backup seance. They weren't sure how playing poker was going to proceed, or even why a Slip of the Cue wanted another method. Every person they asked said they played poker a different way: cards up, cards down, Texas Hold 'Em, California High/Low Split. No one said the same thing twice.

DD&PF set the microphones up for Manon, the piano, and Wayland. They ran the sound through their mixing board. Wayland arranged the colored electrical tape down the side the same way Manon did previously, as backup. Faustine brought her holy water in a sprayer bottle.

Manon frowned at Faustine. "You're supposed to anoint people with it, not spray the water around the room like disinfectant."

Ailill brought his own holy water, which he kept respectably in a bottle. Ailill brought consecrated oil as well, which he gave to Wayland. On the other hand, he also brought his candelabra with candles and several large silk scarves in various designer prints.

The lead guitarist for DD&PF brought a cooler with drinks, in case anybody needed a beer during the exorcism. The bass guitarist for DD&PF brought sandwiches, which made Manon think of Wayland, and then Sebastian. She felt Sebastian's absence, as though the ghost had told them not to invite him. The owners put the left-over cake backstage on a tray. The bass guitarist for DD&PF put Manon and Wayland's cell phones together in a little shrine that folded like a book but stood upright on its own. Since Wayland kept using Manon's after the ghost "gave" it to him, both phones had been Manon's at some point: sapphire with rhinestones hinged to emerald green. Ailill put prayer candles in front of them. The cell phone shrine was located in the front of the auditorium near the poster of the Ferris wheel. They looked for a picture as similar as they could find to the ride at the theme park. Wayland hung yellow marigolds on it, like during the Mexican celebration after Halloween, the Day of the Dead.

Manon sang softly to herself. She made up words to the tune of Row, Row, Row Your Boat:

"Shoo, shoo, shoo, the ghost, make him go away,
    Merrily, merrily, merrily, merrily,
    You can save the day."

Somehow or another, she went flat in the process of singing and modulated to a minor key. Her voice carried through the hall above the others, which was strangely captivating.

So many attendees had different game plans for the seance. *How many different seances there were actually going to be?* Ailill gave Faustine the scarves.

Wayland started to deal the cards on top of the piano. Tadgh walked up to the piano to be dealt in.

"You aren't dealing me in?" Ailill asked.

"You're on ghost detail." Wayland finished dealing, pointing to the mixing board. "One of the hands is for the ghost. Me and Manon are going to touch the cards with our fingertips to see which way the ghost wants to move them."

"How do we recognize what he's saying?" Ailill asked.

"Once we know he's here, we can lay them out according to the alphabet to see what he's saying," Wayland said.

"Do we let the numbers correspond to the letters, or does whichever letter he moves it to count?" Ailill asked.

"I'll put them in order. Whichever one he tells us to move

is the letter he's chosen," Manon said.

"How are we going to interpret the cards?" Faustine asked.

"Red one to ten are the letters 'A' to 'J.' Black one to ten are 'K' to 'Z,'" Wayland said. "Who's writing it down? Ailill?"

Ailill waved his acquiescence with his cell phone before plugging his cell phone into the mixing board. On it were: recordings of the band playing "Love & All Its Glory," hymns, and a demo of "God Save Us from People Who Hate Love Songs." *It would have sounded better as a country tune, but they've already recorded it as a trip-hop number.* He threw in a reading of Psalm 91 for good measure, plus he managed to get a recording of a ram's horn.

"What are we trying to get the ghost to say?" Manon asked.

"Anything he wants to. We merely want him to show up again," Ailill said.

"What are we doing to the ghost once it gets here?" Manon asked.

"What are we doing once he gets here?" Wayland looked reproachfully at her. "Remember he's probably already here and can hear you."

"Lovely thought boy," Ailill said sarcastically, compensating for lost nerves, "lovely thought." He drank his beer in earnest.

"We are going to perform the exorcism that Ailill and I have put together." Faustine moved to the stage without anyone noticing.

"I've got a bottle, in case we can actually make the genie go back into it," Ailill smiled and toasted with his beer.

"It was nice of Fleer Casino to let us have the exorcism here," Faustine said.

"It was best since this was where we saw him materialize before," Ailill said.

The owners of the casino dimmed the stage lights, but

stayed in the back near the doors. Jacob stood on the stage behind Ailill, a couple of feet away. DD&PF hung out by the stage door, which put them between the seance and the stage door like in the previous seance. The friends and family sat in the middle of the auditorium. The families did not bunch up, but strung across the middle of the auditorium from one exit to the other.

Manon started playing "Love & All Its Glory." Ailill and Wayland started to sing. The bass guitarist found an amp to plug into. The drummer hit his tambourine. They sang through it without incident, surprisingly. They braced on the "is never gonna be for me" part, expecting the worst to happen. Nothing.

Then they started playing the cards Wayland had dealt. They played penny poker, so loose change started rattling around. Manon and Wayland touched a couple of the ghost's cards before they felt one move underneath their fingers. They discarded it and dealt the ghost another card. Bidding was a bit trickier. By the time they had both put their fingers on a coin it was hard to tell if they hadn't pushed it themselves. Coins aren't that big.

Oddly enough, the ghost won the first hand.

"It's because I haven't played poker before." Manon shoved the cards towards Wayland to reshuffle.

"You played with me," Tadgh said.

"For instructional purposes," Manon said.

Wayland said to Tadgh, "You said you hadn't been playing with anyone."

"I needed to talk to Manon without everybody knowing about it," Tadgh said.

"He was only over one afternoon. We only talked about poker," Manon said.

"Is poker still on your bucket list then?" Wayland asked.

"I don't know," Manon said.

"Do we play another round, or go for the alphabet?" Ailill asked.

"I'll move the cards over," Manon said.

Ailill played a recording of "Love & All Its Glory" softly in the background while Manon arranged the cards.

"OK, we go through them one at a time," Manon said, "what's your name?"

"Yeah, who are we talking to?" Wayland asked.

Touching the cards, Manon and Wayland spelled out "Bill."

Ailill tensed up while his eyes jerked over to Faustine.

"Are you the only one here?" Manon asked, "How many are here?"

Beneath their fingertips, Manon and Wayland sensed the two of hearts move.

"I take it that means two ghosts are here," Manon said, "when are you going to leave?"

Faustine prompted Manon with notes from Faustine's cell phone.

Ailill silently gave thanks that Manon was taking the initiative, since it was her exorcism.

Manon and Wayland let the cards spell out "write me a song." It took several passes through the deck. Faustine checked the time and realized they took a lot longer with this seance than they had the previous one. But no one had seen "Bill" yet this time either.

"We were on that project already, Bill," Ailill said.

"Bill" would never know the tune was intended to be a throwaway song. Ailill cued "God Save Us from People Who Hate Love Songs."

"This song is dedicated to Bill," Ailill said.

The band started playing along with the recording.

Faustine decided it was time to spray the holy water. She gave everyone on stage a face spritz, and doused the cards a bit. She even sprayed Ailill's beer for good measure.

"We haven't seen him this time," Manon said.

"Look, there." Faustine pointed beside the dessert tray.

There was an old, tall, thin, grizzled man grabbing a bite with his hand from the tray. Then, he walked away through the stage door exit.

"I'm going to go spray the dessert." Faustine ran over to the dessert tray and sprayed holy water on it before looking around to see where "Bill" went.

Scott and Chad stood near their van where they had been waiting.

"Did you see anyone leave?" Faustine asked.

"No. Is it over?"

"It might be." Faustine strode into the pickup and delivery area behind the stage. "Did any of you see that man, older and grizzled looking?"

The lead guitarist for the Phosphorescent Freckles part of DD&PF shelved his guitar, then tried to pack the drummer's cymbals.

"Didn't anyone notice him?" Faustine asked.

The guitarist's face went from mild concern to extreme worry in a couple of seconds.

Scott ran over to her. He didn't want her touching the equipment, but he also didn't want to search for a head in the median of a road again. "What man?"

Chad appeared at the corner of the van at that point. "An old guy appeared out of nowhere," the drummer said, "he wore a black, blue-jean jacket."

"Yeah," Faustine agreed, "it was made out of blue-jean, and it was a black jacket."

"Did you see his face?" Chad asked.

"I don't know. I think it was the ghost," Faustine said.

"Did he say anything?" Chad asked.

Faustine sputtered, flustered and defensive. "I didn't hear

him say anything. He took dessert from the tray and I followed him over here." She pointed at the dessert tray near the stage entrance.

Wayland wandered over to the tray. He counted pieces of cake.

"He took dessert from the tray?" Chad asked.

"Yeah, he grabbed some cake and took off," Faustine said.

"Well, that's one way of finding something sweet inside him," Wayland said.

Meanwhile on the stage, Ailill decided that enough of the seance was over to play the ending since Faustine had left for several minutes. He played the 91st Psalm:

He who dwells in the secret place of the Most High shall abide under the shadow of the Almighty...

Then he played the ram's horn so much, he lost track of how many times he had played it, and forget how many times it was supposed to be played anyway. Then there was silence. Although there was no breeze, the top card on the deck blew over. It was the six of hearts. Ailill made no sudden moves around a potential poltergeist. He sauntered back behind the stage nonchalantly, like he didn't have a care in the world. "Is he still here?"

Scott said, "I haven't seen anything."

"How many pieces of cake did we eat?" Faustine asked.

"I'll do a head count before anyone leaves," Wayland said.

"I'll collect the plates. Were any thrown away yet?" Tadgh asked.

"I think the trash is over there," Ailill said.

"Why would he take any cake?" Chad asked.

"He was doing what the song said," Wayland said.

"Yeah," Faustine said, "let me find something sweet inside you today was right before the chorus of 'Take Me Home.'"

"Has he gone 'Home' home now?" Scott asked Ailill while gesturing with his arm into the blue sky outside the loading and unloading shed, as though Ailill would know because he was the lead singer for a Slip of the Cue. Subconsciously, Scott might not've thought that the other band members could talk.

"Let me count the cake today, since you're all in pieces anyway," Scott sang a little out of tune underneath his breath. He had been writing so much recently he couldn't shut that part of his brain down completely, regardless of the appropriateness of the situation. In the complete silence backstage, his whispered lyrics screamed in the darkness.

"Not now," Wayland hissed at him.

After they did a head count, and a cake piece count, they met to confer.

"Does he have to do what the song said?" the bass guitarist asked.

"What the cards said was 'write me a song,' that means that if we wrote him a song, he would go away," Ailill said. "We already had a song to drive away the demons so we dedicated it to him and sang it."

"Faustine did see him at the dessert tray," Wayland said, "it's possible that he's gone now."

"Do we know that he took a piece of cake?" Manon asked.

"The casino owner said they put out 30 pieces of cake. We have 26 pieces eaten by the band and family members, including those who took two pieces," Wayland said.

"There were three on the table when I was beside it," Faustine said, "but for all I know he was picking up crumbs."

Ailill paced the length of the stage. "We need to do this again so we can see if he's going to come back."

PART THREE

JUST LET TIME PASS

CHAPTER NINE

Sebastian's Dreamscape

Sebastian's dreamscape was a semi-transparent fog that followed the path that Manon repeatedly walked though his mind. Any place he had ever heard a Slip of the Cue song was shrouded in haze. Clouds formed between his memories and lost their sense of attachment to each other, and then to him as well. Like each scene in his mind could really belong to several different movies, as though his past was something he could choose by changing a channel. Since he had never confided in anyone about a Slip of the Cue, there was no one around to argue with about which movie any of these scenes should be in. If all the scenes are from a movie where a Slip of the Cue don't really exit, so be it. Sebastian's life lost its sense of reality after Manon was attacked, which was always referred to as an accident. Covering up what happened was the first step towards his entire life seeming unreal.

Years ago, he first discovered the ice skating rink after going for three straight days listening to every radio station and boom box he passed playing "Love & All Its Glory." Losing his composure, he started running around campus searching for a spot where he couldn't hear that song. He thought he was walking into an old library building, but it turned out to be an old ice skating rink instead. They only played oldies which meant no "Love & All Its Glory," which was current at the time.

His brain fog mercifully dissipated at work. There was an odd dichotomy between the parts of Sebastian's life that were surreal, and the parts that were normal. Sebastian's college job senior year was in marketing. Specifically, he had a student job making fundraising calls for the university's foundation. If he had envisioned his employment after college that project would have been an excellent route to encounter raw contacts. As it was, he couldn't relate to his work. He followed his supervisor's suggestions for cold calls, which increased sales. *Odd that his suggestions would work.* Sebastian hadn't thought that the university marketing team knew what they were doing, but figured he could humor them by following their directions. In his case that meant increased donations. He never comprehended why donors bestowed their money. He played a child's game of do-as-I-do. Fitting in was all he hoped for. He could never fit into a dreamscape world that a songwriter wrote, even if they were friends.

Once he graduated, he continued working for the university's fundraising center part-time, mainly because he didn't have the energy to look for another job. The university's foundation took advantage of the fact that he could travel and give a rousing presentation. When he moved into a supervisory position, he trained others to monitor calls at the foundation's call center. That was more pro-forma. There weren't enough traveling salesmen for the foundation to actually say he monitored anyone. Occasionally, he would give introductory pointers to new associates. Truthfully, since this job was always part-time, no one stayed with it long enough to be Sebastian's competition. Sebastian didn't need the money. He needed work. He needed a cover story. He need enough of a life that he could talk to strangers about so that no one would ask questions about what he really did.

Because it was a part-time position, he didn't require permanent space. Sebastian's nominal office was perpetually moved around. It wasn't supposed to be a mobile unit, but that's the way it ended up. He habitually chatted with the building's receptionist, making sure he could always find where any administrator might move his stuff. There were a few times when he was supposed to have a permanent room assignment, but when he got to work, his stuff had been removed, and no one knew where it was. He had to go around looking for it. He did have supplies, directories, and stacks of paper memos. They were tossed into a closet until he arrived. That way, no one would be tempted to relocated them. He kept the key to his supply closet, but had to check which room he could work in every time he entered campus. He was officially listed as an off-site worker since his primary function was to travel.

Over time this situation led Sebastian to develop his game plan of using the college's ice skating rink as a ploy. Ice skating emotionally moved patrons, improving their mood, propelling them to roam the campus. By contrast, Sebastian had no emotional involvement with ice skating rinks. There was no mental fog over the ice. He could talk up research centers as they walked past them. Patrons were more inclined to write a check for tangible artifacts. Once they saw something physically related to projects needing funding, it felt more real to the philanthropists. Like getting a souvenir from a rock concert in order to prove to your friends that you actually went.

Shopping at the grocery store always felt real to Sebastian, probably because he had to focus on what he was doing, which made him tune out the overhead music, which was usually a little slower and dated anyway. Sebastian pushed his cart along in the grocery store, wondering how he was going to get a presentation assembled for the upcoming songwriting conference he registered for. He hadn't been to a conference in years, and he never attended the major music conferences back when a Slip of the Cue was getting off the ground. The point of attending was locating new business, networking. He couldn't network without a display of his current projects, but the recent photos he took of Manon or DD&PF's concert were not typical situations, nor likely to secure new contracts. Dealing with hyper-inefficient, grossly bureaucratic rock bands transitioning from therapy into a regular touring schedule did not fit the image most independent rock bands had of themselves. While mentally sorting out his work issues, physically Sebastian pushed an empty shopping cart along. Then, he repeated his previous accident, the one that caused his father to discover his weight loss meetings with Faustine. Carefully turning a corner around the end display on the cereal aisle, he rounded the coffee and tea display too fast. This time, he only knocked soda cartons partway into an aisle. He shoved the large cases back into their pyramid monument to corporate marketing. *I wonder if I should apply to a soda company's marketing division…* It would be more normal than keeping a college job for way too long, or working for a rock band. His work with rock bands would be an asset for them, instead of the misunderstood liability it appeared to be in the music industry.

Recovering, Sebastian continued to push his cart along, stopping too long to look at the multi-colored display at the end of the aisle for dieters. Each type of food had its own container. The cups were different sizes and colors. This way dieters never measured the wrong amount of food, like when Faustine ate twice as much rice by mistake. *These containers were custom made for her.* He picked up a couple of sets: a present for Faustine and an additional one for himself. That way, she wouldn't use the wrong size measuring cup for rice again. Someone out there was listening, or else Faustine was not alone in her dieting problems. *Maybe I overreacted to her lack of dieting skills?*

Wouldn't a songwriter need to be connected to their feelings in order to write moving music for the masses? Unfortunately, nobody ever accused this group of songwriters of being in touch with their feelings. The convention banner drooping beside an escalator exclaimed "Songwriters Entente!" No one knew what "entente" meant. Most participants took it as a subtle jab that they should get a thesaurus. The pennant framed their dour faces. There was a hallway full of vendors selling high-priced, songwriting gear. You wouldn't believe what an electronic thesaurus could go for these days! Sebastian crouched at a dinky, black, square table, unaccompanied. He was three times the size of this drink-stand, even hunching over his soda on its petite, red, napkin. The wall-length window beside him was glamorous but not sparkling, no jet setter would be photographed beside it, since it surveyed a drab, grey, half-full parking lot. The afternoon's colorless sky was the most appealing part of the scenery. Sebastian sulked while sitting and glancing around the periphery of the crowd surrounding him, biding his time. He couldn't assimilate the world surrounding him, so he awaited revelation, like waiting for a voiceover in a movie to start explaining a scene. Mysteriously, somewhere within the congregating horde resided an answer to his career. Sebastian would use any analytic method to find the specific person possessing the answer he was looking for.

Unfortunately, Sebastian's marketing strategy for this songwriting conference wasn't clicking, or wasn't "clique-ing." It was simply unacceptable for him to be stranded at a small, square table beside a wall-length window. He arrived at the conference early and attempted to introduce himself to attendees while they registered. Attendees typically straggled in one at a time at conferences. Sebastian planned to ask the new arrivals innocuous questions like, "How many times of you been to this conference?" *Anything to break the ice.* Sebastian smiled to himself over his ice skating joke, since over time, and the process of eliminating any activity that inadvertently involved listening to "Love & All Its Glory," ice skating had become his favorite hobby. Laughing at his own jokes was a habit he picked up off his father.

Sebastian arrived early enough. Tardiness wasn't his problem. Only two or three early arrivals milled in the hallway while he paced, waiting for the conference to start. Those initial arrivals were employees of conference itself. He began the day with limited opportunity for casual conversation. As more typical conference attendees appeared, Sebastian noticed that they came in groups of threes and fours. He stopped breathing as they bunched up around him without acknowledging his presence. *I am here, right? I'm not a figment of my own imagination.* He visualized a snowflake forming, then being trapped inside an icicle. After sufficient numbers arrived, he started breathing again. He started to introduce himself, but those pairs of pairs had congealed into a crowd. There were too many strangers grouped together to talk casually to anyone. Everyone found their own little clique. Unfortunately, it's extremely difficult to break into a clique without making the gang mad.

Sebastian remembered Faustine saying she didn't enjoy

Improvising to Beat the Band

Mexican food, and how she came across. You can say the wrong thing to the wrong gathering totally unintentionally. *Until I know I'm saying the right thing to the right person, I'm not moving.* He retreated to the glass wall. The square, red napkin nested inside the square glass table, both perfectly aligned. Sebastian subconsciously arranged napkins like they were model release forms on a merchandising table. (Any time he had to photograph anyone, he always got a model release, since no one really knew how the photos were going to be used until the marketing campaign was finalized.) Thus decamped, Sebastian breathed deeply. Except that retreating was not the reason that he came to this conference. *Why does anyone come to this conference anyway?*

After three hours, Sebastian still wasn't ready to admit defeat and eat off site. He was still searching for someone to give him a sense for this group. *I wish I had my own display. That way people could mill around me instead of me having to hover around them.* Sebastian's stomach tightened. *I shouldn't be that visible yet. No presentation today. I shouldn't buy a booth at a convention when I don't know who might be attending.* He clenched his jaw. Sponsors are also not supposed to buy a booth at a convention once it's started, but Sebastian eyed some extra space down towards a far exit that he could probably talk somebody out of. There was already a university exhibit showcasing their songwriting classes. A university foundation—Sebastian's marketing day job—having a booth at a songwriting convention was justifiable as finding hard-to-reach prospects. *Who knows, maybe the university has some kind of songwriting program? I know it has a noted poetry program. I'll check. If it does, I'm home free for getting a booth. If it doesn't—but why wouldn't it? —I couldn't try it twice. But only once? I could recover from that. Is there anything about how I'm dressed that would repel songwriters? Should I have worn a suit, or maybe a different color shirt?* If his hang-up wasn't obvious, then he couldn't fathom why he wanted to be there either. *Do I smell funny to them? It's not like I spilled gas on myself when I filled up the car.*

By late afternoon, Sebastian decided to help the conference organizers unload their materials. As a gambit, he couldn't lose. He zigzagged around each of the booths and started asking vendors if they needed help moving their boxes. Radically, each declined. *Well, that's a first.* A no-lose gambit wouldn't harmonize with these songwriters. *Tomorrow I'm handing out business cards to random participants whether they want them or not.* That usually failed to find new contacts, but he required a maneuver allowing him to discover what transpired at this conference.

Their presentations interested him, but were beside the point. He searched, but couldn't find anyone who wanted to have a confab concerning what they learned at any presentation. He physically stretched to overhear conversations beside the cafe. He almost understood their words, but didn't recognize a specific presentation from their chatter. Jumping into a conversation was preposterous. At one point, he thought he might slip into a causerie, since they were discussing a presentation that had recently finished, but one of the women eyeballed him sideways, then suddenly started talking about her flower garden back home. Sebastian couldn't push himself into her conversation at all. *Maybe if I were a conference presenter, I'd meet more people, whoever they are.* Sebastian realized, sitting alone at his square table beside the glass wall, scanning the grey sky in the distance, he was going to have to get a Slip of the Cue to help.

If Sebastian did indeed reek of gasoline, this would be self-emulation. He was striking a match.

---

* * *

Improvising to Beat the Band

When Sebastian was promoting a Slip of the Cue he didn't go anywhere he didn't have a game plan. He scoured every offbeat venue he already knew. He attended churches. He visited libraries. He ate in parks. He went anywhere a standard promoter would not go. He reasoned a Slip of the Cue would never make the big time so he promoted them in places major groups avoided. That strategy made it easy to talk to listeners one-on-one, since there wasn't anybody else around. Sebastian filled their languishing gaps between patrons. Businessmen running gas stations slow down to talk when they don't have customers. When strangers asked him what he was doing there, he would say, "I'm going where the crowd's not!" He couldn't compete with the big time so he didn't attempt it, but his effort was unsurpassed on the local level. So even though he had already made it big, he had no idea how to deal with the coterie. His exertion reminded him of why people hate networking.

The next morning, Sebastian attempted to be slightly more forceful with the conference presenters as they made their way into conference rooms. "I'm new. Can you please describe a typical conference attendee?" Sebastian missed his own non-sequitur, since he didn't expect new people to be like himself. New conference attendees were straightforward and energetic. Songwriters who had been around for a while were low key and laid back. Many successful ones, like Manon, didn't even bother to attend, since the point was to find collaborators to write with. If a songwriter was already booked with songwriting sessions, there would be no need to continue networking. The presenter pretended to ignore him as he stepped into the conference area. The speaker stepped to his side, towards the middle of the hallway. Sebastian continued walking towards him. The speaker resembled a mannequin wearing a nondescript button-down shirt with slacks.

"What's wrong?" the conference presenter asked.

"I haven't been able to introduce myself to anyone here yet. I'm normally excellent at introducing myself to strangers. I wondered what the undercurrent was."

"Well I'm sorry we haven't been more friendly to newcomers, but I think most people have introduced themselves online first before coming here."

"So this conference has a website?"

"Oh it's got a website that's active year round." At that point, Sebastian noticed the conference presenter's face brightening while he stretched out his arms.

"I should've introduced myself online before coming then?"

"That's not necessary." The speaker winced while his ears turned red.

Sebastian realized the presenter needed to return to his immediate task. Besides, Sebastian had broken his own rule about not talking to non-acquaintances for more than a couple of minutes when introducing himself.

This rule was a takeaway from a conference he had attended years ago. In fact, back then, they had gotten into breakout groups during the conference session and given each other "elevator pitches," a few sentences said when meeting a VIP in an elevator, for varying lengths of time. That way each person experienced how listening to sales pitches for different lengths of time made them feel. Sebastian's group decided two minutes worked best for him. They figured it was his height. Shorter speakers tended to have potential customers—in the university foundation's case, potential donors—stop listening sooner.

In any event, Sebastian stepped back towards the wall. *I need to start giving out my business cards, or else I'm going to start throwing them into air like confetti, or giving away free cash.* He learned forward for a moment and handed the conference presenter one. Inappropriate as it was, the conference presenter refused to take his card, nor did he shake hands with Sebastian. *I don't get it. What am I going to do?* Sebastian couldn't fathom what a reasonable capitalist should do when prohibited from handing a stranger his business card.

————————————

During the night, Sebastian studied the website for this unfathomable songwriter's conference. He explored their pages, searching for information for conference attendees. *Where can I upload a photo and write a quick bio?* He read the program, bios of presenters, and the participant interaction that followed. At bottom of the third page was a section titled "Meet and Greet." He would do anything he could to prevent this conference from remaining one great big cold call.

Sebastian remembered a pamphlet he had received at one of his first conferences years ago. Sebastian strained to remember name of it. He vaguely recalled, "Making the Most of Your Conference Attendance." *How did it start?* "Attending a colloquium, yet not forming a single fresh contact until the final session?" Subsequently, Sebastian chided himself if he didn't greet five unknown persons within the first hour of any seminar.

The trick was to pretend that the opening session was definitely your last. Everyone agreed that if it were the very last meeting, and they hadn't made enough contacts and were about to leave, they would say good-bye to at least a half-dozen people on their way out the door. If you don't actually talk to anyone during a conference, that's what's going to happen anyway. Might as well make your first meeting your last meeting and then not worry about it. You've got the ball rolling for the rest of the conference.

Sebastian had never been to a forum where attendees

avoided fresh recruits, yet he had arrived at the "People Who Don't Network" symposium. Sebastian mused about searching for vintage conference pamphlets when he returned home. *What am I forgetting to do?* But in the meantime he needed an edge. Sebastian needed to turn this cold call into a warm call. *Should I start name dropping?* It was the only scheme Sebastian could imagine.

He emailed Wayland that they needed to talk.

Wayland texted back, "About what?"

Sebastian replied, "Gotta talk to you on the phone. Call me." He gave Wayland the hotel phone number and his room number.

Beginning the next morning, Sebastian forced himself to be yet even more dynamic with the conference presenters as they made their way around the auditorium! Sebastian maneuvered as close to the front door as possible. He positioned himself beside the natural stream of traffic. As participants entered the room, they formed a straight line since they were headed in the same direction. Then he took out his cell phone.

"Hey, Ailill, how are you doing?" Ailill's duties as a rock band lead singer had suddenly expanded into giving job references as well. Sebastian angled the phone away from his head. He attempted to look natural by smiling nonchalantly. Fortunately, he only had to hold the phone a foot from his head, sideways, until he secured someone's attention. He turned the speaker phone on and off, like his phone was new and he didn't know how the buttons worked.

"Sebastian, I don't think I've ever thanked you enough for the hard work you did for the band those all years ago. Especially your work with Manon, our songwriter!" Ailill spoke as though he were on stage, going just past a conversational tone.

Sebastian gazed around to see if he had caught anyone's eyes yet. What appeared to be a gaggle of guys, five of them altogether, started watching Sebastian. Two women off to Sebastian's right, but closer to him, tilted their heads sideways to hear better. Additionally a couple of guys, who gave the appearance of attending alone, were within earshot and nodded knowingly in Sebastian's direction.

"I enjoyed working with a Slip of the Cue. The honesty and integrity of the band's music made the tours easy to sell." Ailill lowered his voice to say next part. "So how's it going now?"

Sebastian replied in his normal voice, not matching Ailill's whisper, "I need to go. Several people are coming." His shoulders slumped as he put his cell phone back in his pocket. One of the guys near the door, wearing a rather peculiar plaid, pastel suit, took a step towards Sebastian once he hung up his phone. *That suit would make an excellent cell phone case for Manon.* The other guy right beside him kept on nodding, knowingly. Although the second guy standing by door gave the impression of paying attention, he was lost in his own little world.

One of the two women approached him and said "What do you do?" Rudely, she did not introduce herself before asking. Fans were always overfamiliar, but this was due to songwriters being either completely standoffish or brashly overfamiliar, which was an occupational hazard. Either people wanted them out of the way, or else they wanted to talk about the most dramatic events of their lives with them.

"I do PR work—public relations." At that point, Sebastian's enthusiasm pushed him to hand her his business card. *She took it.* Something familiar finally worked, so he handed the other woman his business card as well. *They took them!*

Sebastian's first success at this conference. Not ideal, but a huge recovery from yesterday. Sebastian had never had anyone refuse to take his business card before, which still unnerved him. He stifled a sigh. "What group are you with?"

"We're songwriters," one woman said.

"We write for different groups," the other woman finished her thought.

The first woman turned away from Sebastian to ask the second woman. "How many people are you working with right now?"

Sebastian inhaled sharply while trying to maintain eye contact with the second songwriter.

"About twenty different music supervisors." The second woman hadn't turned away from Sebastian yet.

"I'm researching bands to do PR work for," Sebastian said, "anyone you know looking for a publicist?"

The women looked at each other.

The first woman said, "the music supervisors are meeting music producers in the dining room."

Sebastian leaned back slightly, shifting his weight to his back foot, leaning away from them, inhaling. *Did I cut them off too quickly?* Possibly, they might have uttered another syllable or two.

The tall, thin man wearing the peculiar pastel, plaid suit remained close to the door for a moment while the women talked. Then, he meandered towards Sebastian, glancing toward the cafe, attempting to emanate a casual air, as though he were going somewhere else.

The young guys from across the room suddenly blurted out, "We're a band."

Sebastian had taken a couple of steps towards the peculiar suit, but changed course and strode towards the young guys, handing the guy who yelled his business card first.

"What's name of your group?" Sebastian asked.

Improvising to Beat the Band

"The Eurille Franklin Orchestra," the winsome, black-haired singer said.

"Let me have your business card." Sebastian wasn't sure he heard band's name correctly, so he wanted to see it. *You're Ellie?* "I can get back to you later. I don't know if we're gonna have much of a chance to talk right now." *Have I asked them everything I need to know?* Sebastian leaned forward on his toes a bit. Just because he managed to get these strangers to open up, didn't mean he was going to be able to close the sale.

Sebastian let the band walk away although he wasn't certain how he was going to continue networking. The man wearing the peculiar suit near the door finally finished approaching him, said "hi," then handed Sebastian a business card, which read "editor." Sebastian had never heard of the publication listed on the business card. Sebastian reached into his bag to get more business cards.

"Thanks for giving me your card." *This guy runs contrary to the other attendees. I need to write down his name.* "Do you think we could talk a bit more later? Over lunch?"

"Are you here by yourself?" the editor asked.

For a moment, Sebastian started to lie, but corrected himself. "Yes, this is my premiere."

"Certainly. Certainly. We should chat a few minutes. Over lunch would be fine." The editor smiled warmly, but then he crossed his arms for no apparent reason. Suddenly aware of his stand-offish position, he dropped his arms to his sides and took a step backwards. *I don't need to be crossing my arms around him. He looked at my elbows when I did it.*

No one else at convention paid any attention to this exchange. Everyone maintained their vegetative state. Their maximum group size remained at three. Sebastian recognized several participants from the previous day. He watched them shuffling around the room in a clockwise fashion. Random groups gossiping while rambling around the hotel. Nobody had chatted with any different acquaintances.

This conference crowd hangs out online, so I should email the reporter, women, and band right after the next presentation. No harm in making sure their email addresses are valid before leaving the conference. Besides, these attendees discreetly coordinate. They certainly aren't making plans out in the open. Are they eating together off site? Sebastian excused himself out of habit—to the thin air surrounding him—and wandered to a side hall. He took out his cell phone, then texted the band he had just met. *What excuse do I have to text them so soon?* Sebastian pressed a key. *We didn't specify where we'd be eating lunch.*

A couple of hours later, lunch occurred at the café counter. Sebastian kept track of the evidence that the conference attendees secretly ate elsewhere and just came back for the meetings. All the places where people were supposed to be eating were filled with people talking business. They wore clothing without any food stains, they didn't carry drinks, nor were there any used napkins in the trash. Plus, the location of food is critical information which cannot be confided to strangers.

The central cafe was a singular spot he could point to and ensure that everybody met in the same place. He spaced his meetings 15 minutes apart. The Franklin Eurille Orchestra arrived first.

"We're going to talk for a few minutes before we go get lunch," the lead singer said.

Sebastian placed his drink on the counter. *Why is it always the lead singer who talks first?*

"We are looking for a PR person to help us with our upcoming tour." He turned to scan his bandmates to ascertain if his story was indeed correct.

"Can you tell me how your band got its name?" *This particular question is the safest route to a conversation.*

"It's our names," the guy standing beside the lead singer

said.

Sebastian took a chance that the second person to talk would be the lead guitarist. "Which is your two names?"

"Yes, I'm Franklin," the lead singer said.

"And I'm Eurille," the lead guitarist said.

Sebastian still heard, "You're Ellie." Apparently, the European guy's name was Ellie.

"The band members were friends first?" Sebastian asked.

Franklin nodded. "We didn't meet as teens. It was later in college."

"Which I'm gathering by your looks was not that long ago?" Sebastian laughed.

He was the only one.

"We graduated several years ago," Franklin said.

"And we need to start touring," Eurille said.

"You're looking for someone to do legwork for you then?" Sebastian asked.

"Yes," Franklin said.

"Great, I'll need to see you guys perform live. Can I get a download of your latest record?"

"I can email you our website's details," Franklin said.

Eurille's eyebrows went up while he pressed his lips into whitened creases, and started blinking rapidly, as though he were telegraphing an S.O.S. to Franklin. "You need to email my sister your resume and references."

Franklin circled around to glance at Eurille, then duplicated the eye brow raise while adding a confirmation smile. "That's a great idea. After she's looked at your photo, and other credentials, we can tell you where to meet."

"Then you'll be hearing from me," Sebastian said.

They smiled and shook hands. Sebastian acted like he was going somewhere else, and the band members started to leave.

"I'll need to take a picture of you," Eurille said, "that way we'll remember how we met."

That's why no one has business cards. They use their cell phones instead! How do they keep from getting people's names mixed up?

"Email us, and then we'll have your email address," Franklin said.

Well that keeps you from having to input a person's name into a database. Sebastian tapped his cell phone, inputing their email address.

The Franklin Eurille Orchestra sounded upbeat amongst themselves as they were walking away. Sebastian strolled away from the bar. The bar's decor was slightly different from the rest of the hotel. It had an art deco look, with accent lights high above in a retro, industrial warehouse, black ceiling. The side hall that Sebastian tentatively wandered down had a more modern look, with incandescent floor lamps, basic white walls, and red and gold trim. Sebastian strolled until he was out of sight, then circled around a column and wandered back over to the café counter. He needed to be gone long enough to keep his next encounter from being awkward.

After half-an-hour, the two, relatively young female songwriters showed up early. One woman ordered a chocolate seltzer at the bar.

"What are you doing at this conference?" the first woman asked.

"I'm trying to get involved in doing PR for bands again," Sebastian said.

"What made you get out of it?" second woman asked.

Internally, Sebastian kicked himself. *Why did I give her an opening?* "My first band didn't need me anymore, and I had other work, so I let it go." *Explaining my hack work for a Slip of the Cue to a songwriter is different from explaining it to another band.* Songwriters had a different set of criteria: they didn't require financial tour support. The only songwriter he knew was Manon. It was worth his while to be able to introduce her to them. Manon's songwriter world was simply limited to Wayland.

A couple of hours later, Sebastian kept staring at the editor's peculiar suit. He pondered the exact words he should say. "That's a great suit, but I can't say why it strikes me."

"Attempting to get prospects to remember meeting me. Many times all I have to work with is what I'm wearing." He smiled broadly.

Sebastian understood. Sebastian's gambit was to dress normally and take prospects to unusual locations instead.

"I can see what you mean." Sebastian returned his smile. "I've had a hard time introducing myself around here."

"Clients can be hard to talk to," the reporter said, "to confirm, did we exchange business cards?"

Is he asking because he watched me try to hand my business cards to everyone? Focusing on business cards because they matter to me? He doesn't seem trapped in his own universe.

"I'm doing public relations for a couple of bands. Do you mind me emailing you the details of their upcoming tours?"

"No, I'd love to hear the details. Anytime you want to email me with any information concerning bands, or upcoming tour dates, or anything related. I'm open to new sources." The editor had not once touched his soda while talking to Sebastian. Sebastian wondered if he was going to leave it when they finished talking. It was a regular glass, not a "to go" paper cup.

Back at home a couple of weeks later, Sebastian was rethinking his game plan concerning Faustine. *Manon can help me.*

"Hey Manon, I need to talk to Faustine for a few minutes,"

Sebastian said, "mind meeting me at church?"

"Am I running interference then?" Manon asked.

"Do you mind?" Sebastian asked.

When Sebastian, Faustine and Manon were in the church parking lot, attempting to avoid recreating their previous clash there, Sebastian presented Faustine with the set of multicolored bowls. Faustine examined the box, then tugged at its cardboard tabs. She discovered the contents were labeled after each food group.

"Now you don't have to worry which measuring cups to use." Sebastian's smug military stance softened to an "at ease" position once Faustine held her new measuring cups. He started to leave.

"Thanks," Faustine said, "color-coded cups were the entire reason for this social call?" She paused. "Why does this mean so much to you?" Sebastian sat his car with the door open. "I mean, you could have told Manon to tell me to look for them. Texted a copy of a picture of them."

"Didn't think of it." Sebastian stood up. He pushed against the roof while tapping his fingers on it, trying to breathe slowly.

Manon watched him across the parking lot. *Is an anxiety attack slowing him down?*

"Why does what I weigh mean so much to you?" Faustine asked.

"I want you to be healthy," he said.

"How long were you two friends before Elodie died?" Manon asked Faustine. She didn't say it loud enough for Sebastian to hear.

"Since we were in college," Faustine said.

"So you were only friends because you were both friends

with Elodie?" Manon asked.

"Who could tell by his actions!"

"This is a little erratic, I'll grant you," Manon said.

Manon waited until they had both left before getting into her car. She realized Elodie's name started with an "E." *I wondered if I should mention it to Ailill?* The six of hearts that blew over during the seance should have corresponded to the letter "E" if aces were high. *Faustine must realize that, but she hasn't said anything.* At least, Manon heard nothing.

———————

Sebastian's title, the Franklin Eurille Orchestra Concert Promoter, dictated making calls on their behalf. Right now, he was trying to arrange an international shipment of t-shirts. After taking a few days to pore over two or three websites suggested by Franklin, he stumbled across a half-dozen more on his own. It seemed more secure to stick with a vendor that Franklin trusted. He ordered samples of the t-shirts online, which arrived absurdly quickly. He needed to make a correction in the type face before they printed a thousand of them, however. Instead of simply sticking to the website interface, he called the vendor. The woman on the other side of the phone line recited her name to Sebastian. It sounded nonsensical to him, but it reminded him of the way Ellie said his name with the personal possessive pronoun wrong. *Bands invent the strangest names.* He needed to write it down, and there was no way he could spell it.

"How do you spell it?" Sebastian's voice was curt.

"E-U-R-I-L-L-E," the woman's voice on the other end of the line said.

Sebastian wasn't sure if it was a stage name or not. *Is she French? Artists and their made-up drivel! But it's her business, and if that's the way she wants to run it, that's the way it is. Deal with it and go on. Is it a mash-up of Europe and Ellie? It sounds more like EuroRail than a musical group. Is she trying to emphasize a connection between America and Europe?* He didn't recognize it from the Franklin Eurille Orchestra since in his mind he abbreviated their name to Franklin Ellie Orchestra. His brain artlessly tossed any name he could not pronounce.

Their initial phone call was rough. If a sooth-sayer appeared to inform him he'd ever say two consecutive words to the woman again, he would look like Manon signing autographs for the first time. Dealing with foreign sales for the band quickly switched from the low gear of being a no-brainer to the high gear of becoming an ordeal. This current problem was fresh and novel, but Sebastian didn't need a thesis for a business white paper or anything. Previously, he had a Slip of the Cue's merchandising affiliations to fall back on. Now, as the gears of commerce spun faster, he flew solo. Sebastian wrote the necessary letter to Eurille. *Let's hope for the best.*

While Scott hammered out the details of DD&PF's writing credits, Sebastian sorted out their merchandising options. If he found a catch-22 with their t-shirts, he would quietly recuse himself. He was looking for an excuse to bail out on them anyway. Sebastian reached out to Eurille for a potential price structure.

"What information's required for a quote? Do you need," Sebastian turned over a brochure, "to see a logo?" Sebastian wondered if there were still price breaks by the number of colors used, or had this business invented other pricing scheme?

"Most clients use us to co-ordinate their shipping. They're usually picky about who they want printing their t-shirts, but don't want them all delivered to the same place."

"Meaning they don't want them stacked in front of their door," Sebastian said.

"Sales taxes require a lot of paperwork to track. It's not a typical accounting program." Eurille had no intention of explaining the chain of events that landed her in this job. Those stories could be evaded until the bitter end.

———————

Eurille moored in Cork, Ireland, employed by her father's small souvenir shop. Her father's shop supplied the local university crowd, kept souvenirs from Blarney Castle, other hot spots in Ireland, plus the local sports teams. Eurille's brothers also worked for her father. On the side, her brothers assembled a home recording studio. They pressed CDs, which sold pleasantly well to the local university students. They also annoyed the rest of their family by using their surname as a first name. Their sister used her surname in business dealings to camouflage being female, an idea leftover from playing rugby. That farce could eventually be discovered. However, once their father, the boys, and their sister all answered to the same name, it was actually impossible to keep track of phone calls or correspondence.

Eurille was used to the idea of merchandising supporting local celebrities. It was a symbiotic relationship. However, her father was not interested in keeping up with his sons' musical potential. Her father never got into it. The music scene wasn't his speciality. Putting your sons' CDs in your shop and telling everyone how proud you were of your kids was one thing, finding the extra time required to become a music publicist was something else. Their father probably could have managed more publicity for them if they had gone into a field more directly related to his line of merchandising. Over the years, he developed athletic contacts in myriad sports. Their father wondered if his sons were interested in music, or simply interested in getting away from him.

Eurille's normal chore was shopkeeping, which resulted in her family having a feel for what would sell. They had enough U.S. visitors to do their own focus groups at the shop. Her brothers' CDs sold well enough in her dad's store. Eurille filled in the gaps between her father and her brothers. She needed to stay occupied, so continuing the family business was an obvious next step. Since her father spent his time on his current business, he didn't have the time to research the music industry. Eurille did. She figured once she had a merchandising gambit down for her family's brand, she could expand to other groups. This way she would be expanding the family business instead of simply replicating it. Several assistants worked for her father, for decades, and they couldn't possibly be replaced. Waiting for one of those positions to open through attrition was unproductive.

Eurille speculated that her first order of business was to determine if her band-merchandising pursuit should be headquartered in Europe. One might think her first order of business would be to get new clients, perhaps from the local university. Her thinking was that she should go to where the bands were, instead of making the bands come to her. She spent weeks researching locations and complicated international business structures. She made a few initial business trips. Finally, she found a booking agent for Aula Maxima at University College Cork and asked their booking agent where a good headquarters might be located. The booking agent thought Eurille should run her subsidiary through her father's shop as long as possible, noting she might not ever require physical space, since the merchandise would be shipped after ordering. She wasn't selling browse-able items. Fans browsed before and after concerts, not in shops.

———————————

Eurille yelled at her brothers for setting her up with a guy in the U.S., which is, for all intents and purposes, a long cross-country bus ride. *I'm going to have to fly. Gross.* She brought a book to read and took a prescription sleep aid. Once her plane touched down in the large metropolitan airport, she took a cab to the city bus depot. That bus travelled to a universe far, far away from downtown. When she got off the bus, still carrying her own bags since she had not bothered to check them, she lumbered towards an extended stay hotel in the distance.

She rented a suite for a month. She remained close to town, since an interstate highway appeared on the horizon, but was as out-of-the-way as she could arrange online, never having been there. But how different could it be? Large cities are extremely similar. No one came out to greet her. She walked through the double-glass doors to check in. Once she got her key, a bell-hop offered to take her bags.

She demurred, "I'm fine."

Inside her room she hung up her clothes and turned on her laptop. She refused to work by cellphone. She texted one of her brothers that she had gotten to the hotel OK. Then she started trying to put things together for her meeting with Sebastian.

If it were merely work, she would have handled it by phone. If it were simply dating, she could have used an internet site. But it was her life, and she needed the cogs to mesh together. A video of a cute guy babbling sweet nothings isn't going to tell you whether or not you approve of where he lives. Much of the context and clarification for a stranger's actions are missing online. *Why did they think I might be interested in him?* Minuscule harm in discovering his story's details. Eurille showered, then threw herself onto the bed. She had an extensive inventory of sights to peruse the next day.

The next morning, Eurille rode the entire bus route from downtown to the end of the line and back. She brought a notebook and drew a map of the area as she went past it. She also made notes about the houses and shops she saw there. She made notes about schools, churches and hospitals. If Sebastian started talking about events from his past, she wanted to be able to place them. She had no desire to be forced into pretending to believe everything Sebastian said. She had no corroborating evidence for anything in his life. To keep from being taken advantage of, she suspended belief during her experiment. If her visit panned out, this location would develop into a short vacation spot. Unbeknownst to her, she ate at the same Sour Cream and Burritos location everyone else ate at when they were anywhere near the hospital on that side of town. She smacked into a touchstone of Sebastian's life.

Eurille spent a couple of days sight-seeing. Making her own map made that process easier. Taking buses through town was a trick she had picked up in college. There were a couple of cathedrals downtown, a university, several upscale malls at the edge of the north side of town, and many scenic views east of town. Points of historical interest were scattered down the bus line. She checked out pubs downtown as well as near the university, in case Sebastian mentioned them. She wanted enough details to be able to tell if he were bluffing during a conversation. Where the bad parts of town were, where the tonier regions started, how much of town was taken over by the university led the checkoff of questions which would not be answered by a simple background search. No one likes getting gnarly surprises when you're past the point of no return. Once Eurille thought she had completely mapped out the area, she journeyed to Sebastian's office to tell him she was in town.

Sebastian, of course, had no idea Eurille was coming. He was in his office making sure signatures were complete on a set of papers he was processing when Eurille knocked and stuck her head inside the door. Sebastian pulled the papers towards his chest which knocked over a small, white styrofoam cup filled with water. He turned to the sink behind him, since his office was in a converted laboratory, and put the papers on a dry area beside the sink. Sebastian took it as a good omen that the water pooled on his desk without hitting any papers. He smiled to himself, which looked strange to Eurille. She merely observed a guy spilling water on his desk and smiling at it. She had no idea what was running through his mind. As Sebastian grabbed paper towels beside the sink, he continued beaming at Eurille.

"Hi, may I help you?" Sebastian circumnavigated his desk, propelling himself towards her, tossing the paper towel in the trash along way. "I don't think we've met." He couldn't place her in his mind. *Maybe she's a former patron?*

"I'm Eurille. We spoke on phone. We were working out t-shirts and other merchandising." They shook hands. "I go by my last name. My brother goes by his first name."

Sebastian stared at her blankly.

"Unless he's in a band. I don't know why he uses our surname in the band. I played a lot of sports growing up. Using my last name is a holdover. I don't think you got my name straight on the phone. You kept trying to order products with the name Ellie on it without the 'r.'"

"I didn't get business cards from your brother when we met. Apparently, few musicians carry them."

"I don't think my dad even has business cards anymore. He emails everyone."

This emerging opportunity was a no-brainer for Sebastian. *I should take her ice skating.* His can't lose gambit was as far removed from a Slip of the Cue as possible.

Sebastian didn't jump to the conclusion Eurille was stalking him. For starters, a lot of money was involved, and her brother's musical dreams were at stake. Given that, coming out to see a vendor in person made sense. Of course, Sebastian was expecting to be taken advantage of at that point, so anything short of a police stake-out appeared demure. His mind double-checked the hours the rink remained open.

"Have you been to the ice rink yet?" Sebastian asked.

"No, I haven't heard of it," Eurille said. *That wasn't on any of the sight-seeing lists.*

"It's close to the university. Our school fields a hockey team. The university won't let non-players anywhere near it, but they still want a spot for high school junior varsity guys to practice and work-out." Sebastian spat out the words all at once. "The hockey fees support an amateur rink. On weekends DJs play a lot of sappy music and couples request songs." *I'm talking too much.* Sebastian slowed his speech down, but he still couldn't stop. "It's close. When do you need to be back?"

It was mid-afternoon.

"Oh, around sunset. I want to be able to see what's around me since I don't have my bearings yet."

"If you're not in a hurry, we can walk there in half-an-hour. We can talk t-shirts, and I can show you our campus, along the way."

As Sebastian walked with Eurille he touched her shoulder to guide her around campus. *What's different about walking with her?* The campus wasn't particularly interesting. Most college campuses have a similar air. *She went to college. They're all really similar.*

"We can get a drink at the student union, or cafeteria, or whatever it's called around here," Eurille said.

"No one calls it anything, except 'food.' Malls aren't important anymore, so they stopped calling it 'the food court' a few years back. Weird that they don't have another name for it yet."

"Any big hangouts I should know about?" *He's got an unresolved dilemma. He hasn't moved away from the university, and stays close to the ice rink. He didn't say he'd played hockey. He spouts details from the university hockey team's financial setup.* Eurille figured he must have unresolved issues with college athletic achievement.

"Do you have friends on the college's hockey team?" The question was Eurille's method of safely asking him why he immersed himself in the team. They walked through a breezeway which held fast food restaurants on either side. "Do they have Latin American cuisine here? I don't see any."

Sebastian looked at her. "They only have fast food on campus. Nothing anyone calls cuisine! I'm not big into Mexican food. The only fast food Mexican joint I know of is Sour Cream and Burritos."

"You attended school here, right?" Eurille allowed for being wrong concerning where Sebastian had gone to college since he worked beside it. He might have moved cross-country originally to be near an educational facility for a job.

"I went to college here. I went to high school up the interstate a bit."

"Have you done much traveling?" *Why doesn't he get out more?*

"I haven't. The group I worked with stayed on tour almost indefinitely since we finished high school. They were on the move constantly. They didn't have a definitive location, so I stayed home. It was cheaper."

They got sodas at a hamburger stand and kept walking. As they strolled past several buildings, Sebastian pointed out what academic pursuits took place in each one. He was careful not to say what classes he had taken, or where they were located. Eurille noticed.

"No one likes their math class. I don't think I could point out the math department building to you at my university using a map." Her face scrunched as she pouted, shaking her hair away from him. She failed to mention the famous mathematician who studied at her university in the 1800s. Her father even sold commemorative memorabilia about him. Tourists from the U.S. laughed hysterically whenever they saw it. Eurille was no fool.

"I guess not." Sebastian took that to mean he should lay off the history of his college. *Is her family anti-intellectual?* This atmosphere contrasted favorably with the introductions he had made when he attended college. A heaviness went missing. He felt lighter even though he was quite a bit older now. "We're almost there."

The white, flat, rectangular building sat apart from the rest of campus. This area was noticeably different. The buildings were shorter and less ornate. On campus, the sidewalk was the only landmass unclaimed by construction. There was an unremarkable grassy park. Relieved students meandered off campus to breath the spacious atmosphere. Short buildings, with lots of underutilized space, welcomed them.

They spent the late afternoon ice skating to every forgotten love song either one of them knew.

———————

Eurille plopped down in one of the overstuffed chairs in her hotel room and held one of the pillows. *How am I going to get*

Improvising to Beat the Band

more information from Sebastian? They were engrossed enough that afternoon for her to sense that he was hiding information. Faustine's aunt would have been proud of her intuition, which was common sense from Faustine's aunt's perspective. He talked about all the wrong things for all the wrong reasons. She placed her water glass down firmly on the dresser while mentally running through a million details, studying herself in the mirror. She removed her gold cross necklace, worn out of habit. She looked at her hands as she placed the necklace in its box. *Am I going to be in town long enough to have my nails done? Where would I go?* Weird random thoughts interfered with her ability to focus on Sebastian. She needed a chance to meet his parents. That would fill in a lot of the blanks he obviously intentionally left missing. *If he's never moved far from home, his parents should live nearby.* No one on an online dating site ever lets you see pictures of their parents, must less their parent's bios, before going out with them. First step though, trying to meet his friends. *But how much do I really need to know before I know he's OK?*

After meeting Eurille, Sebastian spent the entire evening in his backyard listening to his wind harp. He spent hours sauntering around his yard, meditating to the low, haunting sounds it emitted. He remembered her light-tan skirt-suit with a white button-down shirt tucked in. Sebastian tried to remember if she wore a gold necklace. He saw a reflection of light around her neck, but when he looked closer, it disappeared. If she did have a gold chain on, it was delicate, similar to her earrings. Her earrings weren't large enough to see a design.

Sebastian stopped walking for a moment and breathed deeply. If he got the Franklin Eurille Orchestra to meet at his house, Faustine and Manon would see a normal rock band. Since they had seemingly set him up with their sister, he could return the favor and set a friend of theirs up with Faustine. *Then I won't have to worry about what happens to her.*

Eurille returned to her hotel room. *I didn't meet any of Sebastian's co-workers today. If he's a private person, or they're private people, that's fine. But he didn't talk about any of them either.* That omission piqued Eurille's curiosity. He had only mentioned a couple of friends. *What it would take to talk him into introducing them? Maybe at a pub after work?*

Eurille managed a follow-up phone call the next day. "We should get together with your friends sometime." It was a type of question she wouldn't have the guts to ask him in person, she needed the distance over the phone.

Eurille flew back to Ireland with a minimal amount of work accomplished. Sebastian at least knew how to spell their surname correctly, and she saw that he had a day job, even though she didn't really know what it was yet.

The Franklin Eurille Orchestra planned to launch their tour in a small college town. Sebastian started working out a thousand details of marketing. He lined up as many media interviews as possible, ordered band t-shirts, plastic cups, commemorative CDs, then had them delivered to the location of the band's performance. Franklin, the lead singer of the Franklin Eurille Orchestra, called Sebastian and said they wanted him to attend the first concert of their tour. Sebastian agreed, since he hadn't heard the band perform live yet. He thought that the band had given him their last CD, but when he talked to Eurille later, she informed him that there were several older CDs that her brother's band had failed to mention. Eurille slumped over the phone when Sebastian told her he only had one CD of the band.

A new fiscal year had started at the university, so Sebastian's vacation days were reset. He was still too nervous to take any more days off since he had gone to the songwriting conference within the year. Their opening was on a Saturday night. Sebastian would fly in on Friday and leave on Sunday. He would also work in a courtesy call at the college's foundation or recruitment center. He could finesse it so that it still sounded like work.

CHAPTER TEN

DD&PF Go Pro

Sebastian danced to the Franklin Eurille Orchestra's CD for a couple of weeks while finalizing plans for their concert. *It's going to be good to hear them play.*

The lead guitarist planned to drive him to the sports complex where the concert would be performed. Instead of the guitarist showing up, however, a self-driving van did instead. Sebastian received a text from an unknown number telling him to get into the van without further elaboration.

Where's this taking me? Sebastian cracked open the passenger's side door, surprised to see the camera by the steering wheel. The band's music played on the stereo. The car wasn't designed for that road as the steering wheel was on the right side. *Where'd they get a driverless SUV? And why's it made to be driven on the left?* Sebastian clenched his eyes shut as he crouched down in the backseat as the driverless van hurried through the night.

Invisible in the black sky, a drone swooped down from its bird's eye view. The mini-helicopter stalked the right-side rear of the vehicle 10 feet above its roof. Alone on the road, the pitch-black van with a raven drone hovering about it blended uniformly between the stars. The only object visible was the stadium lights. Those lights formed a crescent cutting into the field near the road in the distance. Isolated and tense, Sebastian chanted to himself, *No, no, no, no, no...* The closer he got to the floodlights, the tighter his fists clenched as he leaned further into the crevice between the seat the the door.

Sebastian murmured continuously, as though mere words could direct the van. His powerlessness lingered in his mouth, even though each syllable had his complete focus, *No, no, no, no, no...* The stadium floodlights magnetically drew this modern carriage to them. Sebastian watched the crescent grow wider as they moved closer to the stadium. Averting his eyes from the source of the floodlights, the reluctant passenger focused on the crescent barrier between light and darkness. *No, no, no, no, no...*

About a quarter-mile from the stadium, the square van slowed, then decelerated suddenly as the van hit the tan gravel beside the road. Now the night possessed three colors: black, white, and tan. *This isn't the address I had the band's merchandise delivered to.* The merchandise had been delivered the day before. Stopping didn't mitigate the pull of those monstrous beams. Sebastian covered his face to keep from watching the stadium lights creep closer.

Once the SUV stopped, Sebastian opened the van, and crunching across the tan gravel. Red police lights blinked in the distance. The blue of the police lights blended into the ground and the night sky. Sebastian studied the silhouettes of the band members with the police. Twelve officers paired with three musicians. Resisting arrest meant being dragged along the ground handcuffed, with red and blue lights streaked across their faces.

———————

Eventually...years later...Sebastian granted the editor with the plaid, pastel suit an interview about the incident: "The best thing I could say about the situation is that I didn't know what was happening at the time."

———————————

Sebastian spent the next two days convinced he'd had a nightmare that he thought was real. He ambled around his house in his underwear telling himself that his paranoia about Manon induced it. He made an appointment with the university's counseling office since he thought he'd had a psychotic break. Then, he received an email from the editor, the same one who wore the peculiar suit, asking for comments. He printed it and held it. *You can't have a nightmare and then someone emails you about it.* He kept his appointment with the counselor though because he wanted more information about the mental health effects of fat-free cheese.

Simultaneously, the band disregarded his calls. Sebastian searched for video clips on social media. The band had given an interview with the student newspaper immediately after their arrest, without telling him. Police lights swirled red and blue against the white concert lights from their show in the clip. Sebastian couldn't understand what they were saying. Not because of their accents, which weren't heavy, but because he simply hadn't been told anything. Franklin was talking about not needing immigration papers, and how the U.S. immigration system was corrupt. *How many roadies are being detained?* Sebastian mentally noted to explain to Franklin how the brusque clipping of his voice sounded cavalier.

Sebastian expected a phone call the next morning, indeed several of them. Calls from the band, calls from reporters, calls from their family, a multitude of calls that should start any minute. He waited, glued to the phone which was his modus operandi when he expected an avalanche. In reality, pacing while gripping his cell phone didn't make the band want to call him. Waiting by the phone used to be a specific task. Now Sebastian had to figure out how to wait while he did everything else. There was no official opportunity cost for waiting for the phone to ring anymore. There was no official grieving process for the lost time, like there was no official opportunity cost for having a friend, like Sebastian's friend Elodie, die of anorexia.

Why haven't they called me? If it'd been me, I would've called my public relations specialist at 9 a.m. sharp. It was pushing noon. *How much longer should I wait for a phone call that's up to another person to make? It's out-and-out crazy for them not to have called me already.* The band members were out on bail. He sent a message that he was having a meeting with a major editor that afternoon. Sebastian needed the band to have agreed upon what they wanted him to say. He had no right to manufacture quotes. He conjectured statements, but a list of possibilities is not the same as a band's okay. He was not a band member, nor had he been friends with them before he was hired. He kept his curtain drawn and paced in the near darkness.

One o'clock passed without any word from the Franklin Eurille Orchestra. Since Sebastian was going to have to leave to meet with the editor anyway, he gave himself permission to call them. There was only one person he was allowed to talk to in the band, the band's point person for publicity. Sebastian called him. Then, he called a second time. Due to his familiarity with bands, he was aware that calling them multiple times did nothing. More importantly, they had his phone number and were supposed to call him first. He finally got an email from the point person saying it was okay for Sebastian to meet with the editor, but that was the last communication he had with the Franklin Eurille Orchestra.

Sebastian reasoned the process through, then decided that when he met the editor, he would simply inquire what information the editor needed. He planned to get back to him with the band's answers later, after they had a chance to talk. It was a half-baked solution to a surreal situation.

This situation reminded Sebastian of what occurred to Manon. As soon as Manon hit the floor, the band championed, a Slip of the Cue, stopped talking to him. He had no information the minute this catastrophe happened. That made no sense to him as a publicist. He was supposed to arrive when things collapsed. He was supposed to explain uncomfortable situations to the press. Bands inevitably gave him too much information when things were OK, then the minute they actually needed a public relations person they disappeared. Thankfully, no friendships were currently at risk, unlike when he worked for a Slip of the Cue. He planned on keeping this band as a client. His livelihood remained at stake. *An arrest could be an individual band member's problem, and have nothing to do with band itself, but I'm not certain about these guys.*

Why do I keep on going out to eat for work? Sebastian expected the magazine editor to arrive any minute. *I don't want clients coming over to my house. I don't golf. Nobody but me likes to ice skate.* Mentally, Sebastian took a breath before continuing, even though he needed no extra air to talk to himself. *I'll ask him if he wants to go ice skating later.* Sebastian remembered the time one of his major foundation donors left three kids with him to babysit one afternoon.

Today was an easy day to say no, at least for Sebastian. Rationally, a low exposure band he did public relations work for had been arrested immediately before a concert. For them, it was a big concert. Maybe if band's side of story was firmly established in the paper it wouldn't mean the end of their tour. *There's no such thing as bad publicity.* Sebastian scolded himself for getting back into celebrity chaperoning. *This happens to me every single time.*

Sebastian ordered cheesecake with a strawberry and blueberry flavored water. The food complemented a celebratory atmosphere, which grated against his mood. He faced the stone hearth, decorated with potted daffodils since it was warm weather. The cheesecake contained mint flavored chocolate chips. *Could I have gotten Elodie to eat here?* The stone walls had an allure. He clenched his teeth, then remembered that he was supposed to stop grinding them and put a strawberry in his mouth. *I'm not taking this guy ice skating. If I need a place to hide out, I'm sleeping at the rink. One more false step from anyone, and I'm going into hiding.*

The magazine editor called him as soon as the story broke. Unfortunately, just because he was the band's official media contact, plus being there when they were arrested, didn't mean Sebastian had any meaningful information. He continued waiting for the police to start asking him questions, but then, he always expected the police to question him, even back in high school with Wayland. So far, they never had.

"Hey, how're you doing?" the editor came in with a big, permanent beam plastered on his face. The smile had nothing to do with Sebastian. Sebastian stood to shake the man's hand. They had met once or twice after the songwriting convention in crowded, noisy venues. The restaurant wasn't vacant today, but this was the quietest place they had tried to talk so far.

"How are the guys doing? Any news?" The editor sat down.

Sebastian sighed. "Their arraignment is this month. The

band plans to enter a not guilty plea. Until then, their tour is cancelled." He found this information   in the college newspaper where they were supposed to have performed.

"They're out on bond I take it?"

"Yes, out on bond." Sebastian hadn't planned on mentioning bond. Score one for the editor. Sebastian said as little possible in order to keep the editor from reporting information fans could use to jump to wild conclusions.

"They'll continue touring after the trial?" the editor asked.

Is it the look on my face? Or does the band sell copies? Sebastian swallowed the strawberry.

"The band is currently adjusting its tour dates. Once the new dates are solid, we will post them on the band's website." Truth was, Sebastian wasn't aware of how much longer he was going to be the band's spokesperson. They were obviously exhausting their cash-on-hand for bail. He turned to look out the window. *Maybe that way he can't read my face.* Unbeknownst to him, doubt still showed on his face, and he didn't possess the refined acting ability necessary to circumnavigate his expressions. Sebastian's stomach was clenched too tightly to eat the cheesecake.

The editor looked Sebastian over for a minute. He breathed deeply, then leaned forward. "Several years before you started working with the Franklin Eurille Orchestra, they began to have legal problems." The editor ate a bite of cheesecake. "I believe it's been three or four years now." The editor gestured towards Sebastian using his entire arm. Sebastian's head subsequently involuntarily jerked away from the reporter. "Is the previous issue continuing?" The reporter dramatically paused for Sebastian's reply.

Sebastian sighed and stopped trying to fake it, closing his jaw, and turning back to look at the editor. The editor possessed more history on the band than he did. He couldn't meet his gaze, and turned away again. Sebastian had optimistically asked for this job. The band had two references that Sebastian had confirmed. He figured that sufficed. He didn't do a criminal background check on them, since technically, he was the employee, not the employer. *I should do criminal background checks on everyone I meet.*

"There was an article?" Sebastian's lips were dry. He reached for his drink. Sebastian was no longer aware of what he ordered or was eating. The berry flavored water he had raved over could have been anything.

"I have information, however, I'm not certain it ever appeared in print," the editor said.

"I'm not certain how I'm supposed to know about it then."

"The band is obligated to tell you."

"Strictly speaking, they hired me to help them promote their tour," Sebastian said.

"You're flying blind. I'm not certain how comfortable I'd be working for a band who had not leveled with me about a major issue."

"Today's information is that the tour dates will be adjusted. I will research the other information, then call when there's new material." Sebastian sounded like a criminal defense attorney getting railroaded by a client.

"What made you choose this band?" The reporter's eyes sparkled as he tossed his head to one side.

Sebastian theorized the philosophical direction the reporter was headed. "I decided to get back into the music industry."

"It's a hard field to break into."

"It wasn't before. I mean, when I was younger, we drove around everywhere and asked everyone to listen to the band."

"You went everywhere and talked to everyone." The reporter tilted his head to the other side.

"What are we going to eat?" Sebastian jostled his menu, pointing it towards the editor's closed menu sitting on the dining table. Sebastian remembered not comprehending the conference attendee's food choices, either. One woman ordered a chocolate seltzer at a bar. Yet another cog out of sync at that conference.

"Most people," the reporter leaned further towards him, "are looking for a free ride in this business." The reporter leaned forward so much that he was almost flat on the table.

"What free ride?"

"They're looking for people to do their marketing for them."

"Well, if they're willing to pay someone, I guess it would be okay."

"Don't count on it. If you had a contract, you could sue. Provided you could find them. But the main problem is that they don't know marketing, so they don't know what they'd be paying for anyway. They don't comprehend marketing enough to explain their specific problem to a professional."

"You know marketing. You were only person at that songwriting conference who asked me for my business card."

"Look, the guy who started that conference died a few years ago." The reporter gazed wistfully through the window. He paused to regain his composure, looking down at the table momentarily before looking back up into Sebastian's face. "If it's networking you want, then you want to find a different conference to attend. They haven't been bringing in any new attendees for a while."

That's why no one at the conference acted like they knew why they were there! Sebastian sat up straight.

"Repeat your previous actions that worked. If going around to every fast food restaurant in the U.S. worked for you, then keep doing it." His eyes locked on Sebastian. "Stay away from the new guys if you don't know them. There are reasons they aren't saying anything."

* * *

Improvising to Beat the Band

When Manon's necklace first went missing—over a decade ago now—she didn't realize the implications of the event, figuring it would turn up after a huge spring cleaning. She balked at asking around, afraid of what she might find out. However, fear is no way to either get a necklace back, or find its ultimate resting place. Eventually, she asked Wayland what had happen to her jewelry. She treated him like a local deity, asking him over and over, as though the process of asking him the same question was a magical incantation which would cause her necklace to reappear. The necklace had belonged to her mother. The sentimental value kept bringing her loss back to mind. Simultaneously, her digital recorder went missing. It had completed work on it, plus she mentioned her mother's necklace while recording with it. That's why Manon blamed herself for her mother's necklace disappearance.

Manon was home writing music at her piano in her living room when she heard some rustling at the front door. Manon opened it, to see a yellow sheet of paper stuck on the screen door directly in front of her face. She shuffled around both doors to read a notice from a package delivery company. Manon didn't remember anyone trying to deliver anything. It was odd that they didn't leave the package, and equally odd that she hadn't heard anyone knock. *Did Wayland send another microphone?* The band had been worried about one of the brands of expensive microphones that Manon hadn't gotten around to using yet, but it wasn't clear what their concern was. *Maybe it's paperwork for the car commercial?* There was an unknown person needing to prove a package had been delivered, yet personally remain unfound.

Manon took the yellow rectangle and thoughtlessly crumpled it, placing the yellow ball of paper on her kitchen table. This puzzle mesmerized her. She paced between the kitchen and her piano late into the night. The next day, she looked up the tracking number online. Her search resulted in initials she didn't recognize coming from a state she couldn't make heads or tails of. She didn't sleep that night, staring at the ceiling. The next day, she took the yellow slip to the delivery service office. The delivery service was closed. A white, square note on their door explained their excellent reason: the shopkeeper was hospitalized. Their notice stated their hope to be back the following week. Manon was going to have to sit tight and stare at the crumpled, yellow sheet of paper for three or four more days. Her mind went blank. She decided to email Wayland.

Wayland emailed her back a message saying that of course he didn't know anything. Smoothed flat, the yellow sheet of paper loomed eerily on the kitchen table. The next time she trudged to the delivery service, the delivery man had returned.

"I dropped by last week but no one was here," Manon said.

"I had some boxes fall on me," the delivery man turned shopkeeper said. "Some heavy ones ended up on the top shelf for some reason. I couldn't get anybody to take my shift while I was recovering. Sorry for the inconvenience."

"Are you feeling better now?"

"Oh, I have to wear a brace for a couple of weeks. The doctor said it'll be fine." He returned from the back room. "Here you go," the man smiled, handing her a petite box.

Manon signed for it. *This is a lot smaller than a microphone.* "Is there anyway of finding out who sent it to me? The person I thought it was from didn't know anything about it."

The shopkeeper copied the return address and phone number from the deliver's copy of the paperwork on scratch paper and handed it to Manon. She thanked him.

Improvising to Beat the Band

Manon took the package to her car. Her breathing tightened while she used her cell phone to perform a directory search for the phone number and return address. The search engine kept bringing up white screens. *It must be a bad internet connection.* Manon watched the package sitting in the passenger's side seat for several minutes. *I don't know who sent it. It could be a bomb.* She didn't want to open it alone at home, nor did she want the shopkeeper to open it since he had already been injured. Leaving her car door open, she crouched outside her car trying to open the package. She picked at one piece of packing tape at a time while the box was still on the passenger's side seat. That way she could run for it if the box started to explode. She breathed deeply, started to cry, looked away for a moment, braced her arm against the box, then ripped a large section of tape while pushing the box further inside the car and running the other way. Nothing happened. She slowly walked back to the car. She pushed back the brown wrapping paper and looked at the white jewelry box. She pulled the top a bit. Although it was snug, she didn't feel any wires pulling against the top. She popped the top off and ran. Again, nothing happened. This time after she crept back to the car, she looked inside the box to find her old digital recorder and her mother's keepsake necklace.

Manon cautiously drove home from the post office. At home, she tried to look up the address and phone number on her desktop computer. Her search kept resulting in white, blank screens. Manon picked up some tape before plopping down in her comfy chair in her make-shift foyer near the front door. She stared at her box holding her mother's necklace. It had a hypnotic effect on her. She carefully verified the items by touching their edges. Then, she resealed the box, protecting others form its voodoo. Now people could only come in contact with the outside of the box. She needed to call Wayland, but she had no inclination. She sat motionless, transfixed by the items. *Was this a bad omen?* Manon needed the entire intrigue to be over. She had rejoined normal life; she was writing songs. She was talking to the band again. No one was trying to kill her.

Now what? What would happen if I didn't call Wayland? How long can I pretend this didn't happen? If someone killed her, it would be over with and she wouldn't have to worry about this saga anymore. Paralyzed by fear, she sat and stared at the box, remembering the clerk at the post office in a brace.

"I've had decades of an unknown person attempting to kill me for unknown reasons. I've written my replies to this person, but have no way of sending them." Manon argued with herself while sitting in her overstuffed recliner the rest of the afternoon, clutching a plush, beige, accent pillow, twisting its tassels into knots.

Ice skating dissipated the clouds in Sebastian's head. He mulled over the events from the concert, watching the police take the band away, while he skated laps around the rink. He had only been working with the Franklin Eurille Orchestra for a few months. He thought about returning to work with a Slip of the Cue. Since Manon appeared better, the band might trust him more. However, maybe there was a better plan to reenter his chosen field? The problems with Manon, the ambiguity of her illness or medical emergency, were finished. Without ambiguity, he should resume his life. However, watching the police take his band away, he realized this was not as simple a deal as he had hoped. He had wanted to believe that it was just a Slip of the Cue who had philosophical inconsistencies. Was every band he worked with going to be more problems than they were worth financially?

Demoralized, Sebastian ice-skated. He skated round and round on the rink as he argued round and round in his mind. He picked a time with low foot-traffic. He didn't understand why established ice skating rinks opened at weird times. *Eight in the morning was once popular?* Few skaters meant the DJ played his requests. Mentally, he was still watching the police take the Franklin Eurille Orchestra away. *I've spent half-a-lifetime worrying over the legal ramifications of being involved with a Slip of the Cue. Now, absurdly, I have a position of actual authority with a band whose past I have no recognition of or familiarity with.* Sebastian didn't possess a docket of the band's violations, or which ones were his responsibility. His years of caution clashed with their immediate careless audacity. With this ending, he should have simply continued with a Slip of the Cue.

He didn't even have his own lawyer. *I certainly can't do this as an occupation if I'm going to need my own legal counsel. I doubt DD&PF's tour will ever turn a profit.* Without a legal intervention, Sebastian would continue to piecemeal the legalese he could find about his current situation. There was no chance for an intervention, since it would never occur to Wayland to arrive unexpectedly at Sebastian's house, then drive him to the nearest law office like Wayland did with Manon.

Sebastian noticed that Eurille didn't offer to return to the U.S. to explain why her brothers went missing. In fact, she hadn't contacted him at all, which was curious, since she should want any information they could have communicated to him, had they called. Even more of a problem, the band still had open orders for t-shirts placed. Sebastian was forced to call her.

"Eurille, this is Sebastian. Unless you know where your brothers are hiding, I'm canceling the band's merchandising orders."

"If I knew where they were, I would bill them directly. I'm glad I wasn't planning on having them be my main customer."

"Are you going to explain what's going on? You must know something."

"On the level, I know slightly more than you do since they called my father. I don't have any more details that the police could confirm though."

"Am I still working for them?"

"I think they should be the ones to tell you that. Until then, I would not put any more effort into their account."

"No more billable hours, you mean."

"Yes, that's exactly what I mean."

They talked banally a few more minutes. Sebastian put his land line phone down on the wall beside his kitchen table and stared at it. *The only way the band could cover an unknown, unforeseen, improbable event like this happening was if they had been stockpiling cash reserves. But no one deals in cash anymore.*

After work, Faustine removed her shoes, then sauntered to her kitchen. First, she checked on the milk she was scalding in the crockpot to incubate yogurt with overnight in the oven. She normally didn't eat yogurt because it was too tart, but she had found a dessert yogurt without the L. Acidophilus culture while she was out searching for fat-free ricotta. When she pulled a cookbook off the shelf, dust fell in her face. She brushed her eyes, but couldn't rub the residue completely off her shirt. She flipped through several vintage recipes. She gave up, huffily closed the book, and put it back on the shelf. *Back to veggie pizza.* She opened the refrigerator to ascertain which vegetables remained. She slid open a bin to find peppers, specifically, two red peppers which reminded

Faustine of the séance. They cued her memory of the two of hearts being blown over. Everyone after the séance had been worried since the top card blew over at the end. No one paused to assess what that additional card meant. *Is this ordeal over if there's an extra ghost?* No one brought it up and Faustine hesitated to ask. *I should email Ailill.*

Faustine doused the frying pan with olive oil, then chopped peppers. It was the six of hearts that blew over. *Since aces were high that meant the letter that the card corresponded to was 'E.'* She removed her frozen pizza from the freezer and microwaved it. She pulled cheese out of the refrigerator and started grading it. Aggravated, she tossed the cheese grater into the sink, then threw the cheese into a skillet. *What else could 'E' mean?* A ping interrupted her train of thought to inform her that her pizza was ready. She took the flatbread from the microwave and flipped it upside down on top of the frying pan. Once the toppings had a chance to melt into the regular pizza, she flipped the entire concoction onto a plate. Veggie pizza was her best recipe. She wanted to eat veggie pizza and stay on the diet plan from the weight loss meeting. *I can't believe I measured the rice incorrectly for years.* She took a knife and cut the pizza in fours, braking each quarter apart by hand and eating it a bite at a time. Fussing with the mozzarella made a mess, and occasionally she lost a bite of topping when it fell onto her plate. Mostly it stayed off the floor.

Faustine did not understand having a friendship where she had to figure out if she was allowed to call the person or not. *Protocol wasn't that strict in grade school.* Since she still had a question concerning the séance, Faustine calculated that there was no risk to her social standing if she contacted Ailill. They had worked on the exorcism part of the séance together. She got her cell phone out to text him.

"We never determined what happened to the second card."

Wendolynn Jane Landers

She hit the send button. *Either he gets back to me or he ignores it.*

Being surrounded by courtiers with excess options gets old. Faustine tired of this nonsense with Sebastian, but a feeling nagged her to call anyway.

Ironically, the waitress who took Faustine's order pronounced her name in Spanish. Faustine corrected her, accepting a quick apology. Faustine had forgotten how much she hated ravioli until she had half a pillow of it on a fork headed towards her lips. Once she eyeballed the meat center, she anticipated the bad taste it left in her mouth. Until that moment of no return, it was a forgotten memory. Ravioli was not one of Faustine's comfort foods. She had spent so many years eating butternut squash ravioli she forgot why she never ate ravioli with meat stuffing. *I hate it. It's too spicy.* It wasn't Mexican food, but it was same problem. However, she didn't think she'd change her mind regarding cheese enchiladas even if people started making them with butternut squash.

Having to deal with the real ravioli, spicy, as well as Sebastian, his new date, and Manon, was a bit too much for Faustine. *If we aren't speaking, then why do I have to meet his new girlfriend?* Faustine put her fork down. The fact that the new girl's name was Eurille resonated with her. Her name reminded Faustine of Elodie. *Is he conscious of the similarities, or is his subconscious running his entire life?*

Faustine couldn't follow the entourage's train of thought that afternoon. She was surrounded by garbled sounds that made no sense. Forks clattering on plates matched the high pitched tone of Manon and Eurille's conversation. She decided to wait, eat, then have Manon tell her why she was there. In meantime, she tuned everyone out and stared at her ravioli. *I hate everything here.* She needed to force herself to find something she enjoyed, anything really, or else leave. Their table stretched too remotely from the window to stare at the scenery. She wanted to gaze absentmindedly into the distance and see something humorous, something light to latch onto. If she had foreseen what a disaster lunch was going to be she would have invited her aunt.

Sebastian breathed deeply as he introduced Eurille to Manon. *I hope this works out.* These moments were why he never introduced his friends to his business acquaintances. There was too much at stake, no way to predict what might go wrong, and no way to maneuver the situation back to the way it was before after a fight. So of course Manon had invited Faustine to the luncheon.

"I almost invited you to a conference," Sebastian addressed Faustine.

Faustine didn't realize she was being spoken to. Manon reached over and touched her hand. When she glanced back to the group, away from the window, Manon indicated Sebastian with a nod of her head.

Sebastian realized he needed to repeat himself. "I nearly invited you to a conference I was at."

"Why on earth would you do that?" Faustine smiled forcibly. "We haven't been alone together since I don't know when." Manon searched Sebastian questioningly, too. "I'm not trying to bring up the past while I'm meeting someone new," Faustine glanced over to Eurille, "but there's no way you'd have invited me to any conference."

Later in the dinner, Eurille turned to Sebastian, "You mean the two of you had to go on this diet together?" Then Eurille started pointing at Manon, "and she didn't even know the woman who died? Elodie?" Eurille shook her head, "and you expect to walk away from this relationship, pretending it never happened?"

"Wait 'till you hear everything they did on their bucket list," Manon said. "I still think that making matching Halloween pumpkins was cute. Faustine's was Cinderella and his was Prince Charming."

Sebastian wasn't sure how he ended up talking about "his relationship" with Faustine en plein air in a restaurant. If it were any later in the day, he'd call his father for moral support. *Maybe I'll call him anyway.*

"As along as we're discussing a relationship I didn't know I had, I'm going to call my father. He's retired. You said you wanted to meet him eventually, and he's never met Manon." Sebastian pointed at Manon. "Perfect excuse. Then I won't be outnumbered here. Plus, he saw me when I was screaming mad at her." Sebastian motioned towards Faustine. "He can vouch this is over."

"OK. But I disagree with that last statement. This," Eurille motioned towards Faustine, "should definitely not be over."

"I agree. They haven't dropped it, but they have managed to stop yelling at each other," Manon said.

"If Sebastian gets to invite his father," Faustine started to open her tote bag, "I'm calling my aunt. She's never met Manon either."

Manon and Eurille exchanged glances.

As Sebastian's father arrived, the restaurant manager's face brightened while he walked towards Sebastian with more bounce in his step. "Do you require a separate room, more space?" The manager waved his hand towards a secluded corner.

"I didn't realize you had one. Are they extra?" Sebastian started relocating their party.

Faustine's aunt arrived. Their dinner party turned into an after-hours party, as it moved to a nook in the side of the restaurant. Faustine introduced her aunt to Sebastian, before her aunt met the others, while they stood by the door as the servers carried their plates to the adjoining room. Faustine smiled constantly, which was par for her being nervous. The private room was darker, redder, and more menacing than the rest of the restaurant, acerbated by half the population of the room being unacquainted with the other half.

If I had thrown a proper engagement party for myself and Sebastian, for real instead of make-believe, these are the same folks who would've shown up. Faustine laughed and drank her water. It was awkward, even without hoping for mutual approval.

Once Faustine's aunt met Sebastian's father, Faustine's aunt realized that she had an opportunity to give Elodie's father a sense of closure. She grabbed her cell phone, having programmed Elodie's father's number into it since she didn't want incriminating pieces of paper lying around for Faustine to find. Eventually, Faustine's aunt would come clean about breaking into Faustine's computer, but at the moment she didn't explain.

The servers started to move their party from one room to the next. The manager picked up Faustine's plate and noticed that she had only eaten half-a-bite of her entree. "What's wrong with the ravioli?"

"There's nothing wrong. I don't like spicy food. I thought it would be OK with the sauce on the side, but the filling is too hot."

This was the first time anyone had ever informed the manger that his ravioli was too hot. Fortunately, he looked like a man who could deal with anything.

"How about ranch dressing? Can you normally eat ranch?"

"I can eat ranch dressing on a salad."

"We made a mistake in the kitchen yesterday and picked up parsley instead of cilantro at the store. We can make a chicken taco with parsley instead of cilantro in the salsa with ranch dressing instead of red or green sauce."

"That sounds lovely." Faustine didn't notice that the

manager's excuse was obviously made-up.

The manager briskly departed in a self-assured stride.

"The ravioli didn't have fat-free ricotta in it?" Sebastian suddenly appeared beside her, whispering sternly under his breath while standing by her elbow. Faustine might provide the psychiatric evidence against fat-free ricotta he had been anticipating.

"I didn't see any white cheese anywhere." Faustine tried to look at him while speaking, but he turned his gaze to the others in the party room. "They can't sell fat-free cheese in a restaurant. No one buys it. This is like when they gave you chipotle sauce instead of ranch, only in reverse."

"If this works, you can try selling a ravioli manufacturer on a ranch sauce for chicken ravioli." Sebastian chuckled.

Faustine didn't trust him enough to laugh at his jokes, funny or not. "This has always been a control issue. There's a lot of societal pressure to eat spicy food. This manager isn't hung up on me having to eat his food, his way." Faustine strode towards Manon and Eurille who were standing by the white columns with very realistic plastic ivy, which contrasted with the ruby side wall of the nook.

"Which reminds me, I've got something for you." Sebastian directed his comments towards the now empty area where Faustine had previously been standing, then headed out the door. Nobody knew when to expect him back.

Eurille seized the advantage of Sebastian's absence to interrogate Faustine. *I'm not going to get this opportunity again.* The main difficulty lay in deciding which friend, or relative, of Sebastian's to talk to first. But aside from his father, Faustine seemed to have been friends with him the longest. Given what Faustine told her, it was odd Faustine was not Sebastian's girlfriend. Eurille demanded details. She presumed no one willingly answered simple, direct questions.

"Was he involved with the woman who died?" Eurille asked Faustine.

"No. To best of my knowledge, he wasn't involved with anybody." Making a profound statement of certainty of her knowledge regarding Sebastian's world stopped Faustine cold. Cosmically, she needed to backtrack. After a minute she blurted out, "I don't know anything about any of my friends, so what does it matter!"

Eurille slipped around a corner of the table and glided towards the other side of the room. Faustine took a deep breath, and instead of running after this woman yelled across the room, "At least, she never told me if she was involved with him. But no one ever asks him if he is involved with anybody. I didn't even know Elodie was sick. Sebastian told me after she died. You should ask him." Faustine pointed at the door Sebastian left through, then took her new seat at the table.

Faustine's aunt seized this unique opportunity, hoping to quiz Sebastian's father. She angled around to where he was and pulled up a chair beside him, then asked in a strained sotto voce, "Why don't any of Sebastian's friends know each other?"

Sebastian's father took a moment to think about her question. *I should call my wife.* "I thought they did. I didn't find out his friend from high school was in a rock band until recently." He adjusted his tie. He hadn't taken off his sports coat to eat, and now it was making him hot. "Do you mind if I call my wife? She paid more attention to his motives than me." Sebastian's father took out his cell phone.

Sebastian was gone exactly twenty minutes. He reentered the restaurant and headed to the side room that now housed their close relatives. *These people were the potential babysitters if I had ever had kids.* He walked over to where Faustine was sitting and handed her a box. It contained multicolored cups dieters used to measure their food more easily. "Here, I've been meaning to give you this for a while. It was in my trunk."

"You gave me this already," Faustine said, "did you buy a set for yourself as well?"

"I gave you this already? How can I have given this to you already! I've had it in back of my car this entire time."

"You gave it to me weeks ago," Faustine said.

"I don't know when I gave them to you?"

"Sebastian, I'm not making this up. You already gave me these."

"Then why have I been carrying them around waiting to give them to you?"

"I don't know!"

"I thought you'd be happy to get them. You can use them on your diet."

They had all started eating again, having been successfully relocated from the previous dining area.

Sebastian's father asked him, "Are you still reading women's dieting magazines?"

Everyone in the group turned to stare each time Sebastian and Faustine's would get into a fight in a split-second, over nothing, out of nowhere.

Faustine's aunt attempted impromptu introductions. She was aware Elodie's father had no details concerning his daughter's medical treatment. He had never had a chance to talk to anyone about his daughter's death. Since Faustine's aunt couldn't guess how to tactfully broach the subject, she boorishly started. "These are the guys who started having séances after your daughter died—"

"What was your justification for performing a seance!" Elodie's father glared.

"It was actually an exorcism. It evicted a ghost who had

previously attacked me." Manon cringed at contradicting Faustine's aunt since they had recently been introduced.

"You started having seances after Elodie's death." Faustine's aunt muttered and folded her hands underneath the table. *Was Manon trying to deny it?*

Faustine started to explain. "We participated in the weight loss meeting as a memorial to Elodie. Sebastian made her a wind harp, too."

"Like I was explaining to your aunt, Elodie didn't die of anorexia," Elodie's father said.

Faustine glanced at Sebastian. Sebastian remained silent. Faustine returned Elodie's father's gaze. "Sebastian told me she had died of anorexia."

"She had previously had anorexia, but she had recovered from it," Elodie's father said. "She was well over 100 pounds when she died. She died of the flu or other complications." Elodie's father's eyes pleaded with Faustine.

"Once she started treatment, her doctors didn't want me interfering, so I had to," Elodie's father looked away, "forgo," tears welled in his eyes, "seeing you guys."

"I've heard more information related to what happened than he did," Faustine's aunt said, "now it's over, you should tell him what you know."

Faustine said, "you expect to know an awful lot about people though."

"I told Faustine Elodie had died of anorexia because she had been in treatment for it. You weren't going to tell her," Sebastian said.

"Elodie spent considerable time at the hospital the previous year. She must have picked up a flu bug there. Possibly the Super Flu? If her weight dipped back down, the doctors planned to keep her in the hospital. She arrived mid-afternoon most days for treatment. Once she had stabilized and went to the hospital voluntarily, her doctors started talking to me. They wouldn't give me any details, of course, but I did meet one of her regular doctors once it was over. That's also why I'm sure it wasn't anorexia. The doctors treated me differently once they thought she was out of woods."

This dinner had turned too cosmic crazy for Manon's to deal with. No one noticed when dialed Wayland's number. He picked up on the first ring. Manon named names as to who the dinner attendees were. "It's a restaurant. They won't run out of food. Rations will endure all night."

"I'll be right there. I'm in town. It'll take me 45 minutes to drive across town. Have Sebastian wait for me at least. You go to a hotel. Eurille's staying at one. There's one near where I stayed with Sebastian when we needed to talk. Sebastian would bring sandwiches," Wayland said.

Manon remembered the sandwiches. *I think I still have one in the back of my refrigerator. Wayland has a point. This conclave doesn't have to end until everyone's cleared the air, or has given up on ever comprehending what had happened.*

The conclave lasted through night. Once everyone got wound up, they discovered they had a lot to say. Now it had been a decent length of time since funeral, more critical aspects of that experience were aired. Faustine's aunt was still relentlessly impelled to determine what was wrong with Sebastian.

Sebastian and Wayland booked a room at the hotel Eurille was staying at. Eurille asked Manon and Faustine to stay with her since she had a suite. The entire party moved to the hotel. They ended up with three adjacent hotel rooms. They did most of their talking in the courtyard. Since they had already done a road trip before, this wasn't totally crazy, or out of character. Wayland capitalized on Manon being out with friends. He suggested she invite her sisters.

"I can't explain who these acquaintances are to them."

"Only tell them we're having an impromptu party. They'll want to meet your friends."

"Christmas in July?"

"Thereabouts," Wayland said.

Once no one was keeping secrets, or at least not major ones. There was no reason to keep the stakeholders apart.

Sebastian conferred with his the father the day after the blowout, while they were checking out of the hotel. "Now I know why your blood pressure was so high. Food wasn't the reason. But you're going to have to start managing the stress level in your life differently." Sebastian's father started a soliloquy about a potential editorial for a women's magazine.

CHAPTER ELEVEN

DD&PF have a moment of truth

The lead singer for Dissent Dissonance and Phosphorescent Freckles, Scott, had a moment of truth after a Slip of the Cue's seance and exorcism combination. He drove down the same highway where he and the drummer for DD&PF had seen the disappearing head. They later accepted everyone else's deduction that the head had been from the ghost who attacked Manon. For Scott, it was a moment to accept his mortality. They had managed to keep their band going this long by sheer force of will. *What's gonna happen when we retire?* Silence was his answer. He didn't think they'd ever retire, but it was a sort of normal worry. It sounded like a reasonable concern. It sounded exactly like the sort of reasonable concern that Sebastian would understand. At the next band rehearsal, the lead singer broached the subject.

"We should get Sebastian to do merchandising for us," Scott explained to the drummer, Chad. "You know, more than just concert tickets. Start promoting us."

Chad looked dubious. "Why are you convinced he'd do that?"

"He's still hanging around, trying to find out what's happened to Manon," Scott said, "a Slip of the Cue's not going to let him hang out with them. He's looking for a new angle."

"They've been letting him take publicity photos," Chad said.

"To decide if he'd bludgeon Manon!"

"They never said it was him."

"No, they stopped working with him after it happened instead. Plus, he couldn't work for anyone else either."

"I guess you have a point," Chad asked, "if we get Sebastian, this doesn't mean Manon will come back to us."

The lead singer studied the drummer. "Oh yes it does." He smiled.

"She can't come back while she's working for a Slip of the Cue. They'll have her under an exclusive agreement." This totally bummed the drummer out: he knew those weasels' traps.

"Wayland can't keep her under an exclusive agreement. He's remarried. That point will eventually sink into Manon's thick head." Glee soared in the lead singer's voice.

———

Scott placed sandwiches on the table. Anytime he wasn't certain what to do, he ordered out. The band's scheme was to meet with Sebastian that evening. Scott didn't have time to cook for an entire group of ruffians. He heard the engine of a car rev slightly then stop as it pulled into his driveway. He opened the door, wondering who had arrived first. It was Chad.

"What did you bring?" Scott asked.

"Napkins, paper plates," Chad said.

"We have those. Did you bring anything else?" Scott grabbed his bag and sorted the items in a rush, throwing napkins on the table and tossing the package of paper plates on the kitchen counter.

"It's Sebastian we're talking to," Chad said, "we're not trying to get a big studio advance."

Scott paused a moment before adding, "I'm not nervous." Chad watched Scott bounce on his toes as he said it.

"I brought soda and ice," Chad said, "you can help me take those in, as long as you're not nervous."

Scott ran around to the side of Chad's car, opened the door, and started dragging accouterments inside.

"What else will we need?" Chad asked.

"Nothing. We'll be fine," Scott said. Scott realized he was going to extremes for an acquaintance. This was the important meeting that they'd struggled to get for years. It's supposed to be with a total stranger, not a person's who's already heard your band perform live. Scott braced himself for quite possibly most contentious meeting he would ever have in his life.

Other members of DD&PF sluggishly arrived. Most were older, retired from gigging. Others were part-time members. Few actively toured with the band. Sebastian wanted everyone to be there for the big conversation. For starters, if Scott couldn't get the totality of former members there, his band's request was moot. Secondly, Scott needed to prove who had written which parts of the myriad bits and pieces of songs being sung on tour. As long as they weren't making any money, no one cared if their song fragments got ripped off. But if they started turning a profit, and that's the scenario Scott reviewed with Sebastian on the phone, then all the forgotten fights would dance into plain view. Scott's nerves jangled since these guys had never been physically together. Determining how much, if any, they had matured over the years was complicated since they loathed each other.

Scott taped the meeting in case he did not get everybody's signature. The collected bands were eating for an hour, then listening to Scott's plan. Scott thought that was his best angle.

"You'll have to sign over your rights to whatever work you've done so far," Scott said, "the publisher will want the rights cleared."

"I didn't write anything," one of the guitarists said, "nothing I remember anyway."

"Why don't you guys write new stuff? That way you won't have to put up with us," one of former lead singers said.

"I'm certain there's a form you have to sign regardless. I just don't know what it is," Scott said.

"So you've brought us all over here to tell us we won't make any money if you guys make it big," one of the former rock-n-rollers said from the back of the room.

Once Sebastian got there, emotionally, he felt the cold rain inside the room. "If someone's written part of a song, you can't take away their part of a co-write," Sebastian said, "and you don't have any money to buy anyone out with. You can't claim a song was a work-for-hire after the fact," Sebastian's eyes searched the room, "but as long as everyone's here, you can get a record of who wrote and recorded which parts of the songs you're planning on using."

Scott had a great idea for the bands to break into two groups based on who they were with originally. That way there would be an official record of who wrote what, plus each band wouldn't have to hear the other band's dirty laundry. Scott hoped the formality of the meeting, plus the fact that half the group were strangers to other half, would require decorum.

"Have you guys decided that you're serious?" a piano player asked. If Sebastian hadn't invited him, no one would have even remembered that he had ever been in the group, even though he wrote better intros than anyone. Everyone had forgotten they were still using his melodies. Once the members started rehearsing their own parts, they started to tune out everyone else's.

Dissent Dissonance originally launched with a lead singer, a backup singer on tambourine, two bass guitarists, a lead guitarist, and a drummer. Then the drummer got "ill" and they had to perform without him. The drummer was more than a little annoyed with them since before that concert he had figured he was indispensable. But Scott bought a drum machine for a backup singer to operate on stage. Scott figured that since they had two bass guitarists, they could swing a concert with three in the rhythm section. That experience freaked out the drummer. Instead of thinking how cool his band leader was for keeping them from missing a gig, he figured he was on his way out. For a drummer, he had a bit of a confidence problem.

Concurrently, one of the bass guitarists got the idea that a small band didn't need two musicians playing the same instrument. Somehow, he figured if the band didn't need a drummer, they indubitably didn't need him either. So after the next concert, he was gone too. A hapless move since the drummer planned on coming back until he saw the bass guitarist bail. Then the drummer figured he unquestionably shouldn't come back either. The rolling snowball gathered magnitude.

So after getting extra equipment, in those days drum machines didn't come cheap, Scott found himself with a backup singer, a lead guitarist, and a bass guitarist. Figuring he should continue the forward motion, he booked gigs.

Their drummer and one of the bass guitarists stood in the

middle of the room, surrounded by strangers, without knowing why they were there. It had been a pocketful of years since they had rehearsed with their bands. They were still in contact with a couple of band members, but not all of them. For them, it had more of feel of a high school class reunion. You go to it because Society—whatever that is—tells you you should.

"I don't see why Scott's so worried," the drummer said to the bass guitarist when they were relatively alone at a table. Several large submarine sandwiches were laid out across the table in neat rows. So in that regard, it felt like a high school cafeteria, except in high school they had individual sandwiches instead of sharing one great big one. Meanwhile, Phosphorescent Freckles had a similar nightmare in their space across the room.

Way back, Phosphorescent Freckles—PF—had lost their bass guitarist. When they realized Dissent Dissonance had two, they picked one of them up. They misplaced that bass guitarist's contact information, so they couldn't find him for the party. The PF side of equation lost their original bass guitarist through disinterest. That bass guitarist took a general science class more interesting than their band rehearsal. He reasoned that if the band was more boring than his nondescript science class, he should quit. He decided to realize his potential elsewhere since the band didn't let him do anything any more meaningful than pick at chords. He loved acting and singing, which never occurred with PF. They weren't making money, so switching to acting was acceptable.

Basically, either the garage bands were meeting the creative needs of the players, or else the players left, which seems reasonable until you're the point person putting the gigs together. But they never quizzed a potential player concerning what would make them leave. The closest they came to plumbing the depths of their potential feelings was, "Do you know how to play an instrument?"

───────────────

They got a voice message saying their old bandmates were getting together for a reunion. Since their part of the band had broken up a long time ago, and the last time they had hung out together they were still in school, they weren't sure what to wear.

"I haven't decided that I'm escorting you to this party," one former bandmate said.

"I don't know what they want," the other replied.

"It's a listening party for their new album. They said they were trying to get serious with their music."

"I don't know what their idea of serious is. I remember when the drummer was tossed out for doing drugs. Everybody assumed they were about to be arrested. If he's at the party, they'll be someone using drugs there."

"I doubt it. They're too old."

"Age has nothing to do with it. He was too young to do drugs in junior high. I still don't know where he got the money."

"What do you want to do?"

"I don't want to go."

"Is it reasonable anyone will be arrested?"

"Someone might be," he said. "We can wear disguises. That way, if anyone calls the cops, we can take off without anyone getting our picture."

"I doubt it'll work."

"I'm not showing up looking like myself. If I'm going to be around those guys, I want to look like someone else."

Nothing like the love lost between old friends.

* * *

Improvising to Beat the Band

"Don't you see? This is where it's all going to go wrong." The former bassist currently yelling in the yard wore a kid's cartoon character t-shirt. Nobody had the heart to tell him the nineteen-sixties, or whenever it was he had bought the t-shirt, was over. He was a grown man who shouldn't be wearing too cute clothing. Jokes don't last longer than a decade. The fact that his threadbare t-shirt was no longer funny was completely lost on him.

"How does it go wrong from here?" the current bassist for Dissent Dissonance asked.

"This is when he kept forging ahead after Todd quit, instead of letting the rest of the band have a chance to catch up with him, musically."

"I don't see it way."

"If he had slowed down, given them more time to practice together, Todd wouldn't have quit. He'd still be playing drums. They'd still have two bands instead of one." It's absurd to start an argument when you're wearing a cartoon t-shirt.

"Meaning what?"

"I think those guys in there," he gestured towards the house, "are going to feel railroaded like Todd did and quit. Only this time they'll have a big contract hanging over their head." *This joint band isn't going to keep up with Scott's ambition.*

At that point, a couple of obsolescent members of Phosphorescent Freckles drove up beside several party guests who were milling around, hissing their complaints, and parked on the street. The vintage shareholders from Dissent Dissonance—DD—stopped fighting for a moment to watch them make their graciously late arrival. The driver got out wearing a creepy clown costume. His compatriot disembarked replete with dark shades and a Panama hat. It wasn't a costume party, and they looked nefarious as hell.

"What are you doing!" The current bassist yelled all the way across the lawn, sidewalk, parking lot, and street.

The newcomers paused for a moment. "We're here for the party." The guy with dark sunglasses simply stated the obvious.

"You're not coming in here looking homicidal."

The former bassist nodded his agreement.

"Why? What's wrong?" The Panama hat guy was their point person. Creepy clowns don't talk to strangers.

"This is an important business meeting. You can't show up looking like this is a joke." The current bassist was flying blind. For all he knew, the creepy clown was a psychopath willing to gun them all down.

"We were told this was a party. So we came dressed to have a little fun." The Panama hat guy gregariously concluded his argument.

"Go home and change." The current bassist waved them off.

Sebastian sorted papers in the late afternoon after DD&PF had had their band reunion. Sebastian noticed the party slipping apart after Scott asked the group to split in two, and then write down who had contributed to writing each song. He had a small sheet of paper with tiny illegible scribbles on it. Dissent Dissonance itemized everything song by song, writing the name of each contributor beside it. Phosphorescent Freckles wrote each band member's name down first, then listed which songs he had contributed to beside it. Scott gave Sebastian a master list of names since the handwriting could not be read without having a master list to guess from. As it was, Sebastian still needed to email Scott a couple of questions.

———————

Although Manon could get out and about, she still dealt with people mainly by phone. A lot of her personal life, like conversations, still moved forward non sequitur by non sequitur. Sebastian took a striking pose of her with the stage lights reflected off of the piano. When her proofs came back, she realized that Sebastian was doing public relations work for a Slip of the Cue, even though the band did not officially say so. Wayland had one of the photos blown up into a poster for her. As long as Sebastian was serving as a Slip of the Cue's documentary photographer, Manon concluded that Sebastian should resume his other publicist's duties as well.

"I've been point person for the car ad," Manon said, "but since you're working for a Slip of the Cue, you're in charge now."

"There's no reason for you to quit being point person for the car ad," Sebastian said.

"It's the only footwork I've ever done for the band," said Manon. "I was never sure I was doing it right."

"Well, you couldn't have been doing it wrong, they still kept sending checks," Sebastian said.

"It was previously organized. Anyway, this ad guy has serious problems. You deal with him."

"What problems?"

"I remain unconvinced he was joking."

"What jokes did he tell?"

"Bands should never run sales."

"Did he say why?"

Manon paused. "I didn't understand reason he gave."

"Which was?"

"He called music 'a superior good.'"

"That means people only buy it when they're rich, like a fur coat. I can see how that might compromise your ethics of music," Sebastian said.

"Then you talk to him!"

Manon found herself fulfilling an assemblage of her co-writing duties by phone with Wayland.

"We need to write a song beginning with the letter 'E,'" Wayland said.

"'E' for eggs maybe?" Manon asked. "Sounds like a murder mystery."

"It is," Wayland said. "The ghost turned over two cards at the seance, remember?"

"I wasn't on card watching duty. Faustine was." Manon thought it should be an unforgettable moment in his life.

Nothing wrong with Manon calling Faustine, however unexpected. The problem was that Faustine was getting her hair cut at the time Manon called. The beautician had to cut around Faustine's cell phone while the women talked. There were no photos afterwards to reveal whether Faustine ended up with a rectangle cut into her curls.

DD&PF continued their crusade to obtain Manon as a songwriter.

"I'm not able to convince her," Sebastian said.

Scott kept talking, undeterred. "You should get her to write a song for us," he said. "She's not writing for a Slip of the Cue anymore."

"You don't know," Sebastian said. "She told me she was working with Wayland."

"I most certainly do. She's not sleeping with Wayland anymore. Therefore, she won't be writing with Wayland anymore."

"Their relationship wasn't purely romantic. There were financial obligations holding them together."

"I'm certain she didn't give a damn if they made a dime!" the lead singer said.

"If Manon has to be around Wayland's wife, Manon won't be speaking to you. Your best bet is to get her involved with somebody else," the lead singer said. "That includes getting her involved with Jacob. That involves writing for somebody else. You're not going to have that happen by sitting around waiting for her life to occur spontaneously. While Jacob's off filming the band's current tour, Manon can write songs for their next one." He completely ignored Sebastian as a possible catalyst for Manon's romantic life spontaneously to occur.

"You're gonna have to talk to her yourself if you want to do that. I'm not her agent."

"You'll have to give me her contact email then," Scott said.

"I'll talk to her and see if she'd be willing to discuss it with you," Sebastian said.

———————

Sebastian relayed DD&PF's message anyway, but not in person. There was no need to convince her, so he called.

"Oh my—there's no way," Manon said.

"Keep an open mind," Sebastian said.

"What for!"

"Jacob's working with these guys now. It's best if you can

get along with them."

"Why do I have to get along with them, Sebastian?"

"Manon, imagine working with the band today."

"I've been working with Wayland."

"You've been working with Wayland in order to get your feet back on the ground. They're totally different than when they were kids. For your sake, keep your options open."

"Sebastian, I barely know what's going on with Wayland. There's no way of I could write for another band."

"Watch the video Jacob shot. You'd have a better idea if you could get along with them."

"Sebastian, none of this is necessary. I can live my life fine as it is right now without doing anything."

"Your life is fine without working?"

"Their fans wouldn't accept me as a player."

"If you're introduced as another musician onstage instead of as part of the band no one's going to notice. That's not a deal breaker."

However, Sebastian made sure he talked to his official clients in person. He dropped by DD&PF's headquarters, Scott's house, for a quick chat.

"How should I ask her?" Scott asked.

"I don't think you should ask her for anything," Sebastian said.

"What am I gonna say to start with? That you gave me her email address?"

"I'll tell her you wanted to talk to her regarding songwriting opportunities."

"How should I ask her?"

"If you're asking me a marketing question, a presumptive close is always best," Sebastian said, "but if you're asking me anything specific about Manon, I'm not authorized to tell you." Sebastian wasn't sure his old confidentiality agreement with a Slip of the Cue pertained to Manon currently, but he had so much practice, he pretended he had one with her anyway. Besides, he was too old to say, "None of your business."

Sebastian gave Scott Manon's email address.

Scott emailed Manon some pleasantries. She, in turn, emailed him her phone number. Scott took the exchange as a positive omen and immediately called her.

"We're writing new songs," Scott said. "Have you watched the video Jacob made yet?"

"Not at all," Manon said. "How is that gonna help us write anything together?"

"Well, you can see what sort of work we've been doing," Scott said.

"You're aspiring to dig in the same vein?" Manon asked.

"That's the style we've been traveling with," Scott said.

"So I should give up and watch the video Jacob's got?" Manon said.

"Then reply with your ideas."

Manon was on phone to Jacob. "DD&PF want me to write music for their band. They think I should watch the video you've been making of them."

"I only have unedited footage. I'm not letting it leave the house. Sorry, but watching the video requires traveling to my apartment to view it," Jacob said.

"No chance of you emailing me a copy?"

"My computer is disconnected from the internet," Jacob said.

"You're serious," Manon said.

"As cancer," Jacob said. "Precautions were the reason the project I completed for Wayland was never hacked."

———————————

Jacob picked Manon up at the train station. They didn't say much on way home, and Manon unpacked in silence. She stayed the guest room.

———————————

The next day, Jacob started showing her his video equipment. "You've already seen my digital audio workspace. I haven't shown you my video editing equipment yet." Jacob continued to reside amidst an archeological dig of studio equipment, complete with microphone dinosaur bones. One resembled a Tyrannosaurus rex towering above the studio. The abandoned love seat resided across the room, plush and comfy. Manon sank down into it. She started watching him work. "You can watch me edit, and then you'll see DD&PF perform. The reason behind a documentary instead of a music video is that I can never tell what a band wants. When I'm making a documentary, I have editorial responsibility to report what occurred accurately. There are witnesses. That's not a matter of personal opinion. Unlike a music video where you can go round and round with a band forever."

"I didn't surrender creative control with a Slip of the Cue," Manon said.

Jacob smiled. "That's because Wayland did anything you asked."

"It wasn't that bad!"

Improvising to Beat the Band

"One of the problems you're going to have working with a different band is that you won't have the same give-and-take that you're used to." Jacob moved over to sit beside her on the love seat. He drank a soda, which awkwardly, suddenly, had nowhere to be positioned. He had been working a couple of hours already that morning. Working longer than that without a break resulted in countless editing mistakes. He was ready to call it quits for the day.

"Wayland and I were involved at the time, but our writing relationship was professional," Manon said.

Jacob smiled secretively and contemplated the floor. "I worked with Wayland too, Manon. I'm certain if we talked about the professional aspects of your relationship with him, your experience would be much, much different than mine."

"How could it be so different if it's still songwriting? Recording him could've changed the relationship dynamic."

"Uh-huh, and I bet if we tell stories about working with him, we are going to end up with a radically different set of situations."

"Okay, you go first then. What's your favorite Wayland story?"

"Let's begin with how I got started working with him," Jacob said. "I had to find him between tour dates. The only problem was their tour dates kept changing. Remember, I have to keep the date open as flexibly as possible when working with these guys. I spent two weeks trying to get Wayland to spend only one day with me doing a complete scratch track before we started recording individual tracks."

"That's tour scheduling. We have scheduling issues," Manon said.

"Tell me last time you had a scheduling conflict when you were writing a song with Wayland."

"They weren't busy touring! You were recording Wayland's album after he was famous."

Which was how they spent the next couple of days, Jacob editing video while chatting with Manon sitting right behind him.

"It'd be amusing if I put a documentary together for you guys," Jacob said.

"Why do we need a documentary?" Wayland asked.

"Not merely for Manon," Jacob said.

"Uh-huh, I'm following you, however, any project needs to be capitalized on by the band. What made you think of it?"

"Manon liked the guitar album I made for you," Jacob said.

Wayland laughed. "That is a completely different concept."

"Not really, you guys haven't filmed a documentary yet. It makes sense to make a documentary of your next tour."

"It's reasonable if the band had information it wanted to circulate," Wayland said.

"It doesn't have to be about the band," Jacob said, "it can be music."

"It'd have to be," Wayland said, "because no one in the band will give interviews." If he didn't want it for Manon, this would be extortion.

There are a lot of ways to watch a movie. You can watch it in a theater with friends, alone, at home, while you're working or doing something else. It can be a focal point or background noise. Jacob toyed with the ways an a Slip of the Cue movie could be screened. There were so many different angles depending on which songs the fans wanted to hear.

He didn't have any friends who were fans. Interviewing fans seemed foreign to him. He wasn't a pollster. Reading social media posts brought him closer to a spot where you write movies. But he still couldn't write the movie fans would want him to write. When he read their posts, they didn't speak to him. He had to make a movie the way he experienced their music. His mindset wouldn't stray too far from the beaten path.

For Jacob, a Slip of the Cue's music was more cerebral. He didn't feel it while he was in a crowd dancing. Their music lifted him when he was several feet away from another person. If Jacob produced a music video of the band's opening number, it would feature a young man standing alone in a field of tall, straw-colored weeds, mid-day. The music plays in the distance while a man broods. This is not what the band imagined. The band imagined crowds of women jumping up and down in a dimly lit room at night. Jacob leaned back in his chair, which was ergonomically designed for him to worry a lot, studying the differences between those two shots. More importantly than the feeling those images imparted, the daylight picture of a man was a picture of clarity. Everything known was seen. The midnight dance shot only let specific spots and moments be seen. Since most of image was in darkness, what occurred was implied.

How did Jacob finally start filming the concert tour? Watching a lot of their concerts live. Putting in the face time meant he spent more time with the band than Sebastian did. On the other hand, he wouldn't be doing it forever. He made a point of taking Manon with him. Unfortunately, Jacob had listened to Wayland play the guitar too much. Now Jacob heard Wayland in the mix of sounds the band played and the crowd made all the time. It didn't matter what else was going on, he heard Wayland prominently. Jacob started checking the sound levels for Wayland. Not easy, since Jacob had four microphones on Wayland. Although possible to fix later, he needed to fix it now. *Was Wayland too loud, or was everyone else too soft?* Manon was nearby, so he grabbed her and put his earphones on her. "Listen," he said.

Manon jumped—grabbing and barking at her simply did not occur in her universe. Jacob's nerves took over when he worked. To her, Wayland sounded faint and distant. "I can't hear Wayland," she said, and returned his earphones.

"I hear Wayland loudly. Should I turn him down or not?" Jacob asked.

"I can't hear him at all." Manon remembered those fights with DD&PF. The girlfriend always felt her boyfriend was getting shoved aside sonically, buried in the mix. She should mention it. "I'm not going to be a real judge of how loud Wayland is." She looked at Jacob, trying to use telepathy, in case she had it. "Since we've been involved. Most girlfriends can't judge how loud their significant others are playing."

Jacob looked at her. "I spent a lot of time listening to Wayland play solo guitar on his album."

"Get one of camera guys to listen to it then."

"They don't know how it's supposed to sound."

"It can't be that mysterious. Get them to tell you if they can hear the lead guitar." Manon started walking away. She wasn't being paid to mix this show. *Who's mixing the show anyway?* "You're filming the video."

"Supposedly I am. I'm co-ordinating video and audio production."

"Call whoever normally mixes for them then."

"He's in the back. His name is Carl. Can you go get him for me?"

"I don't know what he looks like."

"Tall, thin, curly brown hair. Lighter than mine."

"I'll see if I can find him." Manon started speed walking

towards the green room.

Manon didn't know who she was looking for. Seriously, she hadn't even met all the band's family members. She found a guy wearing a headset.

"Where's Carl? Jacob can't hear Wayland in mix."

"Okey-doke. Carl is at the mixing station a third of the auditorium back from the stage."

Why doesn't Jacob just call Carl on his headset? They had radio receivers. Are there technical issues that Jacob refuses to admit to? Manon fought a path through the crowd. No one left her any room to scoot between the rows. Many fans were standing and dancing.

"Carl?" Manon needed to be heard without being alarming. No one knows how to do this at a rock concert. Not even one who's spent a year behind a mixing board.

"Carl?" Manon got closer to the board. There was a tall, thin man with curly light-brown hair with a headset in a corner of rectangular space reserved for the mixing artists.

"Carl?" Manon waved over the side of the mixing arena. The man with curly hair jumped and opened his eyes, startled.

"Yes," Carl said.

"Hi, I'm Manon, the writer?" She had no idea what he knew concerning her bio. "Jacob says he hears Wayland too loudly in the mix. He had me listen, but I'm sure I'll think Wayland needs to be louder." She smiled as knowingly demurely as she possibly could.

Carl leaned forward, on top of the mixing board. Subconsciously, he was protecting it. "What I'm hearing is fine. Who did you say you were?"

"I'll let Jacob know it's OK. I write with Wayland. I'm here tonight with Jacob. Sorry to bother you." Manon waved as she exited back though the rows.

Carl didn't figure it out. Best he understood, Jacob sent a

runner who was friends with Wayland to see how the show was going.

For whatever reason, an unknown person started sending Sebastian guitar picks with little messages written on them. "What? They can't email?" He couldn't fathom how to handle it. Somebody had gone through the trouble to hand-punch guitar picks, then put a clear self-adhesive sticker on it with a small message printed in black ink. Easy to hide or disguise. Also easy to ignore. It was a wonder Sebastian got the message at all instead of throwing the pick away.

CHAPTER TWELVE

Who's Manon dating?

Jacob realized mid-conversation with Manon that she only had one job in her entire life. "Manon, what other work have you done besides songwriting?" *I shouldn't be asking this on the phone.* However, Manon still lived on the phone more than in person.

"Nothing. I was in school when I started songwriting and the songs were successful. Then I was incapacitated."

Jacob understood Wayland's reluctance to let her go, considering Manon had nowhere to turn. *But does she want to turn anywhere else!*

"Have you thought about getting another job? Outside of songwriting?"

"Why? Do you have other work to do?"

I can't believe her first reaction is whether I have ulterior motives. She hasn't worked with anyone she hadn't slept with. She thinks she's married to Wayland. It wasn't clear to Jacob how they could divorce. Wayland had moved out and moved on, but since they had no formal relationship, how would they separate? *If Wayland decides to come back to her later, she might not notice he'd been gone.*

"No. I've got enough production staff." He lied. He didn't

have any. He subcontracted work out-of-state, although on rare occasions he employed interns from a private recording school. "You never said anything about wanting to film a music video. You never said anything about wanting to write another song, either."

"Well, I have this talent, and I guess I should be using it," Manon's strained voice trailed off.

"It'd be easier to break off with Wayland if you didn't work with him," Jacob said.

Manon paced the floor at her house, holding her landline. She wondered how much Jacob remembered of their respective childhoods. "Well, growing up it wasn't clear how many women were going to end up working outside the home. Not everyone was in favor of it. There were a lot of women who stayed home to keep house and raise kids and whatnot." Manon was mulling over the wisdom of reminding Jacob that working from home didn't look out-of-place when she was in school.

"Should you get a part-time job? That way you can accomplish a project disconnected from Wayland if you want."

———————

Manon called her sister, Debbie, and told her to come over. In the 20 minutes or so it took Debbie to drive to Manon's house, Manon had fried chicken ready for supper. The smell of food hit Manon's sister first as she walked into the house.

"I haven't been over here since I watched the place for you when you were on vacation," Debbie said.

Manon began setting dinner on the table. The plates were already there, which didn't strike Debbie as unusual. It was similar to how their mother used to set the table for supper.

"Weren't you here for Christmas?" Manon asked.

"No," Debbie said, "Christmas was at Sherrie's house, remember?"

"Duh, that's right. I backtracked to leave presents and make a casserole. You guys stayed at Sherrie's house."

Manon's two sisters and their mother alternated hosting holidays. Manon's house served as storage for those events.

Manon placed the platter of fried chicken on the table, put her hands on her hips and sighed. Holding her potholders imploringly she said, "Jacob thinks I need to get a job."

"Jacob's the guy you went to Illinois with, right?" Debbie evaluated her safest route to the table. She'd have to sit underneath Manon's glare with her head by the potholders. *Would she throw a plate carrying food?* "That's not a bad idea." *How much time does she spend cooped up inside her house?*

Manon sighed then started to hiccup. She forcefully placed her potholders on the kitchen counter. She was down to one hand on her hip. The other dangled at her side while she looked blankly towards the wall. Debbie only took one psychology class during college, then concluded that nothing psychologists attempted ever worked in practice. No academic was going to mangle her sister for the sake of clinical interest. However, getting a job was different. That involved leaving the house.

"I'm calling Sherrie." Debbie grabbed her phone and turned away from Manon for a minute.

Sherrie took a little longer to get to Manon's house, and her two sisters had started eating the chicken before Sherrie got there. Sherrie took too long to park because she forgot the directions. Sherrie drove around the block a couple of times before figuring it out.

Sherrie knocked and walked in. "You've decided to get a job?" The doorway framed her silhouette in the afternoon sunlight.

Manon sighed repeatedly, but remained seated at the table.

"Jacob believes I should get a job."

The first job that came to her sister's mind was playing the piano. Sherrie, the oldest, said, "Are we supposed to figure out if you should accompany Jacob? What band is he in? Or is he a solo act?"

———

Faustine was typing when she glanced up and saw Manon in the hall. Manon had stopped for a moment, then pointed down the hallway while mouthing incomprehensible silent mutterings. Faustine couldn't ascertain why Manon dropped by her office. Manon's lips resembled a child making a fish face, which Faustine didn't comprehend.

"I didn't remember if you said you worked here," Manon's voice was barely audible while she stepped into Faustine's office. "And I was out distributing resumes."

"You're applying for a job here? They've got that online now." *She's had no experience in applying for a job online.* "That's not a bad idea." *Is she still seeing a psychiatrist?* A psychiatrist could force her from the house to get a job. "Was this Wayland's idea?" Faustine was at a loss for any alternate phrasing to inquire.

"No. It was Jacob's. My sisters agreed."

"Did anyone else advise you to get out of the house?"

"You mean Sebastian?"

"I mean," Faustine lowered her voice and mouthed, "Did a psychiatrist tell you to get out of house more?"

"Oh him? No. The psychiatrist I met thought that the hospital had overreacted, although he said I should perform on my own occasionally." Manon started backing away from the office space.

"Ooh, that's interesting. Have you considered it?"

"I'm a lyricist. I don't play guitar. Hauling a piano around is crap."

"But have you considered it?"

"Not anticipating lugging equipment around by myself, no."

"Have you toyed with the idea of starting your own band?" Faustine noticed that she had stopped typing. She flipped back through her notes, trying to re-read what she had written.

"My sisters think that getting a part-time job is mainly my idea, after Jacob suggested it, and I want to humor them. The human resources department is down this hall?" Manon was now back out in the hall, pointing

"Straight down that hall."

"They've redecorated recently," Manon's voice trailed off, "the paint looks new." Manon's eyes deliberated over the exact shade of the recently painted color. When she moved forward again, she stumbled into a room divider spanning half the corridor. She was out of Faustine's line-of-sight. Faustine heard the banging without seeing the accident.

"No Sour Cream and Burritos coupon appeared?" Faustine asked.

"Not yet," Manon said.

"They've been moving the offices around for quite a while now!" Faustine yelled without getting up. "They started renting out part of the building. Everyone has less space and there is a new wall separating our area from where several people used to work."

"Saving money I guess!" Manon yelled back, still out of sight, and kept walking.

Faustine glanced at a flyer on the bulletin board above her computer announcing the next staff party. Faustine had taken the role of office social secretary for the year. The next office party would be held at the open, spacey area at the mall on the north side of town where Sebastian had told her that

Elodie had died. Faustine envisioned an exuberant party taking there. Since she had no excuse to throw one, she became the office social planner in order to arrange it.

Manon was too far down the hall to hear her yell when a plan settled in Faustine's mind. *I'll have to call her later. Manon should volunteer at the hospital, too.*

Faustine called Manon when Faustine got home from work.

"I forgot to tell you, the office party is in the northwest mall. If you're applying, it's a good chance to meet everyone. I think you should come and play piano. Do you have any idea how much you should charge? I have to fill out a form with party expenses, room rental and insurance."

"I'm sorry, what? I'm applying for a normal job, being a secretary. You're sure playing piano wouldn't be an intimidating introduction?"

"This spot in the mall screams for a piano to be played in it. You will not regret it. It's where Sebastian told me Elodie had died. You should see it. Bring Jacob. Wayland ought to have a sense of your appropriate fee. I'd have you play for free, but you've already performed with a Slip of the Cue. If we don't pay you it could be considered a bribe if you get a job."

Manon played jazz improv at Faustine's office party because it was a safe choice. When Manon had asked Wayland if it was OK for her to play a Slip of the Cue numbers he said he didn't know. She wasn't a cover band. In this case, the music she would be allowed to play fell under the band member's agreement. That was one of the pieces of paper she never signed, but should follow anyway. Mercy. She could play cover songs from other bands however, as long as she got them licensed.

Faustine determinedly supervised the event. The mall didn't mind renters setting up promotional booths, which relieved Faustine from many dark visions. A decade prior, a mall required special permission and charged extra. Currently, the mall management focused on increasing foot traffic. Even so, the party essentially had the mall to themselves. *It must be the time of day, or maybe the day of the week. That type of foot traffic issues.* There were a couple hundred mall patrons who wandered past their booths and left their email address to be entered in a raffle. Their marketing and promotion at Faustine's office was relieved that their advertising budget was increased by the amount the social committee had raised for office parties. *I'm glad the ad department chipped in to have the office party off-site.*

The ad department privately doubted this could happen twice since no one would be able to discern if the employees had been forced to fund the ad budget. But while the employees were still content, no one worried.

Manon walked down the long, spacey, time capsule walkway she travelled with Wayland. Being a nurse's aid was the sole entry level job that occurred to her. If she walked around and talked to the hospital attendants, she could find out what they did for entry level jobs. Subsequently, she found the dance instructor before his class began.

"Do you know what kinds of entry level jobs are common

around here?" Manon walked up to him without his realizing that she had walked into the dance room.

"There aren't many entry level jobs around here. Agreed?" The dance instructor nodded his head.

"I've no idea. I've been here, the morgue, and the chapel. I don't know how nurses get started these days."

"If I apply for grant money for an aide position on a short-term basis, will that help you out?"

"What tasks would an aide do?"

"Make my life easier while I fill out forms. I need to document the progress of patients for the clinical trials we are doing. I can't write and stretch at the same time. So I document what I can remember after class, however, it's best to write while the patients are still here, working out."

Once Manon left, the dance instructor pulled a file for a particular grant application out of his computer. It was a yearly grant, and the deadline hadn't passed yet. He smiled. *She arrived at exactly the right time.* The form was partly filled out already. He emailed the missing parts to Manon for her to finish. He called it her job application in his email. No better news for him today. He didn't apply for grant money when he had to hunt for somebody willing to work part-time on a short-term basis. This was a temporary job for a person moving on. Most applicants for a nurses' aide position wanted stability since they had families to support. Manon afforded him a chance to publish a paper. She had another career, so she would not be overly concerned about his academic paper. Truthfully, it was best that she not have an opinion on it.

Instead of Wayland dropping by Sebastian's house to check up on things generally, Ailill decided to save Wayland some legwork and go see Sebastian himself. That would give Ailill an excuse to drop by and see Manon in person without Wayland being around. However, Ailill was unaware of the strict protocol they had been using, and simply banged on Sebastian's front door one evening mid-week without warning.

Sebastian invited him in. "Have you heard the wind harp I set up in the backyard?"

Ailill said, "No, of course not."

Sebastian took him through his house and out his backdoor onto the porch. "You guys need a concert movie. That way people could actually see how one of these works."

Ailill quickly eyeballed Sebastian up and down. Sebastian habitually asked for favors when he was looking for work, but Ailill was in a position to make Sebastian an offer he couldn't refuse, so to speak.

"We make a music video whenever we want to see how our songs react to the video market," Ailill said. "There's not enough demand for a full-length feature." Ailill rubbed his chin. Ailill knew Sebastian understood the band's market demographics.

"Manon hasn't been to one of your concerts." Sebastian's tone was judge and jury.

"Jacob's been filming some concert footage with Manon mixing." Ailill waited for his sentence to be passed down. *I'm not the only one out of the loop.*

"Jacob filmed one of your concerts? He should continue filming the tour so Manon can get the feel of producing. Quite frankly, I still need a feel of producing! I never went to your concerts once you guys started selling out regularly."

Sebastian has to agree to this arrangement. "You're willing to let Jacob film a concert movie for us?"

Sebastian breathed. It was an effort. *Cosmically, if I'm meant to be with Manon, I might die if I set her up with someone else.*

"You're sure you don't want Wayland filming the concert? We can hire a cameraman and have Wayland tell him what to film." Ailill blatantly wanted to cover all bases.

Sebastian glared at Ailill. "Well, I supposed Wayland has the time on his hands, but does Wayland want Jacob following him around? I don't think so."

Ailill paused and scoured the sky for answers. He stopped talking long enough to listen to Sebastian's wind harp, then resumed his thought. "Wayland and Jacob get along fairly well."

"Not that well. Nobody gets along that well!"

"Not as harmonious as I'd hoped?" Ailill started rocking back and forth as he rubbed his chin. *I'm about to lose a lyricist. I feel it coming on. Manon must be using telepathy.*

Ailill hesitated. "You don't think Manon would mind Jacob filming a concert? I mean, if they aren't getting along as well as I think they are, then nobody's getting along at all."

Ailill and Sebastian managed to have a fairly important and intimate conversation without looking at each other. They stood shoulder to shoulder while both looked straight ahead. Every now and then one of them glanced in other's direction without making eye contact, or even looking at their body. The closest they were coming to eye contact was looking at an area near each other's head, three feet away. They didn't even watch the same spots.

"A concert movie may not do what you want it to," Ailill said. "The problem you're discussing isn't solvable."

"Well that's everything I can do," Sebastian said.

"I've been aiming to work this out for years," he spun around and looked at the wind harp, "decades." *Have we found an unlikely ally? Best to be cautiously optimistic.*

* * *

Improvising to Beat the Band

Ailill pushed himself back from Manon's kitchen table a bit. Manon only had one recipe at this point that she felt was fit for company. The chicken was delicious, and he had finished his beer. He decided to explain why she should write songs for his band. Manon got up and was walking away from the kitchen towards her piano. Watching her walk away triggered a fountain of words.

"You know, Manon," Ailill turned to look her square in the eye.

Manon turned mid-stride to look at him sideways.

When Ailill caught her eye, he finished his thought, "I was planning on having you come back and work with us." He said it the same way he would tell her he had cancer.

"Everyone thinks I should work for other bands." *You should have told me you loved me sooner.*

"I don't," Ailill said.

Manon paused before trying to explain, "I've taken a job for six-months." Manon stopped and looked away because she didn't want to finish her plan out loud, "I don't think it'll last much longer than that." Manon couldn't see anything in her life lasting over a year. *No master class in making the good times last.* She was willing to accept that she had gotten lucky and gotten a job, but having things last...?

"I didn't endure this tragedy to let you leave," Ailill said.

Manon stood and looked at him.

"I need other friends in my life." Manon was relived a phrase occurred to her otherwise blank mind. She remembered the days it took her to stare down a blank sheet of paper.

"I need you in my life." There was no mistaking his meaning. Getting another job was not an option.

"Staying home alone has got to go," Manon said.

"You can move near us, if you want. You can move near us, and get a job near where I live, for crying out loud," Ailill's arms involuntarily waved in large, swooping motions.

"If I have other plans," Manon didn't retreat, "then we should set up regular times to check in." They had a customary calling schedule when Manon was in school.

"Are you coming on this tour? Jacob is filming it."

"Shouldn't Jacob be asking me?"

"No. He can't invite his new girlfriend to go on tour with the band he's filming."

A 12-hour flight later, and Ailill was in Ireland for rehearsal.

"Did we ever figure out what the deal was with the second card flipping over?" Ailill watched Wayland unpack his guitar for practice, which wasn't necessary since he kept a guitar in every location he stayed. Yet, Wayland decided he needed to take one additional guitar around with him anyway, for the sake of toting a guitar around. Ailill was not so encumbered.

Wayland said, "Nobody did anything with it."

"Don't know what we would do exactly," Ailill said.

"We were running around counting pieces of cake," Wayland said.

"The ghost appearing was the first order of business," Ailill said.

"But we forgot about the other one."

"I don't know what the card means."

"How did you remember it?"

"Faustine texted me today."

"She waited to mention this?" Wayland asked.

"She hoped to find an appropriate time," Ailill said.

"So, what's the six of hearts supposed to mean anyway?"

"We set up the board so every card matched a letter," Wayland said. "Aces were high. I suppose that means,"

Wayland started counting on his fingers, "that the card matches 'E.'"

"What does 'E' mean?"

"I have no idea."

"I'm texting Faustine and asking her if she knows of any ghosts whose name starts with the letter 'E,'" Ailill said.

———————

The next day, Faustine texted, "The only name I know that starts with an 'E' is Elodie. But since aces were low, shouldn't we be trying to figure out what 'F' means? The ghost's name wasn't "Bill." That's just what we call him."

Ailill replied, "Wayland thought aces were high. I guess that means no one knows for sure if aces were high or low."

———————

Jacob lounged around Manon's kitchen without saying anything. To him, it seemed like the area she felt safest having company in. The most comfortable area in the house was the sofa by her piano. But it had books beside it, underneath it, and on the coffee table which made Jacob think that sitting on it was not safe. Manon talked with her sisters and Ailill while eating at the table, so the table must be fit for company. But the chair was harder than the sofa, so Jacob stretched out a bit and put a foot on the chair beside him.

"Nobody stays with me long." Manon sat down at the table beside him. "So I can't predict anything. I don't know what to expect. By the way, tell me if you notice anything needing cleaning that I've been ignoring. I'm not as tall as your are and don't see the tops of things."

Jacob was tempted to mention the sofa, but reconsidered. "We need to record you. We can do it here since we need a rough track first to see how the songs are going to go." *I'm glad Ailill formulated the idea of recording a companion album to my solo guitar album.* Ailill appreciated how much time Jacob had spent on it with Wayland. The fact the songs weren't finished yet was a dead giveaway that this recording session was open-ended.

Ailill got the bright idea that he should write a song with Manon. *That'll get her out of the house and away from those people who want her to get a regular job for no apparent reason.* She wasn't seeing Jacob at all and a new job would postpone them getting together even longer. *I'll write a song with Manon and have Jacob film the music video of it. That way they'll have to spend a lot of time together filming and editing her vision. I can bring Tadgh so Wayland can vicariously keep up with their soap opera.*

Which is how Ailill and Tadgh ended up in Jacob's guest room, while Jacob and Manon ended up in Jacob's bedroom. Ailill and Tadgh shared a guest bed, staring straight up at the ceiling trying to sleep.

In the silence, Ailill attempted to comprehend that night. "They were sleeping together at the theme park, right?" Ailill said to Tadgh.

"I'm only doing this because I love my mother," Tadgh said.

"Agreed." Ailill tilted his head to address Tadgh. Ailill felt uncomfortable looking away from the person he was addressing. "I'm trying to figure out why they need a chaperone."

"They have a difficult relationship," Tadgh said. "Manon's not moving on right now. She missed the part where she's supposed to be mad at my dad."

"Agreed. But can she just skip the part where she's mad at

him!" Ailill said.

"How should I know?" Tadgh asked. "You're the one who's been married for years."

It was the first night Manon spent in Jacob's bedroom.

Sebastian used the time Ailill spent writing with Manon to get answers about their past from Wayland. They rehashed the same old conversation every time he tried this.

"I'll tell you what I was thinking," Wayland said. "I was scared. We couldn't identify who had attacked her, and everyone figured it was my wife."

"I couldn't believe you thought I had hurt her," Sebastian said. "What were you thinking?"

"No one knew what had happened. Nothing was likely. I knew I didn't do it. I knew my first wife didn't do it." Wayland paused to reload. "Someone else had to have been responsible."

"There must have been a further reason. What was it?" Sebastian asked.

"I figured you were irate about my relationship with Manon," Wayland said.

"Wasn't everyone?" Sebastian asked. "I can't imagine anyone telling you it was a good idea." Sebastian glanced sideways at Wayland as he was driving them down the road on a pleasant sunny summer afternoon. He saw a picnic area on the side of the road and decided to pull over.

"As long as we're on the topic, what were you two thinking with that song anyway?" Sebastian asked.

"Our anti-love anthem?"

"You were in love at the time you wrote "Love & All Its Glory." You may have been in love with more than one person. I've never been in love. I cannot identify with that song even remotely." Sebastian hoped they'd be able to clear the air concerning "Love & All Its Glory." Sebastian didn't rehash Wayland's obvious problem at the time the song was popular, but surely enough time had passed to get straight answers in retrospect.

"It was what I was scared had happened to you," Sebastian said. "I mean, I did a lot of stuff to keep my dad from knowing our rock group existed." Sebastian looked at Wayland. "I did not want to wake up one day and see your face on the cover of the paper!" Sebastian got out of the car. Sebastian concluded by starting to pace beside it. "I ended up working for a normal group." Sebastian started to fidget, and started looking for a random object to move around. There wasn't anything readily available. His eyes darted around the trees and rocks while he shuffled his hands in and out of his pockets. Nervousness was the main reason he had these types of conversations over dinner. A meal came with obvious props. "And now the band I can tell everyone I'm working for goes and gets arrested," Sebastian said. "Even weirder, they won't tell me why."

Jacob sat beside Manon on the love seat. He reclined at an angle, gazing off to the side. He strategized about how to get her to ignore Wayland while ruminating over how she had only worked with him. *She never even worked with Ailill before. Maybe Wayland would tarnish in comparison?* But she never worked with Ailill since that was not their band's style. *What does Wayland tell her about Ailill?* Jacob strained to remember some stories that would build him up a bit. His brain wasn't clockwork. He calmly surveyed the room. Needing a prop, he grabbed his computer reluctantly, because it moved him away from Manon. Out of the corner of his eye, he saw her focus shift towards him as he moved away. If he wasn't in front of her, Manon started to daydream a bit. Jacob wondered if that was her way of dealing with nerves. He tried to remember a story that would make Ailill look good. He could recount it while opening a project on his digital audio workstation. Unfortunately, Jacob couldn't remember anything Ailill had said last week much less anything Ailill had ever said that sounded important or cool. *Have I fallen victim to Manon's biases?*

"Manon, I used Ailill to get to you." Jacob swiveled around to look directly at her. "He helped me with the editing of the documentary."

"Why don't you text him?" Manon asked.

Ailill had taken Tadgh out for the day on an obviously made-up errand.

"No, that won't work. I need him to watch this now."

"You're gonna make him drop everything and come and look at an edit you need? Are you sure you can't email him the clip?" Manon knew Ailill wouldn't come back if he was trying to leave the two of them alone.

Why doesn't she want Ailill there? Is she not as comfortable with him? Maybe he hadn't approved of her and Wayland? I should send Ailill a note saying why I want Ailill to come back sooner than planned. Jacob couldn't get her to focus when they were alone. "I'm telling her we need an edit," Jacob texted, "come help me get her mind off of him."

———

The nouveau studio engineers huddled behind Jacob pondering his computer, editing. Manon remained on the edge of the love seat. She couldn't see the screen. At random intervals she bent to her left side, looking around Tadgh. She decided it was too much effort to get up and squeeze between them. Jacob wanted Ailill to start talking about old band stories in front of Manon.

"How do you decide to make the camera dive at that point?" Jacob asked. He tilted his head towards Manon behind him, and hoped Ailill caught on to his ploy.

Ailill turned around and looked at Manon. "We've done this before at concerts when we've sung about birds flying." Ailill turned back to look at Jacob.

Tadgh wondered if Jacob understood Ailill was clueless when dealing with Manon. He appreciated her well enough to push a product, but he was not at all smooth.

Ailill directed the rest of his commentary towards Tadgh. "Sweeping the camera mimics the feel of a bird swooping. So emotionally, it's portraying the same thing we're singing about verbally." *That's got to be the sort of thing Jacob wants Manon to know.* It wasn't.

Jacob cut back into conversation while he edited the film. Ailill was not as cooperative in person. He was easier for Jacob to move around on the computer screen.

"Tell her about the concert where you did the swooping thing," Jacob said.

"Which part of the concert? While I'm singing?" Ailill asked.

"Did it relate to birds swooping?" Jacob had to turn backwards a bit and looked at Ailill as he said it. "You need to write a song with Ailill."

Manon froze. Everyone looked at her.

"What do you think we should write?" Manon cleared her throat. She couldn't beg off. She wanted to say she only wrote with Wayland, which made no sense. She started songs with Wayland, but ultimately, Ailill ended up in writing process, too. "Obviously, a 'birds swooping' song." Manon laughed. "Aside from that, what's aggravating you?"

"I don't write songs about what's bothering me. I write

songs about what's bothering other people." Ailill looked at Manon.

Manon got the hint. "I'll adapt." Manon's grin acknowledged that he never got first dibs on the songs.

Jacob asked, "Or, how love was lost?"

"That's a little direct." Ailill stared straight at Jacob. Tadgh inhaled sharply and took a step back, away from him. He wasn't expecting any conversation to be particularly direct either.

Jacob watched Ailill. "There are lots of love songs concerning lost love."

"Why do you mention it now?" Ailill's tone bellowed that if Jacob wanted a fight, he was going to get one.

"No need to shout guys," Tadgh said. He was not planning to return Manon to the hospital. They weren't as loud as they were intense.

"Well, I have lost a love, and nobody has asked me about it," Jacob said.

Nobody asked Manon about hers either; it hung in the room.

"What love did you lose?" Ailill asked.

Jacob took several moments to reply. He turned around to face them, then dropped a reference book dramatically on the ottoman between him and Manon.

"I'm divorced," Jacob said.

"Oh my," Manon said. "I had no idea."

"No idea. None," Ailill said.

Tadgh shook his head and looked over at Ailill. "I don't think Wayland knows."

Jacob smiled at Tadgh's side comment to Ailill in his presence. Those two were obviously working together.

"How long has it been?" Ailill asked.

"It's been," Jacob squinted his eyes at a corner of the ceiling, at least five years now." Jacob refocused on their group. "Let's leave it that way." Jacob looked over at Manon. "I've been learning a lot from Manon and what she's going through." His earnest concern shown in his eyes.

Ailill and Manon sat across the table from each other. Ailill looked Manon in the eye, but she glanced down at her notepad. She doodled. Jacob had a glass top kitchen table. He sat at his computer with Tadgh over his shoulder. Although Manon's elbow didn't touch Jacob's, Jacob and Tadgh were physically too close for there to be any intimacy in songwriting. The guys heard everything they said.

"Hey Jacob, we need to go for a walk," Ailill said.

"Why?" Jacob asked.

"We're getting nowhere." Ailill sighed with exasperation and furrowed his brow towards Jacob's back. "Where's nearest corner market?"

"You're not gonna buy her cigarettes." Jacob turned around in his chair while spinning his arms in a circle. He was pointing somewhere away from the window, someplace unseen. "There's a park on this side of the complex."

The bright, spring-green grass made it easy for them to find the park. "You never said goodbye before you went away." Ailill glanced at Manon.

"We've only been alone together once before. Do you realize that?" Manon gave his upper arm a light squeeze.

They were approximately the same height although Ailill was slightly taller. They easily matched each other's walking pace. Their complementary gait helped Manon feel like she was in sync with Ailill.

"I didn't know I was leaving," Manon said.

"You never wanted to be alone with me before," Ailill nudged her with his elbow gently.

"There wasn't much time." She smiled to telegraph to him that she caught his drift. "What are we going to write?" She hesitated, then took his arm. They huddled confidentially while they walked. Not staring at each other soothed them.

"You're new boyfriend says I can't buy you cigarettes," Ailill said. "That's an idea for a song title."

"It was a very versatile moment. I wasn't expecting him to say anything." Manon laughed and shook her head.

"He doesn't realize I don't smoke," Ailill said.

"I think he's assuming the worst. He's trying to be proactive."

"You think being proactive goes with the territory?"

"Let's make a second line, since I don't understand what you mean by that either, and we need to put thing together," Manon said.

"OK. You never said goodbye. You went out for cigarettes. You didn't know you were leaving. There wasn't much time," Ailill said.

"Oh, I don't want it to be a breakup song. I want it to be getting together, or at least being happy." Manon hung onto his arm, but started pulling away towards her side.

"The first time we were alone together, you never said goodbye?" Ailill made a lawyer's counter-argument.

"We can write it for a commemorative occasion," Manon said.

That night, as Manon dreamed, she walked down a dark corridor, although she wasn't searching for light. A mysterious woman occupied the counter at the end of the hallway. Manon stopped and chatted with the woman. Manon started walking away. Once she was out of sight, but not out of earshot, Manon heard the woman say, "I can't believe she's so ugly." Manon stopped, then went back. Manon ranted at the woman nonchalantly sitting behind counter, "I am not ugly! I know I'm not ugly, and I can prove it." The woman behind the counter didn't care. The second woman behind the counter, who she had addressed her remarks to, stood behind her and partially out of sight. Manon recounted to the woman the numerous albums sold with her face on the cover, so she had to be marketable. Then Manon woke up. Manon was uncertain whether she told the woman that her face was symmetrical, which mattered the most.

In Manon's absence, Sebastian decided to see if he could talk to Faustine without fighting. They met in the church parking lot without a chaperone. His car was on one side of the lot. She parked hers on the other. They walked to the center like it was high noon in the Old West.

"Are you sure you need me now?" Faustine wasn't facing Sebastian, and she didn't adjust her posture while making her statement which was disguised as a question. So, she wasn't looking at him out of the corner of her eye as much as she was glancing sideways at him. She was hoping he'd say no, and then they'd be done with it. Fighting after Elodie's funeral could be excused as ignorance. Enough time had passed now. "It took you this long to figure out I had given up on you?"

Sebastian had expected her to go along with him on this. He was a little surprised she had no expectation of doing so, nor wanted to. He spoke calmly, slowly. "All we have to do is figure out how to stop fighting."

———————————

As a Slip of the Cue prepared for a concert, Jacob flew to the show's tropical resort location to discuss filming. Wayland had gotten a text message from Jacob the previous day stating that Manon had gotten a job, and so would not be mixing at the next concert.

Wayland watched Jacob walk past him once or twice without recognizing him. Wayland presumed Jacob was going to bathroom, but then it occurred to him that Jacob might not recognize him without his guitar. Wayland never figured out what to make of not having an identity without holding six pieces of wire together. On the one hand, he induced it. On the other, he understood how models suffered being unrecognized off the runway. Wayland took out his guitar, then Jacob ran up to him.

"So is she working for you?" Wayland ran with the obvious mode of employment for Manon.

"No. She got a job at the hospital." Jacob stood in front of Wayland six feet away. Jacob wasn't sure how close to stand. Fair enough to say he was standing too far away.

"What job?" Wayland started strumming.

"An assistant to a dance instructor," Jacob said.

"Is it full time?" Wayland wasn't too concerned, but Jacob looked frantic. Wayland wondered if Jacob had intended to hire Manon himself.

"No. It's part-time for six months. The dance instructor said that was why he had a hard time filling the position. It's entry level."

"Meaning minimum wage?" Wayland fleshed out Jacob's thought.

"I suppose. Not that it matters. Her sisters wanted her out

of the house."

"Why are Manon's sisters worried about her staying home? I mean, she's stayed home for years."

"That's why I wanted to talk to you in person. I talked her into getting another job. Her sisters agreed and kept talking about it, which made the difference. The only work she's ever done has been for you. I don't think it's healthy."

"Since she's supposed to be moving on." Wayland attempted to focus on his guitar tuner while he spoke and turned the tuning nuts.

"She didn't even notice you were on vacation with your family when we were there at the theme park together. She completely tuned them out."

"Being snake bit may have helped."

Ailill walked up behind Jacob. Wayland nodded over to him before Ailill scared the life out of Jacob by clasping him on his back before Jacob knew he was there.

"Awesome news," Wayland addressed the space over Jacob's shoulder.

Jacob turned around to see.

"What news?" Ailill smiled at Jacob enough to make Jacob feel comfortable

He's treating me like an audience. This is making him uncomfortable. What was Manon's relationship with Ailill anyway!
"I thought you'd be filming concert footage outdoors. Summer air and wearing flip-flops."

"Manon got a job," Wayland said.

"She's working at a hospital," Jacob said.

"She's a nurse? Not same the hospital where Wayland ran around the morgue?" Ailill's brain reached for the worst case scenario first.

"Yes, it's near her. She goes to the chapel there with Faustine," Jacob said.

"Same one," Wayland said.

"What made her decide to get it? She stopped seeing a psychiatrist after a couple of months. There's nothing wrong with her," Ailill said.

"I told to get another job. How was she going to get over Wayland working with him? Plus, the psychiatrist resonated with her," Jacob said.

"She'll be a hospital employee until when?" Ailill's voice rose. *First, she's attacked by banshees. Now, she's working in a hospital. I need my writer back as soon as possible!*

"Six months. It's a grant position. It's part-time." Jacob wished Manon would get a social media account. *But knowing her, she'd only post pictures of her backyard or her piano.*

A sound check guy walked between Wayland and Ailill to find out what was going on. They brushed him off by telling him they'd be ready in five minutes.

Watching an affair from Manon's viewpoint gave Jacob more closure than he ever got from his ex-wife. Jacob never understood why she left. His five-year-old divorce felt brand new. Jacob was in no hurry to get romantically involved with anybody. He related to Manon's reluctance to move on to a new lover. He was fairly certain if his wife had let him, he would have ignored her infidelity even longer. But the guy she was seeing finally gave her an ultimatum, so she left. It was one reason Jacob was not fond of ultimatums. After watching Manon, he doubted that his ex-wife knew why she left either.

Jacob's fuzzy memory of psychology from college centered on make-shift experiments he performed near the university's cafeteria. He remembered a Freudian concept called "transference," where patients kept repeating previous relationships without realizing it. Something in a new relationship, perhaps how someone looks, will trigger a patient's "script" of how they behaved or felt—or trusted someone—in a previous relationship. Now, Jacob was attempting transference from Wayland to himself by playing Wayland's guitar riffs when Manon was around. Jacob rationalized playing Wayland's guitar riffs in order to improve Manon's mood. He didn't want her going out with anybody else who wouldn't be as careful with her mental state. When Manon and Jacob literally slept together at his studio, Jacob woke up with Manon's head on his chest. She was OK with him holding her. Jacob's strategy was simply to keep upping the stakes each time they were alone. Maybe suggesting a shower or bath? He would keep a blanket nearby in case she had flashbacks. He would say it was in case anyone walked in unexpectedly.

When Jacob finally got around to offering a communal shower, his blanket idea almost backfired. Manon had no idea who he thought might walk in. She held it up and looked at him questioningly.

"This is pretty," Manon held up the orange blanket so she could see the embossed sunset. "We can put it up on the towel rack."

Jacob put his hands around her waist. "I don't know if you're going to start having flashbacks. Better to have something to grab just in case."

"The blanket reminds me of when we got our nails done. You had a sunset painted on your toes." Manon reached down and gently touched his toes. "We should get our nails done again sometime."

Manon put drops of a grass scented essential oil in the base of the tub. Jacob rubbed her back with massage lotion while the shower ran. The lotion had a musty, dark scent. She tousled his hair with a handful of the lotion and watched the rivulet of lotion run down the muscles on his back.

———————

"Next time we can go lie down," Manon said.

The scent of the massage lotion continued to waft romantically through the room.

Jacob couldn't foresee what she wanted since he couldn't read her. *Is she ever going to let go of Wayland?* "You didn't need the blanket."

"I don't really have flashbacks. I just don't remember anything."

"Well you never know what's going to trigger your memory."

"Usually nothing does."

Jacob pulled her into his chest and kissed her. *At least there's going to be a next time.* "Chocolate is in the 'fridge." *Let chocolate pave the way into the unknown.*

CHAPTER THIRTEEN

The Sense of the Song

Manon got a facial since that was what she wanted to do after she got a pedicure with Jacob, but didn't mention it at the time. Their shower brought back the long weekend they spent together—minus Wayland and the snakebite. Manon chatted to the beautician that she was on vacation with her former boyfriend when she ended up seeing a psychiatrist.

"Was it your idea to go?" the beautician asked.

"No, it was his," Manon said.

The beautician shook her head. "Sounds like he should have ended up on meds, not you."

After Manon got home from the theme park trip, she took the kitchenwares she picked up with Faustine out of her car, she noticed that her new plates had an orange, abstract design which reminded her of the orange sunset Jacob had painted on his toenails at the nail salon. Now whenever she saw the plates, she reminisced about Jacob. *Maybe I should get him a blanket with an orange sunset on it? I still don't get why he would bring a blanket into the shower, but whatever!* The blanket remained on the towel rack as a souvenir. She bought an extra bottle of the dark, musty scented lotion to have on hand.

* * *

Improvising to Beat the Band

———————

Wayland dropped by Manon's house one lazy afternoon to draft some songs. After an hour or so, they managed to agree on a basic chord structure. Wayland played the chords on his guitar while Manon tried several possible melodies over them on her piano.

Suddenly, Manon stopped playing and turned to him. "We can't write a love song. You've remarried, and you set me up with Jacob."

"We can write a love song! We've been in love. We can still write a love song." Wayland hopelessly repeated himself—like a chorus—while his voice trailed off. There were real reasons Manon was the lyricist.

"Who are we going to write about then? Ailill?" Manon asked.

"No, he has to sing the song. I had a hard enough time playing when the songs were about me," Wayland said.

"You're doing something else onstage and it's distracting. I get it," Manon said.

"'Cause you pointed out that problem back when we got started," Wayland said.

"I still don't remember much stuff," Manon said.

"We can write it about your friends. The ones who aren't speaking to each other anymore."

"We can write what should have been, because the way it ended for them is silly."

"What do we call the Faustine and Sebastian break-up love song then?" Wayland smiled.

"I met them at a weight loss meeting after their friend died of anorexia," Manon said.

"Anorexia in the title is way too over-the-top," Wayland said.

"Angry Anorexics should wait for another day," Manon

said.

"I feel a little weird making a judgement call about Sebastian behind his back. He was a close friend once," Wayland said.

"You didn't speak to him for years because you thought he hit me." Manon didn't understand where this sudden historical revisionism came from.

"It's about what they did after their friend died," Wayland said.

"How the death of one friendship caused death of another," Manon said.

"I don't conclude that the first friendship died. You can still be friends after you're gone. I think it was the loss of control that killed their friendship. That and unclear motivations." Wayland had a definite opinion.

"'After She Died' is a possible song title," Manon said, "we can recount their ordeal after their friend died."

"We can rehash the stuff they did that anyone else might have done in same circumstance," Wayland said.

"No one would have done what they did!" Manon crisply enunciated every syllable.

Dejected, Wayland finished the song idea for her. "What they intended to do was normal, what they actually did was weird. Had their friend ever put a bucket list together for herself?"

"The weird things we do when we're together," Manon absentmindedly started. She glanced towards his eyes, but didn't quite make it. He helped by looking down at his guitar. "To redo the past." An idea sparked within her.

"Maybe we'll get lucky and they won't recognize that it's about them," Wayland said, "'Dieting after She Died' sound like a title to you?"

"That's way too Jane Austen," Manon said, "Sense and Sensibility. Pride and Prejudice. The audience will expect acidic social commentary about women's place in society, or a lack thereof."

"How do you want this song to be taken then?" Wayland asked.

"It's too soon to have a hit again. We can start with an idea carrying less emotional punch."

"A friend of a friend dying for no apparent reason," Wayland strummed his guitar, checking its tuning.

Manon felt the pull of a force bigger than her happening anew.

"Life's a musical journey." Wayland smiled.

"A musical journey," Manon bobbed her head, concurring. "Isn't that a quote, like, from an 1980s political rock band? Maybe U2's Joshua Tree film?"

Wayland strummed the first few chords on his guitar. "Do you think we should open with a full chord?" Wayland strummed a loud full sound. "Or an inversion?" Wayland strummed a melodic chord with separated, spaced out notes. "I've been wanting to put up motivational signs on your ballet mirrors. I saw different motivational signs that the dance instructor put up on the mirrors at the hospital. I think we should put one up on your mirror that says 'Life's a musical journey.'" Wayland kept strumming a minor chord progression.

Manon's brain drew an image of how different her life would have been—lying on her sister's couch alone watching T.V.—if Wayland and his family hadn't intervened. She turned to him and said, "I'm glad you were in love with me."

"Manon, I'm still in love with you." Wayland continued picking a melody without looking at her.

Manon lost her nerve upon reflection. "We can't write a song about Sebastian and Faustine like they were superstars." Manon sputtered while laughing.

"Why not? I don't think they'd know unless we told

them," Wayland said.

"They were on a diet together." Manon emphatically put down her pencil and crossed her arms. "There's no way Sebastian wouldn't recognize himself."

"We can let another band record it if you'd have more privacy that way," Wayland said.

I don't want another band recording my music. This is my project and my friends. I don't want anyone farming it out. "That's ridiculous. No one would mash their names together, Sebastine." Manon smiled, uncrossed her arms, then picked up her pencil.

"Sebastine, they are hereafter proclaimed to be," Wayland said.

After hashing out some preliminary verses, they decided to quit for the evening, and promised to edit it later.

After a couple of months of edits, this is how the song eventually turned out:

Dieting after She Died

First Verse

The weird things we do
   Rewriting the past
   No class to take
   To make the good times lsat

Banshees wrote your bucket list
   Sharing a photo of a daisy
   Disjointed phenomena
   Carried tightly like you're crazy

Improvising to Beat the Band

* * *

Chorus

Nobody fights
   Like you two
   You need a referee
   To spend a night out

Nobody fights
   Like you two
   None of the fantasy
   No anxiety
   How hard could it be?

Second Verse

You were in denial
   Wondering why she died
   Worrying the mundane
   Vacations, ornaments, diets

Learn to make each other
   Breezy, cheery, thrilled
   Your referee quit tonight
   Carefree, merry, full-filled

Chorus

Nobody fights
   Like you two
   You need a referee
   To spend a night out

Nobody fights

Wendolynn Jane Landers

Like you two
None of the fantasy
No anxiety
How hard could it be?

Coda

How hard could it be?
　To be so very happy
　Zappy, happy, zappy

———————————————

The dancers stretched, warming up for class. Visitors wouldn't guess they were in a hospital. There was a blond hardwood floor with mirrors on three walls. Several partition screens crowded the instructors desk. Manon moved them out of the way and lined them up so she could get to the main desk. Dancers weighed-in before aerobic activity. They had lost muscle mass due to anorexia, plus their doctors didn't trust them to exercise on their own: they might exercise for several hours.

Manon connected a couple of large amplifiers on stands to her cell phone. She played a meditation playlist. Covertly, she had a scratch track of "Dieting after She Died" on her cell phone as well. Unobserved, she clicked on the title, so the song also played while she checked the dancers in. She waited for them to figure it out. *Who knows what they'll think?*

The dancers acted like they always did: they bobbed their heads and walked around, trying to stretch a bit before class. Several laughed at the chorus, mouthing the words, "nobody fights," before hugging and wiping a tear.

Manon studied their every move before returning to the meditation playlist.

Although she could barely breathe, Manon played the song once again before the dancers left.

While laughing along with the music, one dancer said, "This is the class…"

Another sang the song's reply, "To make the good times last!"

Although she stood silently, waiting, no one asked Manon anything about the song, or made any comments directly to her.

"It was weird having the women in the dance group hear the song," Manon said.

"Did they like it?" Wayland asked.

"Yeah, they did. I turned it on as they were starting the session. They hugged each other and cried."

"Anyone suspicious?"

"Of me? No. Got clean away."

"You can tell them you wrote the song. It's OK."

"If you say so. By the way, we have the title wrong."

"How so?"

"It's called 'Nobody Fights.'"

"Is that how they were referring to it?"

"Yeah, that's what they called it."

"You'd think writers would know the title to their own work."

"Apparently not."

"Did any of them think it was about anorexia?"

"Not at all," she shook her head, "nope."

Sebastian called himself doing it for Elodie—although who

knows what she would have actually wanted. The deceased shouldn't be blamed for everything. He eventually spent a week in Cork, Ireland, evaluating Eurille's father to determine whether or not to give her father his seal of approval. Sebastian resided in his client's former bedroom and performed many of their old chores while resident. The atmosphere reminded him of Elodie's father's house: grey and somber. There was a better chance of getting familiar with the remains of the Franklin Eurille Orchestra without the band present. If it seemed like Elodie's father could benefit from a vacation with them, he would give his seal of approval. They ran a pro golf shop, not a bed-and-breakfast. *Who knows how much patience they have for strangers?*

Ailill's grandparents lived their whole lives in Ireland. Their son moved to the U.S. when he married a woman who had travelled to Ireland for her education. Ailill was born and raised stateside, except for the summers he spent with his grandparents. He stayed in Ireland sufficient time, once the band started touring, to make it the band's official home base. Wayland had a similar environment. He visited his grandparents in Ireland. His father came to the U.S. on an educational visa, met his mother, and moved to the most landlocked area he could find. Both Wayland and Ailill had been born in the U.S.. Wayland hadn't visited Ireland as much as Ailill. His parents divorced once he finished high school. Wayland's father moved to New York and his mother moved to L.A.. Oddly enough, his parents videoconferenced enough to keep up with their favorite baseball teams, plus maintaining tabs on their kids. One of the many reasons Wayland clung to Manon was that she linked him to a past when his parents were still married. His life blew up in his teens when they divorced. So when the band started touring, Wayland was also open to relocation. The other band members enjoyed the adventure of living in another country, and since they had visa choices (thanks to the band they were business owners, investors, as well as writers) they could come and go fairly easily. They started dating Irish women which eventually led to settling down and raising their families in Ireland. So these guys were not ones to mess around with their paperwork. They knew how to read immigration law. Ailill had been known to adjust tour dates to ensure he resided in Ireland an entire calendar year to keep from having to fill out an additional residency form on his taxes. Reciprocal tax agreements only work when you fill out the forms correctly—even with the favorable tax breaks that writers receive in Ireland. Occasionally, he was tempted to disregard the entire process. He never thought of himself as a dual citizen; he thought of himself as a person with a lot of paperwork to fill out. Sebastian, on the other hand, never left the U.S.. He didn't even know how long they'd let him stay overseas. What was his reason for entering the country, work or vacation? Who knows?

The Franklin Eurille Orchestra had no such paperwork bastion. They had limited resources, and whether or not their business was turning a profit was questionable. Plus they had no fondness for getting their paperwork together on time. They were always sketchy on when and where their tour dates were, and argumentative when asked about them by customs. They weren't like Eurille's father at all.

Eurille's father ran a pro golf shop—anything a serious golfer might need—in West Cork, Ireland. Sebastian realized that being friends with her meant taking golf lessons from the shop's golf pro—a former collegiate star. Sebastian found a time slot on a Thursday morning that didn't need a prearranged foursome. Whoever showed up played together.

"Where's an ice skating rink?" Sebastian counted on the northern climate to bring more skating time.

The golf pro hesitated to humor him. *Someone during a lull would ask about a different sport!* "None around here. Perhaps in Belfast, but I suspect not. Are you traveling to Paris?"

"No, I'm vacationing in Ireland. There's not a rink around Cork?"

"Closed because of insurance hikes. I think there's one in Paris near the Eiffel Tower."

Sebastian inferred that the golf pro didn't go to Paris often. *Probably not a lot of golf near the Eiffel Tower.*

Their conversation was minimal. Sebastian wondered why Eurille's sons went into music instead of sports. He didn't know how close the golf pro was to Eurille's sons. Prudence declared not to ask, only to keep to the task at hand.

Eurille presumed Sebastian would enjoy a vacation in West Cork: a beautiful, scenic tourist trap. An artist came to the golf pro shop on Saturdays to draw souvenir caricatures of the golfers. There was a caricature of the Franklin Eurille Orchestra prominently displayed on a wall near the entrance. Sebastian sent caricatures of himself playing golf to his dad, Manon, and Elodie's father. *I wonder how often the Franklin Eurille Orchestra played in this shop?*

"'Eurille' had a shop on St. Patrick's Street before taking up golf. He's been here at least 10 years. Why do you call him 'Eurille?'"

"His daughter goes by her last name. I do promotional work for her brother's band."

"The boys went off the deep end, didn't they?"

"I'm not authorized to repeat personal details." Sebastian noticed that the pro golfer hadn't been rooting for the band to overturn the U.S. Government.

"I don't buy their story about being worried about U.S. immigration policies."

Improvising to Beat the Band

"I haven't met with them recently. My last information was that the tour dates would be adjusted once their legal problems were behind them."

"Then you're not going to adjust any tour dates. They're always spoiling for a fight."

Sebastian was in the non-disclosure agreement grey area. *Surely an employee of their father was OK to talk to. Surely he knew not to repeat anything they discussed to the press. Obviously stop talking!*

"What were they like growing up?"

"I didn't know them then."

Oddly enough, Sebastian wrote several press releases for the golf pro at Eurille's shop. Not the business he pursued, but it was business.

"I could write them myself, but I don't have the time. I used to write them, but I had to stay up all night to finish. How much do you charge?" the golf pro asked.

Sebastian held the golf pro's business card with elegant gold lettering. *Perfect!* Since the pro golfer had previously tackled publicity on his own, he gave Sebastian a couple of his old press releases, a press contact list, and details about an upcoming tournament. Sebastian spent a night at the hotel writing sample releases on spec. Not what he was expecting.

Sebastian flew back to the U.S., then called Elodie's dad to meet him at Sour Cream and Burritos. They discussed the possibilities of watching a golf tournament overseas. Sebastian had found a nice hotel not too far away from the golf course, great for prospecting for golf clients, so Elodie's father would not be imposing.

Sebastian called Manon and invited himself over. He took the seances as evidence that he was no longer a suspect.

Hopefully, she felt safe being alone with him. Unfortunately, they hadn't gossiped in many, many years. Sebastian started yelling at Manon on her porch across the yard as soon as he stepped out of his car. "Did you get the caricature I sent? Go to Ireland with me! I'm going on vacation there with Elodie's father. There's a hotel near Eurille's golf pro shop. Some golfers want me to represent them at an upcoming tournament."

"Are you still the spokesperson for the whatever-their-names-were band?"

"The Franklin Eurille Orchestra. I don't think so because of how long it's been since I've heard from them. Their family's doing fine." Sebastian still hadn't come in. He was standing by his car. Manon stood in her doorway. "I don't want to send them a letter terminating our agreement while my schedule is still empty." Sebastian slumped a little as he said it. "But once I get enough business, I won't have time to help them rebuild when they resurface. At that point, I'll let them know."

"You don't know where they are?"

"Their folks know they're safe, but won't say anything else."

"Oh come on. That's so weird of them not to tell you."

"Everyone gets told not to talk about anything with anyone else. It's psychotic. I've gotten used to it." Sebastian trekked around Manon's house. "Care if I look in the back? You might have room for a wind harp. Elodie's father wants one, so as long as I'm on a roll, I'm making everyone one. When I make one at your house, I want to talk to you about Faustine. I think I know an editor I can set her up with."

Back at the hospital, the last straggler exited the dance studio.

Improvising to Beat the Band

Manon worked up a sweat and spun a towel over her head like a fan to cool off. She didn't know how to say goodbye to the dance instructor.

"I'm going to be headed to Ireland in a few weeks. A friend of a friend died of anorexia and her father is making a trip to Ireland. My friend wants me to go with him."

"How does this relate to your co-writer?" the dance instructor asked.

"It's in the same country. I'll miss working on this project with you."

"Maybe not, I can search for comparative cultures funding. It could help with the generalizability of the research."

Sebastian drove to Elodie's father's house to help him get his bags together for their trip overseas. Elodie rarely invited him to her parent's house. He had been there possibly once before, sometime around college graduation, and perhaps one other formal occasion, Christmas or Spring Break. The minimal light in the darkened living room was absorbed by the deep color of the soft, plush furniture. Sebastian's golfing caricature displayed over the sofa was out of place. Sebastian realized he didn't know when Elodie's mother had died. From the appearance of the pictures in the living room, it had been more than a decade. The men chatted about golfing from separate rooms while Elodie's father finished packing. Studying the living room, Sebastian made a mental list of questions to ask Elodie's father. The darkness was too intense, so Sebastian was relieved when Elodie's father was finally ready to go.

Sebastian carried Elodie's father's bags to his car. It reminded him of carrying Elodie's coffin. He had put effort into forgetting that afternoon. Usually, he succeeded when trying to push back a memory, but Elodie's father exuded a formal air while packing to leave, which was extremely similar to her funeral. As long as his brain had already gone there, Sebastian asked Elodie's father how the other pallbearers were doing. Sebastian still hoped to ameliorate their loss.

"Fine. They're all doing fine," Elodie's father said.

"I can make an Aeolian harp for your backyard. I've reshaped mine enough times I'm sure I can get one for you to work correctly."

"Sure. That'd be fine," Elodie's father said. It was more of an excuse to invite Sebastian over than either realized. "Have you ever considered going into wind harps?"

They stood around Elodie's father's backyard, which was technically, Elodie's former backyard.

"No, I've only started making them recently. I'm surprised a Slip of the Cue didn't market them, either artistically or from a merchandising perspective," Sebastian said.

"I don't know if they'd have a huge market. They're great outdoors, but most people want their backyard space to be able to do different things. Once you've got a wind harp going, its going to play regardless," Elodie's father said.

"There should be a way of making the string slack unless you wanted it playing. I'll look into it," Sebastian said.

"You can make one for the golf course. I think they'd like one. Maybe near a pro shop, away from the actual course."

"It'd be a good marketing strategy, if they liked it."

"I don't know if they'd let you put your marketing business info on the stand."

"I could put a website address. Most artists do."

"I haven't seen any," Elodie's father said.

"That's because you're looking at older stuff. A website is an additional line. No big deal," Sebastian said.

The wind harp started to play, and they stopped talking.

Improvising to Beat the Band

* * *

Sebastian dreamed of playing golf during his flight, and woke up smiling. *I'm glad we aren't staying with Eurille's family.* He had brushed them off when Eurille had offered. The only "family member" he had gotten to know on his previous trip was the golf pro, and he didn't have much to say about rest of them. Sebastian and Elodie's dad had an early tee time the next morning. The golf pro demanded that Elodie's father know how to play before the tournament. Otherwise, he wouldn't know what he was watching.

After Manon's overseas voyage on a cruise ship with one of her sisters (who flew back), she moved into the house the band bought for visiting musicians, which had been recently redecorated for her arrival. Sebastian dropped by Manon's new abode in Ireland. Everything was new: recording equipment, microphones, sofa, chairs, dishes, carpet. It was surreal for him to see her that fashionably current.

"Someone's sending me guitar picks with the letter 'E' on them," Sebastian said.

Manon thoughtfully paused. "You don't think it's 'Bill' again, so you?"

"I can't say how successful a Slip of the Cue is at pulling off an exorcism since they've never done it before. It's possible that he's returned."

"It's more likely to be somebody else. The card turned over indicated two spirits present. Only one has been accounted for."

"I'm thinking that the 'E' stands for Elodie."

"I never knew her, so I wouldn't know," Manon said, "are

you sure aces were high? Ailill doesn't know."

"No one tells me how to golf! I tell everyone else how to," the golf pro laughed while driving his cart. He drove his cart anywhere he could, meaning he veered off-road more than was prudent. The electric cart forged an erratic path running errands around the golf course before the lesson.

"I've actually only played with you," Sebastian said.

"So makes this your seventh or eighth time then?"

"More like fourth," Sebastian quickly calculated the days. "No, maybe you're right. We played every day Elodie's father was here."

"Have you played much?" The golf pro looked at Manon sitting shotgun.

"This is my first time," Manon said.

"You didn't take her out for a round before coming over? You and your friend's father could have shown her a thing or two." The golf pro had a typical teacher's fight for relevance in their student's lives.

"I don't know enough to show her anything."

"Oh come on. You can show her one thing at least!"

"Maybe one thing."

The golf pro turned to Manon, "You have friends at home who golf?"

"No."

"Great, you can show them how it's done when you get back to the U.S.."

Manon thought of having to teach Faustine to golf because of an overbearing golf pro. "Sebastian, you show Faustine how to golf when you get back."

"See, there you go," the golf pro said.

"Me, you, Faustine, and Elodie's father?" Sebastian eyed

Manon through her side mirror.

"Yeah. Sounds like a show," Manon said.

Manon clenched her fists. She hadn't felt out of her element when she was a dance assistant at the hospital in the U.S., but now, in a foreign country, she thought she might throw up. *I was used to the other hospital, but everything's new here.* Her chest tightened. *I haven't been homesick or had stage fright in a while.* She wasn't expecting it: she hadn't been expecting anything.

The dance instructor, Fred, actually thought she was a physician's assistant. Manon didn't know the difference. Apparently, that had something to do with how long a student stayed in school. Although she had graduated years ago, he felt she was an expert on this particular study, since she had gone through the protocol before. Manon had enough experience to lead a session, but she hadn't been paying enough attention while she was working to feel like she could actually replicate a study. However, Fred had notes about the relevant parts. Manon still wasn't sure what the study was all about. Fred didn't give her a lot of details. He said to let him know if they started doing things that were dissimilar to what they had done in the states. *I'm flying blind.*

She was. It was a double-blind research design.

When she knew she would be staying in Ireland at least six months, she decided to move out of the visitor's quarters and buy her own house. Setting up shop meant recreating her home studio. Since she didn't know how long she would stay, her house was in a property management company's name, along with the studio equipment. Supposedly, she could have other guest writers or recording artists stay there. If she decided to stay, she would transfer the property to her name. If not, the band would have another guest house. This kept people from making rash decisions.

Just when Manon finally set her home studio up the way she wanted it, she had to go out and buy another one: at least she knew where to order it. The same guys arrived as last time, but carrying less equipment, since she was within driving range of a Slip of the Cue's studio. She had to pay extra to have the guys from Indiana fly overseas to set it up. One of the guys setting up her studio was upset by the questions the customs agent asked. Apparently, you couldn't be both working and doing a friend a favor. They normally didn't set up equipment overseas.

Wayland had brought a couple of microphones with him to Manon's abbreviated studio. He had already left a guitar there. She hadn't even gotten her second checklist of how to turn the studio equipment on and off yet before she saw the guitar in its stand in the far corner of the room.

"At least for a while this will save us from lugging microphones around," he said.

"Great, now I won't sit on a plane all day when I need to finish a song." Ailill couldn't believe his good luck at having Manon and his band in the same country.

"We never travelled there that much." Wayland still had a house overseas. Once Manon could work again, the novelty quickly wore off.

"Speak for yourself. There were gobs of songs I never had a chance to draft."

"Write your own songs," Wayland said.

"Or drive across town and polish a song with Manon!"

"We were supposed to finish a song for the next seance. The song to get rid of the poltergeist whose name starts with the letter 'E.'"

"Do you know who it is?"

"Sebastian's friend, the one who died right before Manon started to recover, was named Elodie."

"As far as I'm concerned, this chick can stay. Manon's here, writing, and even has a part-time job to keep her busy while we're touring. I'm done."

"I'm done as long as I don't end up running into the wrong poltergeist in a blind alley day. We're going to have to write a song for Elodie."

"Not any time soon."

"If anything weird starts to happen, we write the song."

"Manon seems to keep a ghost around. If we get rid of 'E,' who knows what demon will show up."

———

Everyone pretended to forget about the last seance. No one felt inclined to endure the hassle again. Everyone suddenly had new projects and yard work to catch up on. Wayland bought new boulders for his yard. Manon was back on her feet and working with the band, which was the point of the original seance anyway. But they all went through the ritual of asking each other if they were simply going to forget about it, in case anyone had strong feelings about getting final resolution. It's not clear something would have been done, except those who didn't care would have stayed clear of the worriers.

Faustine and Ailill were in charge of asking around, having more knowledge than rest about exorcisms. Faustine didn't bother to call a priest. The last priest didn't want the band to perform the previous exorcism. Wayland was the one paying the most attention to the cards, and the most likely to remember that an extra card had been turned over.

Ailill discussed the practicalities of the extra card problem with Faustine. Discussing the problem by text, of course.

Ailill texted, "Wait to see what music Manon writes, then decide if we want to get rid of Elodie."

Faustine replied, "I want my friend to rest in peace, not work for free for your band!"

Ailill texted, "We can give her cut to charity."

This is the ugly underbelly of the band. A ghost is haunting you, and all you care about is whether or not your next album will sell! Having a friend die suddenly gave Faustine more respect for Manon's snake bite. Ailill hadn't experienced a similar abrupt and final disruption.

Wayland had already waited years for resolution to the "Bill" problem. *We'll eventually have a seance for Elodie, especially if something unusual occurs, making everyone believe that an unknown ghost is still floating around. This project won't be finished in a reasonable amount of time.*

After several months, Manon's study ended and she took a cruise back to the U.S.. While at Faustine's office party (the one Manon agreed to perform at while she applied for a job), Faustine transformed into another person in front of Manon's eyes: this stranger enjoyed life.

Faustine stood there in front of Manon, ignoring her, chatting with her co-workers. Manon wondered if she should migrate around the clumps of humanity towards the piano. The freshly polished black wood against glass and tile, all of it gleaming with light, enlivened crowd.

Employees hovered around the buffet, laughing. Sour

Improvising to Beat the Band

Cream and Burritos catered their early afternoon lunch. Faustine requested Ranch House Chicken Tacos to go with their standard Mexican fare.

Manon decided to try out "Dieting after She Died" on this crowd. A Slip of the Cue hadn't performed it yet, and so the song wouldn't be included under any band agreement, signed or unsigned.

Sebastian leaned against the back wall, watching Manon and smiling. *I'm glad she told me.*

Musicians in the rock world rarely appreciate how difficult it is to take portrait level photographs with a thousand fans in front of the camera. Stop action photography helps, but the moment a photographer is looking for onstage can easily occur with a fan jumping absurdly skyward simultaneously. There would be enough crowd interaction to keep Manon from being stilted. The floor-to-ceiling window had plenty of light to prevent shadows from falling on her face when he zoomed in for a close-up.

Faustine invited Elodie's father to her own little block party. It was a direct result of inviting her aunt. Faustine's aunt thought it would be a perfect outing for Elodie's father. Faustine had been inspired by Eurille's attitude when they met at the impromptu extended dinner party: don't let go of people. Sebastian didn't know Elodie's father was coming until he inadvertently took a picture of him in the background.

I'm not going to try to explain this song beforehand. She sang a couple of cover songs she had licensed, then took a moment to double-check that her breathing was steady. *How is Faustine going to react?* Maybe you shouldn't write a song slightly critical of a potential co-worker when you're applying for a job, and she's a reference.

Manon sang and played, singer-songwriter style. *I have until the chorus before she figures it out.* Manon hadn't seen

Sebastian enter. She didn't tell Faustine he was coming. Manon planned to referee once her concert finished. She figured food would keep them busy until then.

Manon smiled and tried to focus on the audience, none of whom she knew. She simply couldn't gauge their reaction while playing. Their round faces made little oval "ohs" while Manon sang. *I have no idea what it could mean. It's one detail too many to focus on. As soon as it's over I'm going to flee the country for several months. Whatever hornet's nest is stirred up can go on without me.* Mid-verse, Manon heard a loud thudding crash of something blunt being dropped in back of room out of sight. It wasn't Faustine, who remained in Manon's line of sight, so Manon kept playing. Manon filled the concert with jazz improv. That kept her from performing cover song after cover song that the audience already knew. Once an hour had passed, which didn't seem as long in retrospect, Manon stopped playing and helped herself to the buffet.

"Take it that song's a work in progress," Sebastian said.

Manon jumped, startled. She hadn't seen Sebastian, and he walked up right behind her. She sighed, then turned to face him.

"Yeah." Manon ate in front of him, obviously not answering his implied question. She looked for his camera equipment to make sure the crash she heard wasn't expensive.

Sebastian realized that Manon was going to make him ask. "It's about me and Faustine, right?"

"It's about any two friends who fight so often they need a referee. The song is from the point-of-view of the referee, instead of the friends. Since it's my song, it's possible the song concerns Wayland and Ailill. Ailill could be adamant about my songwriting solely to keep me available to referee fights between him and Wayland."

"He doesn't fight with Wayland! Besides, his wife can

referee."

Manon stood tall. She leaned forward. *If he's sure it's an invasion of privacy, he can take me to court.*

"I never got you to sign a non-disclosure agreement about me and Faustine," Sebastian said.

"Even if you had, only three witnesses were present for the specifics. Until you announce it to the world, no one will guess. If you have to tell the world before anyone knows, the song is not an invasion of privacy. Writers can always write about their personal experience."

"Your life wrapped in silence, courtesy of Wayland, now bequeathed to me."

"I can only write what I know."

"I'll let you explain this to Faustine. Good luck." Sebastian turned away and cut back though the receiving line which was forming.

Ailill and Wayland flew in to visit Manon and double-check her microphone supply. The metallic-brown unit had been repurposed into a microphone closet. Manon invited Faustine to improve her chances in case of any debate.

Faustine pigeonholed Ailill. "I don't see how you can even contemplate reneging on Elodie's seance."

Not the argument I was expecting, Manon shuffled the microphone boxes around like she was rearranging shoes.

"I definitely ordered a set of microphones with interchangeable tops that screw on and off," Wayland said.

"I haven't seen them," Manon said. Those microphones were simply too expensive to disappear without filling out insurance forms.

Ailill watched Wayland rummaging around Manon's microphone closet. "I don't think she needs them anyway.

She should work with preamps more. This isn't a mic problem. It's a preamp problem."

It sounded like a gibberish problem to Faustine. "The sooner we exorcise the remaining ghost, the sooner Manon will get better."

Manon's sister Sherrie stood behind Ailill in the hall. She couldn't see what Wayland was doing and was mildly concerned. Faustine felt self-conscious not knowing what to say around Manon's sister.

"Will you please tell them that they need to perform another exorcism to get rid of the ghost haunting your sister." Faustine went with a direct appeal. If she triggered an avalanche, it would fall immediately.

"Manon didn't tell me about the other things you guys did. Seances?" Sherrie asked. "I knew you guys had gone on vacation together to celebrate."

"We celebrated Manon being healthy enough to write." Ailill picked at several boxes, then held one up to the light before opening it.

"I dropped by to check on her house while she was gone." Talking about this creeped out Sherrie. It was too similar to moving a deceased person's personal items before a funeral. Sherrie knew Wayland would be the one to break the bad news to Manon's parents if anything fatal happened to her overseas.

Ailill, in turn, was creeped out by the fact that he had spent more time with Sebastian's friend than Manon's sister. Especially since they had graduated from the same high school. Protocol abated.

"Were you in choir in high school?" Ailill asked.

"Yes."

"Did you have Mr. Lee?"

"No, I had Mr. Pence. We went to regionals in California."

"Once we started performing, I quit choir," Ailill said.

Improvising to Beat the Band

Wayland stopped shuffling around and stood with his hands on his hips, contemplating the group bunched by the door. A pause ensued.

"Would Manon need to be present for the seance?" Sherrie asked.

"Whose making arrangements?" Faustine said. "Are we doing it at Fleer Casino again?"

"What if she prefers to stay? Can we give her the option of remaining in the song?" Ailill searched for an alternative. He wanted this door to the afterworld to remain open.

"We only ask when the poltergeist is leaving. We aren't bossing anyone around." Faustine was annoyed by Ailill's forgetfulness. *He's my point-person, my ally. His betrayal erodes our axis of power.*

"No one leaves tonight until I give the all clear. We don't need to keep having these." Wayland searched for the holy grail called Closure.

Manon's sisters had not seen Fleer Casino and Resort. While everyone else acted lackadaisical, they gawked at the gorgeous scenery, paintings, and furnishings. The owners noticed that they appreciated their resort's good taste.

Nothing expensive breaking during the previous seance had pacified the casino owners. They figured that if they played their cards right, so to speak, they would have a great ghost story to tell about a Slip of the Cue. No one pressed the owners to sign a confidentiality agreement. They said their normal hotel agreements would have to suffice, but that they would be on hand in case of an emergency. No way were they giving carte blanche to a seance that could possibly go wrong. A Slip of the Cue emphasized the band was performing an intimate, private concert. The owner's knowledge of seances was spotty.

Sebastian planned on taking pictures. Manon's sisters lacked any confidence concerning their briefing. Faustine imparted significant details on the night's agenda. However, in their mind, those details didn't connect with the physical world. They wondered how the seance worked the first time.

Ailill's designer scarves with their silk print draped across the grand piano occupying center stage. Sebastian photographed Manon waiting beforehand. These were better than the still shots of her comeback concert.

"I hope we don't end up running around counting pieces of cake again," Wayland said.

"It all depends on what the ghost does," Faustine said.

An objective observer would notice the extreme care that had been invested in the gathering. There were the jasmine scented pillar candles beside the taller alter candles. The print on the scarves matched the mystical tokens that Ailill insisted be carefully positioned for maximum effect. How Ailill determined this effect wasn't clear, but no one argued with him. There were fewer strangers here this time. Manon had been coaxed out of hiding in her house for the rest of her life, so less moral support was needed. Wayland's wife's absence stopped bothering anyone.

"Did anyone have any nightmares before this?" Wayland had become acutely aware when he didn't have a headache.

There were no replies.

"One more reason not to have it!" Ailill said.

"How are we warming up tonight? Do I simply deal the cards?" Wayland asked.

"Play a hand with me while Ailill lights the candles," Tadgh said. Since Tadgh saw "Bill" during the last seance, he figured he would be the most likely to see a new apparition. "Faustine, keep your eyes open—starting now."

"I'm watching carefully." Faustine sat in the second row of

the auditorium, safely out of arm's reach of anyone. Manon's sister, Sherrie, was at the opposite end of the row of seats.

"I have forgotten how this goes altogether," Manon said.

"We have to play music to summon the spirit world," Ailill said.

"What are we playing along with 'Dieting after She Died?' It was easy with "Bill." He hated 'Love & All Its Glory,' the drummer said.

"Anybody know what Elodie's favorite a Slip of the Cue song was?" Ailill announced his request to everyone within earshot.

"Aside from 'Love & All Its Glory,' it would've been 'Just Let Time Pass,'" Faustine said.

"We should play 'Tell Me about Love Sometime,'" the drummer said.

"Yeah, we should. Few people here know it," Ailill said.

"It's not finished. I don't have the lead sheet," Manon said.

"We know. We're playing part of it. We'll remember it if it's any good," the drummer said.

"I've not going anywhere near a cell phone until this is over," Manon said.

Tadgh and Wayland finished their game of poker. A Slip of the Cue started playing "Tell Me about Love Sometime" to warm up. Ailill grabbed a four foot long, emerald green, paisley printed, silk scarf to begin a meditative trance dance with once they started "Just Let Time Pass."

"I think we need Manon on piano for "Dieting after She Died." Tell Ailill to move it—" Their drummer reverted into a swearing cacophony.

Manon figured as much and moved over to the piano. "Who's going to hold the cards if I'm playing?"

"We'll deal once the song is through," Wayland said.

"Where's Sebastian?" It finally occurred to Ailill that he hadn't seen him.

"In the back, Ailill," Sebastian said, "with Elodie's father."

"Nervous?" Manon took Faustine's hand, which trembled.

"If it were me, I wouldn't want to be stuck here," Faustine said.

"Your compulsion to diet may end after the seance tonight." Manon started playing.

"Sebastian thinks that I was never actually on one." Faustine turned to search for him towards the rear of the auditorium.

"I know. I was there. Remember?" Manon started playing.

After several minutes of music, Faustine cried. "You guys write complicated songs. They don't sound complicated to begin with," Faustine dabbed at her eyes, "but they are very complicated." Faustine kept her eyes shut through the latest rendition of "Dieting after She Died."

"OK, we ask how many spirits are present, right? That question comes first," Ailill had forgotten the protocol.

Manon maneuvered to the opposite side of the piano, directly across from Wayland. She played with Tadgh and Wayland, and they dealt a hand face down for Elodie.

"We play a hand to see if anyone's here," Wayland said.

"I don't think that's how we did it last time," Ailill said.

The poker players weren't listening. Manon and Wayland tested the cards to see which one the spirit world wanted them to move. They drew a blank.

"I'm not getting anything, Wayland," Manon said.

"I don't feel anything odd tonight," Wayland said, "last time, it felt like an electrical current moving."

"Before, I felt pressure from the edge of the card to move it," Manon said.

"We weren't conducting electricity through the cards, right?"

"Stop trying to talk yourself out of this. We wouldn't be here if you hadn't seen 'Bill,'" their drummer said.

"I'm still not feeling anything. Maybe we should play some more music?"

Manon went back to the piano. They played "God Save Us from People Who Hate Love Songs." Then they played "Dieting after She Died" again.

"Maybe she doesn't play poker?"

They dealt a simple line of cards face down.

"How many spirits are present?" Ailill clenched his eyes shut in order to mustered all the spiritual force he could.

Wayland and Elodie touched all the cards. They had an entire suit on the piano. They never considered how a ghost would communicate a number higher than a dozen. They ran through the cards dealt on top of the piano a couple of times.

"Anything else we should know about? Favorite color? Perfume? Clothes?" Ailill asked.

"Nothing besides what we've gathered." Faustine continued crying and ran out of tissues. She sat there with tears streaming down her face unable to physically stop them with anything.

"Let's wait a few minutes and try it again." *I don't want to come back and try this again in a couple of months.*

They spent an hour trying to contact Elodie, or any other ghost present, to no avail.

"Looks like it's over." Ailill's voice trailed off with disappointment. "Manon's got her cell phone, so she can make notes for "Tell Me about Love Sometime." We need to finish that one." If Manon kept writing without Elodie's spirit's guidance, he wouldn't mind her leaving so much.

Faustine heaved along while streaming tears. Ailill's handed her his scarves. She kept them and eventually took them home that evening.

Sebastian watched Faustine carefully, silently remembering the day he told her Elodie died. *She couldn't cry at all then.*

"Let's take five and see what happens. I don't want to have

to go through the hassle of setting one of these things up again." Faustine didn't stop crying to talk.

"Yeah, maybe we're not paying attention. We could wake up tomorrow and somebody's cellphone is gone again," Wayland said.

"We break to eat and come back in an hour?" Ailill asked.

An hour later, Manon pounded out "Love & All Its Glory" on the piano as hard as she could. Ailill waved long scarves with both hands which made him hard to see. He said he was drying them out. Then they tested the cards again.

"Nothing's different. Nothing's changed," Wayland said.

"I think we can call it. I think it's over," Tadgh said.

"We take a vote on whether we think we've ended it tonight. If anyone's seen or felt anything funny or ghostlike, speak now." Ailill paused, scanned the group to make sure they were with him, then announced the vote. "All in favor of going home?"

Everyone raised their hands.

"Congratulations, Manon. You are officially clear of poltergeists," Ailill said. "Wait a second, the rest of you can go on home, but I want a Slip of the Cue to stay and work on "Tell Me about Love Sometime." I don't want that song floating off into the sonic ether."

So, a Slip of the Cue stayed and finished the first pass of "Tell Me about Love Sometime" the night they knew, or were at least relatively certain, that Elodie had gone away.

PART FOUR

DENOUEMENT

It could have ended differently. Sebastian could have dated Manon, like he always figured he would. Occasionally, he still resented Wayland for the years Manon spent alone. He could have gotten along with Faustine after Elodie died. Maybe something would have happened if they had worked harder at their relationship, like going into therapy. Of course, he might have never spoken to Eurille after her brothers ditched Sebastian mid-tour. But the woman he ended up ice skating with was the woman he stayed with in the end.

After the last seance, in which nothing supernatural occurred, Sebastian took Eurille to Paris to go skating at the Eiffel Tower. They found an excuse to join a golf tournament. Sebastian felt that one tournament should lead to another, so they joined the golfing scene at Cork. That led to promotional work for Sebastian which kept him in Ireland longer. They skated and golfed the rest of their lives together. Sebastian eventually got out of rock-n-roll and into promoting golf full-time. Over time he got used to hearing "Dieting after She Died" on his streaming service, reminding him of the way his life with Faustine unraveled.

Working the psychic developments backwards, Elodie was presumed to have finally departed when Manon played "Dieting after She Died" at Faustine's office party, since Elodie did not appear at her final seance.

Manon stayed in Ireland long enough to keep Ailill from freaking out. Jacob's determination won out in the end. Manon ended up with three places she called home where she could write, her house, Jacob's, and a Slip of the Cue's guest house in Ireland. She found a happier medium between writing about herself versus writing about others.

Faustine remained in relationship limbo. She had her day job, so she stayed busy. Occasionally she met up with Sebastian and Eurille. She kept an eye on Elodie's father until he died. Manon was always hard to find, especially once she started living in three separate places. Faustine occasionally had dinner with one of Manon's sisters at Sour Cream and Burritos. Manon and Wayland's song, "Dieting after She Died," was her only real proof that any of it had ever occurred.

Faustine never knew how her aunt found Elodie's old social media posts since there was only one email from Elodie's father. What her aunt confessed to made no sense.

Improvising to Beat the Band

Turns out Elodie's old social media account was never deleted, or even archived, since they had used her account again so soon after closing it.

DD&PF never took off professionally. They were totally bummed out when Sebastian's career veered towards professional golf in Europe, leaving them searching for another public relations specialist. Scott never gave up, and started a solo career writing background music for movies and television from his home studio.

Sebastian gave the mysterious guitar picks to Manon. He never learned to play guitar, or any other instrument. It also never occurred to him to ask Eurille if one of her brothers had sent the picks as a message while they were in hiding. After all the times they wouldn't return his calls he did not expect encrypted explanations.

Manon never had enough guts to listen to her digital recorder after she got it returned to her by mysterious mail. The package remains sealed in packing tape.

Eurille's brothers whereabouts was later determined to be in South America. They never returned to either the U.S. or Europe. Sebastian figured that Eurille knew more than she divulged about their activities. She and her father flew to visit them only a half-a-dozen times or so through the years.

———————————

A Slip of the Cue, happily, stayed on tour until their final, personal, eternal encore.

———————————

And most importantly, "Bill" never bothered any of them ever again.

PART FIVE

ACKNOWLEDGEMENTS

Please let me express my gratitude to everyone who has purchased a copy of this book, or one of my previous novellas. Financial support from readers is how I can continue writing. It can be hard to turn a profit in this business. I will always be grateful to the unknown reader who bought one of the first digital copies of Dieting after She Died at full price on a "free day." I still do not know how that happened—it shouldn't have been physically possible without extremely high system administrator privilege— since the reader never asked for a refund. It was great motivation at a critical time. I'm also grateful to the secondary retailers who are keeping the paperback novellas available. Looking at those sticker prices, recently as high as $1400, keeps me motivated too.

This book evolved over seven years, from Spring Break of March 2014—when I first started blogging Dieting after She Died on Wordpress based on a dream I had—through April

Wendolynn Jane Landers

2021—when I finished editing the revision of the compilation of the three novellas, Improvising to Beat the Band. This *oeuvre* started off as a blog, then became a series of novellas—which intertwined with my newsletter. Each part of the novel corresponds to a previously self-published novella. I managed to keep to a September deadline for three years running.

I'm grateful to all of the readers along the way—around 700 so far—especially the reviewers. Many thanks to the writers' reviews: Steve M (Earth Seven), Niki Danforth (Ronnie Lake Murder Mystery), Meagan Poetschlag (Wolf's Blood). The reviews of the independent novellas are still available on Amazon and Goodreads, even though the independent novellas are no longer in print. There are currently used hardcopies still in circulation. A big thanks to the Writer's Digest Self-Published Book Awards contest for their extremely usable reviews and advice, including the review that inspired me to rewrite the book yet again. I'd also like to thank the Inklings writer's group, run by Miss Dee Dee, which met at the Vista Grande library in Casa Grande, AZ. Getting feedback from beta readers personally is invaluable.

I'd like to thank the Casa Grande Dispatch, as well as the Arizona City Independent and the Eloy Enterprise for their coverage of the first two novellas. The above-the-fold coverage as I was beginning provided the momentum I needed to keep going. I'd like to thank Central Lutheran Church in Arizona City, AZ, for allowing me to use their space for my first two book launches. The Eloy Santa Cruz Library in Eloy, AZ, has my eternal gratitude for shelving all three books as they came out. Bookmans used bookstore in Tucson, AZ gave me exposure during their author fair, specifically the Bookmans on Grant and Campbell which is now relocated. The Bookmans on Ina was also kind enough to let me play jazz piano improv on more than one occasion, plus take publicity photos. I'm grateful to the Tucson Festival of Books for supporting indie authors through the Indie Author Pavillion, as well as the Tent Talks.

My editor would prefer to not be acknowledged. *Go figure!* I am a hard author to edit—leave it at that.

—Wendolynn "Wendy" Landers
May 22, 2019
Arizona

—Updated dates, and acknowledging another Writer's Digest review on April 18, 2021

Information about the audiobook of Improvising to Beat the Band will be available on my website: www.wendylanders.com. While you are visiting my website, please sign up for my newsletter to receive updates about my upcoming books, short stories, music, plus interesting information about cultural events in central Arizona. Look for musical tracks inspired by Improvising to Beat the Band.

About the Author

Wendolynn Jane Landers started the "Dieting after She Died," series on her self-titled blog in 2014. The first book with the series title was available in paperback in September of 2015. Wendy Landers completed the second book in the series, "LOVE & all its glory IS," in September of 2016. The last book in that series, "Just Let Time Pass," was published in September of 2017. The abridged series compilation, Improvising to Beat the Band, was first available to the public in May of 2019 when the previous novella titles became out-of-print, although there are previously read paperbacks still available. The fictional series chronicles the travails of a popular songwriter, Manon, as she recovers from illness and learns to write again.

Wendy Landers' master's degree is in Applied Social Research, a.k.a "polling." She currently resides in Arizona.

Made in the USA
Las Vegas, NV
21 April 2021